Advance Praise for *Lost in Paris*

"*Lost in Paris* is as delicious as a fresh, colorful macaron. With vivid descriptions, compelling characters, and a fascinating look into the past, Elizabeth Thompson has created a lovely story guaranteed to take readers on a journey they won't forget."

—RaeAnne Thayne, *New York Times* bestselling author of *The Sea Glass Cottage*

"In Elizabeth Thompson's *Lost in Paris*, the magical French capital comes alive in two timelines a century apart. You'll find yourself in both modern-day Paris and the 1920s Paris of Hemingway, Fitzgerald, and Picasso, as a powerful story of secrets across the generations unfolds. If you're a Francophile like I am—or if you're a fan of *Midnight in Paris* or Hemingway's *A Moveable Feast*—you'll eat this story up like a fresh baguette straight from a corner *boulangerie*. A tale of family, heritage, forgiveness, and finding the strength within, *Lost in Paris* sparkles and shines like the City of Light itself."

—Kristin Harmel, *New York Times* bestselling author of *The Book of Lost Names*

"A luscious, layered story of inheritance, heartbreak, reinvention, and family. I adored this book."

—Kristan Higgins, *New York Times* bestselling author of *Always the Last to Know*

"*Lost in Paris* has everything I love in a book: the magic of a romantic location, the intrigue of a family mystery, and the nostalgia of another era. An utterly charming read!"

—Julia Kelly, internationally bestselling author of *The Whispers of War*

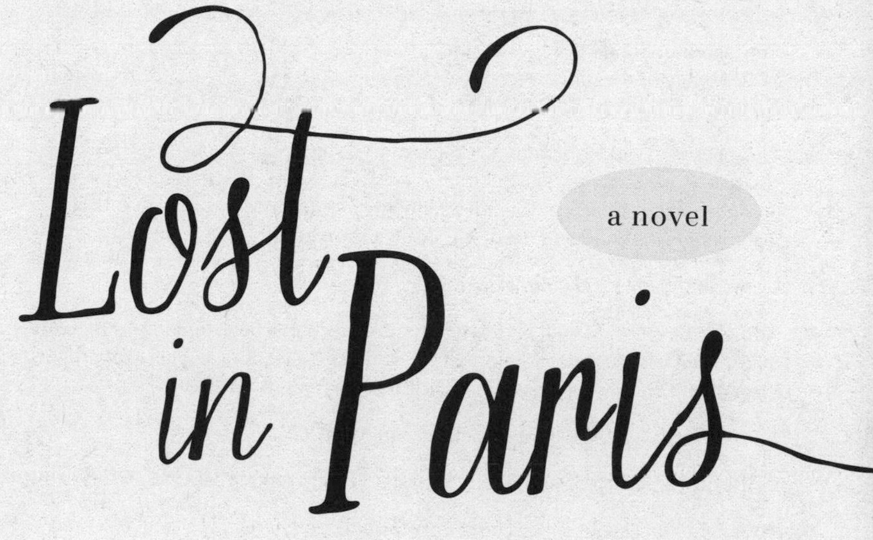

Elizabeth Thompson

GALLERY BOOKS
New York London Toronto Sydney New Delhi

Gallery Books
An Imprint of Simon & Schuster, Inc.
1230 Avenue of the Americas
New York, NY 10020

First Gallery Books trade paperback edition April 2021

Interior design by Davina Mock-Maniscalco

Manufactured in the United States of America

1 3 5 7 9 10 8 6 4 2

Library of Congress Cataloging-in-Publication Data

Names: Thompson, Elizabeth, author.
Title: Lost in Paris / Elizabeth Thompson.
Description: First Gallery Books trade paperback edition. | New York : Gallery Books, 2021. |
Identifiers: LCCN 2020015678 (print) | LCCN 2020015679 (ebook) | ISBN 9781982149086 (trade paperback) | ISBN 9781982149093 (ebook)
Classification: LCC PS3620.H684 L67 2021 (print) | LCC PS3620.H684 (ebook) | DDC 813/.6—dc23
LC record available at https://lccn.loc.gov/2020015678
LC ebook record available at https://lccn.loc.gov/2020015679

ISBN 978-1-9821-4908-6
ISBN 978-1-9821-4909-3 (ebook)

This book is dedicated to Michael for the trips to Paris,
for the lunches and flowers you bring to my desk,
for your encouragement and the champagne celebrations
each step along the way, but mostly for your unconditional love.
Also, to Jennifer for allowing us to show you Paris for the first time,
and to my father, Jim, who made it possible for us to live in France
(and drink champagne).

August 1929
Paris, France

Dear Diary,

In the twilight between sleep and wakefulness, the moment before my lashes fluttered open, I feared it was all a dream.

That I would open my eyes and find myself back in the flat on rue Delambre.

But now that I'm lying atop smooth cotton linens, sunlight streaming through the sheers that cover the tall casement windows, I'm sure it's real.

I'm in the apartment.

Remnants of my birthday celebration litter the marble-topped nightstand: Leftover cake. The opened bottle of champagne. One empty flute, another half-full. The note on the pillow next to mine reads, Good morning, my love. You looked so beautiful sleeping I hated to wake you. I will see you this evening.

I feel like a queen in this four-poster bed with the fluffy duvet covering my naked body.

It is one of those rare instances in life when everything seems good and right and, dare I say, perfect.

I want to live in this moment forever.

For the first time since moving to Paris, I am finally in the position to write and tell my parents I am doing well.

One

December 31, 2018—3:00 p.m.

Bath, England

Clad in OBSTINATE, HEADSTRONG GIRL T-shirts, the "Fitzwillings" laugh and whisper, interrupting my spiel about Sally Lunn's house. Again.

Since I haven't said anything particularly scandalous or funny, I pause, giving the six American women, who are part of a Cleveland-based book club, the opportunity to get it out of their collective system before I wrap up my talk.

We're down to the final two hours of my six-day Ultimate Jane Austen Tour.

I get it.

We've digested a whole lot of Jane.

We've had our fill of cornices with dentils and symmetrical fenestration and *Jane Austen slept here and ate that and promenaded there*.

I make a living leading people to worship at the altar of Austen, but frankly, today I'm over her, too.

In approximately one hour and fifty-eight minutes, I will leave my charges to take to the waters at the Thermae Bath Spa. The moment the handoff is complete, I will be on vacation.

For one glorious week, I will binge on take-out curry and back-to-back episodes of *Love Island*, while lounging in my jammies and feeling smugly superior to the idiots making fools of themselves on national television.

But, I digress.

The Fitzwillings, as they call themselves, are still yammering, and I'm trying not to lose my shit.

I'm weighing my words because I really hate confrontation, when Jerry Sanders, a middle-aged high school English teacher from Wisconsin, says in his teacher voice, "Ladies, is there something you'd like to share with the rest of the group?"

Jerry and the Fitzwillings have been sparring the entire trip. Never mind his bad habit of interjecting into my spiels factoids that are not always correct. He loves to call out everyone who even looks as if they're contemplating talking over me.

"No, we're good, Jerry," says Lucy Fitzwilling. "Thanks, though."

Jerry bares his teeth at her.

It's been happening all week. The Fitzwillings get excited about something and start talking. Jerry calls them out. They stop for a while. Then the cycle repeats.

"As I was saying, Sally Lunn's house is considered the oldest house in Bath, dating back to 1482. Although, Sally didn't live here until the late 1600s. It's a good example of medieval-style architecture. Notice the small stones on the façade and how the windows appear undersized when compared to the elegant building behind us?"

As I pause to let everyone turn around and have a look, my smartwatch buzzes with a call. I glance at my wrist even though I can't talk now.

It's my mother.

Marla and I have a complicated relationship. Other than an awkward five-minute call on Christmas Day, which I initiated, it's been several months since we've spoken—since I flew back to Orlando for my grandmother's funeral at the end of summer.

In addition to wishing her a merry Christmas, I called for an update on how things were proceeding with the sale of Gram's house, which Marla and I jointly inherited and she offered to stage and list. As of last week, she was still sorting through Gram's possessions and grumbling about the clutter she needed to eliminate before we could even think of putting the house on the market.

I didn't feel too bad for her, because as compensation for preparing the house, we agreed that she could keep any of the clutter she wanted or pocket the proceeds of anything she sells.

She lives in Orlando. I live in London. That's the only way it was going to work.

The cold weaves its way through the fabric of my red wool coat. I tighten my scarf and shove my hands into my pockets. I'll call her when I get back to London. Or tomorrow. Maybe.

"Jane Austen frequented Sally Lunn's bakery, which is still famous for its large brioche buns. I hope you're hungry because we'll sample them when we have our tea. In the meantime, you might be interested to know Jane mentioned Sally Lunn's baked goods in a letter to her sister, Cassandra, in 1801. She said, 'Though, to be sure, the keep of two will be more than of one, I will endeavor to make the difference less by disordering my stomach with Bath buns.'"

Two of the Fitzwillings are whispering again. They're eyeballing Jerry.

I talk louder.

"Based on that quote, we can see that Jane was well acquainted with Sally Lunn's buns."

A titter ripples through the group.

"I am, of course, referring to brioche." More laughter. "It's been said that our Jane would often keep a stash of Sally's bakes in her room to supplement the scanty meals served by her aunt Leigh-Perrot, whom Jane and Cassandra visited in Bath."

The ladies are laughing less subtly now, hardly containing their whispers, and Jerry's gaze remains trained on them with sniper-like focus.

It's been a long week. The tour started in London and stretched up to Chatsworth House, famously the location of Darcy's Pemberley in the 2005 *Pride and Prejudice* movie. We gave equal time to Lyme Park in Cheshire, the 1995 Pemberley. We've made all of the relevant stops along the way as we circled back through Bath on day six.

The women are oblivious to Jerry's irritation until he says, "Come on, out with it, ladies. Let us all in on the joke. Tell us what's so funny."

They fall silent, but Jerry is having none of it.

"Really," he says. "We want to know what is so damn hilarious that you keep interrupting Hannah."

"Jerry, it's fine," I say. "I think we've all had enough architecture. Let's go have tea. The reservations are listed under Heart to Heart Tours. I'm sure they won't mind if we're a little early."

I hope.

I herd the group toward the restaurant in a desperate attempt to diffuse the situation.

It works.

We step inside and I give the information to the hostess, who, by the grace of God, has our tables ready.

I let the others go first and that's when I see him. He's sitting at a table all alone, his head bowed over a folio as he writes.

A navy peacoat and a tartan scarf are draped over the empty

chair at the table. He's wearing a black button-down, dark skinny jeans, and boots. His vibe is rock and roll or some other old-soul creative cool, but the intense way he furrows his brow as he writes makes me think of Mr. Darcy himself. I wonder if the Fitzwillings have noticed him.

My watch buzzes another alert and it makes me jump. He must see the movement out of the corner of his eye because he looks up and catches me staring at him. There's a flash of recognition on his face and he squints at me.

He looks familiar . . . vaguely.

Do I know you?

If not, I want to know you.

I scroll through the files in my head. Famous people? No. People I know in Bath? Uh-uh. Other business acquaintances not from Bath? Not that I can remember. Someone from university? No. Guys my roommates have dated or tried to fix me up with? Hardly. People from London? No. Nothing.

It's as if time has stopped around us and we're the only ones in the room. Until I realize the hostess is talking to me.

"Right this way, miss," she says.

I tear my gaze away from his and follow the hostess. In an attempt to center myself, I look at the text on my watch. It's my mother again.

DID YOU GET MY MESSAGE??? CALL ME NOW! VERY IMPORTANT!!!

I'm not sure if her choice of all caps implies actual importance or impatience.

Either way, I can't talk to her right now. After we order, some of the Fitzwillings begin peppering me with questions.

"Hannah, how did you get into this line of work?" Lucy asks. "It's like a dream job. You must have such fun going to work every day."

I adore my boss, Emma, owner of Heart to Heart. She's become more of a friend than a boss. I will never be able to repay her for hiring me as a seasonal employee and keeping me on because I desperately needed work. Not only that, she's given me creative freedom to make the Austen tour what it is today.

It's not her fault that I feel . . . stuck. I'm twenty-seven years old. I can move on whenever I want.

"No, seriously," Lucy presses. "How did you, *an American*, land a cool job like this? I mean, it allows you to live here and work here, right?"

I nod. "I guess I was lucky."

The Fitzwillings are distracted by other conversation. I look over at Brooding Darcy. His head is bowed over his folio again and he's furiously scribbling away. I wonder if I'd imagined our exchange a moment ago.

Then some of the Fitzwillings unleash a clap of laughter over something I missed and he raises his head only to catch me looking at him again.

He levels me with that same unsmiling, unapologetic stare that takes my breath away.

I know I'm not imagining that, but I look away.

After the server delivers our food and beverages, Lucy says, "Hannah, we got interrupted. Tell me how you got the job?"

I sip my tea. "I suppose I didn't choose this career path as much as I needed a job while I was in college."

"You went to college here?" Gloria Fitzwilling asks.

"Yes. I fell in love with the UK after doing a summer abroad here during my undergrad in the US. I returned to do my MA in literature at the University of Bristol, about fifteen miles from where we are right now. That's when Heart to Heart hired me as a seasonal employee. I suppose it was a season that never ended because I'm still here."

Lucy sighs and dreamily pushes an oversized bite of bun into her mouth. It makes her look like a chipmunk.

"I don't blame you," she says around the brioche. "I would so move here if I could. I'd meet a real-life Mr. Darcy and have beautiful Darcy children."

I slant another surreptitious glance at Brooding Darcy's table, but it's empty. Somehow he slipped away and I didn't notice.

Story of my life.

"Oh my *gawd*—yes . . . yes . . . yes!" Polly Fitzwilling throws her head back and cries out orgasmically. "Darcy children means Darcy sex. Yes, please. I'd never get out of bed."

Jerry slams his hand on the table, making the china cups and saucers rattle. "Of all the inane, vapid nonsense." His insult halts conversation at our end. A couple of the Fitzwillings grimace, another presses her lips together. Jerry's wife, Frances, looks embarrassed. Lucy glares at him.

I think the moment will pass, when Lucy says, "Why would you say something so rude, Jerry? We're just having fun. Lighten up a little bit."

My face freezes into what I hope is my practiced, pleasant tour guide expression.

Jerry's face turns red. "You and your friends have been talking through the entire tour. It's safe to say that I'm not the rude one, you stupid cow."

"Okay, no—Nope!" I demand. "We're not going to do this."

"Yes we are." Jerry's chair scrapes the wooden floorboards as he stands and hulks over the table. "I'm sick of their incessant ridiculous babble."

This is a first. I've never had to referee a fight between my charges.

Frances puts a hand on her husband's arm and mutters, "Jerry, please. Sit down."

He bellows, "Shut up, Frances."

The restaurant falls silent. People turn around and stare.

"That's enough." My voice is low but firm. "Let's be respectful of others or they'll ask us to leave."

"I'll make this easy on everyone," he says. "Frances and I will leave."

"Jerry, please sit down," Frances begs. "We haven't finished our tea."

"We're not having tea, Frances. We're leaving. Now."

Watching Jerry take Frances by the arm and quick-walk her out of the dining room triggers a memory I've tried hard to forget.

It was a hot summer night in Orlando. I was thirteen. It was the last time Marla whisked me away from Gram's house, where I lived. Marla promised that this time she would *make things work*. This time, we'd make a life together.

Of course, *making it work* entailed constantly walking on eggshells around her boyfriend, Ed, because I never knew what would make him fly into a rage. It was usually directed at my mother. But not always.

I stand to walk after Jerry and Frances and try to blink away the memory, but not before the mental soundtrack plays: The sharp crack of fist connecting with bone. Emergency sirens. My mother screaming at me as they wheeled her into the ambulance: *This is all your fault, Hannah. This is all on you.*

As cold sweat breaks out on the back of my neck, a vague sense of nausea washes over me. It's been a long time since I thought about that night.

Today's ill-timed phone call from Marla coupled with Jerry's anger allowed the memory to seep through the cracks of the wall I've built between my childhood and my current life.

Outside, I call after Jerry and his wife. He whirls around to face me. "*You* need to learn how to keep your tour under control, Ms. Bond."

This is not a classroom setting where people have to shut up and listen. The women have the right to enjoy the tour in their own way—even if it means giggling and whispering about a fictional character—but pointing that out now won't help.

"Jerry, come back inside. Let Frances finish her tea—"

"Frances doesn't want tea, but I want to talk to your supervisor."

He's thrusting his cell phone at me, jabbing it into my shoulder. I sidestep, trying to avoid the next blow, but my heel catches an uneven piece of cobblestone and I feel myself going down. As adrenaline begins pinpricking my skin from the inside out, a pair of strong hands grabs my torso and rights me before I hit the ground.

"Hey, buddy, take it easy, there." The deep male voice is steeped in a Scottish accent. The words are as strong as the hands that saved me. "There's no reason to shove a lady."

I know it's Brooding Darcy before I turn and see him. He's taller than I realized, and sturdy. Judging by the way he's scowling down at Jerry, he's not playing around.

Clearly Jerry realizes it, too, because he takes a couple of steps back.

"This is none of your business," Jerry says, but his tone isn't quite as nasty as it was a moment ago.

"It becomes my business when I see a man making an arse of himself roughing up a woman on the street. Do we need to call the police to settle it?"

"No, we're good here." Jerry's voice has a defensive edge. "You can go."

A crowd of people has stopped to watch.

"No, you're the one who needs to step away and cool off. I'll stay right here until you do." Darcy doesn't budge, nor does he stop glowering at Jerry, who is clenching his fists and muttering a string of choice words under his breath.

"I don't need this," Jerry says. "Come on, Frances."

I worry about Jerry's wife, that she will bear the brunt of her husband's misplaced anger. I'm opening my mouth to say as much, but Darcy beats me to it.

"Lady, you don't have to go with him."

Frances raises her chin a notch. "I'm fine." She sounds annoyed. "I can handle myself."

She directs the words at me. Like my mother, sometimes people don't know how to accept help when it's offered, much less ask for it.

"Frances, I'm here for you if you need anything."

Her eyes flick from me to Jerry, who is already walking away. She hesitates, and for a moment, I wonder if she'll defect. Then she turns and follows her husband.

"Yeah, your boss is definitely going to hear from me," Jerry bellows over his shoulder as he moves down North Parade Passage, then disappears around the corner.

I need to call Emma before he does.

But first, I turn to Darcy, unsure of what to say.

Because what do you say in a moment like this?

Thanks, but I didn't need to be saved?

What might've happened if he hadn't intervened?

Most of the onlookers have started to disperse, but I'm painfully aware of the handful of stragglers who are still watching curiously, some from the bay window of the Sally Lunn dining room.

I decide on the polite response. "Thank you for your help."

"You're American." His tone is lighter, but his unwavering gaze is still as intense as it was when it was fixed on Jerry. Less angry, more . . .

More what? I don't know.

"That I am." After Jerry's performance, I brace myself for him to tack on a barb about loud, ugly tourists.

"What exactly happened there?" he says. "If you don't mind my asking."

His tartan scarf is tucked inside his navy peacoat. His dark hair is disheveled and on the longish side but in a sexy way that makes me wonder what he looks like when he wakes up in the morning. I blink away the forward thought.

"I'm a tour guide. It's the last day of our tour. He took issue with others talking during my spiels and the way I handled it. Apparently, he thought I could've done a better job. He's off to inform my boss. Which means I need to call her before he does."

I'm caught in the tractor beam of his gaze. Ridiculous, but it totally takes away my breath. My heart thuds against my ribs like a bird trying to break free and soar.

He looks like he wants to say something, but instead, he shakes his head.

"Right, you'd best make that call." He glances at his watch. "And I'd best be on my way or I'll miss my train."

"Thanks again."

"Happy to be of service. Take good care of yourself."

That voice. It's as rich as butterscotch and twice as sweet. As I watch him walk away, I'm thinking I could curl up in that brogue and live a happy life.

That's when I realize I didn't even ask his name.

I open my mouth to call after him, but he's already too far away.

A light snow starts to fall as he's swallowed up by crowds of revelers peering into shop-front windows brimming with holly and ivy and the last of the holiday cheer.

If the Fitzwillings wanted to find Mr. Darcy on this trip, they missed their chance. I want to smile at the thought, but more pressing matters consume me.

Before going back inside, I call Emma, but I get her voicemail. "Em, it's Hannah. I have a situation. It's not life-or-death, just . . . an incident that happened a moment ago. Call me when you get a chance."

In the meantime, I go back inside and apologize to the manager of the Sally Lunn House for the spectacle in the dining room.

I realize that I should make a contingency plan just in case Jerry shows up at Thermae Bath Spa and tries to cause trouble for the ladies. Guys like that are usually all bark, so he probably won't. But you never know. Before Jerry, I'd never had a person on my tour stomp away in a huff.

Heads turn as I walk back to the table, but I focus my energies on my remaining ten charges.

"I'm sorry about that, folks."

"Oh, Hannah!" Tears flood Lucy's eyes. "No, I'm the one who's sorry. I didn't mean for things to go that way. We were only having fun. What in the world is wrong with that man?"

"It's okay. It was his choice to leave. Please don't worry." What else can I say?

As if by divine intervention, my phone vibrates with an incoming call.

"I apologize, but I have to take this. I'll be right back."

I answer before I get outside so Emma's call doesn't sail over to voicemail.

"Hey, Em, thanks for getting back to me so fast. Hold on a moment while I go outside. I'm in Sally Lunn's."

The silence on the other end of the line lasts long enough for me to wonder if the call has been disconnected.

And then I wish it had been.

"No, Hannah, it's not Emma. This is your mother. Why haven't you called me back? I'm in London at Heathrow Airport and I need you to come pick me up."

February 1927
London, England

Dear Diary,

Mum popped in for a visit today.

She made no pretense of what she thought of my new Eton crop hairdo.

In true Constance Braithwaite fashion, she gasped and grabbed a hunk of my hair, going on and on about how I'd ruined my beauty. How no man would want me now because I looked like a boy.

I wanted to tell her the Eton crop was a statement about a woman's self-confidence, and that confidence, in turn, accentuated femininity.

Instead, I murmured that it was just hair. It would grow back.

Lorgnette in hand, Mum moved her disapproving eyes to my chemise, which I'd made myself out of remnant fabric my boss let me take home. I love the loose, straight drop-waist skirt that falls just below my knees. I'd paired it with stockings and laced-up oxford shoes.

The look was inspired by a Coco Chanel design I saw in Vogue *magazine.*

As Mum inspected me, I did a twirl and asked her if she liked my frock. A cheeky move, I know, but I refused to stand there and let her berate me. Her nostrils flared as if she smelled something bad.

Her reaction made me wish I'd worn the golf knickers and tie I had finished sewing last week. Paired with argyle socks, the unfeminine ensemble would've made Mum apoplectic.

I would have wasted my breath if I'd tried to explain that Chanel has liberated women by taking inspiration from men's clothing, which is so much more comfortable and convenient than the restraining styles of the past. Instead, I told her that wealthy women these days pay a lot of money to dress down, and soon, I intend to capitalize on it.

Money is a language she understands.

All she did was shake her head and say she knew my move from Bristol to London would lead to my ruin. The way I looked today was proof.

Then she announced that Allister Hutcheon, the widower undertaker back home, was looking for a wife and had been asking about me.

When I pointed out that Allister Hutcheon was closer to Dad's age than mine, Mum sucked her teeth. She said I was too old for this nonsense. It was time to leave this foolishness behind and return to Bristol while my face was still fair and my virtue was intact. In other words, while I was still marriageable.

I don't need a husband to take care of me and certainly not old Allister Hutcheon. I was so incensed I removed myself to the kitchen and started brewing tea to give myself a moment to calm down.

Everything considered, I've done well for myself. I've made good decisions and enough money to support myself. I've even managed to stash a little under the mattress.

I'd planned to tell Mum during her visit today that I was indeed leaving London, but not to return to Bristol. The way our talk was going, it was clear that I needed to break the news sooner rather than later.

When the tea was ready, I brought it out and blurted the news before my courage could escape me. I informed her I was moving to Paris with my friend Helen to apprentice in the atelier of Coco Chanel.

Mum scooted her chair away from the table. I'll never forget the shriek of wood scraping wood. Nor the way she looked at me with fury in her blue eyes. She gathered her handbag and told me that unless I returned to Bristol with her, I needn't come home ever again. I would not be welcome.

Once she left and her ultimatum settled in, a future life in Bristol flashed before my eyes—the regret of not going to Paris as I wasted away in spinsterhood or, I shudder to think, marriage to Allister Hutcheon.

With that, my choice was crystal clear.

Two

December 31, 2018—5:00 p.m.

Bath Spa railway station

Two hours later, I've deposited the group at Thermae Bath Spa. There was no sign of Jerry and Frances. When I spoke to Emma, she hadn't heard from them, either.

I'd wager that Jerry will simmer all the way back to Wisconsin, where he will fire off a nasty letter to Emma. He may ask for a refund, but that will likely be the end of it.

A cold wind whips around me as I make my way to the Bath train station. British weather is so different from what I grew up with in Florida. Not only does it get much colder in the UK, but there's also fog that descends from out of nowhere and seeps into your bones. Lit by the streetlamps, the misty air shimmers as it couples with the darkness that has fallen around me. It cloaks the evening in a melancholy blue that transports me back to my childhood.

When I was a little girl, "the blue hour" made me wistful and homesick for my mother, who was never there, even on the rare occasion that she was present.

The icy wind cuts through me, and I'm transported back to those nights when I felt hollow and abandoned.

Marla, why are you in London?

When we spoke earlier, she didn't get a chance to explain because Emma beeped in. I told Marla I had to take the call. I did manage to say that I couldn't pick her up. I was out of town working. Because I am.

I didn't mention that I'd be home tonight.

To buy myself some time, I texted that she should check in at the Holiday Inn at Camden Lock until we can meet up. It's affordable and an easy five-minute walk to my flat.

The thought of having her that close, even for a holiday, gives me pause.

Without the Atlantic between us, there is no buffer to keep us from colliding. Just Marla and me, face-to-face, forced to figure out what to do with each other before she inevitably floats out of my life like a balloon let loose from its tether.

But for whatever reason, she's here, and there's nothing I can do about it now.

As I settle into my seat on the train, all I want to do is sleep during the hour-and-forty-five-minute trip from Bath to Paddington station. But my watch buzzes a text alert.

In the split second before I look, I decide that if it's my mother, I will take off the watch and stash it in my purse.

But it's not her; it's a group text from my flatmates Cressida and Tallulah.

Cressida: What time will you be home, Han?

Me: On the train now. Should be home 7:30-ish.

Cressida: I have a man for you tonight . . .

I can virtually hear her voice singing those frightful words.

Me: No thank you.

Cressida: Come on, Han. Zed wants to meet you.

Cressida's blind date track record is horrendous, and a guy with a name like Zed doesn't bode well for improvement. Thank goodness Tallulah chimes in.

Tallulah: What are you wearing to Jemma's party?

Me: Flannel pajamas and fuzzy socks.

Tallulah: Sexy.

Cressida: Not sexy. Don't encourage her. I refuse to let her end the year wearing fuzzy socks. She'd probably stoop to binge-watching *Love Island* if we left her to her own devices.

Tallulah: Right. We will save her from herself.

Me: What's wrong with *Love Island*?

Cressida: We will leave her in Zed's very capable, very large hands.

Me: Hello? Don't talk about me like I'm not here.

Cressida: Okay then. We'll leave you in Zed's care. Did I mention his large hands?

Me: Zed? What kind of guy is named Zed? Sounds like a movie villain.

Cressida: No, he's hot. You want to meet him.

Me: Introduce him to Tallulah.

Tallulah: Tallulah already has a date.

Cressida: Oops g2g. Doorbell.

Cressida's skills for fixing me up on blind dates can be summed up in three words—well, six, really: The Quitter, The Sniffer, and The Stiffer. In order of appearance and offending record.

The Quitter took me to play tennis and then got mad when I beat him.

The Sniffer had a foot fetish.

I kid you not. *A foot fetish*.

I should've caught on earlier than I did because this dude knew way too much about women's shoes than is acceptable for a straight guy. After I excused myself to the kitchen and came back with a bottle of wine, I caught him sniffing my black pump.

Surely that kind of lightning couldn't strike twice. Could it?

Oh yes, it could.

Matt was an emergency room doctor whom Cressida met when she thought she'd broken her ankle. Since she was dating someone, she couldn't wait to introduce us.

Everything started out fine. Matt was prompt and courteous. He'd made a reservation for us at Lumiere and ordered a nice bottle of wine and an array of appetizers for us to share, insisting that I hadn't lived until I'd tried caviar on toast points.

The conversation was flowing—as was the wine—and I thought, *Good job, good taste, no obvious anger issues, not a single mention of ladies' shoes. I could like this guy*.

As he finished his entree—he'd ordered filet and lobster for our mains—he got a call on his cell.

"I'm sorry," he said as he left the table. "It's the hospital. I have to take this."

Five minutes later, he texted.

Listen, love, I'm terribly sorry, but I've been called out on an emergency. Time is of the essence. If you could take care of the tab, I'll make it up to you.

Even before I saw the bottom line on the bill, I knew my one nearly maxed-out credit card couldn't handle the damage we'd racked up.

I swallowed my pride and texted him back.

Matt, I'm sorry, but I didn't bring enough money to cover the bill. I'm happy to pay for my part, but could you call the restaurant and give them a credit card number for your half?

He didn't respond. To make a long, ugly story short, Cressida had to come bail me out. She insisted on paying the entire bill and buying me a drink at the Gilded Lion, a pub down the street from Lumiere, to make up for it.

As we elbowed our way through the crowd, who did I see bellied up to the bar holding court with a pint and twin blondes? Dr. Matthew Brewer. There's no way he could've made it across town in London traffic, tended to his emergency, and gotten back to the pub in that amount of time.

The part I'm most ashamed of—more than a blind date stiffing me with the check—is that I said nothing to him. I didn't present him with the $468.37 bill. I didn't grab his pint and pour it over his head and caution the twins who were hanging on his every word, even though I wanted to, because the thought of causing a scene paralyzed me.

Instead, I said to Cressida before she could spot him, "It's crowded in here. Let's go somewhere else where we can breathe."

Did I mention I'm not big on confrontation?

March 1927
Paris, France

Dear Diary,

Helen and I arrived at the tiny flat we rented on the rue du Cardinal Lemoine. I'm sad to say it is not at all what we expected. It's horrible.

In the dark, we climbed a set of rickety wooden steps outside the main house to the top floor. After ducking through a small door, we had to ignite a kerosene lantern for light. A rodent—or perhaps it was a feral cat—hissed at us as it ran for cover. I wanted to leave, but we had no other place to go. We looked around and saw that the space amounted to nothing more than a small attic room about a quarter of the size of the flat we'd rented in London. This place was drafty and damp and smelled foul—of frying onions and the remnants of an animal that might have died in the walls or under the creaky floorboards. Possibly of relation to the one who greeted us? There was no kitchen, no running water. Just two twin-sized straw-stuffed mattresses atop rusty frames, pushed against separate walls, and a dresser. The landlord has passed off a closet as a loo, but in reality, it's no more than an espace de rangement *with a bucket.*

By the time our ferry crossed from Dover to Calais and the train carried us to Paris, it was after midnight when we knocked on the door of our landlord, Monsieur Arpin. His wife directed us to the apartment and said her husband would call on us tomorrow to collect the rent and make sure we were comfortable.

Comfortable we are not, but I'm happy we don't have to

discuss terms tonight. I'm at once bone-weary and a bundle of nerves over my interview at Mademoiselle Chanel's atelier in the morning.

I will write tomorrow, hopefully with good news and a clearer vision of what the future holds. Now, sleep.

Three

December 31, 2018—7:30 p.m.
London, England

After the train pulls into Paddington station, it takes me another thirty minutes via bus and a short walk from the Camden station stop to get home. I find the flat lit up like the West End.

Even our red lacquered front door seems to glow. I'm putting my key into the lock when I hear laughter through the closed doors and windows.

Someone turns on music. It sounds like a party.

I sigh, crushed by the weight of obligatory socialization even before I enter the flat. I remind myself that it's New Year's Eve. Just because I'm worn out doesn't mean the rest of the world has to tiptoe around me.

Plus, if Cressida and T have friends over, there's a chance I can fly under the radar and sit out Jemma's soirée after all. So bring on the pre-party. The more the merrier.

I let myself in, hang my coat in the hall closet, and toe out of my boots. That's when I hear *her* voice over the music.

Oh my God, no. Please tell me *she's* not here. She doesn't even have my address.

Does she?

"Mom?" I say when I walk into the lounge. "What are you doing here?"

Someone turns down the music.

She jumps up and moves toward me with the agility of a much younger woman.

She's wearing sunglasses. Huge tomato-red plastic frames that clash with her crimson lipstick and auburn hair. The gold quarter-size interlocking *c*'s on the sides of her glasses scream to the world that they're Chanel, but there's something slightly off about them. I'd wager they're knockoffs.

But the spicy-fruity-floral tang of her trademark Coco perfume is 100 percent authentic. She's worn it for years. It mixes with the aroma of the once-fresh Christmas tree that's been languishing in the corner.

"Oh, Hannah! You have the nicest friends. After the cab dropped me off, Cressida and *Taboola* let me come in and they've been taking such good care of me."

"*Taboola*? Mom, her name is Tallulah."

My roommates erupt in fits of laughter. I'm seething.

You're drunk. And you got my mother, the alcoholic, drunk. Or did she forget to tell you about that?

"Oh, sorry. My bad." Marla laughs and dismisses the blunder with a wave of her hand. "They've been simply delightful. They opened a bottle of champagne, and we're all getting in the spirit for tonight's party. I am so happy that we'll get to ring in the New Year together. I really think it's the start of good things."

Marla throws her arms around me, gives me a squeeze, and sets me free. She's too thin, but she still manages to be larger-than-life. Her energy commands attention and draws people to her.

Her long hair falls in rope curls over her shoulders and down her back. She's wearing black leather pants and a sheer black nylon blouse that showcases the lacy black bra underneath. It's just this side of indecent, yet she manages to pull it off.

She's put her own touch on the ensemble with a statement necklace, dangling earrings, and several bangle bracelets on each arm. In true Marla fashion, when it comes to makeup, accessories, and fragrance, more is always . . . more.

I feel frumpy in my khaki cargo pants and red uniform polo shirt with the Heart to Heart logo of two interlocking hearts embroidered over my left breast. Usually, I love wearing a uniform because it takes all the guesswork out of packing for the six-day tours. The pants and shirts stay wrinkle-free. Since I walk an average of 125,000 steps during a tour, cute shoes are out of the question.

"Where's Don?"

Don is Marla's fiancé. I met him at Gram's funeral. My gaze searches the lounge for evidence of him—a suitcase, a coat, all the air being sucked out of the room—but there's nothing.

Marla's mouth flattens into a line. She pushes her frames up onto the bridge of her nose with her index finger. "I left him, Hannah. I called off the wedding."

She squares her shoulders, lifts her chin as if convincing herself that it was the right thing to do. But she's not fooling me.

"I'm a single woman now."

Marla hates to be alone, but I'd be flattering myself if I thought she'd run to me for comfort. Her usual MO is to have another man lined up before cutting the old Joe loose.

Which begs the question, why is she here? And why the hell couldn't it have waited until tomorrow? Or next year?

Before I can ask, Cressida fills the silence. "Hannah, you never told us your mother was so fun. And so lovely."

Marla answers for me. "You're sweet and your home is fabulous.

You girls must be doing well for yourselves." As she turns in a slow circle to take in the flat, I glance around the living room and try to see it through her eyes.

The sleek furniture, the expensive art, the Persian rugs on the parquet floors.

She's right. It's a great place. I totally lucked out when Cressida, whom I'd met at university, asked me to move into the empty bedroom when her former second roommate got promoted and moved to Dubai.

Under normal circumstances, I could never afford a place like this on my salary. None of us could. The townhome belongs to Cressida's family and what I pay in rent basically covers my share of the utilities.

I swear if Marla does anything to jeopardize my living arrangement, I'll never speak to her again.

Oh wait. We don't really speak to begin with.

"They put my bags in your room. I hope that's okay. It'll be like a slumber party, Hannah."

Marla smiles, but I know that behind those sunglasses, her eyes are daring me to throw her out.

"I wish I would've known that you were coming," I say, pausing for an apology or an explanation, then filling the awkward silence when it doesn't come.

"I guess you can stay with us tonight. Then we'll find a nice hotel for the rest of your visit. I only have a full-sized bed, and you know I don't sleep well with others."

Marla raises a brow. I hold my breath, waiting for her to make a wisecrack about that being my problem. How maybe if I loosened up a bit, let myself have fun for a change, my bed wouldn't be quite so empty.

"How long are you in town?" I ask.

"That depends."

"On what?"

She hesitates, and I can tell she's holding something back.

"Okay, two, three nights max. Who knows if I can even find a room, with the holiday. If I do, it will probably cost a fortune. I promise I won't be too much of an imposition."

Cressida and Tallulah are watching us as if we are the cast of a dysfunctional mother-daughter reality show. Like it's the calm before the storm when one of us flips a table or yanks out the other's hair extensions.

No extensions for me, that's for sure, but Marla might have some. Her hair looks a little too perfect after the flight from Florida.

There's no denying that my mother's still a natural beauty underneath all the accessories. Her flawless ivory skin, bone structure, and willowy figure have opened doors for her throughout the years from modeling jobs to wealthy boyfriends to general preferential treatment.

It's her curse and her blessing. If I'm perfectly honest, I can't help but be a little jealous.

I did not inherit her delicate looks. I like to imagine that I got my nose that's a little too big and my lips that are a little too full from my father, though I've never met him. Marla swears she doesn't know who he is. When I was younger and would ask about him, she would say, "Oh, Hannah, don't ask so many questions." As I got older, she added, "It was a crazy time in my life. There were lots of men." As if that was supposed to sate my curiosity.

"Two or three nights?" I ask, snapping back to the present. "You show up and expect us to accommodate you? And on New Year's Eve no less!"

"Oh, come on, Hannah. Surely you can take pity on your ol' *mum* and put up with me for a couple of nights?"

When I don't answer, she laughs. "Your roomies said it would be fine. Didn't you, girls?"

Cressida and T smile but say nothing. It's not the show of support Marla was expecting, and I thank God her fun-mom act doesn't have them completely bamboozled.

That's what I love about my friends. They may not always have the best judgment—case in point, the holy trinity of bad blind dates—but they have good intentions always and my back when it matters.

"Are you en route to somewhere?" I ask, unmoved. There's no way she wouldn't have mentioned this transatlantic trip when we spoke last week, unless she had an ulterior motive. "Surely you didn't fly to London to surprise me on New Year's Eve."

Marla purses her lips. She glances at Cressida and T, who are trying really hard to look like they're not listening. Cressida is flipping through a magazine and T is scrolling through her phone.

"I'm glad you brought that up," Marla says. "Why don't we go somewhere we can talk and I'll fill you in?"

"Or we can give you two some time," Cressida offers. "I need to pick up a bottle of something to take to Jemma's tonight. T, why don't you come and help me pick it out?"

"That's a great idea," T says a little too enthusiastically.

"No, really, you don't have to leave," I insist. The subtext is *please don't go*. Don't leave me alone with her.

She's not a serial killer or anything—don't get me wrong—but she is an emotional vampire, and having Cressida and Tallu here is much-needed moral support.

"No, it's fine, really," Cressida says as she makes her way toward the foyer. "I'd rather pick it up now than wait until later."

"We'll be back in twenty or so," T says. "That should give you girls time to catch up."

They're out the door and then it's just the two of us. My mother and me, staring at each other. Or at least me staring at her bug-eyed sunglasses.

Suddenly, the room feels very cold.

"What is going on, Marla?"

"Why don't we have something to drink?" she says.

"You're drinking again." My voice is flat. A statement, not a question.

She winces and looks wounded. "No, I'm not drinking alcohol, if that's what you're insinuating. Though most people do believe it's bad luck if you don't ring in the New Year with a toast."

The way I remember it, it was always bad luck when she drank. Alcohol landed her in jail and then kept her away after she was released.

"I was suggesting that we share a spot of tea," she says.

I raise my chin, refusing to let her relegate me to the role of disapproving parental figure, even though our roles have always been reversed. When Gram was alive, she did her best to shelter me from my mother. She let me have as much of a normal childhood as possible, but there was nothing she could do on the occasions when Marla would swoop in and take me away.

Before Marla went to jail, Gram didn't have legal custody, because she didn't want to put me through the court battle. When my mother would come around, she always seemed so earnest, swearing that she'd cleaned up her act and the only way she could prove herself was if we gave her a chance. She'd always manage to make us feel like the bad guys—me for not wanting to go with her and Gram for trying to protect me. That was vintage Marla: deflect and play the victim.

"It would've been nice if you'd let me know you were coming," I say.

"I tried. You weren't picking up my calls."

"I mean before you landed in London. You could've mentioned it when we spoke last week."

Marla does a full-body shrug and sighs like I'm being unreasonable.

"When we spoke about Gram's house last week, I had no idea I'd be here."

"How could you not have known? People don't just fly to London on a whim."

Well, most people who aren't Marla need time to plan.

I move into the kitchen and put on the kettle. She follows and parks herself on one of the stools at the marble-topped island.

An empty bottle of champagne and three glasses litter the island's otherwise tidy surface. And she said she wasn't drinking.

At least it was only one bottle split three ways.

I busy myself measuring loose Darjeeling tea into a white ceramic teapot, and grab a small yellow-and-blue creamer pitcher from the refrigerator. I can feel her gaze on me in the quiet. I'm surprised she hasn't filled the silence, which has stretched on for a while now.

"Please take off your sunglasses. I can't see your eyes."

I turn and look at her, arms crossed.

After a few beats, she slides off the glasses to reveal the purple-red remnants of a black eye that even her heavy makeup can't cover.

"What the hell? What happened to your eye?"

She touches it gingerly, then cups her hand around it as if shielding it from my scrutiny.

"How did you hurt your eye?" I ask.

"I ran into a door."

"Really?"

At Gram's funeral, I remember noticing a bruise on her leg and seeing Don pinch her arm in the church when they were having a quiet disagreement. I know she's lying about the door. But the teakettle is whistling. I remove it from the burner and pour the water into the teapot.

"Aren't you fancy?" I know she's trying to change the subject. "I usually drink Lipton."

We sit in silence again until the tea has steeped. I pour it into the mugs and slide one in front of her. Her cup says, THERE IS NOTHING LIKE STAYING AT HOME FOR REAL COMFORT—JANE AUSTEN.

It's a quote from *Emma*.

Marla squints her blue eyes. Her lips move as she reads. "Is this from your work? That tour thing you do?"

"A couple who took my Jane Austen tour last year gave it to me as a thank-you gift. You must have hit the door pretty hard for your eye to bruise like that. Did you have it checked by a doctor?"

"Don't be ridiculous." She blows on her tea and takes a noisy slurp.

"Did Don hit you?"

She sits perfectly still for a long moment before her face crumples, and she nods. "That's why I called off the engagement."

She won't look me in the eyes. Head bowed over her cup, she blows on her tea and slurps again.

"Is that why you came to London?"

"One of the reasons. Hannah, I need your help."

Her words are quiet but matter-of-fact. They lack the usual melodrama she uses when she's trying to convince others of how trying her life is. "I can't go back to Orlando. I'm afraid Don will kill me."

And cue the theatrics.

"You can't move in here." I realize how utterly cold I sound. "I'm sorry. The town house doesn't belong to me. It belongs to Cressida's family."

I start to tell her that I could never find another place like this for the rent I'm paying, but then I realize that would only make Marla more determined to stay.

"I'm not asking to move in with you."

Marla swallows hard, then studies the mug again.

"They must really love you to give you a gift like this."

I sip my tea, unsure of what to say.

"No, seriously," Marla presses. "I'll bet you're really good at what you do."

"I try."

"You're so smart, Hannah. I think you got that from your grandma. It must skip a generation." She holds her mug with both palms, as if warming her hands.

I fight the urge to fill the silence, to ask her about the other reasons she's here.

She said Don was *one of the reasons*.

Since Gram is gone, maybe this is the only place she could go to get away from him. I don't know if she's being dramatic about him wanting to kill her. He certainly left a mark on her face. That's not something to test.

"You can stay for one night. *One*. Not a moment longer."

Tomorrow, I will find her a hotel room and personally move her bags if I have to.

"Thank you, Hannah." She's tearing up. "Oh, thank you."

I half expect her to fling her arm over her forehead and succumb to a case of the vapors.

But suddenly, she sets down her tea.

“Hang on,” she says. “I have something to show you. I’ll be right back.”

“I’ll be right here.”

She ignores my sarcasm and returns a moment later clutching a large manila envelope. She sits down, puts it on the island, and places her clasped hands on top of it.

I take the bait. “What’s that?”

She hands it to me. “This is the other reason I’m here. Open it.”

March 1927
Paris, France

Dear Diary,

The interview was a disaster.

I was so full of hope when I set out this morning toward Mademoiselle Chanel's atelier at 31 rue Cambon to meet Madame Jeanneau, who had responded to my query for a position.

In her letter, she had instructed me to use the steps that led to the back door. I had paused at the top of the stairs when I heard a clatter behind me. A woman pushed past me, threw open the door, and raced into a workroom.

Right in front of everyone, a stern old crone reprimanded the poor, breathless woman, whose name, I learned, was Brigitte. Apparently she was late for work again. Brigitte pleaded with the woman, whom she addressed as Madame Jeanneau. Alas, it was futile, because Madame dismissed her on the spot, saying her services were no longer needed.

Next, Madame Jeanneau turned her ire on me and bellowed, "What do you want?"

I raised my chin, hoping to look more confident than I felt, and told her my name and that I had an appointment to interview for a job. I did not want to celebrate poor Brigitte's misfortune, but I couldn't help but feel hopeful since clearly there was an available position.

She motioned for me to follow her down a hallway papered with fashion sketches that were unmistakably Chanel. For a moment, it was as if Madame was leading me to the inner sanctum of couture, where my dream would come true. I glanced around, half expecting to see Mademoiselle Chanel appear and welcome me with a beatific, Madonna-like smile.

Instead, the stern Madame entered an office, sat behind a desk, and held out her hand, wiggling her fingers. I handed her my sketchbook, praying I'd correctly understood what she was asking.

As she flipped through, I remained standing, waiting for a single word or even the lift of a brow to hint at what she was thinking, but her face remained impassive.

Finally, she closed my book and slid it across the desk. Her gaze raked over me, a slow meander from the top of my head to my feet.

I was determined to let her speak first. Then, fearing I would appear dumb if I remained mute, I blurted my excitement at having a chance to prove myself.

Then, merely trying to lighten the mood, I added that I would always arrive to work on time.

The look on her face made me wish I had remained silent. But she had already moved on, demanding to know where I'd gotten the suit I was wearing.

I was thrilled she'd noticed.

I told her I'd made it specially for the interview. I was so inspired by Mademoiselle Chanel's creations that I had re-created the design to demonstrate my skills.

Madame rose from her desk. She picked up my arm and examined the hem of the sleeve. She yanked open the jacket and examined the lining, scrutinized the collar.

She muttered about my quality work. For a moment I thought I was hired. Then she accused me of stealing the design from Mademoiselle Chanel.

I was so confused I laughed. The charge was so absurd I expected Madame to laugh, too, but she didn't.

My heart pounded as I struggled to understand how something I had sewn to showcase my talent, something Madame had conceded was quality work, made me a thief.

I removed the jacket and told her she could have it. I had never stolen anything from anyone. I simply wanted to prove my capability.

Madame shooed it away, saying I'd demonstrated what I was capable of and it was nothing Mademoiselle Chanel wanted for her atelier.

Then she told me about another designer who'd stolen Chanel's designs and how Mademoiselle had pushed her into a flaming candelabra and set her clothes on fire.

A menacing grin lurked at the corners of Madame's lips as she told me to imagine what Mademoiselle would do to a brazen nobody who had waltzed into her atelier attempting to pass off a filched Chanel suit as her own.

I started to defend myself, but Madame told me to get out and never return.

I gathered my sketchbook and ran from the office. The sewing machines hummed, but the workers were as demure as the dressmakers' dummies scattered about the studio. The smell of desperation hung so thick in the air it seemed capable of oozing down the walls.

As I walked toward the door, Madame said I should notice not one person in the room was wearing a Chanel design.

The sewing machines stopped then, and I felt the weight of every gaze on me. I turned to Madame and said I couldn't tell what they were wearing because their clothing was hidden by ugly grey smocks and frankly grey wasn't my color.

I left the way I'd entered, with my head held high, consoling myself that I was meant to work somewhere I would be valued, where my talent wouldn't be set ablaze.

Four

December 31, 2018—8:45 p.m.

London, England

I undo the clasp of the envelope Marla handed me and peer inside. It contains several papers.

"Go on." Marla points at the bundle with her nose.

I pull out something that looks like a certificate—a deed, maybe? But the writing is in French. A yellowed business card, also in French, is paper-clipped to the upper left corner.

The envelope clunks when I drop it onto the island. There's something else inside, something metal and weighty. I upend it, and a large old-fashioned brass key clatters onto the island's marble top.

I look at Marla for an explanation. "Okay, I give up. What is this?"

"I found it when I was cleaning out Gram's attic. This was in Granny Ivy's cedar chest. There's other stuff that belonged to her, but this is the most important."

Granny Ivy was Gram's mother. My great-grandmother, Marla's grandmother, who lived to be eighty-nine years old. I was only six when she died, but as she used to sew my school clothes, she would reminisce about life in England, where she was born and raised. I don't remember much of what she said, but I like to believe her early influence had something to do with the Anglophile I am today.

Ivy lived with Gram after Ivy's husband, Tom, passed away, so it makes sense that some of her stuff was relegated to the attic after she passed. That would make it part of Gram's modest estate, which mostly consisted of her three-bedroom, one-bath College Park bungalow and its contents. It's the house where I spent most of my time when I was growing up. The only place where I knew safety and stability.

For sentimental reasons, I'd love to keep the house, but Marla made it clear that I'd have to buy her out. She needs money, not memories. Her relationship with her personal finances is about as good as her situation with me. She's always been reckless and impulsive, living for today without a single thought for the future. Maybe that's because she allows her boyfriends to piss away what little cash she manages to save up.

"I still don't understand what this is," I say.

"Remember Patrick Sterling? Gram's attorney?" Marla asks.

"Of course I do." He's the lawyer who handled Gram's will. Marla and I met with him when I was in Orlando.

"I took it to him, and he said it's the deed to an apartment in Paris in Granny Ivy's name. But he says it's ours now."

I practically snort my tea.

"What?" I set down my cup and take a closer look at the certificate. Among French words that I don't understand, I see the name Ivy Braithwaite.

"Mr. Sterling verified this?"

Marla nods and shows me a piece of paper I didn't realize she was holding.

"He looked into it last week and said the French lawyer whose name is on that business card died twenty years ago. But Patrick got in touch with another lawyer from the same firm who will help us. His name is Emile Levesque."

"So this is real?" I ask.

"It appears that way."

"But wait—" I look at the deed again. "When did Granny Ivy come to the States?"

"I don't know. Mom was born in Florida in December 1940."

"Does that mean this place has been sitting vacant since before the war broke out? Or has someone been living there?"

I squint at Marla. She shrugs. "I don't know, Hannah. I'd like to go to Paris and check it out and I'd like for you to come with me. That's the big reason I'm here."

I hear her, but I don't answer her, because I still can't quite wrap my mind around it.

"I don't remember Granny Ivy or Gram mentioning an apartment in Paris. Wouldn't one of them have told us about it? This just doesn't make sense."

"Patrick and the French lawyer say the title is still in her name, and as Gram was her next of kin, it went to her. As per Gram's will, everything passes to us. Of course, he did mention that we have to pay a pretty hefty inheritance tax."

Oh. Okay. Now I see where this is going. With Marla, it always comes down to money.

"So, you're wanting us to sell the place?" I ask.

"I don't know," she says. "I mean, we haven't even seen it yet. And it's . . . Paris. You know?"

"Marla, I don't have money to cover the taxes, if that's why you're here."

Though, since we've jointly inherited the place, technically I'm only responsible for half.

She holds up her hand like a traffic cop. "Don't get ahead of yourself. Eventually we'll have to pay, but Patrick said we have time. Didn't you say you're on vacation soon?"

I mentioned that when we spoke last week. Why is it that she remembers only the things I want her to forget?

I don't answer her. I sit stock-still, staring at the papers in front of me.

"Come to Paris with me, Hannah. It'll be an adventure."

"I don't know."

"Come on. Live a little. Think of it as a treasure hunt with a guaranteed prize. We have the deed right here. At the very least it's a free place to stay. How can you say no?"

"What if someone is living in the apartment? We have no idea what we're walking into."

"That's why I want you to come with me. I'm afraid to go by myself."

I roll my eyes.

So much for adventure. She wants a bodyguard.

"Maybe we could ask the French lawyer to check it out for us," I suggest.

"At a rate of three hundred euros an hour?"

"Well, it's either that or you can walk into the situation blindly."

"*Or you can come to Paris with me.*" Pleadingly, she clasps her hands together over her breastbone.

I close my eyes as I feel my quiet, cozy vacation slipping out of my grasp. I open them again, only to see Marla's puppy dog gaze looking back at me.

And her shiner, which makes my heart hurt.

"We're in this together, Hannah. We jointly inherited the place. I know this is sudden, but you kind of need to come with me."

Excuse me?

"Unless you want to sign away your rights to the place and be done with it?" She smiles.

"Nice try, Marla. Look, I love the idea of spontaneously jetting off to France, but I can't. It's not practical. Not right now."

She scoffs. "We don't have to fly. Paris is practically in your backyard. Let's take the Chunnel. I've always wanted to do that."

She's right. Paris is practically in my backyard. It takes less than two and a half hours to travel via train. I visited the city when I did my study abroad semester years ago, but I haven't been back since, and I've never taken the Chunnel.

I glance down at the certificate or deed or whatever it is that Marla has presented along with her word that this apartment in Paris now belongs to us. I realize that's all I have to go on at this point.

It's New Year's Eve. The law offices—of both Patrick Sterling and our French connection—will likely be closed tomorrow and possibly a few days thereafter.

"I want to wait until I can talk to Mr. Levesque before we go off half-cocked."

I pick up the brass key. It's ornate and looks more like a decoration than our all-access pass into the world of French real estate. Who knows—if someone has been squatting all these years, they've probably changed the locks.

"Wait a minute." A possible snag stops me midthought. "What about property taxes or fees or whatever the French equivalent is? I wonder if Ivy paid them? If not, maybe the government foreclosed."

"I'm glad you reminded me. Patrick asked the French lawyer about that. Hold on—let me get my purse. I had him write it down so that I'd get it exactly right."

She pushes back from the island and clicks off into the living room on her high heels, returning a moment later with her bag, a quilted designer tote that looks about as authentic as her red Chanel sunglasses. I wonder if she bought them from the same corner vendor. She sits down, pulls out another envelope, and extracts a folded paper. I see it's a piece of letterhead stationery with something typed on it.

Marla pulls out a pair of readers and carefully pushes them onto the bridge of her nose, wincing when they settle into place. The glasses draw attention to the bruise. I don't want to look but I can't help it.

Despite everything, the eggplant-and-merlot-colored contusion makes me feel bad for her. How someone could leave a mark on another person is beyond me. She may have been an absentee mother, but she never laid a hand on me . . . despite the way her boyfriends manhandled her.

"Okay, it says here that someone set up an annuity to cover the cost of taxes, and the French attorney confirmed that it's all up-to-date. All we owe is inheritance taxes. He says it's unclear whether inheritance taxes are based on current market value or the last sale price. The French law office can assist us with that, but we still need to get the property appraised. Oh, and I forgot there was this, too."

She reaches inside the neckline of her blouse and pulls out a gold chain. When she holds out the charm, I see it's a delicate gold ring with a small red stone.

"What's that?" I ask.

"It's a ruby ring."

"Where did you get it?"

"It was with the papers and key. The chain is mine, but the ring is too small to put on my finger. I put it here so I wouldn't lose it. I'd like to keep it if you don't mind. I mean, you did say I could keep any of the crap that was left in Mom's attic since I was the one left to clean it out."

She says it in such an offhanded manner it makes me choke out a little bubble of humorless laughter.

She looks offended. "What's so funny?"

I shake my head. I can see from here the ring isn't *crap*. But we did agree she could keep what she found. I hope she doesn't try to pull that with the apartment. "We can't afford to pay inheritance taxes."

"Yes we can," she says with a smile. "When we sell Gram's house in Florida, we'll use the money from the sale to cover it."

Perhaps it will be enough, but I suspect it won't be quite so easy. "Did you ever hear Granny Ivy mention an apartment in Paris?" I repeat.

Marla shakes her head. "Then again, I wasn't around a lot when Granny Ivy moved in with Gram after Grandpa Tom died. I was hoping maybe you'd heard her mention something about it."

I shake my head. "No, I was pretty young when she died. All I know about her past is that she was living in the UK in Bristol when the war broke out. She met Great-Grandpa Tom, who was in the US Air Force. They got married and he sent her back to the States to keep her out of harm's way."

Marla is fishing in the envelope. I have a feeling she's not listening.

"Here," Marla says. "This. It was in the trunk, too."

She hands me a yellowed newspaper clipping. The text is in French, but I recognize the name Andres Armand, the famous French writer who was part of the Gertrude Stein interwar expat scene.

"So, I googled him," Marla says. "The guy in the article. What's his name?" Marla nods to the brittle newspaper clipping in my hand.

"Andres Armand," I say.

She nods. “Apparently, he was sort of a hotshot French writer of the time. Have you heard of him?”

“Of course I have.” I start to say, *Haven’t you?* But obviously she hasn’t. There’s no reason to embarrass her. Then again, not much fazes Marla, so I’d probably come off looking like an asshat.

I have a limited grasp of the French language, but it seems like the article might be about Andres Armand’s death.

I get my phone and pull up a French-to-English translation page and begin typing in the first few lines.

“I was right,” I say aloud.

“About what?”

“This article is a death announcement. Armand was killed toward the beginning of World War II. This is a story about them finding his body. Apparently he died working for the resistance.”

I study the picture at the top of the article. I’d seen his photo many times, but I’d never really looked at him. Armand was a handsome man.

“This was with the deed?” I ask.

Marla nods. “I brought everything that was with it.”

On a whim, I close out of the translator program and search *Andres Armand* and *Gertrude Stein*. Dozens of pages appear. The teaser for the top article reads, “*The Winds of Change*—Novel by Stein Protégé Andres Armand Paints Vivid Portrait of Prewar Paris Life.”

I know about Andres Armand, but I have to admit I’m not an expert on his work. He’s not as well-known as Hemingway or Fitzgerald or one of the American expats that are required reading for every American high schooler.

“I wonder why Granny Ivy saved the clipping with the apartment documents. Was there anything else besides what you’ve shown me?”

Marla shakes her head.

"Maybe she put it with the deed because she wanted to keep all the French stuff together?"

"Maybe," I say. "But why? What did it mean to her?"

It's just an article clipped from a French newspaper. In fact, it may not have meant anything to my great-grandmother.

Ivy had been a reader. Maybe she read Armand. Maybe she was going through an Armand phase at the time of his death, much the same way that I collected Jane Austen memorabilia when I first moved to England. It didn't mean anything except that I enjoyed Austen's work.

"Do you have anything to eat?" Marla asks. "I'm starving."

She gets up and starts opening cabinet doors, setting her sights on an unopened package of Biscoff cookies.

"Put those back," I say. "They're not mine."

She makes a face and begins to tear open the wrapper. "I'll replace them."

She won't. The casual promise—tossed out so nonchalantly it's in the wind the moment it leaves her lips—is one of Marla's greatest hits.

She knows she can get away with it. That's why she does it.

I add Biscoff cookies to my mental grocery list as she stands with one hip cocked against the counter, chomping biscuits with abandon.

I hear the front door open and shut. Cressida and T are back, and they're uncharacteristically silent.

"It's safe to come in," I call, relieved that they're home.

I begin stuffing the Paris paraphernalia back into the envelope because I'm not quite sure how to explain it to them. It still feels a bit fantastical, as if any moment Marla is going to laugh and say, "Just kidding. I really had you going, didn't I?"

"How is everyone?" Cressida asks as if she's walking into a hostage situation.

Tallulah looks just as tentative

"We're fine," I say. "Come in. Want some tea?"

"She's a tough nut." Marla nods in my direction and rolls her eyes. "I still haven't convinced her to come with me. I mean, who needs to be convinced to go to Paris?"

Marla told my friends about the apartment before she talked to me? Why should I be surprised?

I console myself with the reality that if it does pan out, we'll probably end up selling the place and be done with it.

"It's like this," Marla says. "In Orlando, if you travel three hours north, you're in Jacksonville. Three hours south and you're in Clewiston. But from London, you invest the same travel time and you're right smack in the middle of *oh là là*."

"You have to go," T says. "It's Paris, Hannah. I'll go if you don't want to."

I wonder how long it would take for Tallulah to get to know the real Marla, the one standing there smacking on Cressida's cookies. The one who would probably try to stick her with the hotel bill if they got over there and discovered this magical apartment was uninhabitable or, more likely, a myth.

Because what is the likelihood that an apartment that has been sitting vacant for a while is move-in ready?

Or even ours.

It crosses my mind to take Tallulah up on the offer to go in my stead, but I say, "She just sprung this on me. I haven't even had time to digest the situation. There's nothing we can do about it tonight anyway. It's New Year's Eve."

"That's right," Cressida says. "And we have a party to get to. Marla, are you coming?"

"No!" I say before she can answer.

Three heads swivel in my direction.

"I love parties," says Marla.

"You can't go," I say, determined to nip that in the bud. "You weren't invited. You can't just show up."

"Hannah, this is Jemma," says Cressida. "There's no invitation list. There will be so many people there she won't care as long as Marla brings a bottle of something."

"Ha! She doesn't have a bottle to bring."

And a recovering alcoholic doesn't need to be around a bunch of drunks at a party.

"We picked up plenty," says T. "Even something for you so you couldn't use that as an excuse not to go."

"You didn't have to do that. I've had a long week. I want to have a quiet night."

"Well, girls," says Marla. "Let her stay home if she's going to be like that. We know how to have fun."

Visions of Marla dancing on tables with her *bottle of something* snap me back to reality.

Shit.

London was the birthplace of her days as a groupie following around the punk band The Squelching Wellies. I have a sinking feeling that coming here might tempt her to relive her glory days. I need to make sure she doesn't do something stupid.

Babysitting my mother was not how I envisioned spending my vacation . . . or ringing in the New Year. But one of us needs to take responsibility.

"Okay, fine. I'll go."

Cressida claps her hands. "Zed will be so happy."

Ugh. That's right. Okay, fine. I'll meet Zed. It doesn't mean I have to go out with him.

Cressida looks at her watch. “I have to start getting ready.”

As she and T leave the room, they're discussing wardrobe choices. I contemplate what people would do if I did show up in my flannels and fuzzy socks.

Hi, Zed; I'm Hannah.

That would fix the situation.

“Shall I shower first, or do you want to?” Marla asks.

“Go ahead,” I say. “But wash your champagne glass, please. The washing liquid is in that stainless steel pump container to the right of the sink.”

“It's not dirty,” Marla says.

“Didn't you drink champagne with T and Cressida?”

She shakes her head. “I didn't have any. I told you I'm on the wagon.”

“Okay,” I say. “That's good.”

“I'm starting over, Hannah. If I keep doing what I've been doing, I'll keep getting what I've been getting. I'm tired of it.”

“Fair enough,” I say, wanting to believe her but remembering the sting of too many broken promises and sullied declarations in the past.

“So, what about Paris?” she asks. “Are you coming with me?”

March 1927

Paris, France

Dear Diary,

When I entered the garret after my disastrous appointment, I met our landlord, Monsieur Arpin. One glance and I realized he took no more pride in his personal hygiene than he did in the flat's cleanliness.

He needed a shave. He wore grey, grease-spotted trousers and a dirty white sleeveless shirt that was yellowed under the armpits. He smelled of sweat, cigarettes, and whiskey-soaked cabbage.

I held my breath as I brushed past him to stand next to Helen. He leered at us and licked his lips. Muttering, his gaze dropped to Helen's bosom and he had the nerve to say she was the prettier of us, but I would do.

I would do?

At first, I had no idea what he meant, but then he laughed and gave a lascivious wink. It sent a shiver down my spine.

I walked to the door and asked him to leave.

He refused, insisting we settle on the rent. He wanted two months' rent in advance rather than the one month's we had agreed upon in our correspondence.

With a pursed-lip shrug, he claimed circumstances had changed. If we wanted the place, we needed to hand over the money.

He kept muttering in French and holding up two hairy-knuckled fingers with filthy nails. By this time his odeur *had filled the flat, threatening to gag me.*

We tried to reason with him, saying we needed to work to earn the rest. Once we had the money, we would pay.

He refused to budge.

Helen shot me a glance as if telling me to play along.

Her tone changed to something more coquettish and she started proposing . . . alternate arrangements. If I didn't know her so well, I might've worried about what she was getting us in for. Alas, my friend is an actress. She takes on personas and uses them to her advantage. I've seen her do it before, but never in such a dangerous situation.

But it worked. Monsieur Arpin, slack jawed, murmuring about Helen's amiable nature, said he might be persuaded to accommodate us if she was agreeable to certain terms.

I was sick to my stomach as I watched Helen cozy up to the wretch, teasing him with smoldering eyes and a sultry purr.

The Helen that I knew would never trade her body for rent. It was . . . prostitution. I had to keep reminding myself it was just a role. Arpin was fully under her spell.

When he tried to touch her, she sidestepped him, informing him she would dictate the terms of their new arrangement; he was to go away for two days and anticipate the pleasures to come.

When he insisted on sampling the new terms immediately, Helen twisted his arm and lifted her knee to his groin and scolded him.

He was a short, stocky bull of a man, half-crazed with lust. I was afraid if she pushed him too far, he would turn the tables and take what he wanted.

Helen was playing with fire. All he needed to do was push her backward and he could dominate her. But instead, he whimpered in submission.

She held up two fingers and told him that during his two-day wait, he was not to talk to us. If he did, the wait would reset. She would punish him by making him wait another two days.

Then she gave him a shove toward the door, telling him to leave.

Before he could utter another word, Helen shut the door in his face and locked it. I was mesmerized by the power she held over this swine, and petrified by the way she wound him up only to push him out.

Finally, Helen broke character and bowed. Then she made a face and pretended to gag.

I declared her performance award-worthy, telling her that for a moment she had me convinced she meant to deliver on her promise.

What if he called to collect early? He'd already changed the rules on us once. What if he barged in on us in the middle of the night?

Frowning as if she hadn't considered the possibility, Helen said we would find another flat within the next two days. In the meantime, we would move the dresser in front of the door. That way he wouldn't be able to surprise us.

It didn't make me feel better. But Helen sat on one of the beds, applying bloodred lipstick to her mouth, blotting her lips together, and studying her reflection in the compact she'd pulled from her purse as if she didn't have a care in the world.

She turned to me and lifted her left brow in that worldly, knowing way of hers, telling me that since we were in Paris, I needed to understand that men would be men and if we don't outsmart them, they would devour us.

With no security and no money, I was suddenly and shamefully homesick.

Those feelings weren't only spurred because I felt I'd fallen into waters too deep. It wasn't even noon, and Helen was urging me to go to a bar with her. She said we were to meet new friends at a place called Dingo Bar. After all that transpired, I don't understand why Helen was so insistent on going to a bar midmorning.

Come to think of it, I couldn't remember why moving to Paris had ever seemed like a good idea.

Five

December 31, 2018—10:00 p.m.

London, England

By the time we make it across town to Jemma's flat in Chelsea, the party is in full swing. Festive jazz plays over the sound system. The lounge and kitchen are so crammed that people are spilling out into the back garden.

"The key is to invite everyone on the block," Jemma says from her post behind the makeshift bar in the lounge. One thin, tapered hand holds a cigarette; there's a highball glass in the other. "Half the time they don't come, but then at least they don't mind if you have a proper soirée."

She parks her cigarette between her lips, adds ice to a glass, fills it with vodka and a splash of cranberry, and hands it to me. "Drink up, lovie. It's bad luck to ring in the New Year sober."

I touch the glass to hers and take a sip, recalling that Marla said something similar about New Year's luck.

Speaking of the devil, I look around for her, but it appears she's been swallowed up by the party. I wonder if she's having trouble around all this free-flowing liquor.

I throw back the drink and shoulder my way through the

bottleneck in the hallway. I finally make my way through a cloud of smoke and strong perfume into the crisp air of the patio, which is slightly warmed by tall heat lamps and decorated with strings of blinking Christmas lights and randomly placed bunches of mistletoe.

Cressida is out here talking to Danny, a guy she's had an on-again, off-again relationship with for the better part of this year and whom I've never formally met for some reason. She looks posh in her short black dress. With all those beads at the neckline, it has to be expensive. Well, if it's in Cressida's closet, of course it's expensive.

Danny's leather jacket is draped over her shoulders. She's facing him, and his hands are parked on her ass.

Underneath the Christmas lights, the sprayed silver glitter in her blonde hair makes it look iridescent platinum.

"Happy New Year," I say to Danny. He answers with a nod, then turns his chin upward and blows a series of white smoke rings into the inky sky. Danny works in computers and wears horn-rimmed glasses. It's hard to tell if his silence stems from shyness or judgment.

"Have you seen Marla?" I ask my roommate. A jazzy rendition of "Let It Snow" starts to play over the outdoor speakers.

"I saw her earlier." Cressida looks around the patio and teeters a little. Danny pulls her against him. I turn to go.

"Oh, Hannah, by the way, Zed is here. Let's go find him."

"That's okay," I say. "No hurry."

"I'll be right back, love," she says to Danny. "I have someone I want Hannah to meet. Be a doll and refresh my drink?"

She dangles her champagne glass between two perfectly manicured fingers. Danny takes it, leans in, and whispers something in her ear. Cressida laughs, and Danny kisses her.

He'd have to be a fool not to want Cressida. She's smart, funny, rich, and gorgeous. She's the kind of woman who doesn't need a man in her life, which means nearly every man she meets falls in love with her.

Cressida is lost in the kiss, giving me a chance to slip away and avoid the awkward introduction to Zed, who's probably equally unenthusiastic about meeting me. I turn around to make my getaway.

And who do I run into—literally, like, in a breast-to-chest collision?

It's Brooding Darcy from Sally Lunn's house in Bath. Or his identical twin.

"Oh, I'm so sorry," I say. My palms are pressed flat against his pecs and his arm is steadying my waist. "I need to watch where I'm going."

Then he scowls at me, and I know it's him because I'm struck by the same thunderbolt that hit me when I first saw him sitting at Sally Lunn's. I feel myself coming undone again. The same way I felt earlier today.

"It's nice to run into you again. Any more problems with your tour patron?"

And there's that lovely accent.

The scowl wrinkles his forehead and I wonder if that's his normal expression. The male version of resting bitch face.

"No, you must've scared him off. But you left before I could get your name."

"Zed, there you are." Cressida has come up for air and Danny is nowhere to be found. "Hannah, this is Zed. The guy I wanted you to meet."

This is Zed?

Cressida's gaze dips and I realize his arm is still around my waist. In that instant, he pulls away and we both reclaim our personal space.

"I see you two are already . . . acquainted. You didn't need me. You found each other."

She claps her hands like a child who has gotten a pony for her birthday. "I knew you'd hit it off. Zed, ask Hannah. I have a knack for matchmaking."

I laugh out loud thinking about her three disastrous attempts at fixing me up before. But now is not the time to bring that up.

"This is the strangest thing," I say. "Zed, is it?"

He nods. "Actually, it's Aiden Zedrick. Some call me Zed for short."

"Aiden was in Bath earlier today at the Sally Lunn House, where I took my tour group for tea. He helped me with a . . . a *situation*."

"Aye, it was nothing, really." He shifts from one foot to another, looking uncomfortable being the center of attention.

"I thought it was something," I say. "Thanks again."

"It wasn't a problem."

His scowl gives way to bemusement, and my stomach flips.

"You two are adorable," Cressida gushes. "I knew you'd be perfect for each other."

Danny appears behind her with two flutes of champagne.

"Danny, look," she says, leaning into him. "It's Zed and Hannah. Aren't they cute together?"

He doesn't answer, just hands me the other champagne and sweeps Cressida away.

"How do you know Cressida?" I ask Aiden, whom I refuse to call Zed.

"I don't know her very well. I met her through Jemma. I live just down the street. A couple of weeks ago she and Cressida came into my restaurant for dinner."

"You own a restaurant?"

He shrugs sheepishly.

"Not exactly. I'm the executive chef at Lemon and Lavender."

I sip my champagne.

"If you're the executive chef, how did you manage to get New Year's Eve off? Isn't it one of the busiest nights of the year?"

"The restaurant is closed from Christmas Eve through New Year's Day. We reopen January second."

"Were you playing tourist in Bath on your time off?"

"No. I was working. I was on a reconnaissance mission. The owner wants to start offering high tea on Sundays. I made a list of places to check out and Sally Lunn was one of them."

"So you're not really on vacation, then?"

"Eating is not exactly hard work. Especially when someone else cooks."

It's amazingly easy to talk to Aiden. The night passes in a flash and before I know it, the crowd at the party is raucously counting down the end of the year. The music changes to a rockabilly version of "Auld Lang Syne." Those who aren't kissing are blowing noisemakers and yelling "Happy New Year!"

Someone launches a confetti cannon and bits of metallic and rainbow-colored paper float down around us.

Aiden brushes a piece off my forehead, leans in, and kisses me.

It's more than a friendly peck, but it's not exactly the prelude to a hookup. Still, as his lips brush mine, I wonder how a casual New Year's kiss can be so intoxicating. I'm suddenly aware of my hands on his back, of the solid, muscled flesh under his shirt. I want to know him better so I can have more.

But I can't have more right now.

The timing is all wrong.

"Come to the restaurant sometime," he says. "I'll treat you to dinner."

My stomach flips. This sounds promising.

"That would be lovely."

I want to see him again. I want to kiss him again.

"Why don't you, Jem, and Cressida come in tomorrow night? It's officially January first. I'm meaning January second. When we reopen."

"I wish I could, but my mother is in town."

"Bring her."

Hell no.

"It's nice of you to offer, but she and I might be going out of town in the next couple of days."

"Where are you going?"

"Paris."

"Sounds like fun."

I shrug. "It's actually a business trip." *Sort of.*

As we talk, I realize his scowl and his dark features are the only resemblance he bears to Fitzwilliam Darcy. Maybe one of the hazards of my job is reducing everything to a Jane Austen plot.

More proof of how desperately I need a proper vacation.

Alone.

Or at least one without Marla, who seems to be navigating this party fine on her own. I hear her laugh and spy her sitting on an outdoor sectional at the far corner of the patio under a heat lamp.

She's wearing her sunglasses and holding court with a handful of guys. I know one of them. His name is Jesse. He's sitting next to her with his arm casually draped over the back of the sofa, around her, but not on her.

There's enough room that he could lead Marla to believe he's man-stretching, but I know for a fact that's not what he's doing. This is the warm-up to putting the moves on her.

Ew. She could be his mother. Okay, maybe his older sister. But still.

At one time or another, Jesse has tried with varying degrees of success to sleep with most of the women I know at this party. T hooked up with him a couple of times, and he even tried to put the moves on me once. So I know how he operates.

"Come in when you get back from Paris," Aiden says. "It's a standing invitation."

He smiles and my insides melt. I'd better get home before I do something regrettable.

I glance over at Marla. Now Jesse's arm is around her, his hand dangerously close to her breast.

Oh geez, Marla. Really?

"That sounds fabulous," I say. "I'd love to."

"Let me see your phone," he says.

"Why?" I ask.

I hand it to him and he punches in some numbers. His own phone rings.

"I called my phone with your phone. Now we have each other's numbers."

He ensured this isn't one-sided, that either of us could get in touch with the other. It makes me inordinately happy.

"Hannah! Come here!" Marla calls over the music, waving her arms and ruining the moment. "I want you to meet Jesse."

"I'll be right back," I say to Aiden.

I don't want him to meet Marla. Not yet. Probably not ever.

I glare at Jesse as I walk over. "Jesse, I see you've met my *mother*. Marla, I'm ready to go home. Come on."

"No, I'm not letting her go." Jesse puts both arms around her and pulls her against him. I don't know if he's high or drunk or a combination of both, but he's clearly plastered.

"Go ahead without me," Marla says. "I promised Jesse I'd drive him to his house in his car. He's in no condition to get behind the wheel."

"And how are you going to get home?" I ask.

"Hannah, don't worry about me," she says. "I'm a big girl. I can manage."

She sounds like she's sober.

"Remember, they drive on the opposite side of the road here," I say. "Maybe someone else should take Jesse home."

She waves me off. "Don't be such a worrywart. I'll be fine."

I glance at Aiden, still standing where I left him. He smiles at me when our eyes meet.

"Okay, Marla," I say. "Whatever you want to do. I'm leaving."

I return to Aiden to say good night and leave Marla to fend for herself.

March 1927
Paris, France

Dear Diary,

On the way to Dingo Bar, Helen told me she met her new men friends after I'd left for my appointment at the Chanel atelier. She'd gone in search of coffee, made their acquaintance, and they'd invited us to meet them at Dingo.

Helen thinks it's chic to go to a bar in the morning, but I kept wondering what kind of establishment would be open at that hour and what its clientele would be like.

Don't these people have jobs?

Obviously, I'm not the only unemployed wretch in Paris. At least the outing diverted my thoughts from the dreadful Chanel debacle. But it made more glaring the fact that Helen hadn't inquired about the interview. Sometimes she can be so consumed with herself.

She can also be unrelenting when it comes to getting what she wants. For example, after I balked at the outing, she plopped her red cloche hat on my head—she knows how I covet it. She said I could have it if I went with her. She pulled it into place, tugging my hair forward over my cheeks. How could I resist? With that, she grabbed my hand and yanked me out the door. I could've said no, of course, but . . . the hat.

It was a long walk from rue du Cardinal Lemoine to Dingo Bar on rue Delambre in Montparnasse. By the time we'd reached the Jardin du Luxembourg, the fresh air and Helen's effervescence had lifted me out of my mood and I was properly enjoying the mild day and the bright-blue sky. It was such a contrast to the smelly little hovel and the disastrous morning.

Dingo Bar was situated on the ground floor of a white stucco building with shuttered windows and a red awning. Inside, the place was crowded and loud. A jazz quartet played a lively tune. People were dancing, smoking, and drinking as if they were the only things to do at this hour of the morning. The place smelled of sweat, perfume, and stale liquor, which I quickly associated with the aroma of people having a good time. I wondered how many had been there since the night before.

The moment we arrived, Helen spotted one of her fellows seated at a crowded table. He was dark and handsome with intense eyes and an engaging smile.

As we approached, he stood, planted a double kiss on Helen's cheeks, and sculpted enough room for us in the shoulder-to-shoulder seating arrangement.

His name was Pablo. He was a painter from Spain who lived in Paris. Talking over the music, he announced we had just arrived from London, that Helen was an actress, and I was une créatrice de mode.

I started to correct him and tell him that, at this point, I was merely a seamstress, but he was already regaling everyone with the story of how he had stopped Helen on the street that morning and told her she was the most beautiful woman he'd ever met—the muse he'd been searching for his entire life. His soul would be tormented until she allowed him to paint her.

I think he was drunk.

Everyone was talking all at once, mostly speaking English, much to my great relief. Even though I could only catch snippets of conversation, the familiar hum was soothing. The thought of being able to sit here and just listen was a respite. Until Pablo pointed out a smart-looking woman across the table, hanging on every word of the handsome man who sat next to her. Her name was Pauline. Pablo said she was a correspondent for Vogue, *and she had even discovered new fashion talent and had given them their big break by featuring them in the magazine.*

She was someone I needed to know.

Her black bob fell just above her chin. Her bangs cut a sharp line across her forehead, showcasing wide-set eyes. Everything about her—from her flawless makeup to her expensive suit to the emerald earrings swinging from her earlobes—seemed effortlessly stylish.

After I made it down to Pauline's end of the table, her handsome man found a chair for me. He placed it between them.

Pauline introduced him as Ernest, but she called him Hem. She started talking about me as if I weren't there, saying I was pretty—just Hem's type.

It made me uncomfortable, but not as much as when he agreed.

I was relieved when Pauline told him to fetch us a bottle of champagne and he complied.

Then Pauline began asking about my work. I almost couldn't contain myself when she said she'd look at my sketches.

I asked her when she was available, but before she could respond, Hem returned with the champagne. He popped the cork, spewing the liquid at me. People cheered, except for Pauline, who rolled her eyes and handed me a napkin. She told me to ignore Hem, that he was celebrating a newly published book. It had been well received and he was quite full of himself.

As she berated him for making a spectacle of himself and wasting good champagne, it only seemed to egg him on.

He grabbed my hand, pulled me into his arms, and began tangoing with me, weaving us through the tables, pressing his body to mine. I wanted to disappear. I couldn't look at Pauline, but I could feel her eyes burning a hole in my back.

I knew I had to gracefully dance away from Hem or risk losing my connection to Vogue, *but just when I thought I was free, Hem reeled me in and dipped me back. I turned my head to the side just in time for his sloppy, openmouthed kiss to land between my neck and collarbone.*

When he righted me, the world was spinning.

Six

January 1, 2019—11:00 a.m.

London, England

The next morning, the sun smiles at me through the window of my upstairs bedroom, bestowing the promise of a brand-new year. A brand-new decade.

And the promise of Aiden.

Cressida could totally redeem herself with him. He doesn't seem to bear any resemblance to The Stiffer, The Sniffer, or The Quitter. Then again, technically, I found him first. Maybe she shouldn't get credit.

A quick glance at the alarm clock informs me that it's a few minutes past 11:00. I swing my legs over the side of the bed and shove my feet into fleece-lined slippers before pulling on my robe.

The rest of the house is quiet and probably will be until well into the afternoon, given how much fun Cressida and T seemed to be having when I left the party.

I make my way downstairs thinking Marla might have slept on the couch since she got in late, but there's no sign of her or any indication she's been home. My pulse thuds as at least a dozen grim possibilities of where she ended up pop into my mind. Jail? Dumpster? Jesse's bed?

But she does have her cell phone. She could've called.

Did she call? Did I sleep through it?

I speed walk up the stairs to my bedroom and fish my phone out of my purse. There are two texts: one from Marla and one from Aiden.

I look at Aiden's message first.

> Happy New Year. Text me when you get back from Paris. I want to see you.

My stomach flips. Before I can overthink it, I text back.

> Happy New Year to you. Still firming up Paris plans. More soon.

I type an *xo*, but I delete it before sending and move on to Marla's message, which completely deflates my good mood.

> Happy New Year, Hannah. Just wanted you to know that I won't be home tonight. It's not what you think. M.

It's not what you think.

Okay.

What am I supposed to think when Jesse was all over her last night at the party playing grab-a-boob?

On second thought, I don't want to know.

Not my circus. Not my monkeys.

At least she's okay. She let me know she wouldn't be home. She stepped out of her own little world long enough to consider that I might worry if she didn't show up. Part of me is happy I didn't have to share a bed with her after all.

She's a grown woman who can do what she wants.

A grown woman who has slept with a lot of men.

But until now, none of them were my friends.

It's embarrassing when your mother's indiscretions are ripe for post-party gossip.

I should've insisted that she and I stay home.

Then again, if I hadn't gone to the party, I wouldn't have run into Aiden.

I go downstairs and make a cup of coffee, which I take into the bathroom with me, setting it on the vanity next to my phone while I turn on the shower tap.

Twenty minutes later, I emerge with wet hair wrapped in a towel. I've pulled on a cozy exercise outfit, though no exercise is on today's agenda. I have more important matters to tend to, such as finding Marla a place to stay tonight.

What if she wants to stay with Jesse?

I suppose the remedy to that is to get her to Paris to check out this apartment as soon as possible. Maybe this has all been some sick exercise in reverse psychology. I wouldn't put it past her.

As I'm heading toward the kitchen, she startles me with an exuberant "Good morning," and I almost scream.

I press my finger to my lips to silence her and say, "*Shhhhh*, Cressida and T are still sleeping."

Her mouth forms a perfect O and she covers it with her hand. "Sorry," she stage-whispers.

"You didn't come home last night. How did you get in the flat this morning?"

"The front door was unlocked."

"What? Why was it unlocked?" I demand.

"*Shhhh*," she says. "People are sleeping. I wasn't the one who left it unlocked. Don't yell at me."

I make a mental note to remind C and T to be more careful.

Marla opens the refrigerator and peruses the contents. "Do you have any cream?"

She's wearing those ridiculous glasses again this morning. I can't see her eyes, and her curly auburn hair is frizzy. She looks rumpled and pale after her walk of shame.

I imagine it's a snapshot into her Squelching Wellies days.

"Cream? In the little blue-and-yellow pitcher."

"It's empty."

"Well, then we must be out. There might be some skim milk in there."

She tsks her disappointment. "Why bother? All skim does is water down your coffee." She makes herself a cup and leaves it black, then opens the cupboard and helps herself to the rest of Cressida's Biscoff cookies.

I'm not even trying to hide how annoyed I am that she doesn't have the good grace to look contrite about sleeping with Jesse.

Per usual, she's oblivious.

"Do you have to wear your sunglasses in the house?"

"Why does it bother you so much?" She pulls them off and flings them onto the island. "You are cranky this morning. Did things not work out with that guy?"

I blink at her non sequitur, though I know she's talking about Aiden.

"What are you talking about?"

"The guy you were with last night. The one you kissed at mid-night."

She saw us kiss?

I don't want to share details about Aiden with Marla.

Right now, it still feels magical, full of possibility, and I want to savor that feeling for as long as it lasts. Because with my dating history, it usually doesn't.

It would probably be wise for me to get through this Paris ordeal with my mother before I even think of seeing him again.

If he was serious about seeing me again. All I know about him at this point is that he was born and raised in Edinburgh and came to London to attend culinary school.

If I put off calling him, I hope time doesn't turn him into The Ghoster.

Or would that make *me* The Ghoster since I'd be the one who didn't call?

I don't know.

Should dating be this complicated?

"I'm sorry it didn't work out with him," Marla says as she pulls out a stool and sits at the island. "Do you want to talk about it?"

"There's nothing to talk about. It wasn't a date."

"But you kissed him! Oh God—was he bad in bed? Because life is too short for—"

"No! I didn't sleep with him. Unlike you, I don't sleep with every man I meet."

She flinches like I've slapped her in the face, and I'm glad for it. A woman who was sleeping with so many men that she doesn't even know who fathered her child has no right to act injured. I turn my back on her and put another pod in the Nespresso machine.

"I'm not like that anymore, Hannah."

I turn around and face her. For once, she looks me in the eyes. Her bruise is fading, but it still overrides my common sense and makes me feel sorry for her.

"I made a vow when I left for Paris—when I left Don—that this would be a time for *me*. A brand-new start. You know, a chance to get my life together. And maybe even right a few wrongs."

I wonder if she's talking about our relationship, but I don't ask. I'm not that needy. She should know. It's one of the few things she taught me. Don't make yourself vulnerable and you won't get hurt.

"And you lasted, what? Twenty-four hours?" I say. "Or was it even that long? Let's see—what time did your flight leave Orlando?"

"That's rude." She looks offended, but I know her game.

"Marla, I want to believe that you're serious about making a fresh start in Paris, but it's hard when you spend the night with a guy you met on your first night in London."

She's staring into her coffee like it's whiskey and she's drowning her sorrows.

Good. She should look remorseful. What kind of a mother shows up unannounced, invites herself to a party with her daughter's friends, and then stays out all night with a guy who is half her age?

My mother—that's who. She will never change.

Marla laughs, but it's dry and humorless. "You think I slept with Jesse, don't you? Is that what this is all about?" She clucks and rolls her eyes. "Oh, Hannah. Give me a little credit. Jesse could be my son."

"Look, I don't care. You do you, Marla, but don't look me in the eyes and tell me you're changing your ways when you're doing exactly what you've always done."

"It must be nice to be so perfect," Marla mutters.

"I never claimed to be perfect. I just don't put on pretenses and turn around and do exactly what I swore off."

Marla sits up ramrod straight in her chair, lifts her chin a notch, and purses her lips, which are rimmed with the stain of last night's lipstick and liner.

"I'm sorry you feel that way."

This is another one of Marla's go-to tactics. If you can't snow them, guilt them.

"Jesse just broke up with his girlfriend," she says.

I laugh. "Is that what he told you? Jesse doesn't have *girlfriends*. He's a player, Marla. He sold you a load of BS to get you into bed."

"Nope. He was hurting. His girlfriend was at the party with another guy."

"Okay. Whatever. I don't care."

I turn away from her and take out bread for toast. I'm not hungry, but I need something to do.

"Maybe I'm saying it wrong," Marla says. "She wasn't exactly Jesse's girlfriend, but he had been seeing someone and he'd really fallen for her. It's someone you know, as a matter of fact. He had feelings for her, but she didn't feel the same. He was crushed and he needed someone to talk to. So, yes, I was at his apartment last night, and we stayed up talking until five a.m., but then we fell asleep on the couch. With our clothes on."

My mother stays out all night and the next morning she's trying to justify it like a teenager attempting to convince a parent there were no boys at the sleepover. I have no idea if what she's saying is true. I don't care. Well, I do, but I don't want to.

I push two slices of bread into the toaster. "I know her? This woman who supposedly crushed Jesse's soul?"

Marla lifts her chin again, smiling as if daring me to speculate.

I know I'm playing right into her hand, but I ask, "Who is it?"

She nods, and her eyes sparkle as she leans forward, resting her chin on her fist. "Guess."

"I'm not going to guess. Maybe you shouldn't tell me. It might betray a confidence."

Marla blows on her coffee and slurps it. "I wouldn't have brought it up if Jesse had asked me not to tell anyone. Since I'm your mother, don't you think he knows you're the first person I'd tell?"

"You're giving him a lot of credit. He's gorgeous, but I don't know that he thinks that deeply about things like this."

"You're wrong. That's your problem, Hannah. You can be so judgmental. You form conclusions about people and then you brand them. No one's allowed to make a mistake because in Miss Perfect's eyes, they'll carry that stigma forever."

I cross my arms. "I've never claimed to be perfect. That's pretty harsh."

"No worse than you branding me an alcoholic tramp for the rest of my life when I'm working hard to change."

And so goes the endless loop of illogic that is an argument with my mother.

I shake my head.

"At the risk of sounding judgmental, that's the mother I've known all my life. You show up unannounced and you stay out all night. It's optics, Marla. That's what I see. It's the only you I've ever known."

"That's what Gram made you see."

"Leave Gram out of this. She and Granny Ivy were all I had. You were off doing your own thing, living your own life. Do not blame Gram."

"I know Gram was good to you, but there's more to the story than you know."

"Stop. Okay? Just stop."

I want to put my hands over my ears.

If she starts talking smack about my grandmother, I will get her bags and put them out on the curb. Gram was the only mother figure I had when I was growing up. Our life in Orlando may have been boring by Marla's standards, but at least Gram was there for me. Not only did she put a roof over my head and food in my belly, but she also taught me to love literature. She sent me to college. She raised me with *values*.

Oh God, listen to me.

I guess I do sound judgmental.

But I'm *not* a bitch.

Judgmental bitches have no problem confronting people. I relegate the raging to the privacy of my mind.

Because when you speak your mind, people like Marla brand you judgmental. Full circle.

"I'm sorry, Hannah. I know Gram is off-limits. Even though she and I had our differences, I respect that she was good to you."

I shrug.

We sit in silence for a moment.

As I sip my coffee, I ponder how Gram was so tender and warm toward me but so cold toward her own daughter. Marla was hard to love. She was a challenge. I witnessed that with my own eyes, but I can't reconcile the grandmother I knew with the mother Marla claims to have known.

I don't want to dissect the one safe spot of my childhood right now. Contrary to Marla's dig, nobody's perfect. I'm sure Gram had her flaws. But I don't want Marla to smash Gram's clay feet.

Marla's surprise appearance, the did-she-or-didn't-she question of her night with Jesse, and the Paris apartment that we need to sort out together—it's all too much.

"Do you want to call Jesse and ask him about last night?" Marla's inane suggestion pulls me out of my thoughts.

"No. I don't want to talk to Jesse."

"Then you believe me?"

"Okay, fine. Whatever."

I really don't care.

"So then guess who broke Jesse's heart." She leans forward, her brows arched. "I'll give you a clue. You see her every day."

At this point, the guessing game seems the best way back to stable ground.

"I can't think of anyone else I see every day other than Cressida or Tallulah."

Marla's eyes light up and she purses her lips. "You've narrowed it down nicely."

Tallulah had a fling with Jesse last year. It was one-sided on her part. She thought she could change him and wanted it to be more than it was. The tighter she hung on, the more he pulled away. Eventually, everything imploded. She was wrecked over it. I can't imagine Jesse suddenly doing an about-face. . . .

My mind flashes back to a night when we were at the Bull and Thorn pub and Cressida and Jesse seemed extra chummy. He was teaching her to throw darts. He had his arms around her and was helping her aim. At the time, I didn't think anything of it.

"Is it Cressida?"

Marla's face lights up like Camden High Street at Christmas. "I will neither confirm nor deny that."

"Why? I thought you said you weren't betraying Jesse's confidence."

"Yeah, but I'm realizing that I don't know how Cressida would feel about me telling you. She's been so nice to me. I don't want to make her mad. I don't want to rock the boat while I'm here."

"But you just told me."

Marla grimaces and puts her hand over her mouth.

"I guess I did. But you can't say anything, okay?"

"I won't. I mean, it's no big deal. It was only a couple of times, right?"

"No, apparently it was going on for a while. Like most of last year." She grimaces again. "Let's not. I just . . . Let's pretend like I didn't say anything."

Despite her black eye—or maybe because of it—she looks earnest. I want to believe her. I don't want to judge her—or anyone, not even Cressida, for having a secret fling with Jesse.

Maybe I'm an idiot for softening up when a moment ago I was ready to boot Marla out.

Maybe.

I don't know.

At this point we'd all be better off not to test her. The path of least resistance is to get to Paris.

"I was thinking," I say. "Since the meter is ticking on my vacation, it's better for us to go check out the apartment sooner rather than later."

"Absolutely," Marla says. "I'll look into arrangements. Maybe we can leave tomorrow?"

April 1927
Paris, France

Dear Diary,

It's been a few weeks since I've had a chance to write, but I have a good excuse: a lot has happened. Thanks to the guidance of Pablo's friend Luc Fabron, we have found a new living arrangement. It's a small apartment in Montparnasse. It's not fancy, but at least it's clean and free of smelly letches who change the rules at whim.

It turned out the painter Pablo Picasso, who seemed so smitten with Helen, had a young girlfriend . . . and a wife. He has yet to paint Helen. I think she hurt his feelings. That morning at Dingo Bar, he introduced Helen to Luc, another painter. Immediately, Helen threw over Pablo for Luc. It's just as well, given Pablo's reputation for collecting women. And the fact that Helen does not like to share.

Beyond her happiness, meeting Luc was a godsend because he knew of an inexpensive apartment that was available for immediate occupancy. We were able to move in that night. We did not have to risk Monsieur Arpin barging in as we slept.

Much to Luc's delight, we are now his neighbors. He's as smitten with Helen as she is with him. It's too early to tell whether my friend's infatuation will last. Even if it doesn't, Helen has a way of converting tiresome romances into friendships—well, except for Pablo, who seemed full of resentment as he watched Luc take possession of Helen's affections.

I hope Luc understands that if she gets an offer from the

Ballets Russes, she will be gone from his arms faster than he can say, Helen, mon amour.

But for now, they are happy, and we are safe in our new abode.

The afternoon of our first visit to Dingo Bar, we decided to stay away from Monsieur Arpin's place on rue du Cardinal Lemoine until night fell with the hopes that Monsieur Arpin had a nightly routine of drinking himself into an oblivion. Luc and other friends of his (but not Pablo) tagged along to protect us while we gathered our belongings.

I wondered if it was a good idea because by that late hour the men were drunk and seemed to be spoiling for a fight, saying things like, "Let him even look at the two of you and we'll knock him into next week."

I didn't want a scene. I wanted to collect our things and leave Monsieur Arpin and his slum garret in the past. I had bigger fish to fry, such as finding a job so I could earn enough money to cover my share of the rent, which, we discovered, was inexpensive by Paris standards, but cost decidedly more than the place on rue du Cardinal Lemoine. Considering we would no longer be forced to pay the high price of fighting for our dignity, it was worth the extra expense.

Not long after we were settled in the new apartment, I learned that Pauline and Ernest had left Paris before she could look at my designs and make the introductions she'd offered. Apparently they are to be married. After what happened with Hem, I'm not surprised she didn't follow through. Disappointed, yes, but not surprised.

Adele, a woman I met at Dingo Bar, warned me that Hem had

a wandering eye and fast hands. She said he had been married to a woman named Hadley when he met Pauline. According to Adele, it was love at first sight for Pauline, even though she and her sister, Jinny, met Ernest and Hadley together. Apparently, Pauline even went so far as to befriend Hadley to get close to Hem.

This is all to say that perhaps Pauline's helpful demeanor at the bar was less a case of true self-confidence as it was a matter of keeping friends close and romantic rivals closer. She need not worry about me—I have no designs on her man—but it's clear I can't count on her for introductions. Now, I have no choice but to get out there and make the rounds at other fashion houses on my list.

There will be a job for me in this mecca, won't there?

Seven

January 2, 2019—3:00 p.m.
Gare du Nord train station, 10th arrondissement
Paris, France

The next day, Marla and I board the train at St. Pancras station and make the two-hour-and-fifteen-minute trip through the Chunnel to the Gare du Nord in Paris.

"Let's not take the Metro," Marla says when we're standing on the sidewalk paralleling rue de Dunkerque in front of the train station. She points to her phone where she's entered the address of our hotel into Google Maps. "Let's walk."

We reserved a room at a small hotel in the first arrondissement near the Louvre, figuring it was the smart thing to do since we didn't know what we were getting ourselves into. Even though it was a bit far from the apartment, which is in the ninth, the price was right for a modest place with good ratings in a nice part of Paris.

Marla holds out her phone. "It says we're only eleven minutes from the hotel. After being cooped up on that train, I could use some exercise. Want to walk?"

"Sure, I'm up for it."

Before we set out this morning, we called the French law office and were happy to reach Monsieur Levesque's assistant. We arranged to meet him at his office at 4:30. It's 3:00 now, which gives us plenty of time to get to the hotel, check in, and make our way to his office in Montparnasse.

Plus, walking will allow us to see Paris. I'm surprised at how my heart leaps at the opportunity, as if it's breaking free from the cell in which I'd caged my hopes that the apartment would be viable.

I turn in a slow circle, taking in everything: the honking horns of cars and motorcycles on the bustling rue de Dunkerque, shouts and laughs of pedestrians as they pass by on the wide sidewalks, the six-story Haussmann-style buildings that line the street across from the train station.

There's an open window on the second floor of one of the proud stone structures. I can see the silhouette of someone passing in front of it. People live in those apartments nestled atop the shops and red-canopied cafés.

I wonder who they are and how they got there. Will that be me someday? Will I be the one in the apartment and someone else will be standing on the street looking up, wondering how I got there? The thought of living in Paris leaves me breathless. But I'm still cautious. I don't want to get too carried away in case this turns out to be a big nothing.

I force myself to look away and my gaze lands on a small house in front of the Gare du Nord that appears to be tilting or melting into the sidewalk.

"What in the world is that?"

Marla follows my gaze and immediately starts walking toward the structure.

A brass sign stuck in the pavement next to the melting building says it's a sculpture created by an Argentine artist named Leandro Erlich.

It's called the *Maison Fond*.

I was right—it's supposed to look as if it's melting into the pavement. That's exactly the point. It was created for the United Nations 2015 Climate Change Conference as a reminder that global warming has a profound effect on the earth and the lives of future generations.

It also hits me on a more personal level, like an omen of what could be in store for us with the apartment. I hope this trip doesn't melt down into one giant disaster.

Gripping the handle of my suitcase, I turn to Marla. "What are we getting ourselves into?"

Marla fiddles with her phone. "What do you mean?"

"I wonder what the apartment will be like after all these years."

"I guess we'll find out soon," she murmurs, but her attention is trained on her phone. "Okay, well . . . My battery is low. We'd better get a move on and get to the hotel."

Wheeling our bags, Marla and I shoulder our way through the crowds coming and going from the Gare du Nord.

All I can think about is the fact that we've inherited an apartment in *Paris*. I'm smiling like an idiot.

Even when a burly man plows between Marla and me, shoulder checking me before I can get out of his way, I don't care.

We round a corner from the rue de Dunkerque to boulevard de Rochechouart and in a few scant steps, I spy a thin slice of Sacré-Cœur perched high atop the hill in Montmartre. What I can see of its white dome glistens against the brilliant blue sky like a perfectly formed meringue. It takes my breath away.

I grab Marla's arm. "Look." I nod in the direction of the basilica.

Marla and I stop and stare reverently.

"It's beautiful, isn't it?" she says. "Maybe we can go there before we leave?"

I nod. "Have you ever been to Paris?"

"I have." She smiles, but there's a faraway look in her eyes as we resume walking. "A long time ago."

"Good memories?" I'm sensing this might elicit a glimpse into my mother's past, the side of her that I know nothing about except through Gram and Granny Ivy's hushed, disapproving whispers.

Does her dreamy look have something to do with my father? There's so much about Marla's life that's a mystery; it could be anything.

"Yeah, it does bring back good memories," she says. "I was seventeen and I'd run away to follow my favorite band on the road."

"The Squelching Wellies," I fill in. It's my attempt at solidarity.

She slants a surprised glance at me. "Yeah. The Wellies. I caught up with them in London. Paris was the next stop on the tour."

My heart leaps. She was seventeen when she got pregnant, eighteen when she had me. I need to play it cool so I don't scare her off the topic. I decide to keep it conversational and not act too eager. It's easy to do since we're walking side by side, trailing our luggage behind us and dodging other pedestrians.

"How did that work?" I ask.

"What do you mean?"

"I mean, you were so young. Did Gram come with you to Europe for the tour?"

She snorts. "You're kidding, right?"

"No, I'm curious—that's all. Gram was so protective—"

"She was protective of you, Hannah. As far as she was concerned, if I wanted to squander the money I'd saved following a punk band for the summer, that was my business and good riddance."

"So that's what you did?"

"Mmmm . . ." She stops in the middle of the sidewalk and looks at her phone again. "We need to go left . . . somewhere. Wait . . . No, that's not right. Yeah, this is the way. We need to keep following this road."

It's a busy street, more congested than the rue de Dunkerque. This road has four lanes of traffic separated by a wide tree-lined median in the middle. We pass a *crêperie* with wooden tables and chairs out front. There are several shoe shops with carts of athletic footwear outside. There are hotels, tobacco stores, and more restaurants serving everything from sushi to kebabs to curry. I wonder what happened to the French food.

"Were you by yourself?" I ask, determined to resume the conversation.

"When?"

"When you were following The Squelching Wellies."

"No, Hannah. I was adventurous, but I wasn't stupid. My friend Callie came with me, but she only stayed two weeks."

"She left you and went home?"

"Actually, we were only supposed to stay two weeks. That was the original plan, but I wanted to stay longer. What the hell is wrong with my phone?"

She shakes it and nearly drops it.

"I don't know if shaking it like that is such a good idea, Marla."

"The damn thing keeps freezing up on me."

We walk a little farther and that's when I notice that the landscape has changed to a decidedly seedier atmosphere. The storefronts we're passing are shuttered by corrugated metal doors and covered with bright-red graffiti.

The family-friendly bistros have given way to tired-looking neoclassical buildings. I glimpse theaters clearly marked ADULTS ONLY and at least a half dozen sex and lingerie shops.

We are definitely not in postcard Paris anymore.

I wheel my suitcase closer to me and avoid making eye contact with a scantily clad woman who has draped herself along the threshold of an adults-only "bookstore" a few doors down.

"Isn't our hotel in the first arrondissement?"

Marla nods absently.

"The first arrondissement is in the center of the city. Are you sure we're heading the right way? I thought Sacré-Cœur was toward the outer edge of the city."

"I'm just following what the GPS says. Do you want to navigate?"

"Not really. My phone battery is low."

"Then stop complaining." Marla shakes her phone again. "I can't help it if my phone keeps freezing up. I don't know if it's the phone or my service plan."

"Why don't you reboot it? Sometimes that helps. Did you talk to your service provider about an international plan before you made the trip?"

Three men pass us on the sidewalk, do a double take, and slow their pace. I have no idea what they're saying in French, but the way they're elbowing each other, leering and laughing, makes me uncomfortable.

"Let's get out of here," I say to Marla. "I don't like this."

"Oh! Here it goes. We're good. This way."

I figure as long as we walk briskly and don't engage with anyone, we'll be fine. The best way to calm my nerves is to pick up our earlier conversation.

"So Callie was splitting expenses with you, right?"

"Yeah, money was pretty tight. I mean, we were teenagers. We just wanted somewhere cheap to sleep after the concerts. Then the next day we were off on the train to the next show."

She stares straight ahead into the distance, seeing something in her mind's eye that I can only imagine.

"What did you do after Callie went home? Did you room with someone else?"

Marla laughs. "Oh, Hannah, by that time I was 'with the band,' as they used to say."

Oh . . . Oh!

"So, like what? You had a *thing* with one of the band members?"

Was my father one of The Squelching Wellies?

Marla has stopped again. This time we're in front of the iconic red windmill of the Moulin Rouge. She's looking at her phone and frowning. "Oh, for God's sake. I guess I'll try rebooting it like you suggested. How do I do that? No . . . Wait—no need. Service is back. Let's go . . . this way."

I follow her.

"You didn't answer my question. Did you have an affair with one of the band members?"

She waves me off with the hand that's holding her phone. "It's not that simple, Hannah. It was a long time ago. Let's talk about something else. We're in Paris. Let's live in the present, not the past."

I'm not sure if she's irritated by my questions or the spotty cell service. On the train, we exhausted all discussion of the apartment, so I'm out of ideas for small talk.

We walk in silence for the next several blocks.

Finally, we reach a large traffic circle with a statue in the middle and people loitering at its base.

Marla takes an abrupt left and forges ahead. I have to quicken my pace to catch up with her.

Soon, the traffic thins out. The area transitions into a tranquil, tree-lined street with a mix of residences and businesses occupying street-level storefronts. We pass a photocopy shop, a bank, several internet cafés, a grocery, and a couple of pharmacies.

A few minutes later, we round the corner and we're on a pedestrian market street. Cafés and shops spill out onto the curb. Everywhere I look I see artisanal food boutiques, flower vendors, and fruit and vegetable stands. There's a fish market displaying *poisson* on beds of ice. There are souvenir shops offering racks of postcards, Eiffel Tower memorabilia, Notre-Dame gargoyles, and I HEART PARIS hats and scarves that tourists will spend thirty euros on today and toss in the backs of their closets tomorrow. But that's how Paris enchants. I can't blame anyone for wanting to take a piece of the magic home.

Suddenly, I realize we've been walking a long time, so I stop to check my watch. "Marla, we've been at this for almost an hour. I thought you said eleven minutes."

"And we're not going to get there any faster if we complain about it."

"I think we need to stop here and regroup," I say. "Let me see your phone."

She hands it to me. "Fine. If you think you can do better, go for it."

Her phone appears to be frozen again, but from what I can see of the map, we're way north of our hotel in the city center.

"Are you kidding me? We've been walking in the opposite direction of our hotel."

"What?" she says. "No we're not."

She grabs the phone back.

"No. This isn't right," she says. "It's frozen up again. The hotel should be right around the corner."

It better be close since we've gotten our ten thousand steps in via the Seedy Paris walking tour.

I start to say that, but I don't, lest I be labeled judgmental.

"Don't get your panties in a wad," she says. "I'm going to reboot my phone. Maybe that will stop it from freezing on me. Maybe the eleven-minute time was via car?"

Suddenly, as if the universe is willing me to hold my tongue, I smell chocolate. I inhale deeply to make sure my senses aren't playing a trick on me.

There it is—that deep, rich, mouthwatering fragrance. Like manna from heaven.

It's exactly how I remember Paris smelling, like chocolate and bread. Just when I thought that fantasy had been shattered, compliments of the red-light district, I spy the chocolate shop two doors down.

"I'm going in there." I point to the pretty storefront and leave Marla holding her phone at arm's length, waving it around as if that's going to get her better reception.

As I wheel my suitcase inside the shop, I inhale the delectable scent of cocoa and marvel at the masterpieces in the glass cases. Instant mood booster. There are rows and rows of Lucite trays brimming with gorgeous confections in various shapes and colors. Some are wrapped in colorful foil; others are displayed in their full chocolate glory, as if they're waiting to be plucked from the case and savored.

Did I mention that it smells heavenly? Like I've fallen into a chocolate dream.

A woman in a white apron smiles at me from behind the counter.

"Bonjour, madame," I say, trying to sound Parisian. As if I'd fool anyone. All she'd have to do is answer me in French and my deer-in-the-headlights look would give me away.

"Hello." Mercifully, she addresses me in English, and her voice has a delightful lilt that makes the ordinary greeting sound like a beautiful song. "How may I help you?"

"I'll take one of each." I'm joking, of course, but judging by her wide eyes, she thinks I'm serious.

"It all looks so delicious," I add. "How does a person decide?"

"Oh!" She smiles and nods, catching on. "May I recommend the *crème de noisette*? It is . . . how do you say . . . hazelnut cream."

"Yes, please. I'll take a half dozen."

As she selects six perfect pieces of chocolate, I make my way down the display case, wishing I really could taste one of each. I settle on an additional dozen traditional dark chocolate truffles covered in cocoa powder, and a bag of chocolate disks with cacao nibs mixed in.

I'm buying plenty to share with Marla as a show of goodwill.

The woman wraps up my treasures and tucks them into a bag with handles, which she stuffs full of gold tissue paper.

It looks like a gift when she hands the package to me.

I pick up a business card to slip into my purse, in case I want to come back again before I return to London. That's when I notice that the zip code is 75017.

Wait a minute—the seventeen at the end of the zip means we're in the seventeenth arrondissement.

It's been ages since I visited Paris. I don't know my way around the city without a map, but I do know that the hotel where we're staying is not far from the Louvre, which is located in the first arrondissement.

I also remember that Paris has twenty arrondissements. The arrangement starts in the center of the city with the first arrondissement and spirals outward in a clockwise manner, arranged in a snail shell of sorts.

If we're in the seventeenth, we definitely took a wrong turn or two somewhere along the way.

"Merci beaucoup," I say. "Your shop is lovely. You're in the seventeenth arrondissement, right?"

She beams with pride. "*Oui*. We are family owned and have been in this location for nearly thirty years."

"If I wanted to walk from here to the Louvre, how long would it take?"

Her eyes fly wide open and then she purses her lips as if she's seriously considering the question.

"Oooh . . . Forty-five minutes? It would be a long walk."

"Yes, it would."

The moment I exit the shop, Marla says, "Okay, we're lost. I'm sorry. I don't know what happened, but this damn thing sent us the wrong way." She smiles meekly. "Don't be mad. Please."

"I'm not mad." I'm irked at myself for not taking on the navigation responsibility from the start.

"You're mad," she says.

"I'm not mad," I repeat. "But it's after four o'clock. Let's regroup. Call Monsieur Levesque and see if he can meet us at the apartment instead of his office. I'll get us an Uber."

June 1927
Paris, France

Dear Diary,

I've visited all the fashion houses. Each one has turned me down. Some of the ateliers acknowledged my superb sewing skills but claimed my aesthetic didn't align with theirs. That's confusing because my aesthetic rubbed too closely to Chanel's. The others turned me away before I could even introduce myself, claiming they had no openings.

I am beginning to feel desperate. I'm constantly irritated with Helen.

She keeps begging me to come out with her and Luc, accusing me of moping about and being a regular spoilsport.

I try to reason with her: I don't have a job, which means I have no money. I can barely pay for rent, much less drinks.

She insists something will come along. She did not win her Ballets Russes audition, because they only had one opening this time and they selected the niece of a principal dancer. Even so, Helen's not worried. She says she will audition again the next time they need dancers.

I do wish I could be more like my friend—in some ways. She radiates a sunny disposition even when clouds loom overhead. But it's easier to be sunny when you have an income, and she's been dancing in cabarets and modeling for Luc.

Helen is much freer with her body than I am. She's a good person, mind you, but she's an exhibitionist. We have different views of modesty. I button up; she bares all. In the two weeks we've been living in Paris, she has shed any pretense of inhibition she might have presented in London.

As I write this, Helen is lounging about in her robe on the living room sofa, reading the Evening Standard *and leaving very little to the imagination.*

A few moments ago we had a disagreement when I mentioned returning to London if I can't find work. I was trying to be practical and give her fair warning that she might need to find a new flatmate, but she called me defeatist.

She accused me of changing because in London I seemed much braver. She said what if success is right around the corner and I miss the opportunity because I return to Bristol with my tail between my legs?

I have to wonder if she will still sing that tune come the rent day when I can't afford my share. It's one thing to dream and it's another to pay your own way.

I fear we have been living in an altered reality for too long: going to Dingo Bar almost daily and letting men buy us drinks for the pleasure of our company. How much longer will they be so generous? Soon, they will want something in return.

After our tiff, Helen calmed down and said she knows how I can earn money while I continue to look for a situation at a fashion house.

I knew I wasn't going to like what she had to say.

And I didn't.

Luc has a friend, another artist, who needs a model. It doesn't pay much, but it wouldn't require much time. I could still look for the work I wanted.

When I asked if I would have to take off my clothes, Helen laughed at me. Of course I would. He paints the human figure. He couldn't do his job if I kept my coat on.

Embarrassed, I then said I had too much self-respect to flaunt my naked body.

Helen flinched and asked if I was calling her a whore.

Then Helen laughed as if nothing was wrong and started teasing me about being a modest little girl who was afraid for the boys to see my knickers.

I asked her if she ever felt vulnerable without a barrier of clothing between her and Luc.

She said boundaries were her barriers. He wouldn't dare cross her barriers unless she invited him. She insisted that type of control was the ultimate form of self-empowerment.

Then she smiled in such a dreamy manner that I knew she had already given herself to him.

I've never thought about it until now, but the clothing I design is my armor, a barrier between me and the world. I can't imagine laying myself bare for a man to gaze upon as if he were looking at fruit in a bowl.

However, if that fruit belongs to me, and I decide what's forbidden, could I be so brazen if it meant getting what I wanted in the end?

Eight

January 2, 2019—4:20 p.m.

Square la Bruyère, 9th arrondissement

Paris, France

The building is surrounded by an iron fence with an ornate gate. Marla and I debate letting ourselves inside, but Monsieur Levesque, still en route through late-afternoon traffic, said we needed to sign some papers before the apartment would officially be ours. Even though we have the key (assuming it's still functional), we agree to play by the rules and sit restlessly on our suitcases.

As I stare up at the beautiful five-story tan stone building, I take it all in: the Haussmann-style façade with elaborate stonework around large arched windows and iron rails that set off intermittent Juliet balconies.

There's a fountain on the other side of the gate and a bit of garden space between it and the building. Several leafless, mature trees stand like sentries on the grounds. I imagine in summer, when they're lush and green, they will filter the late-afternoon sun and create dappled shade on the walk that extends from where we're standing to the building's front door.

Even though the landscape is winter stark, the place is stately and elegant.

It looks expensive.

I reach into my purse and pull out the paper on which I'd written the apartment's address and double-check that we're in the right place. It appears we are.

With this, my heart thuds. I allow the floodgates I'd guarded to swing wide open. All the hope that I'd denied myself pours out.

The temperature has dropped several degrees, but my cheeks burn as I cast another glance at the apartment building.

I have no idea what shape the place is in, but at least it's still standing.

A black Town Car stops along the curb.

A tall, thin, well-dressed man in his early sixties emerges and extends his hand. "Bonjour, ladies. I apologize for keeping you waiting. Emile Levesque, at your service."

"Bonjour, Monsieur Levesque." I shake his hand. "I am Hannah Bond. This is my mother, Marla Bond. Thank you for agreeing to meet us here on such short notice."

"But of course. It is very nice to finally meet you both in person." He smiles and regards me with warm eyes. I like him instantly.

He opens a leather folio and thumbs through some papers.

"The formalities won't take long. First, allow me to extend my sympathies for your loved one's passing. Monsieur Sterling in Florida communicated that Madame wasn't simply a client to him; she was a friend, and she loved you both very much. That's why her wishes are simple."

She loved us both very much?

I wonder if she really said that or if he's assuming. I hope it's true. I was relieved when I learned that Gram hadn't cut Marla out. Maybe she knew it had the potential to cause my already strained relationship with my mother to implode. I was even more relieved when she hadn't attached stipulations to the inheritance—like us working together. Even though that's what it's come down to, it was our choice. I slant a quick glance at Marla, who seems uncharacteristically demure.

"I am in possession of a copy of Madame's will. She has directed that the two of you shall split everything, which now includes the square la Bruyère apartment. I'm here to accommodate you should you require anything while you are in Paris.

"First, I need your signatures on the paperwork, and there will be the small matter of taxes, but you have ample time before you must pay.

"Now, I imagine you would like to see the property, no?"

We unlock the ornate gate with our key. Monsieur Levesque steps back and motions for us to enter first.

"You checked the place out?" says Marla, after we enter the building. She hesitates in the hallway. "No one is living here, I hope. I don't want to walk in on a bunch of squatters."

Levesque smiles. "I beg your pardon, madame. We are not in possession of a key. We were not able to enter the apartment, but I took the liberty of activating the utilities so you will have heat, light, and water."

Marla laughs her flirty laugh. "That was very nice of you, monsieur."

She arches a coquettish brow and smiles at him. Monsieur Levesque smiles back and takes her suitcase, rolling it to the elevator, which we ride to the second floor. We walk down a short hallway and Levesque stops in front of a door.

"Voilà." He gestures for me to do the honors.

I insert the brass key. My heart thuds as it turns the lock. I try to open the heavy wooden door, but it sticks.

“Allow me.” Monsieur Levesque leans into it until it gives way with a creak and a groan.

Right away, I’m engulfed by the smell—musty, moldy, old. Exactly what you’d imagine a place that has been closed up for decades would smell like. Marla and I pull our scarves over our noses and mouths and forge ahead.

I flip the light switch on the wall in the foyer, but nothing happens.

“I will see to it that my secretary has someone install fresh light bulbs for you as soon as possible,” says Monsieur Levesque.

“Thank you,” I say as I peer into the murky grayness.

As my eyes adjust, I take in the spectacle before me and forget about the smell completely. Highlighted by the slant of afternoon sunlight filtering in through a slit in the drapes, the place appears frozen in time. My heart hammers in my chest.

Batting my way through cobwebs, I walk over to one of the windows and pull back the heavy velvet curtains, stirring up a cloud of dust that makes me cough. It’s impossible to tell the color of the worn drapery, but the thin slices of early-evening light that stream in through the shutters on the tall, arched windows and bounce off a gilded mirror across the room suggest it might have once been burgundy or eggplant. I manage to secure the drape in place with a thick tasseled tieback that’s connected to the wall, even though part of the fringe disintegrates in my hand. Then I open the wooden shutter and turn around to behold a wonderland.

Underneath ash-like dust and gossamer cobwebs lie the remnants of someone’s life. There’s a Sleeping Beauty–like air to the place. Everything appears to be suspended in time, waiting for someone to return. A clock on the wall is stopped at 2:47. A coat hangs on the coatrack. A folded umbrella lists to the side in the patinated copper stand. Men’s shoes sit by the door.

Across the foyer, an ornate mirror is situated above a wooden table. Cobwebs so thick they look like gray cotton candy are caught in the scrolls and crevices.

"Madams, the place appears to be intact and uninhabited, *oui*?" says Levesque, who is hovering in the doorway, covering his mouth and nose with his gloved hand. "However, I fear it is not safe to breathe in the dust. I am happy to help you arrange a cleaning service to make the place hospitable."

When neither Marla nor I answer him, he adds, "Had I a key, I would have had it cleaned before you arrived."

The apartment isn't very large. Beyond the foyer and the living room, there's a bedroom, bathroom, and kitchen I can't wait to explore.

"That is very nice of you, Monsieur Levesque," I say. I hadn't even considered the dust and the mess. I was more concerned about walking into a nest of trespassers. But, even though it's filthy, I'm glad I got to see it just like this.

He nods. "If you don't mind, I will wait for you in the hall."

"Certainly," I say. "We won't be much longer."

Despite its compact floor plan, the place has high ceilings decorated with ornate medallions and gorgeous crown molding.

They don't make one-bedrooms like this anymore, I think to myself.

Even covered in dust and cobwebs, the place is magical. It's fancier and more tasteful than I had imagined. Most important, after all these years, the place still has a soul.

I spy what looks like correspondence on a small writing desk by one of the windows and make my way toward it. The dust is making me tear up. I know Levesque is right—this probably isn't healthy—but I can't tear myself away. I have to find something before we leave—some piece of evidence that proves without a doubt that Ivy lived here.

What I thought was correspondence turns out to be unused

stationery. Situated next to an old-fashioned ink pot and dipping pen, it is strewn over the surface of the desk as if someone would be back to tidy it up. There's also an ornamental hair comb, a couple of books, and a pair of ladies' gloves on the desk.

It strikes me that people spend a lifetime gathering and accumulating objects. In the end, the person leaves, but all the things that were once so important are left behind like detritus.

I lift the gloves off the table to reveal an outline of where they had been. Holding my breath, I drop my scarf from my face and rub my forefinger over the gray and brittle leather to reveal monogrammed letters: IB. Ivy Braithwaite? My heart kicks into high gear. I glance around, feeling guilty, like I'm at a museum and I'm messing with an exhibit I'm not supposed to touch.

Levesque is waiting outside the doorway, looking at his phone.

We probably should leave until we can get someone to help us get the dust under control. Ugh, there are probably hundreds of spiders in here. This is the point where I would usually shudder and run, but my feet are planted as my gaze sweeps over the room, taking in the wonder.

"Monsieur Levesque, may I take these with me?" I hold up the gloves.

"But of course. Everything in the apartment belongs to you and Madame. Take whatever you like."

Realizing suddenly that I've lost track of an uncharacteristically quiet Marla, I guess she's probably in the bedroom.

"We will only be a couple more minutes," I call to Levesque.

"Please take all the time you need."

I feel bad. I should tell him he's free to go, but I don't want him to leave. My French is elementary at best and given that no one has entered this place in decades, if the neighbors call the police or come out to question us, I'd feel better having him here to help explain our case.

"Let me get my mother and we'll go," I offer.

"As you like." He returns his attention to his phone.

I'm moving silently, reverently, through the dust-covered living room when Marla shrieks from beyond the open door.

"Oh my God! Hannah! Come here. Quickly!"

THE PAINTINGS ARE GORGEOUS. There are six of them displayed museum style across one of the bedroom walls. Marla has wiped away the dust on one to reveal a study of a nude woman lying on a bed. She is covered somewhat by bedsheets and looks as if she's staring into the eyes of a lover.

Gazing at the painting, I feel as if I've walked in on an intimate exchange. A lover's promise. Or perhaps the sweet nothings whispered after a night of pleasure.

The painting is quite lovely, if a little risqué. Marla's gaze is fixed on it. Her expression is horrified. I don't understand her stunned reaction. With her history, she's no blushing virgin.

As if reading my mind, she whispers, "Hannah, don't you recognize her?"

I glance at my mother, hoping for a hint.

"Why are you whispering?" I ask.

"It's Granny Ivy," Marla hisses, her voice still hushed. She nods at the painting.

I take a closer look and suddenly everything kaleidoscopes into perspective. Pictures of my great-grandmother as a young woman come to mind and I see that, yes, indeed, the beautiful woman on the bed does resemble Ivy. With her strawberry-blonde hair, she sort of looks like me, too. Like a mix of Marla and me—each of our very best features combined to create one beautiful face.

I turn to my gobsmacked mother. "Obviously you're not the only one in the family who had a wild streak in her younger years."

"I guess not. At least I came by it honestly, but it's just . . ." She shakes her head, at a loss for words.

"Why are you so shocked by this?" I ask.

I'm wondering why I'm *not* surprised by it. Maybe because it's the first clue as to why Ivy never mentioned much about her life in Paris. Was she a painter's model?

I find the possibility utterly thrilling.

As I begin to study the rest of the paintings on the wall, trying to see through the foggy layers of dust, something at the base of the bedside table catches my eye. The cobwebs are thick in that cranny, and I glance around for something to use as a swab.

"Is everything okay, mesdames?" Monsieur Levesque's voice startles me. He's standing in the bedroom's threshold, covering his nose and mouth with his hand.

"The woman in the painting," I say. "She's a relative."

Marla scowls and moves in front of the portrait as if she is protecting Ivy's dignity. Her choppy movements have stirred up a cloud that sends Levesque into a coughing fit.

He leaves the room.

I find a grimy newspaper on the bureau and use it to fight my way through the webs to what looks like a small, leather-bound book.

When I hold it in my hands, I see it's a diary, and I decide to take it with me.

"Marla, come on; we really should go. We need to check into the hotel and we've taken up enough of Monsieur Levesque's time."

"I'm not ready to go." Her voice is petulant.

"Well, then you can stay here by yourself because I'm leaving. We can come back tomorrow and start cleaning."

Holding the gloves and the little book close, I leave Marla rooted to her spot and join Monsieur Levesque in the hallway.

"I hope all this dust hasn't given you an asthma attack," I say.

He smiles. "Everything is fine. Though I should make you aware that I must travel out of town tomorrow. I shall turn you over to the capable hands of my partner, Gabriel Cerny. Here is his card. If you'd like, his assistant will arrange for a cleaning service to meet you at the apartment in the morning. You will be able to better assess the place once it is clean."

"Merci," I say. "That would be very helpful."

He nods and watches as I pull some tissue from my purse, wrap up the dusty gloves and diary, and tuck them into the outer pocket of my suitcase for safe keeping.

"Also, I realized we must check on the annuity that has been covering the taxes all these years. The amount may have been different than what is needed to cover the cost of the fees."

My stomach dips. Great, just what we need. More expenses. Something tells me that if there are property taxes due, the government might not be as lenient about when we pay them as they are about the inheritance taxes.

I fear that we might need to start thinking about putting the place on the market. Because there's no way even with the proceeds of the sale of Gram's house that we'll have enough money to pay for added expenses.

It seems a shame to sell the apartment. If Granny Ivy had kept it, there must've been a reason. It must've meant something to her.

Then again, if she wanted so badly to keep it a secret, maybe the prospect of selling the place was more of a burden than just letting it rot.

Marla joins us in the hallway. "So sorry to keep you waiting."

I'm embarrassed by her brusque tone and feel compelled to cover for her.

"Again, Monsieur Levesque, thank you for accommodating us."

Maybe his associate Monsieur Cerny will be able to point us in the direction of a real estate agent, and preferably someone who speaks our language.

I feel so out of my league. I hope someone doesn't spot a couple of unsuspecting American dopes and take us for a ride. Of course, we could always call Patrick Sterling for help.

Cha-ching, cha-ching. But investing in legal advice would mean protecting ourselves. Better safe than sorry.

My head is spinning and my stomach rumbles. I realize I'm starving. Marla and I never had the chance to eat lunch, and the five-mile walk made me work up an appetite.

"Monsieur Levesque, could you recommend a good restaurant for dinner?" I ask after we exit the building.

I wonder if I should invite him to join us.

"I do not know what type of food you prefer," he says. "Sometimes Americans, they do not enjoy what is French."

"Not all Americans subsist on fast food," Marla snaps.

"It's been a long, emotional day," I say apologetically. "We both need a good dinner. You're welcome to join us."

"Thank you for the invitation, but I am expected at home. There is a bistro not too far from here, Café Breton. You might find it satisfactory. I recommend that you order the plat du jour."

"And what on earth is a plat du jour?" Marla sounds suspicious, as if she's caught him trying to trick us into ordering horse meat or something equally offensive.

"It means the specialty of the day, Marla," I say.

Levesque nods. "*Oui*. It is the finest, freshest ingredients that the chef can locate at the market that morning. From those items he will build the dish. You cannot go wrong."

Levesque tips his hat, bids us adieu, and slips off into the twilight.

The two of us stand there looking at each other; then we turn our faces to the building, staring at the row of windows on the second floor that now belongs to us.

A cold wind whips up some dried leaves that had been resting at our feet. Marla and I both pull our scarves tighter around our necks.

"I don't understand why you had to hurry us out like that," Marla quips. "You could've given me some time since it was our first glimpse of this place."

"You're welcome to go back up there," I say. "We have the key. But frankly, I don't know that it will do you any good to breathe in more dust."

Just the thought of it makes my lungs heave. Personally, I need to digest everything that's happened today before I make any more discoveries.

It was a lot.

"Let's go," I say. "Tomorrow is another day."

"I know tomorrow is another day and the day after tomorrow will be yet another one, but I wanted this moment."

I glance around to see who might be watching the start of a full-on Marla tantrum as we walk away in the direction of the bistro that Levesque suggested.

"You're hungry and cranky," I say. "Let's get you something to eat. Then we'll go back to the hotel, wash off this dust, and get a good night's sleep."

The first thing I plan to do when we get back to the hotel is crack open the diary. My gut tells me it might hold the answers to a few burning questions.

June 1927
Paris, France

Dear Diary,

I've made a new discovery. The best way to distract myself from not having a job is to get out of the apartment. Not only does it put space between Helen and me, but exploring also reminds me that opportunities could be around every corner. I certainly won't find a new situation moping around the apartment, trying to ignore Helen's judging glances.

Today, I set out with no particular destination in mind. Soon, I found myself lingering in the Jardin des Tuileries. With its rows of manicured lime and elm trees and grassy areas offset by gravel paths, the formal garden sits between the Louvre and the place de la Concorde. Since the Tuileries has become one of my favorite places in all of Paris, I've learned a little bit about its history. Did you know that it's the oldest garden in the city? And long before it became a public park, the Tuileries was the site of Catherine de' Medici's royal palace, but the palais *was destroyed during the Paris Commune, long after the queen consort's death.*

I sat on a bench in the midst of the beauty, squinted my eyes, and tried to imagine what it was like when the palais *stood stalwart and proud. For a glorious moment, I escaped my poverty and pretended I was royalty—or at least a member of the court.*

It was all in good fun.

Speaking of fun, I made a new friend today. As I sat there, the sweetest little brown dog ran up and plopped himself onto my feet.

When I bent to scratch behind his ears, he looked up at me with the most soulful black eyes that seemed to say, Where've you been? I've been looking for you. *But all too soon his owners, a girl and a boy, whistled for him from across the park. He licked my hand and scampered off to a joyous reunion. Someday when I'm settled, I should quite like to have a dog of my own.*

By that time, I was so hungry my stomach was growling. I walked along the rue de Rivoli toward home, stopping along the way to admire Joan of Arc's statue in place des Pyramides. After communing with her and Catherine de' Medici, I felt as if I had been bolstered by two strong women.

Even so, by the time I reached Maxim's on rue Royale, it was all I could do to keep from pressing my nose against the window of the fancy restaurant. Despite my dirty shoes, dusty from the park's flint and gravel paths, I approached the front doors, with head held high, and pretended I was arriving for a meal.

That gave me the most wonderful idea. I couldn't afford a sumptuous meal at Maxim's, but I could certainly endeavor to cook something delicious for myself. Helen would be out with Luc by the time I returned home. So as I walked I thought about what I could cook that would be fit for a queen but wouldn't empty my peasant-sized pocketbook. I was so lost in thought I must have taken a wrong turn.

Suddenly, I found myself . . . lost. As I stood, turning in circles, I was taken by the most impressive building. It was a church, but it looked more Roman temple than Parisian cathedral. I was desperate to step into the magnificent structure, but I would have to return another time. Darkness was falling.

Not only did I need to find my way home, but I had to find a market and purchase my dinner.

As I walked away vowing to return, I contemplated what kind of soup would be fit for Catherine de' Medici and Joan of Arc. . . .

Nine

January 2, 2019—8:00 p.m.

Normandy Le Chantier, 1st arrondissement

Paris, France

As we settle into the hotel, a light snow begins to fall outside. The heavy flakes are collecting on the windows of our third-floor room.

In true Parisian fashion, dinner was marked by lovely food and impatient service. Afterward the temperature plummeted so much that we hailed a taxi to take us back to the hotel.

It was just as well; we're both exhausted and ready to call it a day. The room is nice. Very old-world French with the comfort of two full-sized beds and an en suite bath. The hotel offered a discount since I'm in the hospitality industry.

"Do you want to shower first or can I?" Marla asks, standing in the bathroom doorway clutching her toiletry case. She's already staked her claim, but at least she's trying to be polite.

"Go ahead."

I'm happy for her to go first because I'm dying to pull out the diary. I'm not trying to keep it from her. However, I do want to get a first look without her reading over my shoulder.

I'm still trying to wrap my mind around the fact that the apartment was once Ivy's home. The deed doesn't lie, but I can't reconcile the great-grandmother I knew with the woman in those paintings—with the person who lived . . . *here*.

In Paris.

It's weird to think that Granny Ivy might have had a secret life, that she navigated this city and made it her own. But the burning question is why she hid it all these years.

After Marla barricades herself in the bathroom, I retrieve the small book from my suitcase.

I use the tissue in which I'd wrapped it to wipe away as much dust as I can.

The upper left corner of the small blue book's cover is embossed in gold with the year 1940. A piece of satin ribbon is wrapped around the four sides of the diary and tied in a scant bow on the front like a gift.

The dust has settled into the fibers, turning the tie a grayish hue. I imagine it must have once been a soft ballet pink, like a ribbon off a ballerina's pointe shoe, when the author of these pages tied it around the little book with such loving care.

I'm careful as I unfasten it, half expecting the threads to crumble in my fingers like the drapery tie. But it stays intact.

As I open to the first page, the glue that binds the pages cracks, but other than that, the book is in remarkably good shape.

The inside cover is printed with *This is my personal diary for the year 1940.* My heart leaps when I see *Ivy Braithwaite* scrawled in indigo ink. I run my finger over the pretty script. It's Ivy's hand, and it speaks to me clearer than if she were standing here in the flesh.

A link from the past to the matriarch I knew and loved, and when she was close to my age.

I pull back my hand, not wanting to mar the pages with the

dust that clings to the crevices. For a moment, I contemplate waiting until I can clean it up better so I won't damage it.

Then I hear Marla turn on the shower tap, and I realize that the next fifteen minutes might be my last bit of time alone for the next twenty-four hours or so. If I want to look at it uninterrupted, it's now or never.

I thumb through the whole thing quickly at first, noticing that the entries stop on April 16. Then I open to the first page to meet the young woman who brought me here.

January, 1940
Paris, France

Dear Diary,

A new year, a new diary. Usually, this is a happy time, a clean slate, a new beginning. But I don't know what to think. I don't know what this year holds for us. I can hardly bring myself to write of frivolity and pointless fancy, which consumed me this time last year. Now, everything is different. Andres and I didn't even ring in the new decade with a party. Nobody was in the mood. It felt wrong. Instead, we spent a quiet night at home. We were asleep before midnight. The old year slipped away, nudged out by this new period of uncertainty. The silence that permeates all aspects of our life is symbolic of what's happening in the world.

They're calling it a "phony war" because after Hitler invaded Poland in the fall, England and France declared war on Germany. Paris began mobilizing, but since then, there has been no military action. I listen to the news with keen interest and I'm hungry for any word from home. But what I've heard says that all is calm in England.

So many months have gone by without any fighting (and believe me, I think that's a very good thing) that if Andres wasn't so concerned, I'd be inclined not to give this "phony war" much thought. But he is still cross because France won't let him fight—they don't want him because of the deafness in his left ear. Even so, he insists that if France goes to war, he will help on the home front. All he talks about as of late is resistance. I don't ask him to explain the things I eavesdrop at the weekly meetings he holds at his apartment, because it sets him off. Normally, he is such a gentle, loving man. But I suppose waiting in limbo has many people on edge, including myself.

Is it terrible that I am happy Andres won't have to fight in the traditional sense? I suppose I'm selfish and weak. Andres is my weakness, my world. I wish the two of us could exist in this little bubble that is our apartment. I call the place ours, even though it's mine, because he is here almost every night. His apartment has become a meeting spot for the resistance. A place dedicated to secret planning and plotting. That's fine. He stays here with me. I love having him here. Him with his novels and me with my sewing.

I hate to begin the new year—the new decade—on such an uncertain note. Maybe tomorrow I will have happier news to report. Even if Andres cannot see the good in humanity, I will hold enough hope in my heart for both of us.

"What are you reading?"

I jump at the sound of Marla's voice. I'd been so engrossed in the diary I didn't hear the shower stop or the bathroom door open.

She's standing there in the hotel-issued bathrobe, blotting her red hair with a towel.

For a moment, I consider not telling her what I found, because I don't want to share. I'm still trying to process it. Is the Andres Ivy mentions in the diary Andres Armand? She wrote, "Him with his novels . . ." Is that why she saved the newspaper clipping? She speaks of him so intimately. Obviously, even though they had their own apartments, they were living together.

"What?" Marla asks. "You look like you've seen a ghost."

"I found Ivy's diary in the apartment and brought it back with me."

Her eyes widen and she stops towel drying her hair.

"Was it okay to take stuff from the apartment?"

"Monsieur Levesque said it was fine. Why wouldn't it be?"

She blinks at me. Offers a one-shoulder shrug.

"It's our apartment now," I say. "Lock, stock, and barrel. When did you become such a rule follower?"

She snorts.

"It feels weird taking things. Maybe I should've brought some of the paintings here."

"It doesn't mean we have to dismantle the place," I say.

"Oh, I'm sorry; it's okay for you to take the diary, but not for me to take the paintings."

I roll my eyes. "Fine. Bring the paintings here. Where are you going to put them?"

She glances around the room. Nods at a large oil painting of the Eiffel Tower. "We could ask the hotel to remove that one and hang Ivy there."

"That painting is probably bolted to the wall. They're not going to remove it for us. Plus, we're going to check out and move over to the apartment as soon as we can clean up the place."

I feel like I'm negotiating with a child. I'm surprised she hasn't looked to see if the Eiffel Tower painting is, in fact, affixed to the wall.

"How's Ivy's diary?" She lowers herself onto the edge of my bed. "Anything juicy?"

Against my better judgment, I open the book and show her the inside cover where Ivy had written her name.

"If by juicy you mean Ivy talking about the uncertainty of war in Paris, then yes."

"Ivy was here during the war?"

"I don't know. I haven't gotten that far yet. She started the diary on January first. She was sporadic about writing, but she was definitely living in Paris just before the Germans invaded. She mentions an apartment. I guess it's the one on square la Bruyère. She mentions a man named Andres."

Marla's left brow shoots up. "That's exactly what I mean by juicy. I wonder if he's the writer guy from the newspaper clipping?"

"Andres Armand? It could be the writer. She references his novels. Then again, the Andres she mentions might love to read and have a lot of books."

Marla thumbs through the diary and squints at a page. "The diary is for the year 1940?"

I nod.

"Mom was born in December of 1940."

We look at each other and I can virtually read Marla's mind.

A sinking feeling pulls me down. "For Gram to be born in December, Granny Ivy had to conceive in March 1940, a few months after she wrote this entry."

"But wait—was Ivy with Tom when she wrote this? When did she meet Tom?" Marla continues to thumb through the diary and I want to tell her to be careful not to damage it. It's not the latest issue of *Cosmopolitan* magazine.

"A lot of pages are blank. Looks like her last entry was April 16, 1940. Did you see Great-Grandpa Tom's name anywhere?"

"No."

The story we know is Ivy met and married Tom in Bristol just before war broke out. He sent her to the United States to live with his family in Florida.

It never crossed my mind to ask her for specific dates or details. All we knew was that she was a war bride. After that, she lived in Florida for the rest of her life.

There was no reason to dig deeper. We had no reason to question the timeline.

"Why didn't we ask for more details about her life when she was alive?" I say. "When she could've given us the answers?"

Marla tsks. "That's assuming she would've shared this with us. I mean, if she was seeing Tom and this Andres at the same time . . . That's sort of a bombshell, don't you think? Especially back in those days."

"It is. Do you remember Ivy and Tom ever celebrating or even talking about their anniversary?"

Marla wrinkles her nose. "I don't. At the time I didn't pay much attention, but now that I think about it, it seems weird. Then again, when she came to live with Mom after Tom died, I was out of the house a lot."

Marla shrugs and sighs.

I never met Tom. He died before I was born. Since both grandmothers were widows and my mother wasn't married, there wasn't much talk about weddings or anniversaries.

Suddenly, exhaustion takes down my brain like a power outage.

"I'm going to go take a shower and then we both need to get some sleep," I say. "Tomorrow's another day. The diary is not going anywhere, and neither are its clues."

June 1927
Paris, France

Dear Diary,

I am elated! A woman I met when I went out with Helen and Luc tonight told me that the department store Galeries Lafayette was hiring sales floor attendants. Why did I not think of something like this sooner? The place is not so dissimilar to Selfridges, where I worked in London. In fact, it's perfect. At least in the meantime, until I can find work as a designer. I have been so blinded by the need to find work with a couture house that I ignored alternative opportunities.

I will inquire after a position first thing tomorrow. It would be wonderful if I could work in tailoring, but I will take any job that pays a decent wage. When I am gainfully employed, Helen will get off my back about working for Pierre, who, just between you and me, I find to be a most disagreeable fellow. Fingers crossed!

Ten

January 3, 2019—8:00 a.m.

Paris, France

The next morning, we grab a quick breakfast of coffee and fresh croissants at the café next to the hotel. To save money, we've decided to clean the place ourselves rather than hiring the cleaning service as Monsieur Levesque suggested. We ask the concierge to direct us to a hardware store.

He tells us about a shop called Aux Couleurs Modernes.

The last thing I ever imagined I'd search for in Paris was a hardware store. But people do live here, and even Parisians need supplies to fix up their homes. We're already living like locals.

The store is small with crowded metal shelves set up in narrow aisles. We purchase a couple of buckets and mops, rags and paper towels, all-purpose cleaner, rubber gloves, plastic safety goggles to keep the dust out of our eyes, and white dust-filtering masks to keep the dirt from asphyxiating us. We also grab a couple of twin air mattresses to sleep on until we can buy new beds. I shudder to think what might be living in the double that's been there for eighty years.

At the register, I grab two bandannas for our hair—a green one for Marla and a hot-pink one for myself. With the goggles, masks, and scarves, at least our top halves should be sufficiently shielded from the grime.

Marla flirts with one of the shop clerks and lets me pay for our purchases.

Packages in hand, we stop outside of the store to regroup.

"I'll save the receipt so we can add it into the final expenses for the house," I say.

Marla nods. "Maybe we should go back in there and get that wet-and-dry vac we were looking at. We'll be moving around a lot of dust in that apartment. And where there are webs, there are sure to be spiders."

"The dust won't move around very much after water hits it and we pour it down the drain," I say.

Marla crosses her arms and frowns. "Sounds like a recipe for mud. Maybe it would be a good idea to vacuum up the top layer because . . . spiders, Hannah."

When I don't answer, she says, "Here, hold this." She hands me her mop and bucket, which is full of supplies. I nearly drop mine as I try to get a grip on hers. "I'll be right back."

"Are you sure that's a good idea?"

"Hannah, we need it. It's on me."

The model she had been looking at was a five-gallon vacuum that costs about forty-five euros. I don't know how well it will hold up under all the grime, but if she wants to buy it, I won't argue with her.

A few minutes later, she emerges from the shop empty-handed.

"Did you change your mind?"

She reclaims her bucket and mop. "Nope. The charming man at the register offered to deliver it."

She actually bats her eyes at me.

It's a good twenty-minute walk to the apartment. We pass the magnificent Galeries Lafayette department store and église de la Sainte Trinité. I enjoy the chilly morning air and marvel at Paris all around me. There's barely a trace of last night's snow.

I slept remarkably well. After meeting with Monsieur Levesque yesterday and signing the papers, I am finally letting myself believe that this apartment is ours.

I'll battle cobwebs and dust any day if it means we can call the apartment—and all its secret history—our own.

"You're awfully quiet," Marla says as we approach the building and I set down my bucket to unlatch the gate. "What are you thinking about?"

"I'm thinking that last week if you'd asked me how I was going to spend my second day in Paris, I never would've dreamed I'd be hauling a bucket full of cleaning supplies to an old apartment and preparing to spend the day cleaning. I haven't even seen the Eiffel Tower yet."

Marla chuckles. "There's plenty of time for that. I'll bet if you went to the Champs-Élysées and asked the tourists if they'd rather sightsee or clean an apartment that they can keep after the job is done, all of them would take the apartment."

"I'm not complaining. I can't believe we're here."

"We'll get to see everything. After we get our work done."

I start to point out that work-before-play is a very un-Marla-like statement, but I stop myself.

Instead, I say, "All right. I'm holding you to it."

I shift the heavy bucket from one hand to the other as we ride the elevator in silence. Then we stand reverently in front of the heavy wooden door before we open it.

"I think we should suit up out here before we go in," Marla suggests.

"Good idea."

We take the goggles and white masks out of the plastic wrappers, put them on, and help each other cover our hair with the bandannas. After we're all suited up, we realize we resemble a couple of praying mantises. As we're standing there laughing at each other, the door across the hall opens.

An older woman peers out, gasps, murmurs something in French, and slams the door with a loud bang.

"Uh-oh. Do you think she's going to call the police?" I ask.

"Probably. I would if I saw us standing out in the hallway looking like this. Quick, open the door and let's go inside."

We don't waste any time on the temperamental door, unlocking and throwing both of our bodies against it until it finally gives way.

Once we're safe inside with the latch locked, we break out into another fit of laughter.

"No wonder she was startled," Marla says. "Look at us. Wait."

She flips on the foyer light. To my surprise, one bulb in the fixture blinks to life; the other two don't respond. As I'm making a mental note to buy light bulbs, Marla pulls out her cell phone.

"This calls for a selfie."

"No," I protest. "I don't want this on social media. I look awful."

"I promise not to post it." I don't know whether to believe her, but she puts her arm around me and presses her cheek to mine.

Through the funk and odor of rotting time, I can smell her Chanel perfume. And oddly enough, it comforts me.

I realize I can't remember the last time my mother and I took a photo together.

I suppose there's irony in us looking like giant bug people, not like ourselves. So much is changing in our lives, I have to wonder how we will have changed once this weird Paris trip is over.

"I'll text it to you," Marla says.

"Mmm," I say as I make my way through the gloomy dinge of

the living room to the wall of windows. I tie back the rest of the curtains and start opening the shutters. Sunlight pours inside.

I turn around and survey the apartment. Powdery dust motes dance in the air, but I'm happy to see that thanks to the small amount of time we spent here yesterday, most of the cobwebs that had spanned the expanse of the living room are now mostly confined to the light fixtures, crevices of the furniture, and ornate frames on the paintings that hang on the wall.

My phone sounds a text as I open the second set of shutters.

"Promise me you won't delete the picture," Marla commands.

"I won't, but that doesn't mean I'll frame it, either," I say under my breath.

"I'll frame a copy for you." Marla heads toward the third set of windows, throws open the shutters, and sings at the top of her lungs about how she loves Paris in the spring, then waltzes into the bedroom.

It's winter now, but I'm filled with a sudden longing for spring. We have a long way to go before we get there. I wonder where Marla and I will be in the new season. She has a history of quitting in the face of boredom or adversity, or when a shinier new thing comes along.

"Where do we start?" I call. Even though the worst of the cobwebs are down in the living room and bedroom, we still haven't explored the bathroom and kitchen. The magnitude of the job feels more daunting today than it did yesterday.

In the shadows of twilight, the place had an ethereal, surreal look to it. It seemed more like a stage set or a life-sized diorama on one of my Austen tours. But in the unforgiving light of day, it feels real. It's our privilege. Our problem.

When Marla doesn't answer me, I walk into the bedroom.

She is standing in the same place she occupied yesterday,

staring at the collection of gilt-framed paintings on the bedroom wall.

"Did you hear me?" I ask.

"What?" Her voice sounds detached. "Uh, no. Sorry, what did you say?"

I stand next to her and look at the paintings and try to understand what is transfixing her. They're of Ivy, no doubt. Frankly, I find it uncomfortable to stare at my great-grandmother in the nude.

So Granny Ivy was young once and took off her clothes. I'm tempted to ask Marla if she got pregnant with me through immaculate conception. But she seems truly bothered by the art.

I let her have a moment.

Finally, she gestures at the wall and the portraits and says, "This is so strange to me. My grandmother . . . the grandmother I remember was so . . . different from this."

She was stern and matronly.

"I only knew her as a young child knows a great-grandmother. She was always a little . . . frail. She sewed clothes for me and encouraged me to read books and she was passionate about writing letters. Do you remember that?"

"I do." Marla turns to me and looks surprised, as if the memory just occurred to her. "She used to write letters urging leaders of foreign governments to free political prisoners and to enforce human rights."

"I knew it was something important," I say. "I remember the card table that was set up in her bedroom at Gram's house. It was always piled high with envelopes grouped into some semblance of order that only she understood. I remember wanting to connect with her, trying to understand what she was doing. Since letters seemed to be so important to her and she was always writing to others, I decided that I was going to write her a letter. I sat at her table and borrowed some paper and took an envelope from one of her stacks. I guess I messed up the order of the mailing she was working on because I got in trouble. I was never allowed to go into her room again."

"Yeah," Marla muses. "That's how I remember her, too. I think I got in trouble just about every time I was around her. Mean ol' woman."

"She wasn't mean," I say as I try to reconcile the austere woman who freaked out over me using one of her envelopes with the woman in the sensual paintings—the woman who owned this apartment—but it's hard to do.

"Okay, maybe she was a little mean," I concede.

"Well, yeah," Marla says. "Why else would you keep an apartment like this a secret from your family? We could have been vacationing here all these years. Callie and I could've stayed here when we came to Paris that summer."

We're startled by a knock at the door.

Marla's eyes widen and she whispers, "Do you think that lady across the hall called the police?"

"If she thought she saw something suspicious, I hope she did," I say in a full voice as I head toward the door.

"No! Stop!" Marla hisses. "Don't answer it."

"Why not? We're not doing anything wrong. It's not like we broke in. We own the place and we have a lawyer on speed dial."

She blinks at me, seemingly at a loss for words. Because I'm right.

"We should've introduced ourselves to the neighbor. The sooner we let her know we own the apartment, the better. Besides, it might be the guy from the hardware store delivering your vacuum," I call over my shoulder.

There's no peek hole on the door, so I have no choice but to answer it without knowing who is on the other side. I remove the white mask and adjust my posture, holding my chin at a level that I hope projects more confidence than I feel inside, despite my sure words to my mother.

When I open the door, rather than the police or a band of vigilante neighbors, I find a very handsome man dressed in a suit and tie under an open black topcoat.

"Bonjour—uh, good morning." His smile hits me like a thousand-watt bulb. For a moment, I'm at a loss for words as I drink in his tall frame and dark George Clooney–esque good looks. A musky, manly smell mingles with stale cigarettes and expensive cologne, but the way his brown eyes crinkle at the corners and his one incisor tilts rakishly sideways make up for the vague body odor.

"I am Gabriel Cerny." He smiles again, as if I'm supposed to know him. His English is excellent but laced with enough of a French accent to make my toes curl in my sneakers.

And then I remember how I'm dressed, with the ridiculous hot-pink bandanna in my hair and the safety goggles covering my eyes. As I yank them off, I realize I'm not wearing makeup because of the cleaning mission. *Shit.*

"Emile Levesque's colleague?" he prompts. "I have come in his place to offer assistance this morning?"

"Yes, of course; come in, please." I open the door wider, step back, and motion for him to enter. Then I realize that his fancy coat will be a dust magnet. "I'm afraid the place is a little messy. You might ruin your coat. Is that cashmere?"

I resist the urge to reach out and touch it.

He purses his lips and offers a noncommittal shrug that is so very French as he peers in the doorway to assess the place.

He makes a guttural disapproving sound and stays put. "Yes, I see. It is quite dirty. And you are?"

For a split second I misunderstand and think that he's saying I am quite dirty. Then I realize he's asking my name.

"Oh! I'm so sorry; I am Hannah Bond."

"And I'm Marla."

My mother has sidled up next to me to offer her hand. "Bond. Marla Bond." She is in full-on flirt mode. I wonder what happened to the woman who, a moment ago, was standing in the bedroom looking crushed as she gazed at nude paintings of her grandmother.

When Gabriel Cerny takes her hand, I notice he's not wearing a wedding ring and I wonder how long it will be before Marla ends up in his bed.

"Nice to meet you, Mademoiselles Bond."

Marla titters. I notice she looks pretty, having had the foresight to remove her gear and fluff her hair before making her entrance. She's like a rose amidst urban decay.

I guess Gabriel Cerny is somewhere between Marla's age and my own. I'm sure he finds Marla the more attractive of the two of us. I don't even know why that popped into my head, but I send the thought packing as fast as it entered.

Gabriel steps back into the hall. Marla and I follow him.

"It can't be healthy for you to be in that apartment among all that filth," he says. "I shall have my assistant secure a cleaning service for you. I'm sure we can find one by this afternoon to take care of the work for you. A professional crew will have this place tidied up in no time."

"No, thank you," I say. "It's nice of you to offer, but we've already purchased cleaning supplies. Even a vacuum, which should be delivered any minute."

He studies me with eyes that look dubious and amused. Then he blows out a *pffft*. "This is no job for beautiful ladies. You should be out enjoying this magnificent day. It's warmer outside today, but tomorrow, it is supposed to turn bitterly cold. You must seize the moment while you can."

I have no idea what sort of high-maintenance divas he's pegged us for, but I am perfectly happy rolling up my sleeves and getting my hands dirty. Well, maybe not perfectly happy, but you gotta do what you gotta do, and the apartment won't clean itself.

"Isn't he darling, Hannah?" Marla is gushing full-on now. "Bless your heart for worrying about us, honey," she says. "I would love it if you would call in a cleaning crew for us."

This is her steel-magnolia-in-distress persona.

"*Oui*. Right away." Gabriel Cerny is shaking his head as he stares down at the cell phone he has produced from his coat pocket.

Then he's talking into the receiver in rapid French that I do not understand.

After he disconnects the call, he smiles first at Marla, then at me. His gaze lingers on my face—my eyes, my lips, then back to my eyes—and I refuse to let myself squirm.

"A cleaning crew will arrive shortly. *Gratuitement*." He smiles. "It is the pleasure of my law firm to give you this . . . how do you say in American . . . *er* . . . this home-warming gift?"

"Oh, a housewarming present?" Marla's Southern drawl has mysteriously disappeared. Clearly delighted, she slants me a glance that seems to say, *See what I did? Watch and learn*.

Just as Marla has her helpless damsel-in-distress act, Gabriel must use that smolder he's turning on me right now to open doors—and a few legs—for himself.

The little voice inside me that's ever the skeptic rears up and says, *Nothing is free. There's always a catch*.

Even still, if a crew comes in armed with the right tools, they might have the place fit for human habitation in a day or two, which could save us the cost of staying a week in a hotel. Cost-wise, it might be a wash, and I'd be able to stay in the apartment a few nights before I have to return to London.

"Consider it a welcome-to-Paris gift from the law firm Levesque, Racine, and Cerny."

Of course, he says the word *Paris* so that it sounds like *par-ee*, which is so darned charming I hear myself thanking him and telling him he didn't have to do it. To which he shrugs and says, "Why not? I am a partner in the firm. I make the rules."

Ah. Wow. "So, you are the Cerny in Levesque, Racine, and Cerny?" I know he is, but I'm trying to make conversation.

"But of course."

His brow goes up.

"Hannah, he's trying to impress you," Marla says.

I force a smile and make a mental note to call Marla out for this verbal elbowing later. If she got out of raising me, she forfeits the right to embarrass me now.

"When will the cleaning company be here?" Marla asks. "Are we supposed to wait here for them to show? I mean, if they're coming to do the dirty work, there's no sense in us hanging around. Is there a way we could give them Hannah's cell phone number and go get some breakfast? All we had was a croissant, and it is not sticking with me. "

"That is a magnificent idea." Again, Gabriel directs the words to me.

"Breakfast is on us," Marla says. "It's our way of thanking you. It's the least we can do."

Fifty bucks says she'll do the fake purse reach and Gabriel will end up picking up the check.

He arranges for the cleaning service to phone him before they arrive, then calls for his car and takes us to his favorite café in the area.

After we're seated, Gabriel says he's already eaten breakfast. Since I don't have much of an appetite in the morning, I'm still full from the coffee and croissant I had before we went to the hardware store. He and I order café au lait. Marla orders a traditional American breakfast with fried eggs, sausage and bacon, hash browns, and wheat toast (because it's healthier than white).

"You don't have to wait with us, if this is keeping you from something," I say to Gabriel.

Marla kicks me under the table.

I try to suppress a grunt.

"Is something wrong?" Gabriel shifts toward me. He's a little too close, and I catch a whiff of his tobacco-and-coffee-laced breath. I sit back in my seat and make a mental note to chew a piece of gum after I finish my café au lait.

"Nope. Not a thing." I glare at Marla. She's munching on her toast as innocently as a child. "We don't want to tie you up if you need to be somewhere."

He takes a long sip of his coffee, watching me over the top of his cup. He sets it down on the saucer. "That is very gracious of you. But please know that my assistant blocked off my morning for you."

I can see a virtual meter ticking over his head.

"This hidden apartment is somewhat of a novelty, no?" he asks. "I must admit I am quite curious to see it once it is cleaned up."

His phone buzzes and he picks it up, looks at the message. "As a matter of fact, I hope you don't mind, but I have taken the liberty of hiring a photographer to record the before and after." He points to his phone. "She is ready to meet us at the apartment when we are finished."

"The before and after?" Marla asks.

Gabriel nods. "It is not every day that one opens the door to a place such as this that has been lost to time. It is a city treasure."

Now it makes more sense why a named partner of a law firm

would clear his schedule to help us "get settled in" and clean up this grimy apartment. There's something in it for him and his firm. Of course, the history buff in me is thrilled at the prospect of having a record of the way it looks before we scrub away the past. Despite my skepticism, it seems like a win-win.

Marla frowns. "Let me be very up-front. We don't have money to blow on a professional photographer. The one I hired for my last wedding cost an arm and a leg. So, if Levesque, Racine, and Cerny wants to spring for pictures, knock yourself out, but I—er, we—can't chip in."

Marla punctuates the statement by slurping her coffee.

Gabriel answers with that pursed-lip shrug. "My firm is happy to cover the cost of the photographer."

"Do you have other plans for those pictures beyond saving them for posterity?" I ask.

"If you are willing, we could offer them to the press," he says. "If you want to sell the place, it will go a long way toward driving up the price you could demand. Everyone wants to own a piece of history. Some are willing to pay extra to obtain it."

"Whoa, slow down there." Marla pauses, the final forkful of egg and potatoes hovering midair. "Nobody said anything about selling the place."

"Well, we might have to," I say.

"We haven't even had a chance to really get in there and see what it's all about," she says before shoveling the food into her mouth.

"Fair enough," he says. "You need not decide whether or not you want to sell the place now. The media will be interested in learning of the apartment's existence whenever you are ready to release the news."

"Of course, the press will be good publicity for Levesque, Racine, and Cerny?" I say.

"*Absolument*." There's a challenging glint in his eyes. "Do you mind?"

Marla and I look at each other.

"Perhaps we can negotiate a price break in the final legal fees," I say.

Gabriel nods and his face slowly gives way to a smile. "I like a woman with a good business head."

He leans back in his chair, taking the white coffee cup with him. His eyes linger on mine a bit too long. I can't quite discern if it's sexy or predatory . . . or just French. Whatever it is, it makes my stomach stir again.

June 1927
Paris, France

Dear Diary,

I didn't get the job at Galeries Lafayette. The man in charge was very frank that my French was not strong enough to work with the public. They had no openings in tailoring.

I left the interview distraught, Helen's defense of naked bodies ringing in my ears.

Is she right? Are bodies merely flesh and bones, and nothing sacred?

Before I returned to the apartment, I spent an eternity walking around, trying to sort out my options. I wandered past the Palais Garnier, the opera house where Helen is so desperate to perform someday with the ballet. Even though she is no stranger to rejection, she says she will not lose faith in realizing her dream.

I found myself back at the église de la Madeleine, the church with the fabulous Roman-looking façade that I had stumbled upon the other evening when I got lost. This time my intentions were more purposeful. I had come to pray, even though I am not Catholic. I felt drawn there the other day when I lost my way. This time, I went inside and got down on my knees amidst the gilded splendor. I figured God answers prayers no matter your religion. I asked him to send me a sign about what I should do next.

Then I returned to the Tuileries garden, where I watched children launch small boats in the pond and walked past groups of old men playing boules. *My favorite area is dotted with ancient statues that have withstood the test and trials of time.*

I paused in front of the Nymphe. *She stood as naked and proud as the other sculptures, mostly of men wearing clothes. There was a dog at her bare feet and it made me think of the sweet little creature I met the last time I was there. The* Nymphe*'s head was bent as if she were gazing down at me, saying,* I persevered. You can, too . . . if you're strong enough.

Alas, she stood high upon her pedestal, carved of marble. I am but skin and bone. Breasts and bottom.

I feel like a lost kitten who has strayed away from her home, and Paris is the tomcat waiting to pounce. I'm not equipped to run with the strays, even though I've become one myself since leaving London.

As I stood there, I swore I heard the Nymphe *whisper, "We are one and the same, you and I. You will be fine, but you must not be so proud."*

When I returned to the apartment at dusk, Luc's friend Pierre Jean, the painter, was there. He offered me the job as his model.

I'd asked for a sign for what I should do next, though I'm hard-pressed to believe this one came from God.

Eleven

January 3, 2019—10:00 a.m.

Paris, France

After Gabriel picks up the check for breakfast—as predicted—his driver takes us back to the apartment.

On the way there, I watch the Paris morning unfold out the window like scenes from a rom-com. People walking dogs with leashes in one hand and to-go cups in the other. A woman running and pushing a baby jogger. An older man ambling along with a bulging mesh grocery bag on the crook of his elbow and a long baguette tucked under his arm.

When we arrive at the apartment, the photographer, a willowy blonde, is waiting for us outside of the gate. Two guys are helping her. One is arranging a lighting umbrella and the other is holding a couple of camera bodies at the ready.

It makes so much sense to professionally photograph the place. I can't believe I hadn't thought about it until now. Gabriel was right. Much more than a family heirloom, the apartment is a piece of history frozen in time that deserves to be documented. The realization makes my inner history nerd sing.

Until Gabriel leans in and kisses the blonde on both cheeks,

French style, then lingers a little too long in her personal space. She doesn't seem to mind.

"Hannah Bond and Marla Bond, may I introduce you to Anastasia Girard. She does not speak English, but I am sure that will not be a problem."

Tall and beautiful, with large hazel eyes and a pouty mouth, Anastasia looks as if she would be as confident in front of the camera or on the cover of a magazine as she seems to be in real life.

I sense a vibe that she and Gabriel might have been involved once . . . or even now?

They'd make a beautiful couple. I'm mesmerized by their interaction. The subtle ebb and flow of flirtation, the way Anastasia angles her perfect chin down and gazes up at Gabriel through long, dark eyelashes. The way Gabriel's gaze lingers on her face, caressing it without even touching it. The chemistry that pulses between them is breathtaking.

If they haven't had a *thing*, they're ripe for one.

"Anastasia says she is pleased to meet you. She is ready to go inside when you are," Gabriel offers.

"You're going to stay and translate, then?" Marla says to him.

Gabriel gazes at Anastasia, who is putting her cameras in their cases for the short trip inside. She seems careful, which bodes well for her treatment of the apartment.

"I'm sure you have other things to do," I say. "My French is limited, but I can speak enough to get by. Plus, I have a translation app. I think we can manage."

Gabriel waves off the out I've given him. "I am happy to stay. As I said, I set aside the morning for you. However, let me call the office."

He steps away for a moment and makes the call. When he returns, he says something to Anastasia in French. She turns and looks at Marla and me and nods.

We go inside.

It's a small elevator. Anastasia steps in with her camera equipment. Marla offers to ride with her and unlock the door.

When the empty elevator returns, Gabriel motions for the assistants to enter next, leaving the two of us alone. It would've been a tight squeeze, but the four of us could've fit. I am happy to wait and talk to Gabriel.

"You really should check out the Musée Rodin before you return to London," he says. "It is the most wonderful place. One of my favorites in all of Paris. It is a collection of Rodin's sculptures. There is a lovely garden, which might not boast its full glory in the heart of winter, but it is still full of beauty, a perfect place to sit outside and enjoy Paris."

"Isn't the museum housed in a mansion?"

"Yes, it is. It's called the Hôtel Biron and it was built in the early eighteenth century."

"Did Rodin live there?"

"He did, but he did not have the place all to himself. At the time it had been subdivided and he rented several rooms on the ground floor. After he died, the place was nearly destroyed to build apartments, but they saved it and turned it into a museum honoring him. It has been the Musée Rodin for more than a century."

"You know a lot about it."

"As I said, it is one of my favorite spots in Paris. I hope you will visit."

"I hope so, too," I say. "Someday, anyway. I don't have a lot of free time this visit."

"How long are you in Paris?"

"I have to be back in London by next Tuesday. For work."

"And what is it that you do for work?"

"I give tours about Jane Austen throughout the British countryside. I take Austen fans to all the places they've read about in her novels."

"Ah, that is intriguing. I assume your clientele is mostly women?"

"Women and a few husbands who have unwittingly agreed to come along for the ride."

"I take it you are a reader," he says.

After seeing him flirt with artsy, gorgeous Anastasia, I've never felt like more of a bookworm, but I am who I am.

"I love to read. All kinds of books."

"I do, too," he says. "I prefer biographies myself. I love reading about interesting lives and the people who have lived them. Your job is very interesting, no?"

"It has its moments. I love meeting the people on my tours. I have a chance to get to know them because often we are together in relatively close quarters for the better part of a week as we tour the countryside. I've learned a lot about human nature."

He smiles at me and for a moment it feels as if his gaze is caressing me the same way it caressed Anastasia moments ago.

Then the elevator arrives and breaks the spell. We get in and silently make the trip up one floor. Before the doors open, I can hear Marla's voice.

"You can't photograph the paintings in the bedroom," she yells. "Do you understand what I'm saying?"

When I get inside, I find her standing in the bedroom waving her arms like a referee.

"No photographs of the pictures on the bedroom wall." She's raised her voice again, as if talking loudly will help Anastasia understand her better. But Anastasia shrugs and looks pleadingly at Gabriel, who is standing beside me.

"Is there a problem?" he asks. "*Quel est le problème?*"

"*Quel* problem is I don't want her to photograph the paintings in the bedroom. They're off-limits."

"Ah," Gabriel says. Then he and Anastasia have a short conversation in French, which I don't understand because they're speaking fast.

Finally, Gabriel says, "Anastasia thought you didn't want her to photograph the apartment."

"That's not what I said," Marla hisses.

"I know that and you know that," I say, "but Anastasia doesn't understand you, just like you didn't understand what she was saying to you. Mind your manners."

Marla snorts and crosses her arms. "Maybe we shouldn't do this today. I mean, it was thrust on us out of the blue. We haven't even had time to comb through the inside of the apartment ourselves."

"Let's go out here." I motion for her to follow me out of the apartment and into the hallway so we can speak privately.

On my way out, I say to Gabriel, "I'm sorry. Give us a moment and we'll be right back."

I lock eyes with Anastasia, who is regarding us as if we're a couple of escaped lunatics. Who can blame her? Marla is making me feel a bit deranged at the moment.

Once we're out of the apartment and in the hallway, I say to her, "If she doesn't take the photographs today—in fact, right now—the cleaning crew will be here and we won't get 'before' photos."

"And why is it so bloody important to photograph the mess?" She's shouting again.

"Because this is kind of a big deal." I'm talking in a quiet voice to set an example, but Marla isn't big on nonverbal cues. "And lower your voice, please. We don't need to make a scene."

Marla throws up her hands and presses the elevator call button.

When the doors open, she steps inside. I do, too. We ride down in silence.

On the ground floor, we exit the elevator and I hold open the lobby door and allow Marla to pass through first. Once we're outside breathing in the brisk morning air, my head clears enough to talk sensibly.

"Do you want to tell me what's going on?" I ask. "There's more to this than you not wanting people in the apartment, isn't there?"

Marla shrugs.

"Please tell me what you're thinking. It matters."

Marla stops in front of a concrete bench and drops onto it. Her eyes are glistening with tears.

"What's going on, Mom?"

She does a double take.

"I like it when you call me Mom."

I don't know what to say, so I don't say anything. I lower myself onto the bench next to her and wait patiently for her to speak.

"When I was growing up," she finally says, "I always felt like the odd one out. You had Gram. Granny Ivy was mad protective of Mom and you, of course." She shakes her head. "It's . . . never mind."

"No, keep going."

She opens her mouth to continue but closes it again as if she can't find the words.

"So, discovering this place sort of felt like a second chance to be part of that triangle?" I ask.

She shrugs. Blinks.

"It's a chance to turn that triangle the three of you had into a square where I'm included. Does that sound dumb?"

"It doesn't sound dumb." I smile at her and I don't know what comes over me, but I reach out and put my hand on hers. I half expect her to pull away, but she doesn't.

"It's just that this . . . this apartment feels like something for you and me. A gift from Granny Ivy and Mom—although, I don't know that Mom even knew about it. It doesn't matter. It feels like Ivy's way of reaching out to pull you and me together. I remember something that Granny Ivy said to me once. Mom and I were in a really bad place. It was the day before I was leaving for Europe with my friend Callie. Mom and I weren't speaking. It was really bad. That afternoon while Mom was at work, Ivy stopped in my bedroom doorway and said, 'Lovie, I know your mum isn't happy with your summer plans, but between you and me, I'm glad you're going. Most people go about their lives as if they have all the time in the world. But they don't and they only realize it after it's too late. Be careful, but go out there and get whatever it is you're chasing.'"

Marla's voice breaks on the last word. She swallows hard and then clears her throat. I don't want to breathe for fear that she'll stop talking.

"I wish I would've asked her what she meant," she continues. "Because looking back on it now, I think it might have had something to do with her time in Paris. But I was so self-absorbed, all I could think was, 'Finally someone in this house is on my side.'

"It doesn't matter now. You and me . . . We've never done well when others were involved. Since I arrived in London, I feel like we've been making such progress, but now there's all this stuff coming at us from the outside. I know we need to clean the place up and it would be cool to have before and after pictures, but I don't know that I'm ready to share our treasure with the world just yet."

"I get it. I totally get it. For the first time in our lives, we're on the same page." Even if it feels a little tenuous. A little fragile. "I want to protect that, too. But this is our only chance to get pictures of how the place looks now, and just because we take the pictures doesn't mean we have to publicize them immediately. I'll talk to Gabriel about drawing up release paperwork. You can't blame him for wanting the photos, but we are his clients at the end of the day, and I doubt he's going to do anything rash to jeopardize that."

"Oh, Hannah, you always see the best in people. How do you do that?" Marla laughs. "I guess you're not old enough to be jaded and cynical like I am."

She reaches up and touches my face. "You're so pretty and you don't even know it."

We sit there a moment.

Her words have thrown me. It's a totally un-Marla-like thing to say. I feel as if I'm living in an alternate Parisian reality. A decidedly non–Jane Austen dream.

ABOUT AN HOUR LATER, as Anastasia is wrapping up her shoot, the cleaning crew arrives.

"There is no sense in you remaining here while the work is in progress," Gabriel says to us. "Why don't you use the opportunity to step outside and enjoy the day? When you return, the place will be transformed."

He snaps his fingers in the air as if that's how the magic will happen.

"Thanks, but I'm not leaving," says Marla. "Um, excuse me."

She motions to one of the crew members who has taken an industrial vacuum to the dusty sofa. "Please be careful there. That couch is old. You're being too rough."

The woman must understand because she slows down and vacuums less vigorously.

"See, this is why I can't leave this place unattended," Marla says. "Why don't you two go? In fact, Gabriel, why don't you take Hannah somewhere and show her the sights? I think it would be a good break for all of us. She was saying she wanted to see the Eiffel Tower."

With her next breath, Marla shouts at one of the workers. "Hey, be careful with that. It's a very old lamp, not a soccer ball."

Gabriel laughs as Marla moves in the direction of the offender.

"I'm sorry about that," I say. "She means no disrespect."

"No apologies necessary." He arches his left brow. "Or perhaps I should have said you can make it up to me by allowing me to show you the Musée Rodin this afternoon and maybe the Eiffel Tower, too?"

"I'll think about it," I say. "Right now, I need to return a work email."

"I thought you were on vacation?" Gabriel says.

"I am, but I'm sure you understand work doesn't take a holiday just because you do."

He nods and leaves me to conduct my business.

A few minutes later, as I'm finishing up, Marla steps out of the bedroom, her arms full with three gilded framed paintings. No doubt the ones of Ivy. She walks over to the sofa table, carefully lays each one down, and begins gently dusting one of them. A woman obsessed.

I relay Gabriel's plan and confirm she's okay being here solo.

"That's a wonderful idea," she says, holding the painting in both hands and examining it in the sunlight. She leans in. "He's cute, Hannah."

He's only a few feet away doing something on his phone, but I'm glad the vacuums are making enough noise to muffle Marla's words. He must sense that we're talking about him, because he smiles at us and closes the distance.

"I'll have my cell phone with me," I say. "Call if you need anything. Is your phone charged?"

"Of course it is. I'm not a child."

I give her the side-eye.

"I'm young at heart," she says. "Now, you go be *young*. It's time you start acting your age.

"Take this daughter of mine away from here and teach her how to have fun," Marla says to Gabriel as the woman running the vacuum switches it off. Her words virtually ring in the room, dancing off the walls, twirling and swirling with the dust motes that the cleaners have stirred up.

Gabriel grins his Clooney smile. "I am happy to oblige. I am a very good teacher."

July 1927
Paris, France

Dear Diary,

It's been a week now, but posing for Pierre is still awkward. I doubt it will get easier lying naked in front of a stranger with a lousy disposition who refuses to play by the rules.

Today, he crossed the very clear line I drew before accepting the job.

Helen warned me he might. Lo and behold, one week in and he felt emboldened to take freedoms with my naked body.

Here's what happened: I was having trouble arranging myself into the pose he was trying to describe. He came over and took my left arm and placed it over my head. Then he lifted my chin to a precise angle. As he did, his hand trailed down my neck, past my collarbone. Before I knew it, he was cupping my breast.

I smacked his hand away, jumped off the divan, and grabbed my clothes, telling him he was never permitted to touch me.

He smiled sheepishly, murmuring that it was my fault for being so alluring. I had tempted him. How was he supposed to help himself?

I told him he could help himself to a new model because my work with him was finished.

I have never dressed so quickly in my life.

When he realized I was serious, he begged me to stay, saying without me he could not finish the series. I told him he should've thought of that before taking such liberties.

Then he slumped down on his stool and put his head in his hands, mumbling to himself. Je suis un idiot.

He is an idiot. I did not dispute him. Instead, I grabbed my handbag and sketchbook and walked out the door.

He ran after me, begging me to reconsider. When I kept walking, he told me I could take the rest of the day off and he would pay me for a full day if I would come back tomorrow. Then, we would start anew. He told me that he knew I was not like the others and he would never touch me again.

I slowed my pace.

The next thing I knew he'd raced back into the studio and came out rattling the rusted can he keeps on the shelf. He handed me a fistful of coins. I stopped, but I refused to look at him. I kept my gaze pinned on the coins in his outstretched palm.

He said it was more than what we had agreed, but he wanted me to have it to make up for his blunder.

He transferred the coins into my hand and begged me to come back tomorrow.

I told him I couldn't because I felt unsafe alone with him.

Then he sweetened the pot by offering to introduce me to someone who could open doors to the world of Paris fashion. He said the meeting would happen tomorrow evening.

I told him I would think about it. The last thing I want is to feel indebted to Pierre, but would accepting his help be any less dignified than retreating to Bristol? Because that is what I will have to do if I don't return to Pierre's atelier. Even so, as I write this, I do not know if I will return tomorrow or pack my bags for home.

Twelve

January 3, 2019—11:30 a.m.
Paris, France

I go back to the hotel and take a quick shower to rinse off the apartment dust. I have just enough time before Gabriel collects me for our adventure to put on some makeup and change into my velvet wrap dress. Cressida helped me pick it out. It's red and hot pink with bold black letters stenciled into the pattern. Paired with black tights and boots, it's sophisticated enough to wear to a Paris museum.

We take our time meandering through the old mansion that houses the Musée Rodin, following the black-and-white checkerboard marble entryway to the grand staircase that leads us up to the second floor. As we cross the creaky parquet floor, Gabriel tells me the history of the house.

The grand casement windows allow the perfect amount of light to stream in and showcase the sculptures. We linger in front of *The Kiss*, a breathtaking marble sculpture of a nude couple locked in a passionate embrace.

I clasp my hands behind my back to keep from reaching out and touching the smooth milky surface. I want to trace the areas where their bodies are joined, forever held together by the stone from which Rodin tried to set them free.

"Have I succeeded in teaching you how to have fun yet?" Gabriel asks.

A frisson of awareness skitters through my body.

"I'm having a wonderful time," I say. "Of course, Rodin's work is tremendous, but it's such a treat to see the inside of the house. I could almost imagine what life was like when Abraham Peyrenc de Moras lived here with his wife."

Gabriel tells me the house was long considered the most spectacular in the neighborhood because it was freestanding—it didn't share walls with other homes, as is the case with so many homes in Paris. It was also unusual because it had one of the most beautiful gardens in the city, which remains today in all its seven-acre splendor.

"Isn't looking at an ancient *manoir* too much like work for you?" Gabriel asks.

"I never met a big house I didn't love. This is no more work for me than it must be for you to escort a client to the Musée Rodin. Did you find it less enjoyable with me in tow?"

I turn and face him.

"Oh, that's right. Today, you are a client." His gaze smolders. "However, since Emile Levesque was your original point of contact, when he returns, I will send you back to his capable hands. Voila! You will no longer be my client and that will leave my hands free to serve you in other ways."

I laugh at his forwardness, giving him the benefit of the doubt that something must've gotten lost in translation.

"What exactly are you thinking of doing with those capable hands?"

He raises his left brow knowingly. His gaze falls to the V neckline of my dress and lingers. I'm suddenly feeling quite out of my depth.

"What I meant is I have served you in a professional capacity. When Levesque returns, I will be at your service as a . . . friend." Gabriel looks at his watch. "In fact, Levesque is probably back in town by now. I guess that means I am no longer on duty."

I waver at the new tenor of our conversation. If I let it, it could drift into very personal territory.

I'm not sure I want that.

But I'm not sure that I don't.

Gabriel is so attractive on so many different levels—physically, emotionally, intellectually. It's like the trifecta of sexy.

My mouth goes dry, and I wish I could paw through my purse for a piece of gum.

This guy is French and older, which translates to experienced. What in the world does he want with someone like me?

Okay, never mind. I know what he wants, but I'm not sure if I'm up for the emotional roller coaster of a hookup right now.

Aiden pops into my mind and I feel weirdly guilty. We haven't even been on a date, beyond the blind date that really wasn't a blind date.

He should not figure into this . . . whatever *this* is with Gabriel. A no-strings-attached chance to have fun? A short-lived Paris fling with my attorney with benefits?

The start of something bigger?

It's been such a long time since the last time . . . since Charlie . . . and I know how *that* ended.

Maybe I'm overthinking something good.

God, here I go. I need to stop. I need to go with the flow.

"But you're a named partner. Doesn't that still make me your client in the grand scheme of things?"

He reaches out and sweeps a lock of my hair off my cheek, tucks it behind my ear. I can smell his earthiness and the phantom scent of nicotine on his fingers, even though he has never smoked in front of me. My cheek tingles where he touched it.

"It means you are Levesque's client and you are my friend. No? Are you not my friend, Hannah? Because I think we could be very good friends."

His voice is low and sexy, and I melt a little more inside. I can't make my brain come up with a witty reply to keep this banter going.

That's my curse. Queen of the comeback, I am not. Give me a few hours and I can craft the perfect thing to say, but sadly a late comeback is a dead comeback.

"Would you allow me to cook dinner for you tonight, Hannah? One friend cooking for the other?"

I can't abandon Marla tonight. It was one thing to leave her at the apartment bossing around the cleaning crew, but it's quite another to desert her on our second night in Paris when we should be strategizing our next moves.

"Look, I had a nice time with you today," he says. "I have enjoyed talking to you. You are as interesting as you are beautiful and I want the conversation to continue. That is all. Please know my intentions are pure. Think about it."

He doesn't bring it up again as we stroll around the gardens. Nor does he mention it on the ride back to the apartment.

When I get out of the car, he follows me. He pulls a pen and a leather-bound notepad from the breast pocket of his coat, writes something, and hands me the paper. "I would be happy to send a car for you tonight, but I don't want to pressure you. This is my address. I would love to cook for you. I will prepare a meal for two and hope for the best. If you do not show, I will understand." He shrugs. "I will have leftovers for tomorrow night. And another sad night of eating all alone."

"Somehow I doubt that," I say, glancing at the paper, on which he has scrawled an address and the time—7:00 p.m. His handwriting is neat and bold. It matches his personality perfectly.

"It is true. I love to cook, but I hate to cook for myself because I hate to eat alone."

"No pressure, huh?" I smile.

He shakes his head. "Absolutely no pressure. I am simply telling you the truth. I will not push you, but it bears repeating that I have had such a lovely time with you today, Hannah, and I do hope to see you tonight."

He leans in, and for a split second, I think he's going to kiss me on the lips, but he whispers a soft kiss on my cheek.

Without another word, he gets into his car and leaves.

It is late afternoon as I let myself into the lobby of the apartment building. I'm in another world as I press the call button for the elevator and take the short ride up to the next floor.

But I land firmly back to earth when I walk into the clean apartment. It looks like a different place dust- and cobweb-free—like the difference between Kansas and Oz. I'm speechless as I take in everything as if for the first time. The shoes are still sitting by the door, only now I can see the worn leather and fraying laces clearly. Rather than the ashy gray of before, they're a deep, rich cognac brown.

The jacket hanging on the coat tree is a vibrant cobalt blue. The umbrella is magnificent yellow. Everything has been cleaned and returned to its original place, and I'm sure I have Marla to thank for that.

As if on cue, she appears in the living room. "Well, what do you think? She cleans up pretty good, doesn't she?" Marla is standing with her hands on her hips, gazing around the room and looking pleased with herself.

As she should.

"It's unbelievable," I say. "How long have they been gone?"

"They left about a half hour ago. A van came and whisked them away."

"That's efficient. I'm glad we didn't try to clean this place ourselves. We would've barely made a dent."

"It was a nice gift from Gabriel," Marla says. "Speaking of . . . How was your afternoon? I'm surprised to see you back so soon."

I glance at my watch. "We were out for more than four hours."

She tsks. "And you had the whole night ahead of you."

Her insinuation of failure irks me.

"He wants to cook for me tonight." The words fly out of my mouth before I can stop them.

Her eyes grow wide.

"He's cooking? At his place?"

I wait for her to invite herself.

"Well, that's more like it." Her brow arches and the corners of her mouth curl upward. "You know what that means, right? I hope you brought your sexy underwear."

"Marla, really? Stop it. Just don't."

I have exactly one pair of sexy undies. They're in London in the way back of my dresser, where they've remained since the day I purchased them. I don't even remember why I got them. I think they still have the tags.

"You didn't bring your sexy panties, did you?" she says.

"We came here to work."

"It's Paris, Hannah. How could you not bring good underwear?"

She says this the way some parents might admonish their daughters for getting a bad grade or denting the car.

"I'm sorry to be such a mortal disappointment to you, Mother."

She makes a weary face to show how deeply I've wounded her. "You can't wear granny panties on a date in Paris with a Frenchman.

I guess we'll have to buy you something new on the way back to the hotel."

After missing all those years of back-to-school shopping, my mother is making it up to me by taking me shopping for sexy underwear. Cool.

"Gabriel is not going to see my underwear tonight. That is, if I even go."

"Hannah, you have to go."

"No, I don't."

Marla clears her throat. "What I mean is a night out is exactly what you need. Gabriel is a good-looking man. He seems interested in you. You're in Paris. Why not live a little? Since I've vowed to become a new woman in Paris, it's only fair that you work on yourself, too."

AS WE CLOSE UP the apartment and get ready to go back to the hotel, Marla holds out her phone. "Look, it's only a thirteen-minute walk from here to the Galeries Lafayette department store."

"Is this the GPS you used yesterday at the train station?"

Marla gives me the stink eye.

All kidding aside, I really don't want to buy new underwear. Gabriel tempts me in the most primal way. My cotton granny panties will be my chastity belt. For extra protection, I won't shave my legs, either.

"Now we know where to go if we need to go shopping," I deflect. "What? Why are you looking at me like that?"

"Hannah, you need to go shopping. You need new underwear."

"I don't think so."

"Hannah, I'm going to be blunt with you because I don't want you to embarrass yourself. Frenchmen aren't like the English boys you've been dating. Frenchmen expect a certain level of . . . sophistication."

English boys?

First, I contemplate asking her how she knows so much about Frenchmen and sophistication. But I really don't want to know. Then I consider telling her there hasn't been an English boy since Charlie, but she doesn't know about him and I don't want to explain.

Instead, I say nothing and think more about my options for tonight.

I just met Gabriel. He's our lawyer, and just because he's sexy as hell and I'm thinking of letting him cook for me doesn't mean I want him for dessert.

But what if I do?

It's been a very long, dry season.

I can't believe I've let Marla get into my head, but I think about what she said about loosening up, and I have to admit she's not wrong.

We take the short walk to the Galeries Lafayette. The department store occupies an entire city block. It's a stunning sight both inside and out. Four floors are organized around an enormous Neo Byzantine–style dome made of ethereal stained glass. The overall feel is art deco. Gold leaf arches and railings shimmer in the natural light flooding in through the dome, making the merchandise in the great hall glisten and sparkle like diamonds.

I'm gaping, turning in a slow circle, taking it all in like a tourist.

We make our way to the lingerie department on the fourth floor. It's huge and seems to have everything from workout clothing and sleepwear to stockings, garters, slips, panties, and bras in every conceivable level of opacity and sensuality.

Marla commandeers a saleswoman, Yvette. They tag-team me,

pointing out options and extolling the virtues of expensive panties for self-empowerment.

"Think of it this way," says Yvette in perfect English. "If you wear your good undergarments every day, even to the market, you have a sweet secret that is your own. It belongs to you. If you choose to share that secret with another person, all the better."

Yvette is a different breed of woman than me. She probably has an entire wardrobe of sexy.

"Plus," Marla chimes in, "that way you're always prepared."

"Okay, okay. You've convinced me." I point to a feminine violet-blue bra and matching panties. Yvette finds my size and I go into the fitting room, relieved when she doesn't trail in after me.

I'm seduced. I love the set, with its delicate sparkles and intricate embroidery. It makes me feel feminine and, yes, sexy.

Marla wins this round.

When Yvette finishes wrapping my purchase, Marla asks, "Which way to the Grand Marnier Palace?"

Yvette cocks her head to the side. Her glossy brown hair falls over her slight shoulder and her blue eyes look puzzled. "*Excusez-moi?* Urr—I beg your pardon. I do not understand."

"The Grand Marnier Palace," Marla enunciates. "It's a big, fancy building. It's supposed to be right around here somewhere. This store is huge, so I don't want to exit the wrong door. We could be walking in circles for days just to get a drink."

The woman shrugs. "I am sorry. I do not know of such a place."

Exasperated, Marla holds out her phone. "See, it says right here—"

"Ah, le Palais Garnier," says Yvette.

"Isn't that what I said, the uh . . . Pa-lay . . . Grand Marnier?" Her brow knits as she tries to imitate Yvette's French pronunciation of *palace*.

Yvette suppresses a smile and looks at me knowingly before giving us directions. We thank her, and as we turn to leave, Marla asks, "They serve drinks at this hour, right?"

"Madame, le Palais Garnier is an opera house," Yvette says sweetly. "If you drop by the box office, I am sure they will be happy to tell you what they offer and when you can visit."

"An opera house?" Marla's hand flies to her mouth and a small laugh escapes. "I thought it was like Grand Marnier's headquarters or something. You know, the Palace of Grand Marnier. My bad." Her cheeks turn pink. "It used to be my favorite drink. I wanted to take Hannah there for a cocktail before her date. Oh, coffee for me, of course."

She shrugs, and it's kind of endearing to see her thrown off her game.

I get it. This underwear shopping trip was her way of passing the baton to me. Though she and I have always marched to different drums, she's still my mother, and she still has a few things she wants to teach me.

July 1927
Paris, France

Dear Diary,

Against my better judgment, I returned to Pierre's studio the next day.

Instantly, I wondered if I'd made the right decision because instead of showing proper contrition for his inappropriate actions, Pierre's disposition was sullen and irritable. He acted as if I were the one who had wronged him, saying because we hadn't worked a full day yesterday he was behind and didn't have time for distracting chitchat. That was fine with me because I really didn't want to talk to him, either.

The studio was cold and he refused to light a fire or give me a break to stretch my legs, which were falling asleep because they were curled under me.

He kept saying, Cinq minutes de plus. *Five more minutes.*

After an hour had passed, I stood on wobbly legs and pulled on my robe.

He made a guttural growling noise and tossed away his brush. Grudgingly, he agreed to light a fire so we could get back to work. He claimed he needed to finish this study of me before the end of the day so he could get back on track to meet his deadline.

I don't think he realized I had him over a barrel. If I walked out, he wouldn't be able to finish the series he was preparing for the exhibit.

Of course, if I left, I would be without a job and he wouldn't introduce me to his person he'd promised could open doors. Although, now that I'd had time to think about it, I wondered if he really knew such a person.

Once the fire was roaring, he rapped his brush on the easel and yelled, "Back to work! Vite!"

I told him he needed to check his tone. Because he was acting so foul, I lingered over my sketchbook and finished drawing the dress I'd been holding in my mind all morning.

He started banging around the studio, and I finally laid down my pencil. I told him that his ill temper was uncalled for, and I believed this arrangement would not work after all. Perhaps we should call it quits.

After that, he was all business, and I felt emboldened to ask about this evening's meeting.

He told me he would take me to a salon where there were many influential people.

I wasn't sure what he meant by influential people, or, for that matter, what he meant by a salon.

He told me it was a place where painters and writers and creative minds gathered. It was at the home of an American woman named Gertrude Stein. She opened her home for people to call on Saturday evenings. He said she was always interested in meeting new people and sharing ideas. Pierre said I might meet someone there who would look at my sketches.

Okay. While it wasn't the key to the locked door that he had offered yesterday, it was something.

Because I don't trust Pierre, I will have Helen accompany me tonight when we meet him at his studio before we walk to Ms. Stein's home. Wish us luck.

Thirteen

January 3, 2019—7:00 p.m.
Paris, France

I take a cab to the sixteenth arrondissement address that Gabriel wrote down. Even though he offered to send a car, I felt more in control of the situation providing my own transportation. Dressed in a black sweater dress and knee-high boots, I arrive shortly after 7:00 p.m. and linger out front for a moment, taking in the splendor. His home is gorgeous. It's a nineteenth-century apartment building, carved out of the locally sourced light-gray limestone that gives Paris buildings their distinctive look.

I'm not an expert on Parisian real estate, but even I know that this is the expensive neighborhood.

After the doorman allows me in, he instructs me to take the elevator up to the third floor. When Gabriel answers the door, he greets me with a quick kiss on the lips.

"I'm so happy you're here."

His eyes sparkle as he helps me out of my coat. He hangs it in the foyer closet, and his gaze slowly meanders the length of my body.

"You look stunning," he says as he takes my purse and places it on the shelf above my coat.

Since I'd already worn my one nice outfit to the museum today, I borrowed a stretchy little black dress from Marla. Gabriel seems to appreciate the way it clings to all the places that make me self-conscious.

I hope he can't tell I'm holding my breath and doing my best to suck in my stomach. The only thing worse than my granny panties would've been Spanx. Do they even sell such a thing in Paris?

Finally, he closes the closet door, puts his hand on the small of my back, and ushers me into the living room. I'm hyperaware of his touch and the smell of his aftershave. It's crisp and clean with hints of tobacco. It makes me want to lean in and breathe deeper.

I'm glad I ended up shaving my legs.

When I step into the living room, I notice that his home lives up to the neighborhood's reputation.

From what I can see, it's about three times the size of Ivy's ninth arrondissement apartment, and it has all the charming, old-world Parisian fixtures one would imagine—the kind that make a home look both old and brand-new at the same time.

The paint is fresh and bright white, and the Murano glass chandelier in the foyer sparkles as if it was recently cleaned. Who knows? Maybe the cleaning crew stopped by Gabriel's place after they left square la Bruyère.

Then I'm struck by the aroma perfuming the air.

My stomach growls. "Something smells delicious."

He smiles at the compliment and looks downright boyish in his black Henley and blue jeans. I like this more casual side of him.

"I hope you're hungry. I have prepared a feast for us."

Which means he was pretty confident I would show up tonight. I'm glad I did.

I'm glad I didn't miss the chance to see this place. To see the floor-to-ceiling casement windows from the inside. I notice that they're covered by shutters and flowing white sheers, so I can't see outside where I once stood, but it's dark out there anyway and it's warm and inviting in here. A grand piano sits in front of the windows in one corner. Across the room there's a fire in the fireplace, which is one of those modern gas-and-glass models built into the marble surround. It gives the room a contemporary touch that reminds you that, yes, these walls have seen the ages, but the current custodian enjoys all the latest conveniences. And has very good taste, as evidenced by the large white couch-and–chaise lounge combo with a fur throw draped casually over the back—perfect for lounging or cuddling.

"Sit down, please," Gabriel says. "How do you say . . . make yourself at home?"

"Make yourself at home!"

I know it was a corny thing to say, but when I get nervous, my inner nerd springs to life. I'm relieved he chuckles as he leaves the room.

Rather than sitting, I take the opportunity to take in the room with its high ceilings, crowned with expensive-looking medallions and sculpted molding. Its details are similarly French to the ones in Ivy's apartment, but here they're elevated to the next level. It's all white on white—white ceiling, white fixtures, white walls, white shutters and drapes, white furniture—except for the Murano glass chandelier and the deep-red Persian rugs that top the parquet floors.

I notice no trace of cigarettes or ashtrays, which probably means he doesn't smoke in the house.

Points for him.

He's still smiling when he returns with champagne in a silver bucket and two crystal flutes. He sets everything on the coffee table, which is carved out of marble and laid with a scape of large hardback coffee-table books, a massive fresh floral arrangement in a gleaming silver dish, and a grouping of towering silver candlesticks in graduated sizes. The place looks straight from the pages of *Architectural Digest*.

"I hope you like bubbles," he says as he coaxes the cork from the bottle with a controlled *pffft* and a nearly inaudible pop.

He pours two glasses and hands me one, then touches his glass to mine.

"To you. I am so very glad we're doing this."

"I am, too."

The way Gabriel looks at me reminds me I'm wearing the lacy violet-blue thong and matching bra under my dress. I'm not sure how much longer I'll want to keep my silky little secret to myself.

He gestures to the sofa. "Please make yourself at home and enjoy the fire while I go in and check on dinner."

"Can I help you with anything?" I ask.

He shakes his head. "Everything is done. It's simple food. Coq au vin and *pomme de terre*. It needs to cook a few minutes more."

I feel odd sitting alone in the cavernous room.

I take my champagne over to the built-in bookshelves that line the walls on either side of the fireplace. They are crammed full of books—and not the generic leather-bound variety for show that designers often use to accessorize fancy places like this.

Some shelves house large art and photography books. Several volumes detailing the history of France occupy another shelf. They're situated among small sculptures and colorfully painted bowls and sterling silver chalices. There's a framed black-and-white photo of a much younger Gabriel with four other people. I pick it up for a closer look at the older man and woman, who could be his mother and father. And a boy and a girl who could be his brother and sister. Yes, I can see the resemblance. The dark wavy hair, the deep-set, dark eyes, the same strong features. This has to be his family.

I hear footsteps behind me and turn, photo in one hand, champagne flute in the other, a smile at the ready as I start to ask Gabriel about the people in the picture.

Only, it's not Gabriel standing behind me.

A small, thin, well-dressed woman with short dark hair who looks like she could have just stepped out of the salon is regarding me with a quizzical expression. Her arms are crossed and in the crook of one hangs a crocodile Birkin bag. I'm no fashion expert, but even I know about this bag, and I'm 99 percent sure it's real.

She says something to me in rapid French that I don't understand.

"I'm sorry, my French is not very strong. *Parlez-vous anglais, s'il vous plaît?*"

She raises her chin and actually looks down her aquiline nose at me. "Ah, I see. You are American."

Her English is perfect.

"Yes, I am." I return the photo to the shelf.

"And you are?" she asks.

It takes me a moment to realize she's asking my name. "I am Hannah Bond." Foolishly, I set my champagne flute on the coffee table, close the distance between us, and offer my hand in greeting.

She regards my outstretched fingers for a moment before uncrossing her arms and giving my hand a perfunctory squeeze and recrossing her arms.

"I did not realize my husband was entertaining a dinner guest this evening."

Her husband?

"The chicken should be ready in fifteen minutes," Gabriel calls from the kitchen. "I've opened a bottle of burgundy for us to enjoy with the meal. Do you like red wine?"

He enters the room with a goblet in hand. "Here's a sip to try. If you don't care for it, I'll open—" He stops short as soon as he sees the woman.

His wife?

"Veronique," he says. "I was not expecting you home tonight."

"Yes. I see." Her expression is neutral as she looks back and forth between Gabriel and me, her head still held high.

Veronique is his wife. Nice. It's slowly sinking in. Only it doesn't make any sense.

Nothing inappropriate has happened. Except for my new underwear and the peck on the lips, which was pretty chaste by French standards.

I don't know whether to stay or go. I wish one of them would say something to give me an indication of what I should do. If I leave too hastily, it implies that hanky-panky was on tonight's menu. But if I stay—well, the situation feels more and more awkward as each second ticks by.

"So, Hannah is your flavor of the moment?" Her voice is lilting and amused.

"Excuse me?" I ask, willing to give her the benefit of the doubt. Maybe her English isn't as perfect as I first thought. "I am Gabriel's client."

"I know, honey, they all are."

Honey?

"Let me guess," she continues. "He has prepared coq au vin for you and given you a sob story about how he loves to cook but hates to eat alone?"

She must read the astonishment on my face because she barks out a laugh.

"Do not feel bad. You are not the first. His law practice is like a garden that keeps producing fresh crops of . . . how shall I say . . . dinner guests." She gives my body a once-over and shakes her head.

Then she waves her hand as if she can make me disappear. Her large diamond ring glints in the light. Gabriel is frozen in place. The glass of wine he was bringing me to taste is suspended as if he's offering a toast.

Veronique sets her bag on the sofa, walks to a bar cart with a decanter and crystal glasses, and pours herself a drink of amber liquid.

"I should go," I say to Gabriel while her back is turned.

He nods and at least has the decency to look sorry. I grab the wine from his hand, knock it back, and return the empty glass.

As soon as I disappear into the foyer to retrieve my purse and coat from the closet, Veronique lights into him in rapid-fire French.

I don't need Google Translate to understand exactly what she's saying.

July 1927
Paris, France

Dear Diary,

Helen had other plans and could not accompany me to meet Pierre tonight. I strongly considered staying in for the evening, because I worried that arriving alone would give him the wrong idea. Alas, as the clock ticked closer to seven, all I could think was how I do not fancy being a painter's model forever. If I am to find a more advantageous situation, I must explore every opportunity. Pierre had promised an introduction, and I would be foolish not to take it.

I'm so happy I went, despite the evening getting off to an unfortunate start.

More about that in a moment.

We were the first guests to arrive at Miss Stein's home. I quickly realized the heavyset man in the armchair by the fireplace was not a man at all, but a woman with terrible fashion sense and an unfortunate haircut that was more Julius Caesar than Eton crop.

She greeted Pierre by name. Her American accent clued me in that she was our host.

Pierre had the nerve to introduce me as his model. He did not mention that I was an aspiring fashion designer. After the introduction, I became invisible. I wondered if he had misled me, because it was curious that someone as inelegant as Miss Stein would have an interest in, much less connections to, the fashion world.

The longer Pierre prattled on about the form and symbolism in his current paintings, the more irritated I became with him. To quell my mood, I glanced about the tidy room, taking in the paintings and drawings displayed on the walls, some stacked two or three high. I am by no means a connoisseur, but the massive collection looked impressive.

Aside from the art, the home was not fancy. Yet everything—the books, the statuary, the flowers in vases—seemed to have a purpose.

Maybe that's why I felt so out of place.

Especially when Miss Stein began talking to Pierre about me as if I weren't there, telling him I was quite comely and that she was eager to call at his studio to view the paintings and perhaps add one to her collection.

When I agreed to model for Pierre, I hadn't considered that a rendering of my naked body might hang in someone's home in full view—in a place like this.

I tried to find my voice and explain that I was more than a model, but Miss Stein interrupted me to introduce her partner, Alice Toklas, the tiny, wiry woman sitting on the small chair across the hearth from her. I didn't understand what she meant by partner. Did they invest in art together? Or perhaps another business venture? I meant to ask Pierre on the way home, but he ended up leaving without me. Can you believe that?

Before that happened, others arrived. At the first break in conversation, I gathered all my courage and addressed Miss Stein. "Pierre tells me you are acquainted with leaders in the fashion world?"

She squinted at me as if she didn't understand and asked Alice to fetch me some tea and make me comfortable. I thought she was inviting me to join the circle of men that was forming around her, but soon I realized I was not to converse with her and the men; I was to join Alice at the ladies' table.

Foolishly, I tried to snare Pierre's gaze, but he was deep in an animated conversation with another man. The next thing I knew, Pierre had stalked out of the room, looking angry. The man he'd been talking to went after him looking just as disgruntled.

The lone curio that did not have a place in this room, I decided it was time for me to leave.

In the foyer, I glanced around for Pierre, but he was not there. Then suddenly, the front door swung open. The man Pierre had been arguing with nearly knocked me down in his haste.

He excused himself. I asked him if he knew where Pierre had gone.

He asked if I was a friend of Pierre's. I was so irritated I said not anymore.

He laughed a laugh that reached all the way to his gold-flecked brown eyes and said that anyone who disliked the man was a friend of his. He took my hand and introduced himself as Andres Armand.

That's when I realized he was quite possibly the most handsome man I'd ever met.

He offered to escort me home because he said it wasn't safe for a young woman to walk alone after dark. When I asked him why should I trust him, he told me he hoped I would give him a chance to prove himself worthy.

I have never believed in love at first sight. Until now.

I wanted to trust Monsieur Armand. Maybe it was his

handsome face or the fine way he dressed. Though, Jack the Ripper was rumored to have been an aristocrat.

Even so, I allowed him to walk me home. My heart broke when he bid me adieu without asking to call on me again. He knows where I live, but I fear I might never see him again . . . unless I venture back to Miss Stein's salon, which appeals to me about as much as posing naked for Pierre Jean.

To see the charming Andres Armand again, though, I might risk it.

Fourteen

January 3, 2019—8:45 p.m.

Paris, France

"Why are you home so early?" Marla asks as I let myself into the hotel room. She looks from the TV to the clock on the nightstand between the full-sized beds.

"Gabriel is married."

I figure there's no sense pretending.

"What?" My mother's mouth falls open and she pushes to a sitting position. She looks truly horrified.

I nod. "His wife, Veronique, came home before we even had a chance to sit down for dinner."

"Tell me what happened."

I sit down on my bed, remove my boots, then lean against the headboard and hug my knees to my chest. "Obviously he wasn't expecting her. The worst part is that I'm not his first 'dinner guest,' as she called me. Not that being the first would make it any better. Marla, what kind of a man invites another woman to the home he shares with his wife while she's away? It was so awkward. I feel so dirty."

"Did something happen?" Marla sits up. "He didn't—"

"No. Nothing happened. But if she hadn't come home so early, who knows where things might have ended up?"

Marla stands and starts pacing. "I'm furious. I'm going to call that law office tomorrow and report him."

"Marla, he's a named partner. Really, it's fine. Nothing happened. He invited me over for dinner. I went of my own volition and then I left. He didn't touch me. End of story."

"Well, then, we are changing law firms first thing tomorrow."

"Marla, no. That would be too messy. He mentioned that Monsieur Levesque is back in town and will be our point person. I'll bet we'll never hear from Gabriel Cerny again."

THE NEXT DAY, MARLA and I check out of the hotel and move into the apartment. The plan is to spend the rest of our time here going through the contents of Ivy's place—looking in every drawer, searching every nook and cranny for more information about her secret life.

Maybe it should be enough that we inherited the apartment, but one thing Marla and I agree on is that we want to know more about Ivy's life in Paris. It's the first time my mother and I have had a common goal.

Today, with my new direction, I won't dwell on the fact that I lost an entire day of my weeklong vacation—valuable time—playing with a married man rather than spending it at the apartment getting the lay of the land and taking inventory.

I don't like that I'm behind, but it gives me a renewed sense of purpose. Today, I dig in with vigor.

We find photo albums stashed on shelves and clothing hanging in the closet: two pairs of men's pants and three shirts, a few dresses, a red cloche hat, and a long, camel-colored coat with faux fur edging the sleeves and collar.

The garments are dusty, but they're in remarkably good shape. They look like back room thrift store pickings. I remove them one by one to examine them. The piece that tugs at my heart is a stunning black drop-waist dress trimmed in soft gray silk with the most delicate beaded flowers embroidered around the hem, neckline, and cuffs.

It was Ivy through and through.

She died when I was six, but a few months before, to celebrate my graduation from kindergarten into "big-girl school," she embroidered similar beaded pearlescent flowers around the neckline of my favorite pink sweater. It was like wearing the most wonderful necklace, and I thought I was so grown-up. It's one of my most beloved memories of Granny Ivy.

I start to call out to Marla to come look, but I don't.

She wouldn't remember, because she wasn't there.

I make a mental note to have the items cleaned. In the meantime, I hang the dress back in the closet and turn my attention to five more diaries I find stashed away on the closet shelf. Jackpot. I take them into the living room and sit at the desk, where I thumb through the earliest volume and skim a part that has her talking about first arriving in Paris and having a difficult time finding a job, ultimately taking work as a painter's model.

That must be where the paintings in the bedroom came from.

I put down the diary.

I'm wasting precious time sitting here reading when I should be searching. I only have three more days—two and a half if you count travel time—before I have to return to London and go back to work. I can take the diaries with me and read them later. Right now, I need to see what other treasures I can find in the apartment.

When I booked the ticket, I made a return reservation for myself, not fathoming that this shrine to Ivy's life would be a real thing.

Honestly, since Marla was involved, I expected nothing.

Speaking of the devil, I hear her humming "I Love Paris" to herself in the bedroom.

I walk around the common area, opening drawers, closets, and cupboards, taking inventory of the contents. In the living room, among other things, I find an old deck of playing cards still in its box, a heavy glass ashtray, and a world atlas. In the bathroom, I find a brittle robe hanging on a hook on the back of the door. There's an empty cut glass bottle with a faded label that reads EAU DE LAVANDE AMBRÉE PURE and a sliver of petrified soap next to a silver-handled shaving brush. One of the more curious things I uncover in the kitchen, shoved in the back of a cabinet, is a set of five rectangular cookie tins painted to look like a train when set end to end. The first tin is the engine, the next three are cars transporting both human and animal passengers, and the last is the caboose complete with a waving conductor.

I keep reminding myself that I'm supposed to be here. I'm not snooping, despite how weird it feels to pilfer through someone else's belongings, looking at what was left behind. I can't escape the feeling that someone might burst into the room at any second and stop me.

Maybe it's because I don't really know what I'm looking for.

Finally, after I've been at it for a couple of hours, I silently bid Ivy's ghost to give us some clues. I'm squinting at a faded grocery list that I found wadded up in a kitchen drawer when Marla calls from the bedroom. "Hannah, come here and look at this. I think I might have found something."

I get up from where I've been sitting on the floor and walk into the bedroom. Marla is holding a stack of yellowing papers as thick as a phone book.

"This was under the bed. What do you make of it?"

I take the tome from her. It appears to be a manuscript of some sort written in French on a typewriter and held together by a rotting rubber band, which crumbles and falls away as soon as I take the stack from Marla and start thumbing through the pages.

There's no cover page. No name anywhere on the manuscript—at least not from what I can see at a glance.

The yellowed paper feels brittle and fragile, like dry autumn leaves. I don't want to rip through it.

"This might be something," I say. "But I don't know."

A few French words jump off the page at me, but I can't make sense of it as a whole. I bring it into the living room.

"Where are you going?" Marla trails after me.

"One thing I learned from the tours I lead is that we need to touch things like this as little as possible."

"How are we going to look at it unless we touch it?"

"Marla, I can see by looking at the papers that they're fragile. Dirt and oil on our hands will only make them deteriorate faster."

She rolls her eyes. "Okay, excuse me while I get my X-ray glasses."

"You're hysterical. But I'm serious. While we're figuring out what we have here, we need to treat it with care, and that includes keeping our hands off it until I can get us some gloves and an acid-free box to store it in."

"And then what?"

"I don't know. We'll cross that bridge when we come to it."

We stand and stare at the stack of pages as if we're waiting for it to answer our questions.

"Okay, I know we shouldn't get too excited, but remember that obit clipping that was with the deed?"

Marla nods.

"The person was Andres Armand."

"Right, we think he's the Andres in Ivy's diary," Marla says.

"He was a writer. Even though he was French, he hung with the American expats in Paris between the wars. What if this is his work?"

Marla's eyes are wide. "Do you think it is? You're the one who's the expert in dead writers."

"I have no idea. I'm not that familiar with his work. Who knows? If it is his, it's probably a draft of something that's already published."

"Maybe we need to go to the bookstore or the library and see if we can get copies of his old work and compare," Marla suggests.

"That's a great idea. I want to do an internet search to see if I can figure out how many books he wrote. Then we can take it from there."

A quick online search on my phone turns up a website for the Andres Armand Foundation, which is headquartered in Antibes. The site says Armand wrote twelve books over his lifetime. A respectable number. Though it would take some time to compare the French text in the manuscript to his body of work, it would be doable . . . in all our spare time.

I jot down the names of the books and plan to purchase the original French-text versions before I go back to work.

"Too bad we can't borrow them from the library," Marla says. "Since neither of us speaks French, what are we going to do with twelve French books after we're done comparing?"

"Maybe that would be a good way to start learning the language," I say. "You realize you're going to be living here for the time being, right?"

Marla gives me a blank look. "Reading those books is like asking me to solve a calculus equation without knowing basic math."

"You have to start somewhere," I say.

"That's an awfully expensive outlay for a bunch of books that might not even turn out to be useful. I mean, what if this isn't his work? Or what if it's not something that's been published before?"

My pulse picks up. "If this is unpublished work by Andres Armand, that would be pretty significant."

"Would it be worth something? I mean, would it be valuable?"

"Discovering a previously unpublished manuscript by an author of note would definitely be valuable. I'm not sure how much it would be worth, though. It's not like a painting by Picasso that could be auctioned off."

"Why couldn't a manuscript be auctioned?" Marla asks.

Resisting the urge to lift the first page, I clasp my hands. "I don't know. This isn't my area of expertise."

"But you're book smart, Hannah. You've never come across anything like this on your tours?"

"No, I haven't. I know some literary history, sure, but antiquities publishing is its own beast. We need to find an expert who can tells us if this is an Andres Armand book, either published or not, and what to do with it if it is."

She gives me a stern look. "Do not call that horrible cheating man."

"I won't call Gabriel. I don't want to talk to him after last night."

"I think we should enlist Levesque's help."

I get my phone out of my purse and call the main number at the firm.

The receptionist passes me along to Levesque's secretary, who says he's tied up this afternoon and will call us Monday, unless it's an emergency. If so, Monsieur Cerny might be able to help.

"No! It's not an emergency. Monday will be fine."

Why is Gabriel always available while Monsieur Levesque seems to never stop working?

I blink away the frustration and explain what we've found, hoping that when he calls us back, he will be able to guide us.

Fifteen minutes later, my phone rings.

"*Mon amour*," says Gabriel. "Levesque's secretary said you called. How may I help you?"

"You can't. I'll wait until Monsieur Levesque gets back."

"I understand you have found an interesting manuscript? If that is the case, I am the one in the office best equipped to help you. Emile would simply turn the task over to me anyway."

"Thank you, but, as I said, I'd rather wait and talk to Monsieur Levesque. Perhaps he can tell me where to get help outside the firm."

There is silence on the other end of the line. It lasts long enough for me to think we've been disconnected.

I'm about to push the End Call button when he says, "You are angry with me. Please do not be."

Ugh. Technically, nothing happened. We could pretend that we were simply client and attorney having a business dinner.

But we both know that's not true. He misled me, and it proves how bad a judge of character I am when it comes to men. I can't blame Gabriel on Cressida, though he has definitely earned a place in my Date From Hell Hall of Fame as The Cheater.

"Your wife is beautiful, Gabriel. You're a lucky man."

"Hannah, is that . . . *that man*?" Marla sputters, catching on. "Why are you talking to him after what he did to you? Let me have the phone. I have some things to say to him."

I hold up a hand to silence her and turn my back when she persists.

"Hannah, my wife and I have an arrangement. She travels excessively and while she is gone, I am free to do as I please."

From the look on Veronique's face, I would venture to guess

that she's not as on board with their arrangement as he thinks she is, but it's not my business. I will never allow myself to be alone with him again, but based on his ties to the arts community, he might be our best bet at finding an expert in interwar literature.

"That's between you and your wife, Gabriel. Thank you for offering to help, but Marla and I can wait to talk to Monsieur Levesque."

"Tell me about the manuscript," he says. "Does it appear to be an antique?"

"Yes. So, you can see it's not exactly an emergency. The manuscript has waited many years. We can wait a few more days."

"Ah, as I said, Emile will simply refer you to me. I am the consultant for all things having to do with the arts and antiquities. So, it appears as if you're stuck with me. I am very happy to help you find someone who can look at it. I will connect you with the right person. You won't even have to see me again. Since you are upset, it is the least I can do to make it up to you—to prove that I am truly sorry for making you uncomfortable. Please trust me, Hannah."

July 1927
Paris, France

Dear Diary,

I took Sunday off, but today, when I arrived at Pierre's studio, I asked him what happened on Saturday night. I deserved to know why he'd left me at Miss Stein's salon without the courtesy of a goodbye.

Though we did not work yesterday, it appeared that Pierre did not benefit from the rest. He was quite irritable and disagreeable.

When I asked him again to explain why he left me in a stranger's home, he rubbed his red eyes and raked his fingers through his greasy hair. I suspected he'd been bitten by the Green Fairy or worse.

Absinthe is illegal in Paris. Even so, it's everywhere. Hiding in plain sight. The same holds true for the fairy's good friends, opium and cocaine. One need not look very hard to find them, especially within the circles Pierre and Helen run.

It was clear that Pierre was unrepentant and didn't wish to talk about abandoning me. All he said was he had run into an unexpected conflict and was confident I would see myself home.

I shouldn't be too mad, because if he had done the right thing and walked me home, I might not have met Monsieur Armand. My heart skips a beat every time I think of him. But Pierre doesn't need to know that.

We had been working for an hour when someone knocked on the studio door. Pierre erupted and threw his brush against the wall, cursing and demanding the person go away and let him work.

But then the door opened and my heart nearly stopped when Monsieur Armand stormed into the room.

He did a double take, tipped his hat, and said it was lovely to see me again.

I wanted to disappear into the crevices of the floorboards. Seeing this man who treated me so kindly and with such respect the other night made what I was doing suddenly feel shameful and wrong. I grabbed my robe and hugged it to myself as the two began arguing in rapid French.

Finally, Pierre went to his rusty can and counted out francs, muttering to himself the entire time.

He threw coins at Armand, who stooped to collect the money.

Armand then addressed Pierre in English, saying his debt to Mademoiselle Leon was settled. That she would be happy to receive what she was owed, though Pierre shouldn't need someone to call to collect his debts in the first place.

He turned to go but not before warning me of Pierre's reputation for taking advantage of his models. He said that's why he always seems to need a new one.

Pierre began shouting at him, and I wanted to cover my ears, but Andres Armand remained composed. Again, he tipped his hat to me as a gentleman would to a lady and took his leave.

After Monsieur Armand left, Pierre threw a can of turpentine at the door, leaving a muddy, oily splat on the wood.

I had to ask him if what Monsieur Armand said was true.

Pierre called him a jackass and told me not to believe a word he'd said.

When I asked him what happened to the model he'd used before me, Pierre said it was none of my concern and demanded we get back to work.

But it was my concern if what Monsieur Armand said was true. The only thing worse than posing naked for a man like Pierre was doing it for no compensation.

He blinked and asked how I knew Andres Armand.

I told him I'd met him at Miss Stein's Saturday night. But I wasn't about to let him change the subject. I demanded pay for the next two days up front.

He then started growling about how he had no money because Armand and I had taken it all.

I told him if that was the case, I would leave, too.

Pierre flew into a rage, throwing things, then storming out, leaving me in the room alone with the door wide open.

By the time I had dressed, he had not returned, so I gave my portrait a little wink and marched out of that dreary studio.

Fifteen

January 6, 2019—10:00 a.m.

Paris, France

I've taken Gabriel at his word that he will keep things strictly professional. He's a married man. Hard stop. There will be no more breakfasts at his favorite café, or tours of museums, or dinners for two. We will only speak of the manuscript and who can help us figure out if it's the work of Andres Armand.

Marla doesn't want to speak to him, much less work with him. When I told her I wasn't afraid of him, that I could handle myself, she washed her hands of the manuscript. She wants nothing to do with him or the authenticating process.

As far as I'm concerned, that's just as well. I'm sure she finds this book talk boring.

After telling Gabriel my hunch that the manuscript might be the unpublished work of Andres Armand, he showed up at the apartment, on a Sunday, no less, wanting to see the treasure with his own eyes.

I want to ask him what Veronique is doing on this lovely Sunday morning, but he distracts me with the hint that he knows someone who might be able to help us—a professor of literature at the Sorbonne.

"If this manuscript turns out to be important, we will need to safeguard it," he says. "It is not a good idea to simply turn it over to someone whom you have just met—even if they are affiliated with the university. You don't know people's motives."

"Not everyone's motives are pure," Marla murmurs. "That's for sure."

I give her a look that says, *Knock it off*. There's no sense in rehashing what happened the other night.

"Who is this professor you're recommending?" I ask. "Is he not honest?"

Gabriel shrugs in that way I found endearing when I first met him, but now it seems affected.

"One would hope. Still, you must be careful, Hannah. Your manuscript could easily get lost and *poof*." He snaps his fingers like a magician who has made the woman in the box disappear. "There goes your precious find. And you have little recourse."

He suggests I copy each page of the manuscript. He offers to hire someone to do it for us, and this time there is no mention of it being on the house. It's better that way, because I don't want Levesque, Racine, and Cerny to have any claim to the book should it prove to be authentic.

I know I'm being extra cautious, but my gut is telling me this stack of typed pages might turn out to be something.

Still, Marla and I can't afford to shell out for fancy photocopies and we don't know how someone else will handle the fragile pages, so Gabriel and I establish that it's documentation enough—at least for now—for me to take clear photos of every page with my iPhone. I get to work.

• • •

GABRIEL CALLS HIS SORBONNE contact first thing Monday morning. Professeur Louis Descartes is available to meet this afternoon; I invite Marla to join us, but she declines. She's in the middle of sorting through Ivy's dresser drawers and doesn't want to stop.

"I mean, if you need me, of course I'll go, but you keep making a point of saying you can handle yourself. Frankly, I'd rather not see the French skunk again, even if he is pretending to be helpful." Her gaze sweeps over the pile of underwear and stockings and garter belts she's deposited on one of the air mattresses. "You'll be in a public place. It's not as if he's going to try something in the middle of the Sorbonne."

She's right. We'll be in public, I'm a big girl, and everything will be fine. Still, I can't help but feel like Marla is bailing on me again.

Why am I surprised?

Gabriel offers to pick me up. While it would be nice to have a chauffeur carry me door-to-door to and from the Sorbonne, I tell him I'll meet him there.

He's at the university when I arrive, waiting in the reception area outside of Professeur Descartes's office. His eyes light up when he sees me, and he stands. After saying something in French to the receptionist, he makes small talk with me, mostly about the manuscript and the impending meeting with the professor. It's as if nothing happened the other night.

I'm glad. There's nothing to talk about.

However, I do wonder what happened between him and his wife after I left.

Did Veronique storm out, or did the two of them enjoy the coq au vin that Gabriel had prepared for me?

Was it some sort of kinky role-play act to keep their marriage exciting? You know how sometimes couples will go to a bar separately and pretend to pick each other up? Maybe Gabriel and Veronique arrange for him to invite another woman over for dinner, and she walks in on them. They pretend to fight and then . . .

Never mind. I don't really care what they do. As long as it doesn't involve me.

When Professeur Descartes is ready for us, his assistant shows us into the office.

Gabriel serves as our translator.

Descartes acts unimpressed as he dons the extra pair of white gloves I picked up before the meeting. The manuscript is now housed in an acid-free box.

Descartes says something to Gabriel in a tone that doesn't seem to bode well.

"What did he say?" I ask.

"He says he does not want to speculate. It could take some time. He must read the work and figure out if it is a draft of one of Armand's previously published works. If not, he will compare it to those works and see if the styles are similar. For now, he has everything he needs and will be in touch when he has an answer."

Gabriel has him sign a receipt that he received the manuscript and would take all necessary precautions to protect it. I ask Gabriel to give him my cell number and contact me directly when he is finished.

With that, Descartes stands and unceremoniously walks to his office door and opens it, the universal sign for *end of meeting*. No time for questions or discussion.

Once we're outside, I realize we didn't discuss fees or expenses. "How much is this going to cost?" I ask. "I meant to ask him before we left, but my head is spinning with so many questions, and of course, there's the language barrier."

Gabriel's car is waiting for him.

"No worries," says Gabriel, edging toward the vehicle. "He will contact you should any potential expenses arise. He will do what he can through the Sorbonne. However, should he need to seek outside council, there might be fees."

I smile through the painful thought of additional financial outlay.

I have no idea where we will find the money, but we will. Or I will. Somehow. It's for a good cause. Or at least that's what I keep telling myself.

Even though I don't want to ask Gabriel for favors, I realize I'll need someone to step in if I'm not in Paris when Professeur Descartes finishes because I'd rather not have Marla toting a potentially valuable manuscript around the city.

"I'm going home tomorrow," I say. "I'll be available by phone, but I'll need some notice if Professeur Descartes makes any discoveries and wants to meet in person, or needs me to pick up the manuscript."

"If he finishes before you can get away, I will send someone from the office to pick it up *tout de suite*," Gabriel says.

At least we seem to be in unspoken agreement that we shouldn't entrust it to Marla, who might inadvertently leave it on the Metro or in a café if she got distracted flirting with a guy.

The best part: Gabriel volunteered. I didn't have to ask him.

"You are going back to work?"

I nod. "I start back Wednesday. I have to make money to cover that inheritance tax."

I almost add *and legal fees*, but the last thing I want is to sound like I'm fishing for freebies.

• • •

"HOW DID EVERYTHING GO?" Marla asks when I walk in the front door. "Does he think it's the real thing?"

"It might take a while before we know anything. Lots of reading and comparing. You know, all sorts of academic stuff."

"Boring." Marla feigns a yawn and returns her attention to a wooden box full of what appears to be costume jewelry. She swirls her hand through the bobbles. It sounds like a wind chime.

I laugh. "You didn't think I was going to come back with a definitive answer, did you?"

She shrugs. "I was hoping. I don't know how that stuff works. I didn't know if they have some kind of database where they can plug in the words and get an answer."

"That would be nice, wouldn't it? If this book has already been published, there will be a record of it. That will be easy. If not, all they can do is compare style and do some sort of test on the paper and ink. And maybe even try to figure out what kind of a typewriter it was written on."

My gaze darts around the living room. "You didn't happen to come across a typewriter while you were taking inventory, did you?"

"Nope. I didn't see one."

She picks a rhinestone-studded brooch out of the box and holds it up to the light.

"What are your plans?" I ask.

"What do you mean?"

"I mean, my vacation is almost over. I'm leaving tomorrow. Are you comfortable staying here by yourself?"

She drops the brooch back into the box and resumes swirling.

"I guess so. I'm certainly not going back to Orlando, and you made it clear you don't have room for me in London."

I start to suggest she could always find her own place, but I don't.

"You'll have to go back to Florida sometime—after Gram's house closes."

"When that time comes, you can come with me."

She's right. We will both have to sign the papers when we sell the house.

"What are you going to do in the meantime? I mean, do you have money to get by?"

She sets the jewelry box on the coffee table and sits up, pushing herself forward to the edge of the couch seat and gripping the seat cushions as if for support.

"I have a little bit, but I'll have to get a job eventually. I'm not sure how to do that here. I mean, since I'm a property owner, does some kind of a visa come with it?"

"I don't know," I say. "You'll need to look into that. You do realize even if you live here, this place belongs to both of us."

When we jointly inherited Gram's house, Marla wouldn't hear of us keeping it. She needed money, not memories. I, of course, would've been hanging on to the place solely for the memories. It was my childhood home. When I suggested we rent it out, she wanted no part of that, either. The only arrangement she would entertain was me buying out her half or putting the house on the market.

I wonder if she's remembering that now.

"What are you saying?" She squints at me.

"I'm saying given the inheritance tax and the high cost of living in Paris, maybe you shouldn't get too comfortable here. We might need to rent the place out or eventually sell it."

"I can't even think about that," she says. "We've worked so hard this week to get it into livable shape; doesn't it seem a shame to let someone else move in? Hannah, I feel so at home here. For the first time in my life, I feel connected to a place. I feel a connection to you and Ivy. It's all we have left of her. This is our legacy. We can't just turn it over to someone else."

"Remember what you said about Gram's place? You insisted I needed to buy you out or we needed to sell it—"

"Hannah, you know I am not in a position to buy you out. I thought we'd made so much progress. I thought this apartment had brought us together."

Here we go, plucking the heartstrings to distract from the fact that she's trying to skirt the very rule she made: buy the other one out or sell.

No negotiation. No discussion.

"I know what you're thinking," she says. "I can read it on your face."

"Why should I pay rent in London while you're living in Paris rent-free. How is that equitable?"

"Don't think of it as me living rent-free in Paris. Think of it as me being the custodian of our investment—of our legacy."

Of course, she evades the question.

"Did you really want to hang on to Gram's house?" she asks. "Did it mean that much to you?"

I shrug. It's not an easy yes-or-no answer. I wanted to keep it for sentimental reasons, but the practical side of me knew keeping a house in Orlando wasn't . . . well, it wasn't practical. "It was my last tie to Gram."

Marla rolls her eyes.

"You know rude gestures like that are not helping, right?" I say. "They're not winning you any points."

"I'm not trying to win points, Hannah. I'm trying to stay in Paris."

"It's always all about you, isn't it?"

"Oh, Hannah."

She gets up and walks to the window and looks out. Her back is to me, reminding me of all the other times in the past when she turned her back when things got hard.

"I wanted to keep Gram's house, but you wouldn't even discuss it."

She whirls around to face me, but she's smiling rather than wearing the pigheaded glare I was expecting. "That's it! That's the answer. You keep the Orlando house and I'll keep the Paris apartment. I don't know why I didn't think of that before."

A bark of bitter laughter escapes my throat and threatens to turn into a genuine fit of histrionics.

"Okay, I know you're not serious—"

"I am serious." She has the audacity to look offended. "It's the answer to our problem."

"You realize this apartment is worth at least five times the value of Gram's house. I know you're smart enough to have figured that out."

There's something in the way her eyes shift that makes me realize she might not have thought of it.

"I know that. But money aside, if you think about it in sentimental terms, it would really be the answer to our problems."

"Our problems? No it won't. If we keep this place, and that's a big *if*, we'll need every penny of the proceeds from Gram's place—and probably more—to pay the inheritance taxes on this apartment."

She's looking at me, but I know she's not listening. She's staring off into the middle distance. Her gaze has a faraway look that I recognize from long ago, back in the days when Gram would get on her case about something, usually having to do with me. Marla would be there physically, but her mind was somewhere else.

I don't need this. I have a happy life in London. Granted, by her standards, maybe it's not the most exciting life, but it works for me. Think of the things I could do if I had my half of the proceeds from Gram's house in Florida and half the net of the Paris apartment.

I could pretty much write my own ticket.

July 1927
Paris, France

Dear Diary,

I'm happy to report that after leaving Pierre's studio, I found work.

As it turned out, salvation was at my doorstep. Or just below it.

The boulangerie *beneath our apartment was in need of a counter girl for the first shift. They hired me on the spot, which proves it's always good practice to be nice to your neighbors.*

The day starts early. I report at 4:45 in the morning. The pay is a pittance, but it's something. It will leave my afternoons free to sew and search for fashion work.

I shared the good news about my new job with Helen when she got home from Luc's studio, and she insisted I come with her and Luc to celebrate at Dingo Bar.

I urged her to go without me and have a good night. To celebrate for me. Because my alarm clock would awaken me early, and there was the uncomfortable possibility of running into Pierre.

Before the words had left my mouth, Helen was already shaking her head. She would not hear of it. She said I could not avoid Pierre forever. She promised that Luc would not allow Pierre to harass me.

Since we've been in Paris, I've learned to stand up to Helen, but that night I actually did want to have some fun. Because it felt like the first time since moving here I had something to celebrate. Why not enjoy myself?

When we arrived at Dingo Bar, the place was lively and

festive. The music was loud and people were drinking and dancing. I'm starting to recognize the regulars who are fixtures of the place.

True to their word, Helen and Luc stood guard, even though there was no sign of Pierre. Immediately I relaxed and drank champagne and talked to a handsome blond man named Scott, who, as it turns out, is a famous author.

I have heard of his book, The Great Gatsby, *though I haven't yet read it. How exciting to meet someone famous!*

Helen and I were flirting with Scott when a commotion arose. I turned to see a petite blonde holding a champagne flute and stomping toward us on top of the tables. She was stepping on people's hands and knocking over drinks in her determination to reach us. People were shouting and cussing, but she seemed oblivious.

She stopped before us and asked Scott to be a darling and help her down. As if it were perfectly normal to walk on tabletops in a bar.

As he lifted her down, Scott asked her what in the Sam Hill she was doing up there on the tables. She claimed it was the only way she could get to him. That there were too many people and tables between them, that nobody would keep her from the man she loved.

She introduced herself to us as Zelda, Scott's wife.

When we had a moment, Helen pulled me aside and told me that she'd heard Scott had had an affair with a beautiful young American starlet. Now, Zelda is rabidly jealous of him even looking at another woman.

I can't say I blame her, but Helen and I didn't get to talk about it very long because that's when I saw Andres Armand across the crowded room. His height and his dark good looks made him stand out like a spotlight had illuminated him in the crowd.

His gaze connected with mine and my heart thudded in the most unexpected way. The next thing I knew, he was standing next to us and Zelda was squealing like her long-lost best friend had appeared. She linked her arm through Andres's and I wondered if Scott would get jealous because Zelda was gushing on and on about how Andres was the most talented writer she'd ever met. She made us swear we would not tell Scott because she would deny ever having said it, even though it was the God's honest truth. Scott, of course, was standing right there and would've needed to be unconscious not to hear her. When he didn't react, Zelda introduced Andres to us.

Helen wasn't aware he was the very man I'd met at Miss Stein's salon and again in Pierre's studio.

He turned to me and lifted my fingers to his lips the way he had at Miss Stein's home. Only this time, he dusted them with a featherlight kiss.

I was swept away.

By then Zelda had drifted off to dance the Charleston with a man who wasn't Scott. Andres and I spent the rest of the evening talking. Pierre's name did not come up the entire night, nor did my modeling for him. We were too busy speaking of art and books and my new job at the boulangerie.

He was the perfect gentleman. Even when he walked me home again, as he had after the salon. I willed my traitorous heart to stop fluttering, to remember its place, because a man like Monsieur Armand wouldn't be interested in an unsophisticated girl from Bristol. He must've realized that, too, because once again, he didn't ask to see me again after we reached my door.

If I were smart, I would put Andres Armand out of my mind forever. My head knows that, but my heart can't forget him.

Sixteen

January 8, 2019—11:00 a.m.
London, England

Marla and I come to a temporary compromise on what to do with the apartment. We decide, for the time being, not to decide.

Even so, I think she insisted on coming back to London with me because she is afraid I'll try to sell the apartment out from under her while we're apart.

So, here we are. I need to get back to normal, and she's at loose ends.

Since I don't want to leave her to her own devices at the London flat, I take her to the Heart to Heart tour offices, where I'm meeting my boss, Emma, for a catch-up before I go back to work tomorrow. I'm hoping Marla will want to slide into one of the city tours and give me a breather.

"This is where you work?" Marla asks, wide-eyed, as she looks around the suite on Buckingham Palace Road. "Where do you keep the busses?"

"This is where the corporate office is housed. We contract the busses from another company and they meet us at predetermined sites, depending on the tour. It wouldn't make financial sense to keep our own fleet."

Violet, the receptionist to whom I've just introduced my mother, smiles at me.

"Oh." Marla looks disappointed. "I thought a tour company would own a whole farm of busses. I was hoping they'd be those cute red ones you see all over town."

"We also have walking tours," Violet says. "In fact, would you like to choose one of these that starts at the top of the hour? I'll arrange for you to go while Hannah meets with Emma. It would be on the house. Here, I can show you what's available."

"Thanks, Violet," I say. "That's a good idea. I might be a while."

Marla shakes her head. "I'll just sit out here and wait for you. I won't bother anyone."

She plants herself on the love seat in the reception area and picks up a magazine that's lying amidst brochures advertising the various Heart to Heart offerings.

"It will give me a chance to catch up on the celebrity gossip I've missed. But wait, Hannah—is there a brochure for the tour you give?"

I'm touched that she's interested. I walk over to the rack next to the reception desk and select the pamphlet showcasing the various Jane Austen packages. It's in between brochures for the Shakespeare and Cotswolds tours.

"So, the people who take your tour don't meet you here? I'm trying to visualize you at work."

She closes her eyes.

"Nope. Sorry to disappoint you, but I'm rarely in the office. I'm mostly out in the field. It depends on which tour I'm conducting, but most of the time I meet my charges at Kensington Palace Gardens and we head out of town from there. Sometimes I'm on the road for the better part of a week."

"No wonder you don't have a man." Marla laughs and shakes her head in the direction of Violet, who is doing her best to look neutral. "How can she expect to meet anyone if she's always away?"

"She's one of our best guides," Violet says.

I want to hug her. But Marla is right. It is hard to maintain a relationship when I'm on the road more than I'm at home. I think of Aiden and wonder if I should take him up on the meal he offered now that I'm back.

I brush aside the flashback to the last man who wanted to cook for me—Gabriel. At least I know with near certainty that Aiden isn't married. But since I'm gone so much for work and I'll be spending a lot of my free time in Paris, should I even bother to call him?

It feels complicated.

"Em's off the phone," says Violet. "You can go in now."

"Marla, I shouldn't be too long. Are you going to be all right out here?"

"Of course. I'll just sit here and read." She waves the Jane Austen brochure. "Now, go on. Off with you."

She's not a toddler who needs constant supervision. Even though sometimes it feels that way. But Violet is on a call and Marla is sitting there with one leg tucked underneath her, reading the pamphlet like it's a best-seller.

I knock lightly on Emma's door to announce myself before pushing it open and stepping inside.

"Hannah, I'm so glad you're back." Emma stands and gives me a hug. "How was your vacation?"

"Different from what I'd planned." I tell her about Marla's surprise visit.

Emma's mouth forms a perfect O.

"Was this a good surprise, then?"

"Let's say it was unexpected. We ended up going to Paris."

"How lovely."

"And bizarre," I add.

I tell Emma about the turn of events with the apartment and about Granny Ivy's secret life. When I stop for a breath, Emma's jaw is hanging open.

"Hannah, that is fantastic. It's like a movie plot."

"I found a series of my great-grandmother's diaries in the apartment." I fish around in my bag and pull out the one I've been reading. "Take a look at this."

I thumb to the part where Ivy and her roommate, Helen, go to Dingo Bar on their first morning in Paris, and hand it to Emma.

"Read this and tell me what you think."

She reads silently, her eyes growing wider with each line.

"Pablo? Hem? Pauline Pfeiffer? You must be kidding."

Naturally, one of the big reasons Emma and I get on so well is our mutual love of literature. That's why she started her tour company, whose tagline is "Why just read a book when you can live it?" Of course, it has expanded to include nonliterary tours, but the heart and soul of Heart to Heart remains the tours that feature books and authors.

"No big deal—you inherited an apartment in Paris, and your great-grandmother used to hang out with the expats." She laughs as if she can hardly believe it. I understand her reaction. I still haven't fully wrapped my mind around it.

"I don't have definitive proof, but she says so in these diaries. And it's not like she's saying, 'Oooh, look at me with Ernest Hemingway. I'm so cool.' She writes about them as if she's just met them and doesn't realize who she's with. Of course, at that time, she wouldn't have understood because they weren't legends yet."

"What year is this?" Emma lowers her head and looks at the page for a clue.

"Look at the outside of the diary. It says 1927."

She flips the cover over, runs her finger across the embossed numbers.

"So, by 1927, Hemingway would have already published *The Sun Also Rises*. He was pretty well-known in his circle but was still trying to make a name for himself as a writer."

"That was around the time that he was divorcing Hadley and marrying Pauline."

"Hannah, this is crazy," Emma says as she continues to scan the diary's pages.

"That's not the half of it." I tell her about the clipping of Andres Armand and the manuscript we discovered. "I have no idea if it's the real deal, but the law firm that's assisting us with the legalities of inheriting the apartment helped us locate a scholar who is looking over the manuscript to see if he can authenticate it."

Emma continues to read for a moment. Then she looks up at me. "Please tell me you're not intending to leave and move to Paris permanently."

I shrug. "Honestly, Emma, I have no idea what I'm doing next. My mother wants to stay in the apartment. She doesn't have a history of being the most practical person in the world. I don't know what she'll face when it comes to obtaining visas—and we have the small matter of inheritance tax to contend with—but one of the first things that she and I have agreed on in a long time is that we can't let go of this apartment. I mean, she wanted to hang on to it from the start, but I'm realizing how important it is to keep it in the family."

Of course, I haven't admitted this to Marla yet because I'm trying to manage both of our expectations.

"I don't blame you," Emma says. "I would feel the same way if I were in your position."

All of a sudden, I'm gripped by a crazy idea. Before I can even think it through, I hear myself saying, "I'm not sure if this would work out or if it's even something you'd be interested in, but what if we expanded Heart to Heart into the Paris market? What if we offered an interwar, expat tour? You know, Hemingway, Zelda and Scott, the whole Gertrude Stein and Sylvia Beach shebang?"

Emma squints at me for a moment. I can see the wheels turning in her mind. "What exactly are you thinking?"

"I'm sort of flying by the seat of my pants here," I say. "But think about it. Paris in the twenties and thirties was a crazy time. It was such a rich period of literary history. I think the Parisian expat circle would make for a great tour."

Emma pauses for a moment and then nods. "Hannah, you did a stellar job developing the Jane Austen tour division of Heart to Heart. If anyone can lead the charge into Paris, it's you." She waves her hand as if to give me the green light. "We need to figure out the basics and get permits and such, but Hannah, this is bloody brilliant. We'll need to bring someone on to take over your Austen tours, but besides that, I need to know that you're ready to relocate to Paris."

"I am."

I am?

"I guess I need to put together a game plan," I say.

My head is spinning.

Twenty minutes and lots of logistics later, Emma walks out with me to meet Marla, who has abandoned the Austen excursion brochure for one that features a tour of celebrity homes in the Greater London area. I'm not surprised.

"That one seems right up your alley," I say after I introduce her to Emma.

"Yeah, it looks fun," she says, sounding a little preoccupied. I'm glad because it means she's not peppering Emma with questions and embarrassing stories. "This tour wasn't running today," Marla says. "Otherwise, I would've taken up Violet on her offer."

"It's a good one," Emma says. "Come back any time and we'll get you on it. On the house. Lovely to meet you, Marla, but I must run and make some phone calls."

Em's excited smile tells me the calls will be all about the Paris project.

"May I keep this?" Marla calls to Violet, who is on a phone call, and holds up the brochure.

Violet nods and gives her a thumbs-up as we head out the door.

"It looks like you and Violet became fast friends," I say.

"We did. She's nice. She turned me on to this tour after she saw me reading *Hello!* and the *Daily Mail.* Emma seems nice, too."

When we're in the elevator and on the way down, Marla opens the brochure and points to something. "Look at this."

I lean in and see she's pointing to stop number five on the tour, the home of British musician Martin Gaynor. I have no idea why I'm supposed to care.

"I can get you on that tour tomorrow if you'd like to go."

"Nah." Marla laughs and then sighs as she looks at the brochure. "You don't have any idea who he is, do you, Hannah?"

"Martin Gaynor? Sure I do. He's an old British punk rocker."

"I guess you could call him that." She's smiling like she has a secret she wants me to beg her to share.

"Okay, I'll bite. Was Martin Gaynor one of the guys you followed on tour?"

"One of them," Marla says. "Back in the day, he was the lead singer of The Squelching Wellies. I've been inside that house." She taps the paper with a chipped red nail. "Well, once, anyway."

"Maybe you should look up your old friend and say hello."

I wasn't being serious, but instantly I regret putting the idea out there. Since she's been doing so well, I'm not sure it would be a good idea for her to go for a ride down groupie lane.

Would seeing Martin Gaynor, middle-aged bad-boy punk rocker, throw her off the straight-and-narrow path of rehabilitation?

"No, I don't think so. He wouldn't remember me. Back in those days, there were a lot of women."

It's not just the familiar words, a take on what she used to say to me when I'd ask about my father—*There were a lot of men, Hannah*—but also the wistful way she says them that makes me wonder.

"Is Martin Gaynor my father?" I ask as we step out of the building into the chilly afternoon.

"What?" Marla snaps. "No, Hannah. Don't be ridiculous."

She followed The Squelching Wellies for a summer and came home pregnant with me, and she admitted to having been inside the front man's house. It's as logical an assumption as one plus one equals two. But I'm not going to fight with her.

"You know what would be fun?" she asks.

I'm almost afraid to ask, but I do. "What would be fun?"

"Let's go by his house."

"Are you serious?"

She nods.

"Are you going to knock on the door and reintroduce yourself?"

"Of course not, smarty-pants. The last time I was there—well, the only time—it had more security than the White House. I want to go by and see it."

"So, let me make sure I'm understanding this right. With all his money, Martin Gaynor still lives in the same house that he lived in when you two were teenagers?"

"It wasn't that long ago, Hannah, and he's a little bit older than I am. But even if he wasn't, why would it be so odd for him to still live in the same home?"

"Because people who stay in the same houses—even if they're magnificent mansions—are more the type to settle down than I imagine a young punk rocker who has suddenly come into a lot of money would be."

"Obviously you haven't seen the house, have you?"

"No, I haven't. Someone else handles the celebrity home tours. I've never been on that one."

Marla's eyes sparkle. "It's a great place. Maybe it's time you got out of your comfort zone and tried something different. Let's go by the house so you can see it."

"Only if you'll knock on the door."

She purses her lips and tilts her head to the side. "Maybe I will. If we can figure out a way to sneak past the gates."

As we take a cab to the Richmond Hill home in southwest London, I ask Marla what became of The Squelching Wellies.

She looks confused. "What do you mean?"

Help me out, Marla. I'm trying to make conversation.

"I mean, are they still a band? Do they still tour or release music or did they break up? I've heard of them in passing, but since punk rock was never really my scene, I don't know much about them."

Once she starts talking, she tells me more than I really wanted to know. Essentially the Wellies, who were originally from Wellington, were part of the early 1990s British music scene, and at the height of their popularity, they were on par with The Smiths.

"They were part of this new resurgence of punk music and it

resonated with me and what I was going through at the time," Marla says. "You know, it spoke to me. I wanted to rebel and basically their music became the soundtrack of my life. And then I got pregnant with you and things changed. The band broke up at some point, but that was after I stopped keeping track." She shrugs and turns her head to stare out the window. In profile, she looks so wistful it makes me miss the glory days for her.

"Really?" I ask. "Even after following them around Europe, you just quit them? You didn't even listen to their music?"

She turns back to me. "I had a kid. It wasn't exactly lullaby music."

I don't challenge her on that—even though I'd bet she never played me any lullabies—and we ride in silence the rest of the way.

The house is as magnificent as Marla described, set closer to the main road than I expected and surrounded by a tall wrought-iron fence. Really, all you had to do was shimmy up the iron posts, avoid impaling yourself on the pointed finials, and drop down into the world of Martin Gaynor, punk rock sex god.

"You've really been inside this house?" I ask as we stand on the sidewalk peering through the bars of the gate at the yellow-stone, Italianate mansion. Its deep-set front door is flanked by twin white-trimmed bay windows that rise all the way to the second floor. To our backs is the summit of Richmond Hill. Between the summit and the house is a narrow one-way road, bordered by the sidewalk on which we're standing.

From the front, the house doesn't look very large, but I suspect what it lacks in width it makes up for in depth.

"It looks smaller than I remember." There's a dreamy quality to Marla's words, as if she's here in body, but her mind is somewhere in the past.

"What's it like?"

She gives me a one-shoulder shrug. "It's a big, fancy house. Probably exactly what you're imagining."

"I'm not really imagining anything. That's why I'm asking you for details."

"I'm sure it's been remodeled after all this time."

The air is damp. The soundtrack to the gray afternoon is the occasional honking car and snippets of conversation from passersby who seem unaware of or unaffected by the fact that they're in the vicinity of punk rock royalty.

"Were you in love with him?" I ask.

"Martin?" Marla blinks incredulously. "No, Hannah. No way."

I hold up my hands. "Well, you did follow him around Europe for a summer. Just saying."

"Everyone wanted Martin. He was . . ."

She smiles and shakes her head and steps away from the gate. "I'm ready to leave when you are."

"Wait, no. We came all the way out here. You have to at least ring the bell."

She gives me major side-eye, then walks back to the gatepost and presses the button on the intercom. As she does, the gate begins to open.

Marla jumps back and curses under her breath. She starts power walking away from the house and I follow her. Once we're a few yards down the sidewalk, we both break into a fit of giggles, holding on to each other as we try to catch our breath.

"Oh my God, did that button open the gate?" I ask. "If so, why would he bother with the fence?"

Marla sighs. "He's been out of the limelight for a while now. Maybe he doesn't need security like he used to."

Or maybe he does. Out of the corner of my eye, I see the nose of a dark Bugatti emerging from Martin Gaynor's driveway. It stops before turning onto the street in the opposite direction of where we're standing.

The car window slides down to reveal a middle-aged man with a long, thin pale face, spiky black hair, and Wayfarer sunglasses peering out at us. He pulls his glasses down on his nose and stares for a moment.

I grab Marla's arm and nod in the direction of the car. She turns around and freezes in her tracks.

"That's him," she whispers.

He rolls up the window, and we watch him drive away.

"MARTIN GAYNOR IS SEXY as fuck," says Cressida. "How can you say he's not, Tallulah?"

I fear she and Tallu will come to blows as we sit around the kitchen island sipping tea and debating the hotness of Martin Gaynor.

T wrinkles her nose. "He's so tall and gaunt. He looks like a walking skeleton." She shudders. "To each her own, I guess."

"Marla's opinion is the only one that matters here," Cressida says. "Was he good in bed?"

"I didn't sleep with him," Marla insists.

"Oh, come on," says Cressida. "How could you not? I would've. In a heartbeat."

"Of course you would," says Tallulah.

"At least she owns it," I say.

Tallulah smiles and shakes her head. "I would love to stay and continue this important debate, but unfortunately I have other things to do. I'll see you tonight. Let's all go out."

We toss out some ideas.

Tallulah glances at the time on her phone. "I really need to run. Text me the plan."

The moment T leaves the room Cressida is back to Martin Gaynor. "Do you think he recognized you? I mean, you said he stopped and stared."

"Oh, I don't know. Probably not. More likely, he was wondering who the two crazy chicks were prowling around outside his house. He probably didn't like it that we were playing around with the intercom button. I never could resist a dare, though."

Marla smiles at me.

"Okay then, I dare you to go back and talk to him," says Cressida. "Better yet, I dare you to sleep with him."

Marla laughs and stands. She takes her teacup to the sink.

"That might be tough, because it looks like Marla and I are moving to Paris," I intervene, hoping to steer Marla away from temptation. "At least temporarily."

Cressida gapes at me.

"Are you moving into the apartment?" Cressida asks.

I nod. "Em is letting me start an expat art-and-literary tour in Paris."

"That's wonderful," cries Marla. "You didn't tell me."

"I know," I say. "We were preoccupied with creeping on Martin Gaynor."

"Hannah, I'm so proud of you," Marla says. "That's a promotion for you, isn't it?"

"I guess it is."

"And it's a long time coming and so well deserved," says Cressida. "Brava!"

Marla and I bring her up to speed on the apartment, the diaries, and the manuscript.

Cressida gasps and claps and peppers us with questions, which, at this point, we're not prepared to answer, because there are still a lot of things we don't know.

"I will continue to pay rent here, of course. I won't leave you high and dry."

"You're such a love, Hannah, but that won't be necessary. You'll have enough on your plate getting yourself moved and settled in Paris and starting the tour there."

"Yeah, but I'd like to keep this place as a safety net until I'm sure the Paris tour works out. If it doesn't, I'll be back."

Makeup-free, with her blonde hair piled high in a messy bun on top of her head, Cressida sighs. "Not to worry. T and I won't be in the market for a new flatmate anytime soon. How could we ever replace you?"

A lump forms in my throat as I think about starting over. Sure, the tour is a good opportunity, but it seems the older I get, the more difficult it is to make new friends like Tallu and Cressida. The three of us came together so naturally it's difficult to imagine that happening again in Paris, especially given the language barrier and my new workload.

"We should have a dinner party," says Cressida.

"We're leaving tomorrow morning," I say. Even though my schedule is a bit freeform right now, I have a lot of work ahead of me and I don't want to take advantage of Cressida's and T's good natures by imposing a fourth roommate on them for more than a night.

"Well, then, we shouldn't waste any time. Let's do it tonight."

This. This spontaneity right here is one of the things I'll miss the most about living with my girls.

"Okay. If you're sure. I think a dinner party sounds fun," I say. "What can I do?"

"You leave it all up to me," says Cressida. "You and Marla will be the guests of honor as we celebrate your new Paris adventure. I'll text Tallu. We'll get it sorted while you two make yourself scarce and come back at . . ." She looks at her Cartier Tank watch. "Be back at six o'clock sharp, ready to celebrate."

I go into my room and pack some things to take to Paris since I'll be there for the foreseeable future. I'll have the rest of my belongings shipped after I know the new tour will work out. But really, what I want to do right now is go back to the office and talk more with Em about the venture.

I hate to leave Marla on her own, but she'll be unsupervised after we move in together and I'm at work so she might as well get used to it. I find her in the living room reading a magazine. "Han, if you don't mind, I have an errand to run. I'll see you back here at six, okay?"

Problem solved.

I take a dress, boots, and my makeup bag with me to the office because Cressida gives fair warning that we will not be allowed back in the house until six o'clock as we are the guests of honor and she wants to surprise us.

Then I grab the bus to the office.

It's cold outside and the windows are fogging up. Still, as the bus rattles to a stop to pick up more passengers, I know that Aiden's restaurant, Lemon and Lavender, is located down the street on the next block.

I wonder if Cressida will invite him tonight. It's such short notice; he's probably working. I revisit my dilemma of whether or not I should ring him now that I know that I'll be living in Paris. I mean, really, what's the point?

Even so, I use the sleeve of my coat to wipe off the condensation on the window to get a better look. It's a gray, misty day and I see what I expected: knots of people gathered on the corner waiting for the signal to cross. Others are chancing a jaywalk. One man wearing a black hoodie sprints toward the bus.

If I squint my eyes, I can pretend it's Aiden. That he makes it just in time. Our eyes meet as he climbs the steps, breathing heavily after his run. He smiles and claims the empty seat next to me, saying, "We must stop meeting like this."

But when the straggler enters the bus, I see it's not a man. It's a rather surly-looking woman. She grunts at the driver and takes a seat toward the front. As we pull away from the stop, the seat next to me is still empty and so are any Lemon and Lavender hopes of seeing Aiden again.

July 1927
Paris, France

Dear Diary,

Tuesday afternoon, when I got home from my first day at the boulangerie, *a bouquet of the most beautiful peonies I've ever seen was waiting for me with a note that said Andres would call on me Friday at 7:00.*

For the past three days, the minutes masqueraded as hours, the days lingered like months, as I passed the time until I could see him again. I had no idea where we were going or what we would be doing, but I didn't care. I would go anywhere with him . . . or I could be content doing nothing at all. As long as we are together.

Since I didn't have the money to whip up a new dress for the occasion, I decided to distract myself by jazzing up one of my old frocks, embroidering beaded flowers on the collar and cuffs. It's tedious work, but it occupies my mind and keeps my hands busy.

When Helen saw how I'd transformed the garment, she proclaimed the dress looked brand-new, as if I'd paid a fortune for it.

She said I should march myself back to Mademoiselle Chanel's and show my work to Madame Jeanneau. Helen was sure the old crone would beg me to come work for her.

Helen's sweet belief in me made me smile. I think I will be perfectly happy working my shift at the boulangerie *and furthering my own designs for now. Perhaps someday I will give Chanel a run for her money.*

Finally, Friday arrived! When Andres knocked at my door, he regarded me with that same dreamy smile that swept me off my feet the first time I saw him at Miss Stein's salon.

It turned out he was taking me to another salon. This one was at the home of an American poet, Natalie Barney, who lives on rue Jacob.

I hesitated, hoping that he had not misunderstood who I am. I told him I am not a writer or an artist in the traditional sense of the word. I attended Miss Stein's salon as Pierre's guest.

Andres made a sound deep in his throat at the mention of Pierre's name.

To lighten the mood, I asked him if Miss Barney would exile me to the women's table like Miss Stein. He laughed and assured me Miss Barney's gatherings were very welcoming to ladies.

When we arrived, Zelda Fitzgerald was the first person to greet us. Just as she had at Dingo Bar, she rose up on tiptoes and kissed Andres on both cheeks, gushing about what a handsome devil he was. Then she smiled at me and commented that Andres and I were becoming an item.

Zelda Fitzgerald is a flirt, but I rather like her. Despite her spirited ways, she's obviously devoted to Scott. When the two are together, they light up the room. I can't take my eyes off them, and what's more is the lengths to which they go to capture the other's attention. I still can't decide if it is a beautiful, elaborate display of love or sheer madness.

Probably both.

I am beginning to believe that an otherwise sane and thoughtful person can become intoxicated and seduced by Paris simply by breathing her air.

That's my excuse, anyway.

When Scott joined our little circle, he greeted us and immediately fell into conversation with Andres. Zelda said usually Scott doesn't deign himself to attend Natalie Barney's salon, but tonight a special reading would take place. She pointed out that all the men were there. Except for Hemingway, because he was much too manly a man to join what was usually a ladies' salon.

I felt comfortable enough to ask what she meant by Ernest not wanting to attend this salon. He was a regular at Miss Stein's.

Zelda threw back her head and laughed, explaining that Gertrude Stein might have all the female parts, but she was more of a man than most of the boys in Paris and that's why Hem is so friendly with her.

Apparently Ernest and Pauline are married now. I can't help but think of that day at Dingo Bar when he'd pulled me away from Pauline and danced me around the place. I still believe he would've kissed me on the lips had I not turned my head. I'm sure it was all a game to him. Just as flirting seems to be for Zelda.

I am starting to believe it is the national pastime of Paris.

The biggest surprise of the night—and certainly the sweetest treat—was when Andres recited some of his own writing. I'd never read his work, but now I can't wait to dive into the small book of French poetry he'd read from at the salon and given to me at the end of the evening.

My heart is full. I have slipped under his spell.

Seventeen

January 8, 2019—5:45 p.m.

London, England

I leave the Heart to Heart office with a game plan.

We will call the Paris tour Les Années Folles. It means "the crazy years," a term coined to describe the rich social, artistic, and cultural changes happening in Paris in the 1920s. Even though I haven't yet read through all of Ivy's diary entries, I am certain they will come in handy.

Borrowing a page from the Tenement Museum in New York City, I will make Ivy the central figure and tour guests will follow her as she grows from British immigrant to bohemian woman living the expatriate life in Paris, rubbing elbows with the likes of Ernest Hemingway, Zelda and Scott Fitzgerald, James Joyce, and Sylvia Beach.

I'll keep the itinerary a short two days at first, during which we'll visit as many of the Lost Generation haunts as we can, such as Dingo Bar, Gertrude Stein's home, Shakespeare and Company, Café de Flore, and the Ritz.

I have my work cut out for me, but for now, I'm excited to press pause and enjoy my going-away party.

At the office, I changed into the dress I brought, touched up my makeup, and hailed a cab so I wouldn't have to endure the long, lumbering bus ride home. It's a little splurge I feel I owe myself as I embark on this new path.

When I arrive at the flat, night has already settled over Albert Street. The golden light glowing in the front windows reminds me of New Year's Eve when I got home and discovered Marla here. It's hard to believe how things have changed in a week. It feels like years.

Which reminds me: I wonder if Marla is home yet.

The moment I open the door, I'm greeted by the aroma of something delicious—garlicky, savory, utterly divine. My stomach growls in appreciation as I shut the door behind me. I shrug out of my coat and hang it in the hall closet before I enter the living room.

Édith Piaf is crooning "La Vie en Rose" from the speakers. I see that Cressida and T have decorated with dozens of tiny twinkling Eiffel Tower lights strung from one corner of the dining room to the other, crossing in the middle. I have no idea where they found them on such short order, but they are fabulous.

I breathe through a sudden, unexpected pang of premature homesickness.

I hear muffled conversation, the sound of a champagne cork popping, and a wave of laughter. I move to the kitchen and stand in the doorway. For a few beats, I see my friends—Cressida, Jemma, and Tallu—before they see me. Cressida has invited Danny, but there's no sign of Jesse, much to my relief.

I know I'm not saying goodbye to this place or these people forever, but I want to imprint this moment on my memory forever—the convivial sounds, the delicious aromas, the good energy that flows like the champagne they're pouring.

Then Aiden comes out of the pantry carrying a bag of onions, and my heart lurches. Dressed in black jeans and a black shirt, he's even cuter than I remember. His longish dark hair and pale skin give him the appeal of a bad boy, only he's anything but.

He's the first to spy me.

"There she is," he says, his Scottish brogue making the words sound as rich as foie gras and a hundred times more delectable. Cressida, Jemma, and T turn and greet me with gusto augmented by multiple flutes of bubbly.

"Here's your going-away present," Cressida says, gesturing to Aiden like a game show model. "Aiden has agreed to cook dinner. Isn't that fabulous?"

The butterflies in my stomach are borderline painful.

He sets down the onions and brushes off his hands, but he doesn't move to close the distance between us. Of course, there's also a kitchen island and four people blocking the way. Still, I notice something a little reserved in his eyes.

Maybe I should've told him I was in town before Cressida and T broke the news. But I assumed he'd be at Lemon and Lavender tonight, and I'm leaving tomorrow to return to Paris indefinitely.

"I figured since I couldn't get you to come to the restaurant anytime soon, I'd better bring the feast to you. A moveable feast seems fitting since you're leaving us for Paris."

The butterflies swarm.

"That's clever, Aiden. Thank you."

He smiles and begins peeling an onion.

"Is Marla back yet?" I ask.

"Oh, I thought maybe she met you at the office after doing her errand?" Cressida says.

I shake my head. "No, I was there all afternoon. She didn't stop by."

“I’m sure she’ll be here soon,” T says. She hands me a glass of champagne. “I can’t believe you’re leaving us, Han.”

I’m overcome by a sudden rush of shyness as I feel Aiden’s gaze on me. Then Jemma gets up from her seat at the island and offers him one of two shots of tequila she’s poured, which he waves off. She proceeds to down both and whispers something in his ear.

She looks pretty tonight, rocking a 1920s vibe with her jet-black hair cut into a sleek bob with bangs. Her flawless porcelain skin is the perfect canvas for her smoky eyes and bloodred lipstick.

He’s at least a foot taller than Jemma. She looks tiny standing next to him as he smiles down at her. He offers her a taste of whatever it is that smells so good on the stove. She puts one hand on his bicep and the other over her heart, closes her eyes, and moans.

“Oh, Aiden. Oh my God. *Mmmmm* . . . What is this? It’s better than sex.”

Everyone laughs, clearly eager to have what Jemma’s having, but Cressida quips, “Jemma, obviously you’re sleeping with the wrong people.”

Jemma holds onto Aiden’s arm with both hands and gazes up at him. “That’s just occurring to me.”

Puh-lease. I have no right to be bothered by Jemma’s innuendo, but I can’t help it.

“It’s just simple beef bourguignon.” Aiden slants a glance at me and looks a little embarrassed for Jemma. “I figured a good, hearty French stew would be the perfect dinner on this cold night before we send Hannah off to Paris.”

Jemma is Cressida’s friend. T and I have gotten to know her through Cres, but we’ve always found her to be somewhat of an enigma. Nice enough, but distant.

As Jemma and Aiden stand together at the stove, it's clear they would make a beautiful couple.

I have this premonition of getting an invitation to their wedding.

Just like what happened with Charlie. Only this time, the talk would be about how Jemma and Aiden had been friends and neighbors until *that night that changed everything*. Jemma would coo from her place at the bridal table, "It was his beef bourguignon. One taste and I knew I couldn't live without him. Just think, if he hadn't cooked that going-away dinner for Hannah, I might never have tasted true love."

The guests would sigh and clap and tap their champagne flutes with silverware until the couple kissed.

Then Aiden would tut. "We would've found our way to each other eventually. Nothing can stop true love, but here's to Hannah for speeding things up, and here's to Cressida for getting the matchmaking wrong *again*."

It occurs to me that I've never given Charlie a name for the Date From Hell Hall of Fame. He was more long-term than the others, but he still deserves the dubious honor. Let's go with The Heartbreaker, since he broke up with me out of the blue after we'd been together for three years and then disappeared from my life until a save-the-date card arrived in the mail six months later.

What would Aiden's Hall of Fame name be? Not The Ghoster, since he's here tonight. The Chef? Hard to say since he hasn't really done anything wrong.

"I'm here. I'm here. So sorry I'm late." Marla's words yank me out of my thoughts. She rushes into the kitchen at a half jog, her high heels clicking on the wooden floor. Her red curls look wind tousled and her cheeks are flushed.

"I meant to be back an hour ago, but, well . . . you know how it goes."

I've never been so happy to see her in my life. It's such a strange feeling, but she's a welcome distraction from what's cooking between Aiden and Jemma. It's on the tip of my tongue to ask what kept her, but she's going on about the London traffic with the group, and really, it's not my business where she's been or what she was doing. Just like Jemma and Aiden aren't my concern.

Still, I wish I understood what changed between them over the past week. On New Year's Eve, Cressida was certain that Aiden Zedrick was my soul mate, and I was open to the possibility. Now Jemma is all but humping his leg. I mean, it's fine, but I don't get it. If Jemma had prior claim—if something had been brewing between the two of them—I wish Cressida would've told me. Even better, I wish she wouldn't have invited him here tonight.

Then Jemma leans in and whispers in Aiden's ear again.

This sucks.

I turn my back on them—literally—and try to fall into the conversation about traffic that's still somehow going strong. If I'd been wistful about leaving London to relocate to Paris twenty minutes ago, I'm not now.

THE DINNER IS DELICIOUS.

We start with a mesclun salad with goat cheese, pumpkin seeds, yellow beets, and a traditional vinaigrette, then move to French onion soup followed by the beef bourguignon with plenty of crusty French bread that Aiden baked himself. Of course, the wine is flowing and everyone has had too much.

Jemma is seated to Aiden's left, and I'm on his right. Earlier, I caught her switching the place cards that Cressida had set out.

T had originally been in the place that Jemma claimed.

I'm surprised Jem didn't move me, which makes me wonder if

she's aware of the plans that Cressida had for Aiden and me. If she didn't know, that would make things slightly more forgivable, but still disappointing.

Since I sat toward the center of the table, I was drawn into many different conversations and mercifully didn't have to rely on small talk with Aiden.

To be honest, I was too busy talking and eating to notice whether Jemma clung to him during dinner or if she spoke to anyone else.

Even though it's after eleven by the time we finish dinner, we decide to go to a club called Fugue and dance. I'm not in the mood, but everyone else is so enthusiastic I don't have the heart to be the lone stick-in-the-mud. This is the last time in a long while that I'll be able to go out with my friends, so I might as well make the most of it.

When we go out en masse, everyone dances in a big group. It's fun—cathartic, really.

We tumble onto the dance floor and move with abandon. The DJ is playing remixed eighties pop. Tallu and Marla are dancing with their arms over their heads. Cressida is twirling like a dervish, miraculously not bumping into anyone—or if she does, they don't seem to mind. Danny is doing a hipster dance with economic, but effective movements.

And surprise, surprise, Jemma is hanging all over Aiden, looking quite unsteady on her feet.

She stumbles back a few steps off the dance floor and knocks into a blonde girl, making her spill her drink.

The blonde looks pissed—in the American sense of the word.

Aiden leans into my ear. "I'm going to buy that woman another drink. Will you look after Jemma? She's tanked up. I'll get her some water while I'm at it. Would you like something?"

What I'd really like is to know what's going on with you and Jemma.

"Some water would be great, thanks."

He disappears into the crowd, and Jemma starts to trail after him. Taking my babysitting job seriously, I redirect her to an empty banquette.

We're all pretty lit, but that's when I notice how wasted Jemma is.

Her eyes are unfocused and she's swaying in her seat.

"Are you okay?" I ask, touching her arm to steady her.

"I want to go home," she moans.

She starts to stand but flops right back down on the banquette.

"My legs don't work," she slurs. "Watch."

Again, she tries to stand with the same result. This time she puts her head in her hands.

"Jemma, are you okay?" She doesn't answer.

"Are you going to be sick?"

"I can't tell. The room is spinning too fast. I don't think I can find the loo."

I try to help her to her feet, intending to walk her to the bathroom, but she's deadweight. I know we'll never make it.

"*Ugh*—oh no—" she moans.

I know what's about to happen. "I need your bucket," I shout to a group of guys at the table next to us.

I can't wait for them to comprehend my request, so I grab the bucket full of ice that's been cooling multiple bottles of beer. I'm barely able to dump the remaining bottles and ice on the floor amidst their angry protests before I shove the bucket in front of Jemma's face—just in the nick of time.

The owners of the beer go from gripes to gasps of awe and delighted disgust.

"Sorry," I say. "I'll get you a clean ice bucket."

"No problem," says one of the guys, watching Jemma sit with her head over the sullied one. "Bloody fast reflexes."

"It would've been down Stu's back," says another.

"We'll get ourselves a fresh one," says the guy named Stu. "You've got your hands full."

A moment later, Aiden delivers the drink to the blonde and returns with two waters.

"Someone needs to take her home," I say, accepting the cold bottle.

"I will," Aiden says. "I live near her, and I need to go anyway. I have an early meeting."

"Do you need help?" I ask, not sure what I'm offering. Maybe just a chance to have some time with him.

"Thanks, but I'll grab a cab, get her settled in, and then I'll walk home from her place. It's not far. Only a few blocks."

We stand there, the awkwardness pulsing between us as strong as the electronic music.

"Thanks for the dinner, Aiden. It was delicious."

"My pleasure. I'm sorry we didn't get to spend more time together."

I nod.

"Good luck with your new venture, Hannah. I'll call you."

Right. I wish he hadn't said that as I watch him walk away—probably forever—with Jemma draped all over him.

July 1927
Paris, France

Dear Diary,

Andres was waiting for me when I got off work today. He said he wanted to take me somewhere special. He was so exuberant that I had to argue with him before he would give me a moment to fix my hair and my face and put on a clean dress after my shift at the boulangerie.

Before I knew it, he had whisked me away to the most delightful little bookshop on rue de l'Odéon. It is called Shakespeare and Company and it sells English books. I felt as if I had fallen down a rabbit hole and landed in London.

It was magnificent.

The shop window showcased dozens of volumes of Andres's book, Un Homme de Parole, *and I could hardly tear myself away from the beauty of the display to enter the shop. It suddenly hit me that he was someone important.*

I kept saying, "Andres, that is you. That is your novel."

He nodded proudly and said that both he and James Joyce, among others, owed their start to the generous woman inside the shop whom he was most anxious for me to meet.

We entered the stuffy shop and a thin American woman with dense, wavy brown hair the color of a mink stood and greeted us.

Andres introduced her as Sylvia Beach, the shop's proprietress, and she greeted me so warmly I at once felt at home and as if I had made a new friend.

The shop was as warm as she was with its stately wooden

furniture and shelves upon shelves of books. In the rare place a bookshelf did not claim a wall, beguiling paintings and drawings decorated the space.

Before I could look around much, Sylvia asked me what I enjoyed reading. I must admit being put on the spot like that caused my mind to go blank. I couldn't recall a single author I had recently enjoyed. All I could think of was Vogue magazine. That seemed so plebeian. So common. Not that I should pretend to be someone I am not. But I want to be worthy of Andres and I feared such an answer might embarrass not only me, but him as well.

Then I recalled Scott Fitzgerald's Gatsby and told her I was dying to read it. Before I knew it, Sylvia was pressing a copy into my hands, telling me to take it with me. I hesitated because I had not thought to bring money with me; I had been in such a rush to leave the apartment with Andres.

However, when I tried to hand the book back to her, she wouldn't take it. She told me I could borrow it. If I liked it and wanted to own it, I could pay her later. If I didn't think it worthy of my library, I could simply return it at no cost. No questions asked.

I must remember to embroider a bookmark for her to express my gratitude.

I can't wait to dig into Gatsby so I have something to talk to Zelda about next time I see her.

Eighteen

January 9, 2019—10:30 a.m.

Paris, France

It's a glorious day for January. Chilly enough for a jacket but pleasant enough for a good long walk. It's as if Paris has donned her finest to welcome us back.

Armed with a guidebook and a list of points of interest based on Ivy's diaries, we head to the left bank. Starting at Shakespeare and Company bookstore, we walk to 20 rue Jacob, the home of the American playwright, poet, and novelist Natalie Clifford Barney, who used to hold salons in the same vein as Gertrude Stein's. From there, we find our way to Stein's own famous residence at 27 rue de Fleurus. Along the way, we pass by rue de Buci in the Saint-Germain-des-Prés district, a buzzy place with cafés and open markets where vendors sell everything from boutique clothing and flowers to cheese and meats, fruits, vegetables, and olives. We stop by Dingo Bar, La Closerie des Lilas, and the brasserie Les Deux Magots—one of Ivy's favorite lunch spots.

I try to imagine my great-grandmother walking these streets, making Paris her own. What I wouldn't give for her to be here now, giving us this tour. More than that, I wish I understood why she thought she had to keep this part of her life a secret from Marla and Gram.

On the way home, we walk along the left bank of the Seine, through the part that is crowded with merchants who sell used and antiquarian books. I've recently learned they're called *bouquinistes*.

"I think I should bring them here," I say, gesturing to the stalls. "The green boxes on the walls with all the books have UNESCO status."

Marla answers me with a blank stare. It dawns on me that she's a good person to bounce my ideas off of because if she gets it or is entertained, then the average person probably would be, too.

That's not meant as a slight to her. I fully own the fact that I am a book nerd. Not everyone gets excited about *bouquinistes* or UNESCO World Heritage designations, and I want this tour to be interesting for everyone.

"Do you know what that means?" I ask.

She shrugs and focuses even more intently on the souvenirs laid out before her in one of the stalls.

"I'm not judging you," I say in my most nonjudgmental voice.

"You wouldn't say that if you weren't. But go ahead. What is so great about these *bookanistas*? Are they the nerdy sisters of the fashionistas?"

She snickers at her own joke, picks up an old book, and thumbs through it.

"It's not *bookanista.* It's pronounced *boo-kee-neest*," I enunciate.

"And you said you're not judging me." Marla snorts. "I see."

She returns the book and moves on down the line of vendors.

"I want to know if you understand," I say as I trail after her. "I need to know if the content for this tour makes sense. I'm asking for your opinion."

She turns to me and her face softens. "Okay, try me."

"Really?" I ask.

She nods.

"Okay." I clear my throat. "I read last night that these bookstalls have been here for more than five hundred years. There are about nine hundred of these green boxes in the designated areas on both sides of the river." I rap on the top of one, which is raised to create a canopy. Behind it, I can see Notre-Dame Cathedral.

Marla lifts a brow. "Hmm. That's interesting. That's a long time."

"Exactly! Think about it. Hemingway, Fitzgerald, Joyce, and Pound used to walk right where we're walking and look at the wares like we are right now, searching for books of other authors or maybe even their own work."

"That works," Marla says. "Especially if you drive home the fact that the writers used to come here. You could tell them to squint their eyes and pretend like it's 1927."

"That's a great idea."

For a moment, Marla and I stand side by side, squinting at the people milling about. Some are bartering with the vendors; others have their noses in a book.

"You might want to explain the Costco thing a little better," she says.

"The what?"

"You said they had some kind of Costco designation."

It takes everything I have not to laugh. I put my hand over my mouth. Marla looks confused.

"What's so funny?"

"It's UNESCO, not Costco. That means the United Nations designated this area and its green boxes as a World Heritage site. This area is considered a protected landmark."

Marla raises her brows. I'm determined to keep her interested.

"Someone, I don't know who, said the Seine is the only river in the world that runs between two bookshelves."

"That's cute. I think your tour people would be interested in knowing that. But just a little bit of constructive input? You might want to enunciate a little better. I could've sworn you said Costco."

Or maybe she wasn't listening.

"Look, I'm just saying." Marla crosses her arms. "I'm not suggesting you dumb it down, but don't make people feel stupid by using hoity-toity terms like *booka . . . booka—*"

"*Boo-kee-neest.*"

She rolls her eyes. "That's exactly what I mean."

I say, "There's nothing wrong with not knowing something as long as you're open to learning."

She stays quiet.

"I didn't mean to hurt your feelings. If it makes you feel better, I didn't know any of this until I started researching it for the tour."

"Hmm." She's flipping through a stack of vintage postcards. "Maybe it's not so much what you say, Hannah, but how you say it."

It's a bitter pill, but I pause to swallow it.

Before I can respond, Marla holds up a small blue box that she's picked up from one of the stalls.

"Look at this," she says.

The picture on the front of the package looks like a daily desk calendar. The type you rip the pages off every day to reveal something new.

Marla takes the plastic tray out of the box and begins thumbing through and laughing to herself.

"What's so funny?" I ask.

"It's a French phrase-a-day calendar." She flips another page. "I was thinking it might be a good way to learn to speak French. We could make a point of working the phrases into our daily conversation. You might even share a French phrase with your tour. Like this one: *Le trajet en voiture ne prend que trente minutes*. It means, 'The trip by car only takes thirty minutes.'"

"How does telling them they could see everything by car in thirty minutes help my business when it's a walking tour that will last two days?"

"Oh, Hannah, you're missing the point." She turns to the woman tending the bookstall and reads from the calendar, "*Voulez-vous un peu plus de fromage?*"

The woman frowns and looks at Marla like she's said something vulgar. I'm not quite sure she hasn't, because her accent is more Central Florida than French.

"What did you say to her?"

"Would you like more cheese?" She holds up the calendar and points, looking proud of herself. "That's what it says right here."

"*Souhaitez-vous acheter le calendrier, madame?*" asks the bookstall woman.

Marla's head swivels toward me. "What did she say?"

"I think she asked you if you would like to purchase the calendar."

Marla turns to the vendor and smiles. "Yes, please. I would love to buy it."

After she completes the transaction, we walk along the quay. Marla is like a kid with a new toy, flipping through and trying out random phrases.

"*Veuillez double cliquer pour accéder au menu*. That means, 'Please double-click to access the menu.'"

She laughs, clearly delighted. "*Voilà une belle salade de tomates*," she says with a flourish. "Here is a beautiful tomato salad."

I laugh at the absurdity. I can't help it.

"Oh wait—look. Here's one that really would be useful for you: *N'oubliez pas de donner un pourboire au guide touristique*."

"I have no idea what you just said. Your accent is incredibly terrible."

"I said, 'Don't forget to tip the tour guide.'"

"Okay, that one was good."

She cocks her head to the side and holds her finger in the air like a know-it-all. Then she shoves the little calendar back into its box and tucks it away in her purse.

We walk along in silence for a few minutes.

"I'll need to get a job since I'm moving here."

"You might want to talk to Monsieur Levesque about that. I'm not sure what's involved in getting a visa."

"How did you do it?" she asks. "It seems like you're not having to jump through any hoops to work here."

"That's the beauty of working for Emma. Her tour company is well established. She cut through the red tape so I could work in England, and she'll do the same thing here in Paris."

"Well, why couldn't she pull some strings for me? Think about it, Hannah. Couldn't you use an assistant? It will be hard for you to run a one-woman office, coordinating and running the tours. Who's going to answer the phones? I could be your Violet."

"We have the original Violet in the London home office for that. She can do a lot for me remotely."

"Okay, but there will be lots of other things to do here. Why do you always think you have to do everything yourself? It's okay to ask for help."

As much as I hate to admit it, her words strike a nerve. She all but designed me not to ask for help. She was the one who made me believe that I couldn't trust anyone. The one who made me afraid to rely on anyone but myself. And, okay, Gram. I could always rely on Gram.

Marla doesn't seem to get that yet.

On the horizon, I see the Eiffel Tower stretching up like a beacon at the end of the long stretch of green Champ de Mars. Along the way we glimpse the gold dome of Napoleon's tomb.

Now that Gram is gone, Marla is the only person I have. Marla and the ghost of Ivy.

What would it be like to work with Marla? Work *and* live with her?

I shudder. It's a frightening prospect. However, she seems to be sincere about changing her ways.

Even this walk through Paris has a different vibe from when we got lost in Pigalle that first day.

I'm opening my mouth to concede just that when Marla's phone rings.

"Who in the world is calling me?" she says as she pulls her cell out of her purse, squints at the number, and answers with a tentative, "Hello?"

Her face goes from suspect to wide-eyed.

"Oh my, well, hello indeed. I really didn't expect to hear from you, but I'm glad you called."

She makes eye contact with me, then turns and walks away a few feet, but I can still hear her. "Per chance can I call you later? I can't really talk right now. I'm out in the middle of Paris with my daughter."

She nods. "Yes, sure . . . Right . . . Uh-huh . . . Okay, I'll call you then. Oh, at this number, right?"

She smiles. "Okay, wonderful . . . I am thrilled to hear from you."

I think I hear her say something about London, but I can't be sure because a woman walks by pushing a stroller with a crying baby.

The only other thing I hear Marla say is, "Bonjour, for now."

I think she means to say *adieu*, but I'm too distracted by the way she smiles at the phone to correct her.

"Who was that?" I ask.

"No one." She slides the phone back into her purse. "It was a wrong number."

"I heard you say you were thrilled to hear from them. I'm fairly certain you wouldn't be thrilled to hear from a wrong number or a telemarketer. Unless that's your new way of making friends."

"Hannah, maybe it's none of your business. Did you ever consider that? I don't have to tell you everything, you know."

"You do need to be straight with me if we're thinking about living and working together. Are you reconnecting with Don?"

"Don?" She looks genuinely taken aback. "You have nothing to worry about with him. I blocked his number. He doesn't know where I am so there's no way he can get in touch with me. That's how serious I am about starting over."

"I don't want to get in your business, but I have a right to know what's going on. You gave me your word that living in our apartment would mark a big change for you. If there's a new man, I deserve to know about it."

We're at a standoff. Literally. She's standing there with the river lapping behind her, crossing her arms and staring me down like it's a contest to see who will blink first.

Then *my* phone rings.

I almost don't answer it. Aiden called me today when we were on the train returning to Paris. He left a message saying it was nice to see me and he was sorry we didn't get to talk more. He told me to call him. I still haven't decided if I want to. The Jemma situation muddies the water. Plus, even if there is no him and Jemma, there is Paris and me.

It appears to be a French number.

"Hello?"

"*Allo*, may I speak to Hannah Bond, *s'il vous plaît*?" It's a woman speaking heavily accented English.

"This is she."

"Mademoiselle Bond, this is Brigette from Professeur Louis Descartes's office at the Sorbonne. He asked me to call you and tell you that his finding is inconclusive. The work is not one of Andres Armand's previously published books. It could be something unpublished, but Professeur Descartes cannot be one hundred percent certain. He said that he's done all he can do, and you are free to retrieve the papers at your earliest convenience."

I'm stunned, and Brigette hangs up before I can ask, *Now what?*

"What's wrong, Hannah?" Marla asks. "Is it bad news?"

"It was Professeur Descartes's assistant calling to say that they can't be sure the manuscript is the work of Andres Armand. So, they're done. We can pick it up. I think he just blew us off."

"Well, what are we supposed to do now?" Marla asks.

"That's what I'd like to know."

"As much as I hate to involve the filthy *salopard*," says Marla, "maybe we should call Gabriel and ask if he knows anyone else who can help us."

"How did you learn to cuss in French?"

"He's a bastard. That's why I looked up the word. Gabriel Cerny, inspiring women to cuss, one slimy move at a time."

She looks pleased with herself. It's not lost on me that Marla has used this opportunity to redirect the spotlight away from her phone call. But she's right on one account: Gabriel is probably our best bet for figuring out our next move.

Surely someone out there can tell us for sure whether or not this is authentic Armand. I place the call to Gabriel and leave a voicemail explaining the situation.

In the meantime, I need to keep reading Ivy's diaries and look for someone to translate the manuscript for me.

I know the identity of the author must be hidden somewhere in those pages.

November 1927
Paris, France

Dear Diary,

I wonder how Andres gets any writing done.

When I ask, he says creativity works in mysterious ways. Words don't flow like water from a faucet. He can't turn it on and off at will. He insists that to write something truly great, a writer needs to give the idea time to marinate before it develops full flavor.

He is very lucky that he has a trust fund to support his marinating. Nevertheless, he is always so generous, surprising me with flowers and candy.

Lately, he has been urging me to quit my job at the boulangerie *and move in with him. As much as I'd love to, I can't take him up on the offer. What if something happened? It took me long enough to find this position. As meager as it is, it allows me to support myself.*

Tonight illustrated exactly how fast life can change course.

At the beginning of the night, everything was fine. We ran into Scott and Zelda at Harry's Bar. We were a loud bunch, having fun and singing at the tops of our lungs and talking over each other and the music, everyone trying to make a point, like birds cawing all at once.

When we left, Zelda swiped a bottle of champagne from the bar. We passed it around as we made our way to Dingo Bar.

Zelda was whining about being hungry, demanding that she needed something to eat before she passed out in the middle of the street, which would've been a feat because we were on the walkway.

To distract her, as we passed a young boy who was loading

leftover baguettes from a boulangerie *into the basket of his tricycle, Scott hopped on the small bike and took off down the walk.*

We all doubled over with laughter as he peddled furiously, his long legs bent at such a ridiculous angle that he looked like a circus clown careening down the fancy walk, barely avoiding hitting several pedestrians in the process.

When the boy caught up to him and tried to pull him off the trike, Scott toppled over. The next thing we knew, he was on the pavement and the boy was pummeling him with his tiny fists and yelling words that were much too vulgar for a garçon.

Scott was fine, of course. The only danger he was in was of busting a gut from laughing so hard.

The boy rode off on his little tricycle and we were getting on our merry way when Pierre seemed to appear from out of nowhere.

He stood in front of me, blocking my way. I hadn't seen him since that day at his studio when I walked out. And after all this time, he was spoiling for a fight.

He insisted I owed him money since I didn't finish the job for which I was hired. He bellowed on about not being able to complete the painting series, insisting it was my fault that he'd missed the submission deadline.

I told him I didn't owe him a centime. He had not paid me beyond the six paintings he had completed. It was his own fault that he missed the deadline. He could've used the completed paintings as reference.

As soon as I'd said my piece, he unleashed a string of vile words that made me pale. Andres puffed up and stepped between us, and Zelda grabbed my arm and led me into a nearby restaurant. As I walked away, I glanced over my shoulder in time to see Andres landing a punch on Pierre's jaw, which sent him falling backward.

By the time Zelda and I returned, Andres and Pierre were nowhere in sight. Andres had asked Scott to see me home.

Now that I'm home, sleep eludes me. I can't close my eyes until I hear from Andres that he's safe and Pierre hasn't pulled some dirty trick.

Nineteen

January 9, 2019—4:00 p.m.

Paris, France

We've been back in the apartment a couple of hours when Gabriel returns my call.

"I am sorry Louis Descartes disappointed you," he says. "He could have worked harder on the case if you ask me. Then again, he does not study Armand exclusively. Did you retrieve the manuscript?"

"Yes. We took a cab to the Sorbonne and picked it up right after Brigette called. I figured it was better not to leave it lying about the office too long."

As I'm explaining why I'm in Paris, not London, Marla walks in from the kitchen holding two glasses.

"Gabriel, I've put you on speaker. Marla is here."

"Bonjour, Marla." His voice sounds seductive.

My mother rolls her eyes at his greeting and hands me a glass of sparkling water before plunking down on the other end of the sofa.

"I've had a chance to do some research," he continues. "That is why it took me a while to telephone you. I have located a retired professor from the University of Oxford. A Dr. George Campbell. He lives in London. He fancies himself an Armand expert. I spoke with him and he is willing to take a look at the book as soon as we can bring it to him. I am happy to accompany you."

"Hannah is busy." Marla's tone is chilly. "She got promoted and is starting a brand-new book tour here in Paris. Since she doesn't have time to bother with this, I can take it to London. I don't need you to go with me, Gabriel."

"We can talk about that later, Marla." I shift so my body is angled away from her, hoping she'll take the hint to be quiet. I guess I shouldn't have put the call on speaker.

"But you're so busy with work, Hannah. This is a way I can help."

When neither Gabriel nor I answer right away, Marla says, "Are you saying you don't think I'm capable?"

I glance at her. She's sitting forward on the couch. The sun is streaming in through the window and highlighting the worry lines around her mouth and eyes. "We can talk about it after we're off the phone. Gabriel doesn't need to be part of this discussion."

"I would prefer Gabriel wasn't involved at all."

It's my turn to roll my eyes at her. I mouth, *Stop*.

She sits back with a *harrumph*.

"I will let the two of you talk it through," Gabriel says. "I am happy to ask my assistant to secure an appointment for you with Dr. Campbell. When you decide what you'd like for me to do, please let me know."

After I thank him and disconnect the call, Marla says, "Why don't you trust me?"

"That's not the problem."

"Well, then what is the problem, Hannah?"

I sigh.

"Did you have to be so rude to Gabriel?"

"You know how I feel about him. I can't believe you're sticking up for him after what he did to you."

"He didn't do anything to me. He might have tried, but he didn't succeed. So get over it and mind your manners."

"That doesn't mean I'll let him accompany me to London."

I don't remember deciding she would be the one to go to London.

"And as I said," Marla continues, "you're busy with work. This is a way that I can help you."

I didn't mean to make a face, but I guess I did. Marla puts her hands on her hips. "What?"

"Nothing."

"No, it's something. Why don't you trust me?"

"Have you heard the story about Ernest Hemingway's first wife, Hadley, losing one of his manuscripts?" I ask.

Marla shakes her head. "No, but do tell, please. You have a book-related story for every occasion, don't you?"

So what if I do?

"It was 1922 and Ernest and his first wife, Hadley, were still newlyweds. They hadn't been living in Paris very long. She was taking the train to meet him in Switzerland and had put the typed pages of his work in a satchel. It was his early Nick Adams stories about life in Michigan. He'd been working on them for months.

"Apparently, Hadley found her place on the train, stowed her bags, then got up to buy some refreshments for the trip. When she returned, her bag was gone and so was all of her husband's hard work."

"Are you telling me this because you think I might pull a Hadley and lose the manuscript?"

Yes. But—

"What if we printed out copies of the manuscript from the photos you took with your phone?" Marla suggests. "I can take the copy to London for a first read. If the manuscript is as fragile as you say, we should probably keep the original somewhere safe anyway."

Actually, she's right. Even though we took photos of each page, we really should have a printed copy at the ready. That way we can keep the original under lock and key until absolutely necessary.

"If we do that, we can mail the package to Dr. Campbell. But I need to make sure he'll accept a photocopy for the first read."

"I'd really like to take it to him in person," Marla insists. "What if it gets lost in the mail?"

Instead of arguing with her, I call Gabriel back and ask about submitting a photocopy.

"I will inquire, though I don't see why not," he says. "As long as it is a clean, easy-to-read reproduction. On this pass, he will be looking to see if the prose matches Armand's style."

"True," I say. "But how should we print it? I guess I could buy a printer and ink."

Gabriel is silent for a moment. Then he says, "Ah! I have an idea. If you drop by my office, I will have my assistant, Ophelia, connect your phone to our copy machine and print it out for you."

"That sounds like a big job."

"It should not take long. The copier is state-of-the-art."

"I'm embarrassed to ask, but what will that cost? The manuscript is more than two hundred pages. I'm not sure I can afford to pay an attorney's hourly rate for photocopies. Could you direct me to a self-service print shop?"

"Nonsense. We will not charge you. If you come soon, Ophelia will do it while you wait. It should only take fifteen minutes."

GABRIEL'S OFFICE IS LOCATED on the twenty-second floor of a skyscraper called the Tour Montparnasse. The sleek lines of the building strike a sharp, no-nonsense contrast to the city's famously ornate old-world architecture. An added bonus: it's located right at the Montparnasse Bienvenüe Metro stop.

It doesn't get any easier than that, especially since the weather had turned colder. Marla stays at the apartment to start a pot of chili for our dinner, and I'm relieved for the break. I could use some time away from her.

The elevator opens directly into a reception area, where a woman is sitting behind a mahogany desk. She smiles at me.

"Bonjour. Puis-je vous aider avec quelque chose?"

I ask her if she speaks English and she nods.

"Thank you. I am Hannah Bond. Gabriel Cerny is expecting me."

"One moment, please. I shall let him know you have arrived." She picks up the phone, dials, and speaks into the receiver in a low voice.

The reception area is surrounded by floor-to-ceiling windows on three sides. Expensive-looking cordovan leather love seats and chairs are grouped around mahogany coffee tables that complement the main desk. Oil paintings in heavy gold frames adorn the walls. A well-dressed woman is seated on one of the chairs. Her purse is on her lap, and she's clutching a manila envelope with both hands as if it might fly away if she loosens her grip. We are the only two in the reception area.

"Monsieur Cerny will be right with you," says the receptionist.

I walk to the closest window and look out at the most incredible view of Paris. What mesmerizes me is the postcard-perfect view of the rooftops—a stunning patchwork of white, silver, and gray—stretching as far as the eye can see.

This is my city now, though I'm still waiting for it to feel real.

In the distance, I spy two of the most recognizable landmarks in the city: the gold-domed roof of Les Invalides and the Eiffel

Tower. Across the Seine, on the right bank, the Arc de Triomphe stands tall and proud.

I close my eyes for a moment. When I reopen them, the sun glints off the gilded dome as if Napoleon, who is buried inside, is winking at me to say, *This is as real as it gets.*

"Hannah? *Ellllooo*, Hannah?"

Gabriel has appeared beside me, looking as handsome as ever in his tailored suit, crisp white shirt, and blue tie. "It is a magnificent view, is it not?"

I didn't expect him to come fetch me himself.

"It is," I say. "It rivals the Eiffel Tower."

"Some would say it is better. You can't see the Eiffel Tower from the Eiffel Tower, can you?"

We laugh and he holds out his hand. "Your phone, mademoiselle?"

I retrieve it from my bag and hand it to him.

"Thanks so much for doing this, Gabriel."

"It is my pleasure. Come. You will wait in my office while Ophelia prints the copies. It should not take long."

"I don't want to keep you from your work, Gabriel. I'm happy to wait out here."

"Nonsense. You will be more comfortable with me."

He turns and walks away and I follow him.

As we make our way down the halls, we are intercepted by a pretty brunette dressed in a tight navy blue pencil skirt and white blouse. Her hair is swept up into a French twist. Her lips, which are painted candy red, curve into a smile as Gabriel says something to her in French and hands off the phone.

Ophelia, I presume. Before Gabriel can introduce her, she disappears obediently down another hallway.

I follow him in the opposite direction. "Here we are."

He stops in front of a paneled mahogany door and gestures for me to enter first.

His corner office is larger than the whole la Bruyère apartment. It smells of furniture polish and old money. The floors are marble. The decor echoes the cordovan leather and wood of the reception area, but the pieces are antique, not of the matchy-matchy offices-to-go variety. I'm drawn to the window to check out this vantage point.

"Why is your desk arranged so that your back is to the view?"

I turn around and see that Gabriel is standing at a credenza, pouring something that looks like Scotch or cognac from a decanter into two lowball glasses.

He shrugs. "I am so rarely at my desk. When I am, I must concentrate on my work, not the landscape. When I want to enjoy the view, that is when I take the elevator to the observation deck at the top of the building. Take your coat off. It is warm in here. You'll get overheated."

It is a tad warm. As I shrug out of my coat, I wonder if I'll ever get so used to Paris that the landscape, as he calls it, will become a bore. I hope not. I want the city to keep its magic.

He crosses the room, hands me one of the glasses, and takes my coat and purse. Since I don't have my phone, I'm not sure what time it is, but as the saying goes, it's five o'clock somewhere. When in France, do as the Frenchman with the expensive liqueur does.

"Let's sit over here," Gabriel says. "*Le canapé* . . . er, how do you say . . . the couch takes advantage of the view. I do think you will like it."

He drapes my coat over the back of the sofa, sets my purse on top of it, and gestures for me to take a seat.

I don't love his use of *takes advantage*. It reminds me of the night he took advantage of his wife's absence and almost took advantage of me.

But this is different. This is his office. Ophelia should be back any minute with the copies and my phone. I realize I feel a little unarmed without the latter.

Rather than sitting, I stay at the window, admiring the Eiffel Tower in the golden late-afternoon light.

Gabriel stands beside me, a little too close.

I take a small step away, pretending to zoom in on something in the distance.

I rack my brain for a banal touristy question to ask him to keep things friendly, but before I can get the words out, he smooths a strand of hair off my face, trailing his fingers across my cheekbone.

I flinch, sloshing my drink. "What are you doing?"

"You are so beautiful, Hannah," he says.

I step away to put some space between us. "And you are married, Gabriel. I thought I made myself clear. I'm not interested in married men."

He laughs. "You American women do love to play the virtuous good girl, don't you? Hannah, you don't need to pretend with me. We both know we want this."

He grabs the collar of my blouse and pulls me toward him. The fabric rips.

In the split second before his lips land on mine, I toss my drink in his face.

"Fuck!" He backhands my glass and it shatters on the marble floor. "You bitch. Why did you do that?"

He swipes at the cognac, wiping it off his face, out of his eyes. He blinks rapidly like I've blinded him and curses me with guttural French.

I don't wait to see what happens next. I grab my coat and purse from the couch, leave the office, and speed-walk down the hallway in the direction of Ophelia. I grab my phone from her without explanation.

I was hoping the Metro ride home would give me time to collect myself. But after leaving Gabriel's office, a storm moved in. As I wait for the train, bitter cold seeps into my bones and no matter how tightly I pull my coat around myself, I can't stop shivering.

Back at the apartment, Marla takes one look at me and gasps.

"What happened to your blouse? It's torn."

The smell of simmering chili permeates the air. I feel sick to my stomach as I tell her what happened and brace myself for the onslaught of *I told you so*'s.

But they don't come. Instead, she hugs me and tells me it's not my fault.

"From now on," she says, "we will not communicate with Gabriel Cerny. I don't care if he is the only person on earth who can get this manuscript authenticated. If that smug son of a bitch so much as looks at you again, I swear a glass of liquor in the face is going to seem like a facial compared to what I'll throw at him. In fact, I think we should go to the police."

I shake my head.

"He assaulted you, Hannah."

"It's just a torn blouse. He didn't hurt me—" A sob escapes my throat and I hate myself for being so weak—for so stupidly trusting him. I hate myself even more because I fear that if I do file a police report, the firm will drop us and come collecting with fury. If that happens, we will be forced to sell the apartment to settle.

If there's a silver lining to all this, though, for the first time in my life I know without a doubt that my mother has my back.

I can't say it's worth being assaulted, but it's worth something.

November 1927
Paris, France

Dear Diary,

After the scene with Pierre and Andres last night, I barely slept a wink, hoping that Andres would come to my door and tell me all was well.

He did not show up.

After work today, I was ready to scour the city for him and throw myself at his mercy, because I now know I cannot bear to live without him.

However, when I entered the apartment after my shift, the first thing I saw was the six portraits Pierre had painted of me lined up along the wall.

I was utterly confused and more than a little frightened. I wanted to hide them before anyone else could see.

But the note on the table distracted me.

My love,

I purchased the paintings. They are my gift to you. If I have any say, you will never find yourself in the predicament of working for such an insufferable man again. Do I have a say, Ivy?

Love,
Andres

Twenty

January 11, 2019—7:00 p.m.

Paris, France

The day after the incident with Gabriel, I spoke to Monsieur Levesque and told him what had happened. I tossed and turned the night before, feeling sick to my stomach as I debated how much to reveal, but it finally hit me that I am not the guilty party. I have nothing to be ashamed of.

I told Levesque I would not take the matter to the authorities as long as he assured me that Gabriel Cerny would no longer handle any of our business with the firm.

He promised he would do one better: we would not be billed for any hours we had worked with Cerny. Levesque also promised to take the issue to the partners.

Within an hour Levesque called me back with Dr. Campbell's contact information, and now, a day later, Marla is on a train barreling its way toward London to bring him a copy of the manuscript. We'd ended up biting the bullet and printing photos of each page ourselves at a local print shop.

Really, we could've mailed the copy, but Marla insisted on going in person. I couldn't blame her for wanting to get away for a few days.

More selfishly, I'd been looking forward to some time by myself. The apartment is beginning to feel like home. There are reminders of Granny Ivy everywhere. It's nice to be able to sit in stillness surrounded by her belongings and meditate on what she must have been like as a young woman.

I have settled onto the couch with the 1929 diary when my phone rings. I answer it without even looking at the number because I am expecting an update from Marla. She should be arriving at St. Pancras station in London right about now.

"Hannah, thank God. I was beginning to think you were avoiding me."

Gooseflesh forms on my arms at the sound of the Scottish accent.

"Aiden, hello. I'm sorry I haven't called you back. It's been . . ." I don't quite know what to say. *It's been weird. I've been busy with work and fending off randy Frenchmen. You're in London; I'm in Paris—oh, and how's Jemma?*

"I'm in Paris on business. I know how busy you are, but I hope you have time to see a friend."

A friend. I'm not sure if that makes things better or worse.

"Of course. I'd love to see you. How long are you here?"

"Just tonight. Are you free for dinner? There's a fun event I think you might enjoy."

We make plans for him to come by the apartment at 7:00 p.m. He was cryptic about the dinner, but it's something work related and I am to dress in all black. Nothing too fancy, but it must be all black. Head to toe.

We chat for a while. Long enough for me to pique his curiosity about the apartment. I can't blame him. I'm still discovering new treasures in this trove.

Soon, it's time to get ready.

After I shower, I can't find my brush, which I need to blow-dry my hair. It's odd because I don't remember removing it from the bathroom. I end up using my fingers because I've wasted so much time looking for it that I'm cutting it dangerously close to not being ready when Aiden arrives.

When I go to brush my teeth, I can't find my toothbrush.

My favorite lipstick is missing, too.

One thing might be misplaced, but three things missing? That's weird.

I shoot Marla a quick text.

Can't find my hairbrush, toothbrush, and lipstick. Have you seen them?

No one else has been in the apartment. Maybe she moved them?

While I've been working, she's done a good job keeping things picked up. We have to be neat since we're living in such close quarters. I'm surprised by her level of tidiness.

I wait for her reply, but nothing comes.

Aiden will be here in ten minutes. I resort to the old toothpaste-on-the-finger trick and gargle with mouthwash.

As I dress, taking underwear from the dresser, I see the sexy undies I bought in the Galeries Lafayette before dinner with Gabriel. It feels triggering. I push them to the back of the drawer in favor of a pair of granny panties, as Marla lovingly calls my French-cut cotton briefs.

What does it say about you when your mother's lingerie drawer whispers boudoir and yours screams big-box store?

It doesn't really matter, I think, as I pull on Marla's little black dress—the same one I wore to Gabriel's—because I'm not in the habit of showing off my drawers to *friends*.

I fish another tube of lipstick out of the bottom of my purse. It's not my usual color, but it will have to do. I'm swiping it on as Aiden knocks on the door.

My heartbeat kicks up and I almost smudge.

Other than the attorneys, photographer, and the cleaning crew, Aiden is my first official guest at the apartment. When I answer the door and see him standing there in all his dark, smoldering glory, I have the same visceral reaction I had the first time I saw him. My heart is still beating like crazy. My mouth goes dry, but my hands get a little damp. I wipe them on the skirt of my dress, a motion that I hope looks like I'm smoothing it into place.

"Aiden," I say. "Welcome to Paris."

He greets me with a kiss on the cheek and I remember New Year's Eve . . . the kiss we shared that seemed like so much more than a friendly peck . . . the party at Jemma's house . . . the way drunk Jemma was all over him at my going-away dinner.

He wouldn't call me if something was going on between them, would he?

Then again, Gabriel was married, and that didn't stop him.

"Come in." I step back and motion for him to enter.

He smells good. A mixture of soap and leather with notes of green grass and cedar. I breathe in deeply as the sleeve of his jacket brushes my arm, conjuring the goose bumps all over again.

Where is my resolve to not go all weak-kneed over this *friend*?

"You can hang your jacket on the coat tree."

As he slips out of it, I say, "See the coat hanging there? It was here when we first opened the apartment doors. You should've seen it. It was covered with cobwebs and dust. We sent it out to have it cleaned and then returned it to its original place. It seemed only right to keep things as my great-grandmother left them."

Aiden shakes his head, clearly still astounded. "Quite a story you've got here."

"Well, Marla and I are still piecing things together, but I suppose it's not every day that you discover an apartment in Paris that's been in your family for generations that you never knew about."

He smiles and follows me into the living room.

When we stop in the middle of the room, he looks around and whistles.

"Wow. This is amazing. And it's all yours?"

"Well, mine and Marla's. I have photos of what the place looked like when we first arrived, before we had it cleaned. Would you like to see?"

"Absolutely."

"Have a seat."

As he settles himself onto the sofa, I go to the desk and pull out the large manila envelope that holds copies of the before-and-after photos.

The difference is astounding.

"Is it all right if I sit here? I feel like I'm in a museum. Like I shouldn't touch anything."

"I know; I still feel that way and we've been here awhile. Here we go. Before and after."

I hand him the photos. Even though the shot of the apartment before it was cleaned is a color photograph, it almost looks black-and-white on account of the ash and dust. It looks like something out of a movie set—*Sleeping Beauty* or a film about an abandoned and long-forgotten house.

Only this is real life.

"I guess you don't really need the photos that were taken after the cleaning crew worked its magic since you're sitting right here. Why don't you let me give you a tour?"

I show him through the rooms—the kitchen, bathroom, bedroom, and the living room and foyer, which he's already seen. It doesn't take us very long, but he listens reverently as I point out the apartment's finer features. I note that the only change Marla and I have made is swapping out the old mattress for two air mattresses, which we then replaced with twin beds after we returned from London.

"It's challenging sharing a bedroom with my mother, but this is how it will be until we figure things out."

"That's a lot of togetherness."

I exaggerate a nod.

"Speaking of, where is Marla?"

I tell him about the manuscript and Marla insisting on heading up that mission.

"Wow. I'd say you do have a couple of things going on in your life. Are you going to announce the find to the public? It could bring a lot of attention to your new tour."

"I suppose we will when we have some concrete answers. But right now, there's too much happening to factor in the curious public. By the way, what kind of business brings you to Paris?" I ask, worried I've been rambling.

"Food business, of course. And the dinner we're going to have tonight."

"It's the food capital of the world." *Wait, is it?* I should stick with subjects I know. "How did things turn out with Jemma?"

He seems puzzled by the non sequitur.

"The night I was in town. After the dinner you cooked and we all went out dancing."

"Oh." He shrugs noncommittally. "I'm guessing she was spectacularly hungover the next day."

"You haven't spoken to her since?"

"No. Why? Is everything okay?"

"I'm guessing it is. I just thought . . ."

I feel ridiculous having brought it up.

He laughs. "What is it?"

"She seemed a little . . . how do I say it?"

"I don't know, Hannah. Maybe you should just say it?"

"Interested in you."

"Interested in *me*?"

"Never mind. Would you like something to drink?"

"You can't say 'never mind' when clearly something is on your mind."

"Okay. The way she acted made me wonder if you two are seeing each other. Or if she was interested in seeing you. It's fine if you are. I don't want to get in the middle of things. She and Cressida are good friends. Do you know what I mean?"

"Not really. I'm a wee bit confused. Why would you think Jemma and I are dating when I thought I made it clear that I'm interested in you?"

"You are?"

"I am. Is that okay with you?"

I nod.

"I'm glad, because it's good to see you, Hannah."

My head is spinning. It feels like *a lot*. When I thought Jemma was in the picture—that I'd lost him to her—I resigned myself to not having a chance. But now . . .

"Of course, we can take things slowly," he says.

"Slow would be good."

My mind flashes back to Charlie telling me he wasn't sure he'd ever be ready to marry. I've spent the last few years convincing myself that relationships and me, we weren't meant to be.

You give your heart to someone. You lose yourself in them body and soul. Then one day three years later, you wake up to an empty bed and realize their foot was only ever halfway in the door. It can do a number on you. You start to believe that nothing in life is permanent, that you can't take anyone or anything at face value.

As if I needed a reminder.

Other than Gram, no one in my life has actually been who they seemed.

My mother had better things to do than raise me, and now here she is trying to make up for lost time.

My father was never in the picture.

Charlie was a bust.

And even Granny Ivy had a secret life.

"You're not married, are you?" I blurt out.

He laughs quizzically and it's a sound that touches me to the core of my soul. "Nope."

"Just checking."

"Let's get out of here," he says. "I think you're going to like this dinner."

"Sounds fun," I say. "If we have time afterward, I'll give you a supersecret sneak preview of the brand-new Années Folles tour."

"Années Folles?"

"'The crazy years.' It's what the interwar period in Paris was called, and it's the name I'm giving my new tour. Are you up for a little bit of crazy, Aiden?"

February 1929
Paris, France

Dear Diary,

Today is my birthday! Never have I seen such a romantic gesture as the effort Andres made.

No, it's not a proposal. He still doesn't believe in marriage. Monogamy, yes. He vows I am the only woman for him and he doesn't need a certificate forcing him to be true.

One would think we'd reached an impasse, but listen to this . . .

This evening, he rented a horse and carriage and after he took me to Maxim's for dinner, we set out with a bottle of champagne and what looked like a box that would hold a small cake, for what I thought would be a nighttime tour of the city. That would've been the sweetest gift in itself, but there was so much more.

His gift to me even overshadowed my birthday dinner, and you know how I've longed to dine at Maxim's.

I thought it curious when the coach veered deeper into the right bank's more residential neighborhoods. Usually, the sleepy streets aren't our idea of fun, but I was happy to be with him and it was interesting to see this side of Paris—with its tree-lined streets and handsome homes.

Suddenly, the carriage stopped in front of a pretty building that was set back off the road. A stately wrought-iron fence surrounded it and the sweetest little garden. A lone stone bench sat waiting off the main walkway.

Andres hopped out of the carriage and helped me down.

He used a key to unlock the gate.

I followed, peppering him with questions.

He pressed his index finger to his lips and said I would understand soon enough.

Another key let us inside the double front doors to a reception area with marble floors. He led me up the grand staircase. Finally, we stood in front of a polished wooden door, which he unlocked. Before I knew what was happening, he scooped me into his arms and carried me over the threshold.

Inside the apartment, a banner hung over the fireplace. It read "Happy Birthday, My Love! Welcome Home!"

Then he handed me the keys and said he thought I could use an apartment of my own since Helen is traveling so much after winning a spot in the Ballets Russes.

I glanced at the stately floor-to-ceiling windows and the regal crown molding. At the sofa that commanded the center of the room and the delicate writing desk, which graced the wall between the tall windows.

I told him it was a lovely place, and so nice of him to find and furnish it for me, but I could not afford it. I could barely afford my current apartment, and that place wasn't nearly as grand as this one.

Then he said the most curious thing. I would find the new place much more affordable than my current rental because this place was paid for in full. He had set up a fund to cover the taxes and utilities. I would find my new home had everything I needed: a modern kitchen, the latest in indoor plumbing, and a soaking tub.

He teased that I might find the commute to the boulangerie *a bit longer, but I could always quit and focus on my clothing creations.*

I was at a loss for words. It was a lovely gift, but how could I accept it? It dawned on me that perhaps this was a way of tricking me to move in with him.

I thanked him again but reminded him I had no intentions of being a kept woman.

Then he really shocked me. He said he didn't understand how I could consider myself a kept woman since I owned the place. He reached into the breast pocket of his coat and pulled out an envelope.

Tucked inside was the deed to the apartment—with my name on it. The place is mine to do with as I please. It belongs to me, even if I decide to kick him out of my life tomorrow or sell the place and move back to Bristol. Those last words were his, not mine. How could I throw him out when I love him so very much?

I was sure there had to be a catch, but I could not find one.

Soon, my full heart overflowed and I could not contain the tears. I threw my arms around him.

He scooped me up and carried me into the bedroom and made love to me until the moon was high in the inky sky.

We did take a break to eat the birthday cake and drink the champagne he'd brought. He lit the candles and sang the birthday song—wearing nothing more than his own birthday suit.

It was one of those rare instances in life when everything seemed right and good and, dare I say, perfect. Right now, as I write, he is softly snoring beside me.

I want to live in this moment forever. However, reality elbows its way in, deflating my bliss. I must contact my parents.

Before I left London, I gave my mother the address of the rue du Cardinal Lemoine apartment. However, given my mother's propensity for showing up unannounced at the most inopportune moments, I dared not tell her the first apartment was such a disaster that Helen and I had been forced to move. I never sent her the address of the second apartment because she was likely to show up simply to wag her finger in my face and remind me of how I'd failed. She would have delighted in being right and rubbing my nose in the fact that I was not clever enough nor talented enough to secure a position in the atelier of Mademoiselle Chanel.

If she had learned of my work for Pierre . . . I shudder to imagine what might have happened.

Still, the fact remains my own mother threw me out. She made it clear I was no longer welcome in her home. If she had changed her mind—if she had cared one iota—she could have found me in Paris, but she didn't.

But, dear diary, I refuse to dwell on that sad truth because for the first time since moving to Paris, I am settled and deeply happy. I am finally in the position to write and tell my parents I am doing well.

I shall post a note home tomorrow.

Twenty-One

January 14, 2019—3:00 p.m.

Paris, France

Marla was gone for four days. By the time she returned, Aiden has come and gone and I don't have to try to explain something I don't yet understand myself.

I needed the time to sort things out without her demanding to know why I've been so distracted.

I didn't want to talk about it, which would've made her all the more determined to pry it out of me.

The truth is, I think I may have royally screwed things up with Aiden.

It started off as a beautiful night. The dinner was a fundraiser planned by the food industry to raise scholarship money for those who want to study the culinary arts but can't afford tuition. It was called Dîner Dans le Noir—Dinner in the Black—which had a double meaning because we were all dressed in black and the scholarships would keep students from going into debt. The event was held in a mansion in the seventh arrondissement called Maison des Polytechniciens. Built in 1703, over the years, it has been the private residence of several different wealthy families. Currently, it's owned by the Association of Friends of Polytechnicians, which lends it out for private events.

Everyone was dressed in black and the place was lit by candlelight. The food was delicious. Aiden was . . . well, he was Aiden.

After we left the dinner, I was regretting not wearing my lingerie because I was tempted to ask him to come over. Especially after we took a detour and he kissed me on the quay of the Seine.

He'd said he'd always wanted to do that.

I was thinking, *Please don't let this one be too good to be true*.

As we walked and talked, getting closer to the apartment, I was pointing out potential stops for the tour. He offered to fly in and orchestrate a dinner for the end of the first day of the inaugural tour. He said we could call it the "moveable feast."

At first, I thought he was kidding. I mean, how would that even work?

So I brushed it off—okay, maybe I kind of laughed it off. Not in a mean way. Or at least I didn't intend for it to come across that way. But let's just say that by the time we got to my door, the mood was different.

He lightly kissed me good night and went back to his hotel, and now I feel weird.

I'm not sure if I hurt his feelings by rebuffing his dinner idea. But you know what? It's my tour. I don't tell him how to run his restaurant.

I have a lot riding on making this tour a success, and I need to stick to what I know.

It's only been a few days, but I haven't heard from him since he got back to London. Maybe I won't. Who knows? Maybe he'll enter the Date From Hell Hall of Fame as The Egotist.

Then again, maybe that's harsh. Especially when he's never been a date from hell, and this time it was just as much my fault as anyone's. I've been pretending to be too busy to call or text him, and now Marla's home and that's my current excuse for not reaching out.

"I spoke to Emma while I was in London," Marla says from the bedroom where she is unpacking her bag. "She is going to call you, but she said if you're willing to let me be your assistant, she sees no reason why y'all can't hire me. She also thinks it's absurd that you always try to be such an island, Hannah. You don't have to do everything yourself."

I'm sitting at the desk in the living room, finalizing the tour route and pretending like I'm not wallowing over Aiden. I set down my pen.

"I'm not afraid to ask for help, and I don't appreciate you talking about me to my boss. Why would you do that?"

This is a prime example of why working and living together isn't a good idea. It makes me furious to think that Marla would zero in on what might be considered a professional weakness and use it against me.

Marla walks into the living room and stands by the desk. Her hands are on her hips and she's wearing that look that I've learned means, *I see your challenge, and I'm upping the ante*.

"Talking about you? This isn't even about you, Hannah. It's about me getting a job in Paris so I can support myself."

She sticks out her bottom lip like a child who is about to throw a tantrum.

"You're right. It's not about me. It's never been about me, Marla. My entire life it's always been about you. *You* couldn't raise me because *you* got pregnant too young. *You* couldn't tell me about my father because *you* slept with too many men. You'd take me from Gram when *you* were ready for me. Then you'd give me back when *you* had something else you'd rather do. We're selling Gram's house because *you* need the money. Now you're here because there's a cool apartment in Paris that gives *you* the chance to start over and you want me to give you a job so *you* can stay—"

My voice catches. My throat is burning, and I'm afraid that if I say another word, I'm going to cry.

I sit there frozen, barely breathing, willing myself to get a grip.

She stands there looking shell-shocked.

Finally, I find my voice. "I can't do this right now. I need to go for a walk."

I get up and go into the bedroom to get my coat. Marla follows me.

"We need to talk about this, Hannah. We're not going to solve anything if you keep running away."

"If I keep running away? Says the woman who, once upon a time, couldn't stand to live in the same house as her only daughter. That's rich, Marla, coming from a woman who cherished her freedom above all else. Well, you might think all we need to do is talk about things, and *poof*, everything will be perfect. But that's not working for me. It's not that simple."

She shrugs, then swipes at the moisture that's collecting in her eyes. "You're right. I was a lousy mother. There's no taking it back because I can't change the past, but what I thought I could do was make it up to you by being there for you going forward."

I want to scream at her, but the fury is stuck in my throat.

Instead, the words come out a whisper. "What makes you think I need you now? You think you can fall into my life because you're finally ready and we can pick up like nothing ever happened? I'm a grown woman. This whole bonding exercise has been an interesting experiment, but I have my own life that I've designed without you. I don't have room for you, and I certainly don't need you."

I hate myself—not for saying I don't need her, but for feeling bad for saying it.

As I walk into the foyer, I shrug into my coat and pull my gloves out of the pockets.

"Hannah, we are all the family you and I have left. I realized this after Gram died. I didn't get a chance to make amends with her. But there's still a chance for us. I'm sorry I was a horrible mother. There are a lot of things you don't know. I wish we could start over and you would give me a chance to make it up to you."

"What don't I know?"

She doesn't answer me.

A moment ago, she sounded so earnest. So serious. As if it would be that easy to let go of all the hurt and betrayal. When really, it's more of a fool me once, shame on you; fool me twice, shame on me for hitching my life to the Marla carnival train when I knew better. Because I know exactly what she's all about.

I should let it go. Yet I hear myself saying, "If you think it will help, tell me what I don't know. Enlighten me."

She does that thing where she opens her mouth to say something, then thinks better of it and clams up.

"What if it wouldn't necessarily make everything better?" she finally says.

"What does that even mean? Why do you always talk in riddles?"

"I don't mean to confuse you, Hannah. I just don't want to say the wrong thing."

"Well, don't say anything, then. I'm going for a walk."

"No, Hannah; I'll go. You were working. The only reason you were going out was to get away from me. Let me go."

She reaches for her purse, which is on the table in the foyer. The strap buckles, spilling the contents onto the floor.

"That's my hairbrush! Why is it in your purse?"

"Oh. I'm sorry. I guess I was in such a hurry to catch the train that I grabbed it by mistake."

"I texted you and asked if you had it. Why didn't you tell me you did? Would you happen to have my toothbrush and lipstick, too?"

She drops down onto the floor and picks up her purse, then pulls out a plastic bag with a zip closure and hands it to me.

My toothbrush.

"Well, that's gross," I say. "How could you mistake my toothbrush for yours?"

She digs deeper into her bag and pulls out my missing lipstick.

"Really?"

"I'm sorry."

I'm close to boiling again. "I really need to take a walk before I say something I'll regret. When I get back, we need to have a talk."

We need to set some boundaries, put up some metaphorical walls in this one-bedroom. Because our future depends on it.

I STAY OUT LONG enough to put things into perspective and cool off.

I'm irritated that Marla helped herself to my things and went to Emma behind my back, but the rational part of me also feels bad about not giving her a chance.

The bottom line is she needs a job or all the expenses will fall to me.

It would be selfish if I stood in her way.

On the other hand, I know how Marla is. I haven't even hired her and she already steamrolled me to get to Emma. I worry that if she worked for me, she wouldn't respect my authority.

An idea hits me. What if we put her in charge of sales? It would give me more time to focus on the tour content and operations. Marla would be good at sales. Look at how she has me questioning my better judgment right now.

As further incentive, we could make the pay commission based. That way she has to work.

I sit on the bench in the courtyard of our apartment and call Emma. I'm relieved when she answers.

"Is there room in the budget for a small office?" I ask. Because there is no way I can live and work with Marla in the confines of this small apartment.

"We can probably swing it," Emma says.

"If we can lease that separate space, I'll hire Marla on a probationary basis. What would you think of putting her in charge of sales? She could work on commission and receive a percentage for each seat she books."

Emma loves the idea. I promise her I will supervise Marla and keep on top of the bookings to make sure we're running in the black. With that, it's done. The only thing left is to tell Marla.

I let myself into the apartment. Marla is in the kitchen running water. She shuts off the tap and sings, "Hellooo? Hannah, is that you?"

Her voice sounds perfectly normal. Like a mother in the kitchen making her child an after-school snack. At least that's what I imagine it would be like.

Gram was always working at the library when I got out of school. I would go there and hang out and do my homework and eat the snack I packed for myself in my lunch box that morning.

But sometimes I'd go to my friend Marcy's house after school. Her mom didn't work and always had some kind of food ready for us—like pizza rolls or cheese and crackers or PB&J sandwiches. It was such a foreign world, and I loved it.

"Yeah, it's me," I say.

Marla comes into the room, wiping her hands on a kitchen towel.

"You okay?" she asks tentatively.

I nod.

Silence hangs between us like a stanchion.

"Do you want some tea?" she asks. "I just put the kettle on and I was going to brew a cup. I brought back some Biscoff cookies—the ones Cressida likes."

"Sure," I say. I'm cold and her busying herself in the kitchen will buy me some time to figure out what I want to say. How to say it.

By the time she returns with tea and all the fixings on a tray, I have three thoughts lined up.

"First, we absolutely need to set some boundaries. I'm usually happy to share, but you have to ask before you help yourself to my stuff."

She sets the tray on a cocktail table and nods earnestly. "I'm sorry."

"Second, you said there are a lot of things I don't know about your relationship with Gram. Will you tell me?"

She looks resistant.

"I need to know. I know you said it wouldn't necessarily make things better, but really, anything is better than being kept in the dark."

Marla leans forward on the damask-covered wingback chair and squeezes a lemon wedge into her teacup. She lifts the cup and saucer and tucks her leg under her body. She takes her time blowing on the hot liquid and slurping at it.

I let her form her thoughts.

Finally, she says, "You never knew your Grandfather William. My dad."

I nod.

"I'm sorry you didn't, because he was a hell of a man. We were so close."

Marla has a faraway look in her eyes. I don't say a word. I almost don't even want to breathe for fear she'll stopping talking.

"I guess you could say I was the ultimate daddy's girl. I had him wrapped around my little finger. At least that's what Gram used to say."

She pauses and I can see the sadness closing in.

"One night, I decided I wanted ice cream. I thought I couldn't go on if I didn't have some cookies-and-cream ice cream from this place in Winter Park. But Gram said no, absolutely not. I was grounded and she saw right through the ice-cream ploy that was really an excuse to get out of the house and hang out with my friends for a while. She had me pegged. There was a boy who worked at the ice-cream shop that I had a crush on—now I don't even remember his name . . . Ricky or Robby or something like that. I'd just gotten my driver's license and the day after that I got the worst report card of my school career. Gram grounded me and she was not letting me get out of it—even for a few hours. I pitched a big fit. There was a lot of door slamming and tears and teeth gnashing. But she wouldn't budge. Not even after Daddy tried to win me a reprieve. In fact, he got a little mad at Gram, saying she was being too harsh. He wanted a compromise. If I did my homework, then I should be able to get ice cream. He believed in positive reinforcement. So then the fight transferred from Gram and me to Daddy and Gram.

"He ended up saying if she wasn't going to let me get ice cream, he was going to go get me some."

A tear slips from the corner of her eye and meanders down her cheek.

"He got in a bad wreck. Someone blew through a red light and hit him broadside. And he didn't—" She hiccups. "He didn't make it."

My breath hitches. I knew Grandpa William died in a car accident, but I'd never heard the circumstances surrounding it.

"After he died, I went off the deep end and Gram didn't know how to handle me or how to go on without him. After Daddy's accident, something broke between us. Our relationship already felt like a fraying thread. That day, it snapped. She blamed me. Not outright. It was one of those passive-aggressive grudges. From then on, Gram didn't care what I did. Before, it sometimes felt as if she and I were in a competition for Daddy's attention—not in a creepy way. Daddy was the most generous gentleman you'd ever meet. But I always felt like Mama turned things into a competition. Or maybe I did. I don't know. I didn't mean to."

It's the first time I can remember her referring to Gram as Mama.

"It was as if she'd checked out. So, that summer, I went to Europe and followed the Wellies. When I came home pregnant with you, even that didn't wake her up from her sleepwalking. Until you were born. Then, it was as if she showered you with all the love she couldn't give me but that she'd been storing up. Not too long after that, Grandpa Tom died and Ivy moved in with Gram. The three of you were as tight as three peas. There was no place for me.

"Hannah, at least when I left you with her, I was sure you were with someone who loved you. When Daddy died, he left me all alone. Mama was just as happy for me to stay away.

"I know this might sound like a lame excuse, but I didn't know how to be a mother because I'd never had a very good example to follow."

We sit there in silence as dusk settles over the apartment, making the shadows long and the light dim.

"I'm trying to reconcile the Gram who raised me, the woman who was so loving and caring, even if she wasn't very outwardly demonstrative," I say, "with someone who iced out her own daughter."

"That's why I said me telling you this might not help things," Marla says. "Maybe I shouldn't have told you."

I shake my head. "Not telling me doesn't change the way things were. I'm not quite sure what to do with this information right now. I need time to process it."

"I know you do, and that's fine. If it helps at all, I think that you—the way you acted, the way you loved her—you were the person Gram always wished I would've been. That's why you, Gram, and Granny Ivy all got along so well."

I nod. I don't really agree, but I hear her. And I want her to know that.

As I digest what she's told me, I let a few more minutes of silence hang between us before launching into my final point, and I'm glad to have some good news for her.

"The third thing I wanted to say was if I were to hire you, you'd have to respect the fact that I would be your boss."

Through the hazy ambient light I see her blink. She sits up straighter, adjusts her posture.

"You can't think of me as your daughter," I continue. "If I ask you to do something, you can't second-guess me. Do you understand what I'm saying?"

She nods with the vigor of someone trying to save her own life.

"Hannah, I promise. I will be a model employee. I'll be at your beck and call."

"If I hire you, it will be for a sales position. Is that something you'd want to do?"

"You mean selling seats on the tour?"

I raise my brows. "Yes. That's exactly what you'd be doing. I need this tour to be a success right out of the gate and the only way that's going to happen is if we are booked out for months at a time."

"I think I'd be good at that," Marla says.

"I do, too. I'm going to hire you on a probationary basis to see how you do between now and the first tour—"

Marla's phone rings. I'm a little irritated when she answers it in the middle of what she should think of as a job interview.

"Hello? . . . Oh! Hello, Dr. Campbell; this is Marla. It's good to hear from you so quickly. How can I help you?"

Marla puts the phone on speaker so I can hear what he's saying.

"I've had a chance to read through the copy of the manuscript you delivered the other day," he says. "While it's quite early in the process, my gut feeling will not let me rule out that it could be the work of Andres Armand. However, I can't quite authenticate it at this point. Would it be possible for me to have a look at the actual manuscript?"

Marla looks to me.

"Hello, Dr. Campbell. I'm Hannah Bond, Marla's daughter. She put you on speaker so I could hear the call. We would be happy to return with the original."

We make arrangements to call him back once we know when we can make the trip.

"Wow, that was fast," I say after we disconnect the call.

"At least he didn't give us a big, fat shrug like we got from Professor Sore-Bone," Marla says. I stifle a laugh at her play on words. "What exactly will it mean if Dr. Campbell thinks this is the work of Andres Armand?"

"It will mean a newly discovered Armand book. Then we'll have to figure out what to do with it. Do we consult literary agents ourselves or do we partner with the Armand foundation? If Armand has descendants, we need to find out if they have any claim on the book. I have no idea what copyright laws say about who owns the manuscript. It might even fall in the public domain, for all I know."

"Maybe Monsieur Levesque can help us figure it out," Marla suggests.

"Or more likely he can direct us to someone who can. In the meantime, I'll keep reading Ivy's diaries. I know she and Andres had a relationship, but did he live here, too? I can't imagine who else all the men's stuff would belong to, but Ivy seemed so adamant about not living with him outside of marriage.

"It seems like she was good about journaling for the first three years or so and then there are long stretches when either she didn't write or the diaries are missing. And then we have the partial diary from 1940 that was there by the bed, which is more about the impending war than anything else."

"Don't you think that people mostly write in diaries when times are hard?" Marla says. "The rest of the time you're living life and you're too busy to pour out your heart on the page. But the day-to-day, that's the juicy stuff. It's like that saying about how life is what happens when you're making other plans." She stops and takes a deep breath, then clears her throat. "That's why I'm trying to live in every moment right now, Hannah. I know I can't go back and change the past, but I'm grateful for this chance to have you in my life now. Thank you for letting me prove myself to you through this job. I promise you I won't mess up."

I don't quite know what to say. Especially when Marla starts crying.

"I don't mean to get all emotional on you." She sniffs, looks up, and fans her face with her hands. "Never mind me. Carry on. Nothing to see here. Time to start prepping for London."

Frankly, I'm taken aback by her gratitude.

"Sounds good to me. I was thinking—maybe we should make a trip to Bristol while we're there to see if we can go through marriage records. Something's still not sitting right with me about the timeline."

April 1929
Paris, France

Dear Diary,

I am bereft and without words.

A letter from my cousin Abigail arrived. All I am able to do is copy it here, because even after reading the news several times, I still can't believe it's true.

Dear Ivy,

I tried to reach you at rue du Cardinal Lemoine, the only address your parents had for you. However, my letters were returned as recipient unknown. Until now, I did not know how to find you.

I am now writing with a heavy heart to inform you that your parents have passed. Your father died of apoplexy last July. Your mother could not bear to be without him. It is believed she died of a broken heart barely three months later.

They have both been laid to rest in Canford Cemetery. The next time you are home, I do hope you will pay your respects to them.

Your cousin,
Abigail Braithwaite

Twenty-Two

January 16, 2019—1:00 p.m.

London, England

Two days later, armed with a release supplied by Levesque for Dr. Campbell to sign before we turn over the original manuscript, we take the train to England. For someone who hadn't spent much time in Paris before the apartment came into my life, I feel quite cosmopolitan traveling back and forth between Paris and London so often.

We meet Dr. Campbell at his flat in Stockwell. It's the second floor of a brick row house. The place is clean but cluttered with an overflow of books and papers stacked on every flat surface. He has to clear off two chairs for us to sit down.

He's a small, stooped man with silver hair and thick glasses that magnify kind brown eyes. He signs the paperwork without hesitation. When we turn over the box, his whole face lights up like we've handed him the Holy Grail.

"Ah, so this is the baby."

He sits on the sofa, pulls on the cloth gloves I've provided, and opens the box like he's unwrapping a Christmas gift.

He lifts the first page up to the light and squints at it. He makes some noises that I can't quite decipher as good or bad.

"As you know, I've already read the story and the style is consistent with Armand's work. Now I want to enlist the help of a handful of colleagues. I'd like to try to date the paper and see if we can figure out what kind of typewriter was used to ensure it all corresponds with the time period. It may take a while before we can give you an answer one way or the other, but I will keep you updated."

As we're leaving, Dr. Campbell says, "Say, have you thought of contacting the Andres Armand Foundation?"

Marla and I look at each other.

"Yes, we have considered it. But we don't exactly know how they're supposed to fit into the picture."

"I have a contact there," Dr. Campbell says. "One of Andres's descendants by the name of Étienne Armand. I'll touch base with him and see what he has to say."

IN THE CAB, ON the way back to Cressida and Tallu's flat, Marla and I are giddy at the possibility of authenticating the manuscript. But Dr. Campbell said it would take a while, so I redirect my thoughts to the more pressing tour. I've been thinking about something Emma said about me using the same formula for Les Années Folles that I used for the Jane Austen tours.

Sure, the structure worked for Austen, but I have a nagging feeling that I should think outside of the box for this one. I have so much original, personal material in Ivy's diaries. It would be a shame if I didn't use it. But there's something else, too.

I text Aiden.

I'm in town tonight. Spur-of-the-moment trip or I would've let you know sooner. Are you free?

It takes him less than a minute to respond, but the seconds feel like an hour. When I see the text bubbles dancing, my heart jumps to my throat.

I'm working tonight, but come by the restaurant for dinner.

Meeting him at the restaurant is the best of both worlds. I get to see him, but there will be none of the awkwardness of being alone. I still don't know what I'm looking for with this . . . friendship? Relationship?

Hannah: What time?
Aiden: If you can come later, I can spend more time with you. Might even be able to eat with you. 10 p.m.?
Hannah: It's a date.

My heart is thudding with a combination of relief that I didn't screw things up when he was in Paris and anticipation of seeing him again. I'm hoping he's still game to do the tour dinner. After I thought about it, I realized it would be a unique way to celebrate the launch. The dinner might be a one-off, but it would make the inaugural tour special.

Just because he can't be there to do the dinner at the end of every tour doesn't mean I have to cut off the idea at the knees. Who knows? If it works this one time, maybe I can hire a local chef to make it a regular thing.

"Why do you look so dreamy?" Marla asks.

"Nothing." I shove my phone into my open purse on my lap.

"Was that Aiden?" she asks.

I nod. "I'm going to see him tonight. I can't remember if I told you, but he was in Paris last weekend when you went to London."

"Really?" Her brows shoot up. "And?"

"There is no *and*," I say, because I know exactly what she's getting at, "except that he offered to create a meal for the first evening of the tour. He suggested calling it a 'moveable feast.'"

"Oh, like that book," Marla says.

"Yes, like Hemingway's book."

We ride in silence for a while.

"What are you doing tonight?" I ask her.

"I'm not sure. Cressida and Tallulah both have dates. I'll probably call it an early night since we have a train to catch at the crack of dawn."

"Sounds like a good idea. I won't be out too late, even though I'm starting late."

When I leave the flat at 9:30 to take a cab to Lemon and Lavender, Marla is snug in her flannel jammies, watching TV, and nursing a cup of herbal tea.

THE COMPACT RESTAURANT IS exactly as I'd imagined: Red-lacquered tables with mismatched chairs painted in a rainbow of bright colors. Matisse- and Cézanne-inspired art on the lavender walls. There's a cozy fire in the French-country-style fireplace. The warmth reaches all the way back to the snug table for two in the far corner where Aiden and I enjoy our dinner.

"Here's my thought," he says when I ask him to tell me more about his dream moveable feast. "What if we serve it picnic style on the Champ de Mars under the lights of the Eiffel Tower?"

"That sounds promising." I take a bite of the Grand Marnier

soufflé he prepared for us for dessert. It's like tasting heaven on a spoon. "Would it be too cold to eat outside?"

"I could prepare a menu that would warm up everyone. Who doesn't want to have a picnic under the Eiffel Tower no matter the temperature?"

I want to have a picnic under the Eiffel Tower, I think. Especially since I've been in Paris for weeks now and I've only seen it in the distance.

"We could start with some onion soup or foie gras on a crispy baguette and then move on to cassoulet," he says. "I have a great recipe. I could serve a mixed-greens salad with a Dijon vinaigrette and we could end with crème brûlée. What do you think?"

"I think it sounds delicious, but you'd better give me a budget. And where are you going to cook this feast? I'd love to offer my apartment, but the setup is circa interwar. Marla and I have been subsisting mostly on cafés and takeout and the occasional one-pot meal she prepares."

"Where I cook is the last thing you need to be concerned with. Don't worry about me. I have my resources."

Our gazes snare and he's radiating the same electric warmth as the first time I saw him. He doesn't seem to be nursing a grudge over the way the evening ended when he was in Paris. I'd fully prepared myself for him to use it as an excuse to push me away.

"So, you're saying I should trust you?" I say.

"Well, yeah. Have I ever given you reason not to?"

No, Aiden, you haven't. But I still worry that one day I'll discover you're like all the rest.

"I usually don't give people a chance to let me down when it comes to work, but lately I've been throwing caution to the wind."

"How so?"

I tell him about hiring Marla.

"My mother and I have a complicated history, but she's proving she really wants to make things right. Am I stupid for trusting her?"

"I'm sensing trust doesn't come easily to you."

"Trust and I have a fraught relationship. But I won't bore you with that."

"You wouldn't be boring me," he says. "I'd really like to hear about it. I want to know more about what makes you . . . you."

I don't quite know where to start or whether I should laugh it off and steer the conversation in another direction.

"Do you really want to know what makes me the damaged person I am?"

I cringe. The words sounded much better in my head and that's exactly why I'd rather not get into it—

"I really do want to know." He smiles and reaches for my hand. "Don't think of it as damage. Think of it as texture."

I take a deep breath and jump off the high dive before I can chicken out.

"Basically, my grandmother raised me. I'm just discovering that my great-grandmother—her mom—had this secret life no one knew about. It's weird. You live with someone and you think you know them. Then you find out there was a secret side to them you never knew at all. That they were keeping something this big. I don't even know what I think about it yet. Add to that the fact that I've never known my father. And I spent a lot of years with someone once, but he . . . he—"

The word gets stuck behind the lump in my throat.

"Let's just say things didn't work out . . ."

"Hannah, I'm sorry."

"No, don't be. It was for the best. We dated for three years and one night our conversation meandered down the dreaded where-is-this-relationship-going path and he told me he didn't see a future for us. He said I'd helped him realize that he never wanted to get married. So we broke up. It was amiable and very adult. There wasn't a big fight. I didn't cause a scene or create a lot of drama. It was like one day we were a couple and I thought we were heading for forever, and the next I discovered that he wanted something completely different than I did. I was sad, of course, because I loved him. He said he still loved me, but there was no sense in dragging out the inevitable."

"Do you still talk to him?"

"Oh no. Here's the kicker. He ended up marrying someone else less than a year later. And he had the audacity to invite me to the wedding."

I hope my laugh doesn't sound bitter.

It's hard to read Aiden's expression. I hope I haven't overshared, but I feel like I have. I hate feeling this exposed. I glance at my watch. "Oh, look at the time. It's been a lovely evening, but I need to go. Aiden, thank you."

I stand to leave. I realize we are the only two left in the restaurant besides servers and other staff.

"Let me take you home."

"No. Thank you, but I'll be fine. Get me a quote for the food for the tour dinner and I'll see if it works with our budget."

He hesitates. "I won't let you down, Hannah."

I'm not sure if he's talking personally or professionally, but I want it to be both, and my neediness makes me want to run as fast as I can.

When I get home around midnight, Marla is nowhere to be found. I wonder where she's gone, but I'm too tired to text.

Either Cressida or Tallu comes in around 2:00. The other comes in about forty-five minutes later.

Even after they've settled in, there's still no sign of Marla. I lie awake, thinking about the heartbreak she has suffered in her own right. What a toll it must've taken to feel responsible for her father's death and know that's the reason her own mother emotionally canceled her.

That kind of grief has to change you. It must break you apart and put you back together again differently, practically rewriting your DNA.

Or maybe Gram passed the gene that keeps people from sustaining healthy relationships to Marla and Marla passed it to me. As I drift off to sleep, I wonder if that's why Aiden scares me.

THE NEXT MORNING MARLA and I board the train to Bristol. When we're settled and the train pulls out of the station, I ask her where she was last night.

She promptly brushes me off.

I press the issue, giving her a taste of her own nosy, nudgy medicine. "Please tell me you didn't hook up with Jesse."

She pulls a face. "Oh, Hannah, of course not. I told you, it's not like that with him."

I don't believe her, but, you know what—?

"Okay, Marla, fine. I don't want to know."

"I am not attracted to him, and even if I were, Tallulah and Cressida have a prior claim. He's off-limits. I firmly live by the rule, sisters before misters."

I almost snort the mocha I purchased before we boarded the train. "Tallu and Cressida are not your sisters."

I want to add, they could be your daughters, and for that matter, if you're so honorable, why was it not *daughters before rotters* back in the day? Because you threw me over for some gems, Mom.

But she waves me off, leans her head against the train window, and sleeps the rest of the way to Bristol.

After we arrive, we find no trace of Tom and Ivy's marriage record in the city hall. Though we do find death certificates for Angus and Constance Braithwaite, Ivy's parents. They passed away within three months of each other. Angus passed first, on July 27, 1928. Constance followed in October.

"Are you sure Ivy and Tom were married in Bristol?" Brie, the desk clerk, asks.

"I thought so," I say. "That's what my great-grandmother always said. This was Ivy's hometown."

"Have you tried searching the GRO records online?" Brie suggests.

She must read our confusion. "GRO is the General Register Office. It's a database where all civil registration of births, adoptions, marriages, deaths, and such are recorded."

Brie scribbles something on a small scrap of white paper and passes it to me across the desk. It's a website.

"It's quite easy to use and very complete. It contains all the records dating back to 1837. If your granny's information exists, it should be there."

Marla and I thank Brie and make our way out of the municipal building.

"Well, that's great," I say as I tuck the slip of paper into my purse. "We could've simply done an internet search rather than make the trip."

"Maybe. If you knew where to look," said Marla. "Sometimes the internet can feel like the ultimate wild goose chase. While we're here, we might as well have a look around."

But first we go to a pub and look up the web address that Brie provided. With the names and the year—1940—we discover that Ivy Braithwaite and Thomas Norton were married May 22, 1940. It was a Wednesday.

They were married in London, not in Bristol, but that's not the first thing on our minds.

"Gram was born on December 4, 1940," I say.

Marla counts on her fingers. "That means she was probably conceived in March 1940."

Marla and I look at each other. "In the first entry in her 1940 diary—the one I found on the floor by the bed—Ivy talked about spending a quiet New Year's Eve with Andres, and she didn't leave Paris for the UK until mid-April."

"Yep," Marla says. "Are you thinking what I'm thinking?"

"I'm thinking that Tom Norton was not Gram's father. I'm thinking that Ivy was pregnant with Andres's baby before she married Tom."

WE'RE MOSTLY SILENT OVER the fish and chips we order for lunch. I could really use a pint or two right about now, but I don't want to drink in front of Marla. Instead we order bottles of J2O. Orange and passion fruit for her. Apple and mango for me.

Sometime later, as we finish our meal, Marla says, "I noticed that the address on the death record for Granny Ivy's parents was Whitchurch Road." She drains her glass. "Why don't we go see where they lived? It might not give us any clues about her marriage, but it would be good to put things in context."

It's a great idea—I'd hate to write this trip off as a total waste.

We hire a cab and soon enough, we're standing in front of the two-story white-stone home where Ivy was raised. It appears to have been split into two apartments. The houses in the surrounding neighborhood seem to be more modern, but if I squint my eyes, I can imagine how it must've looked when my great-grandmother lived there.

I went to university in Bristol and I can't believe I never thought to visit Ivy's childhood home. It never crossed my mind.

"I wonder what happened to the place after Angus and Constance passed," Marla muses.

I watch my mother standing there gazing at the home with reverence. I remember the way the paintings of Ivy distressed her. It's humbling, really. In her own quirky way, she is more affected by the past than I am. Or maybe it's that she is the one who slows down long enough to connect to the heartbeat of our ancestors.

I think about how my mother was shut out as a teen. Gram never forgave her the one mistake—or circumstances prevented them from forgiving each other and moving on. Now, it seems pretty clear that Ivy was living with her own secret pain, too.

Marla reaches out and gives my hand a quick squeeze. "This is our past, Hannah. And I think there's more for us to discover back in France."

I want so badly to trust my mother and start anew—to give her the second chance she never got from her own mother. I'm not quite there yet, but I can feel the ice around my heart thawing.

January 1930
Paris, France

Dear Diary,

My parents' death nearly broke me.

Andres insists I should cling to the good memories. I wish it were that easy. The trouble is there aren't that many good memories. My parents and I weren't terribly close. I always thought someday we would find our way to each other, after they realized my need to get away from Bristol wasn't to escape them. It was about finding myself.

Now we will never have that chance.

Some days, that's all I can think about. It's worse when I'm alone with my thoughts. Today it felt as if the walls were closing in. I had to get out of the apartment.

I didn't know where I was going, but I found myself at Harry's Bar. I was nursing a café au lait while I sketched, when I realized Zelda Fitzgerald was calling my name. She invited herself to join me, saying I looked as sad as she felt. I wasn't in the mood for company, but she ordered a bottle of champagne and two glasses, and the next thing I knew, she had pulled my sketchbook right out of my hands and began perusing my designs. I would've been offended, but by the time the waiter returned, Zelda had commissioned me to sew her a new wardrobe.

She confided that she was in such a funk, the only way she could lift her spirits was by indulging in her second-favorite pastime—beautiful clothes. I asked her why not her favorite?

She bemoaned that was no longer an option. The dance

company for the Teatro di San Carlo *in Naples, Italy, had invited her to dance with them, but Scott had forbidden her to accept the offer. He couldn't bear to be away from her, yet he refused to follow her to Italy.*

Zelda said ballet and pretty things were what kept her sane. Since her dream of being a ballerina had been ripped from her life, she needed something else to make her world beautiful. She decided the only thing that would heal her wounded soul was if I designed a collection just for her. She promised to pay me more than anyone had offered in the past.

In the meantime, she said, we would have to search for happiness at the bottom of the champagne bottle.

By the time we'd finished, we were sozzled. One moment we'd been toasting her new wardrobe, and the next minute, Zelda was a mess, crying into her hands, claiming that Scott had not only robbed her of the ballet, but he had also stolen her writing. She swore Scott had read her diaries and used her words in his books, passing her writing off as his own.

She said he was determined to drive her crazy.

I can't get the image of Zelda's mascara-stained face out of my mind.

The worst part is that I don't know if I believe her. Perhaps I don't want to because there are many parallels between Zelda and Scott and Andres and me. Andres the writer, me the diarist with stifled creative aspirations.

The difference is Andres is exceedingly supportive of my endeavors, and as for my intermittent diary scribblings . . . you know they are not witty enough for anyone to covet.

It's difficult to believe Scott would do that to his wife, but it was just as difficult to see Zelda falling apart in front of me. She implored me not to tie myself to Andres in marriage so that nothing would prevent me from leaving him when I was ready.

I have no plans to leave Andres, despite Zelda's warning. I didn't tell her that, but I did ask if she was thinking of leaving Scott. She said no, that neither of them could survive this world without the other. It will be 'til death do them part.

Then she stood up from the table and pirouetted into a curtsy like a ballerina at curtain call. For a moment she acted as if she were basking in the praise of an adoring audience.

The waiter broke the spell when he asked her if everything was okay. She blinked at him and said it most certainly was not. We were out of champagne. She ordered another bottle and told him to send the bill to Scott. Then she sat down at the table and said to me, "If I can't have ballet, I will always have champagne. Ivy, darling, let us drink a toast to the few little things we have left."

Twenty-Three

January 23, 2019—4:00 p.m.

Paris, France

How many tour bookings do we have now?" I ask Marla when she walks into the office.

I've rented a small storefront on the boulevard Saint-Michel in the Latin Quarter. We could've found cheaper accommodations, but this one is right in the heart of a touristy area and it was available immediately. I figure the walk-in traffic will be worth the higher rent.

"I'm not sure," she murmurs absently as she sits down at her desk and begins typing something on her phone. "I'll check after I finish this."

The inaugural tour leaves exactly ten days from today, and last I heard, Marla had booked two months' worth of two-day tours. With all of the permitting in place, I've lined up two days' worth of content, including stops at Gertrude Stein's and Natalie Barney's homes, browsing at Shakespeare and Company, a trek through the Tuileries, coffee at Café de Flore, and lunch at Les Deux Magots. One night we will enjoy Aiden's moveable feast, and the other night we will have an early dinner at Auberge de Venise Montparnasse, which used to be Dingo American Bar, where Ivy and her friends spent so much of their time.

There is a host of other places that Ivy mentions in her diaries that I'd love to work in (she seems to have been a regular at Harry's Bar), but we are almost overscheduled.

I will adopt the persona of Ivy Braithwaite as I present the tour. I've almost memorized my spiels. For someone who never wanted to be an actor, I'm having way too much fun pretending to be someone else.

"What are you doing?" I ask Marla. I've tried not to ride her too hard about her job. She did well booking the first eight weeks. But now I need her to pick up the pace and book out several more months. Her paycheck depends on her performance, so you'd think I wouldn't have to ask her for reports, but she has yet to fill me in on whether the seeds she's planted with various travel agencies and tour-booking sites have paid off.

"Can you at least give me a hint as to how you're doing with bookings for the rest of the year?" I ask.

"What?" she looks up from her phone as if just realizing I'm in the room.

"Our tour bookings?" I say as I push a yellow pin into the Paris city map that's hanging on the bulletin board on the wall. The yellow pins represent possible alternate stops on the tour. "The clients you're supposed to be getting."

"Oh . . . yeah . . . I need to call Glen at Tripadvisor and see if he's gotten our second ad up yet."

I glance at her over my shoulder. Her fingers are flying across her phone screen again. I turn back to my map.

"If you don't know if the ad is running yet, that means you have no idea if it has generated bookings. Marla, I need hard numbers soon. We have a lot riding on the first six months of tours. It will make or break us. What are you working on over there?"

"Well, I know this probably isn't an opportune time to bring this up, but I need to go out of town for a couple of days."

I turn around and face her. "Where do you need to go?"

"It's complicated, Hannah."

As if that's supposed to placate me with less than two weeks before the tour starts.

"Well, if it's complicated, maybe it should wait until after we get the tour up and running. I really need all hands on deck for the next month and I need you to focus."

She chews her bottom lip.

"My trip can't wait."

"Just tell me what it is."

"I'd rather not."

I shake my head because I can't believe we're even having this conversation.

"Do you remember what we talked about when I hired you? I told you I was afraid something like this would happen. I don't enjoy being a hardnose, Marla, but I need you to focus all your efforts on helping me get this tour off the ground. If you can't tell me why you want time off right now, then what am I supposed to do? What would you do if you were in my place?"

"Hannah . . ." She studies something on her phone for a moment, then types a quick message. Finally, she looks up.

"Okay. I'll tell you. I was wanting to keep it a secret until I looked into it more, to make sure it wasn't a wild goose chase. But I suppose you need to know. I looked into the Andres Armand Foundation that Dr. Campbell mentioned. I was able to locate that Étienne Armand he spoke of. Not only does he run the foundation, it turns out he's

Andres Armand's great-nephew. I've set a meeting with him to discuss the authenticity of the manuscript. If it pans out that Andres wrote it, it could be a really cool element to add to the tour."

That's true, but I'm not sure we'll be ready to announce the discovery in ten days, much less incorporate it into the tour.

"When is your meeting?" I ask.

"It's tomorrow."

"Is there any way you can push it off a few weeks? At least until after the tour launches?" I ask. "I know it's important, but right now, we need to put the tour first."

"Will it be any easier to get away after everything is rolling?" Marla asks. "I think we're going to be even busier."

She has a point.

When I hesitate, she says, "This is about family, Hannah, or at least someone who was important to Granny Ivy. Maybe you need to rethink your priorities."

I bristle inside, but I do my best to keep a neutral face.

"How long will you be gone?"

"I could make it a quick trip. Say, down and back in the same day. Leave tomorrow morning and then come back tomorrow night."

"But Marla, even if you take the TGV, the trip down there will take hours. It's not like going from Paris to London. How can you get there, meet with Étienne Armand, and get back in the same day? Plus, don't forget we have that presentation to Procope brasserie on Saturday afternoon between the lunch and dinner rushes."

"No worries, if I can't do the round trip in one day, I'll catch an early train Friday morning. So, really, since I'm working Saturday helping you with the presentation, Friday should be my day off. And since the trip is about the manuscript, which could help the tour, it's sort of work related."

"Sort of. It's not an essential trip right now given everything else we have on our plates. A few days ago, we agreed that we would work hard and be extra focused until the tour launches. Then we will all be due some extra time off."

It's the truth. She agreed to it, but she has that determined look on her face that says she's already made up her mind. She's going to Antibes.

"Will you get me the tour numbers before you go?" I say. "Emma will ask and I'd like to know where we stand on bookings. Two months of tours is a good start, but we can't build a business on that."

"Sure thing."

We've barely finished the conversation when she's texting again. My gut tells me she's not texting with Étienne Armand.

Something doesn't smell right.

But giving her due credit, Marla has surprised me in some regards. I want to believe I can count on her. I'll never know unless I allow her to show me.

"Okay, go ahead and make the trip to Antibes, as long as you're back for the Procope presentation. Is that a deal?"

"Absolutely. As soon as I look at the train schedule, I'll send you my itinerary."

She turns her attention back to her phone.

"Thanks, that would be great," I say. "But before you do that, I need to talk to you about something else. Can you please give me your full attention for a moment?"

She keeps tap-tap-tapping away, her gaze pinned to her phone. "Sure, what is it?"

I refuse to speak until Marla stops whatever she's doing on her phone. After the silence stretches on for a while, she looks up at me, blinking as if she missed something.

"I'm waiting for you," I say. "Are you finished?"

"Of course." She puts her phone down and sits up straight.

"Tallu called. She lost her job in London," I say. "I've offered her a temporary job helping with the launch. If she likes working for Heart to Heart and living in Paris, I'll keep her on to help you with bookings."

Marla's face brightens. "Does that mean I'll be her boss?"

"No, if she stays on permanently, it will mean you'll be working together to book the rest of the tours we need to schedule."

Marla frowns. "I hope she realizes she can't horn in on the groundwork I've already laid. I've worked hard to establish my territory."

That's exactly the competitive fire I was hoping to stoke.

"I'm sure T will understand that. I'll let the two of you work it out, but I have to level with you. I need bookings. We're ten days out and you haven't shown me anything beyond the first two months of tours."

"Fine," she says curtly as she stands and gathers her purse. "I'll get you numbers before I leave tomorrow. But right now, I have something else I need to take care of."

SURPRISE, SURPRISE. NOT ONLY did Marla not make it down to Antibes and back in a day, like she thought she could do, but she's been away three full days. She left on the twenty-fourth. It's early evening of the twenty-sixth and she appears to have fallen off the grid.

She was a no-show for today's Procope presentation where I introduced Heart to Heart and Les Années Folles tour to the manager, with the goal of securing a discount in exchange for making the brasserie a meal stop on the tour.

I managed without her, of course, just as I have my entire life.

It's clear nothing has changed. Marla promises the moon and

then does as she pleases. I have no idea what she's up to. The only explanation she offered for the delay was a quick text yesterday saying the trip was taking longer than she expected. When I asked why, she texted that she would fill me in when she got home. Frankly, right now, I don't have the time or energy to worry about her. I need to invest the best of myself in the business.

She did give me the numbers before she left. In total, we have almost three months of bookings locked down. But a lot of them came from the main Heart to Heart office, not Marla.

It's good to know I have Tallulah up my sleeve. I can count on her. She's arriving tomorrow. I can't wait to see her. Right now, her phone is propped up on a pillow. We're FaceTimeing as she packs for the trip.

"Did it feel weird not to go to work this week?" I ask.

"Nah, it's a relief."

"The good thing about this temporary position is if you fall in love with Paris and Heart to Heart, I can make your position permanent. The harder you work, the more you get paid. You'll be doing me a favor by igniting Marla's competitive streak. She was doing great for the first couple of weeks, but she's been a bit scattered this week."

"Hello, love. I miss you." I hear Cressida's voice in the background. She leans in so I can see her pretty face and then she picks up the phone. "I'm so jealous that T gets to see your new place. When can I come?"

"Anytime you want. As long as you don't mind sleeping on an air mattress."

Cressida claps her hands, which shakes the phone and gives me a view of T's bedroom ceiling. "Yay! It will be like glamping. All I care about is seeing you and the sooner the better. I'll figure out when I can come and let you know. Of course, if it would be better for you, I can stay in a hotel. Oh! And speaking of hotels, why on earth isn't Marla staying with us while she's in London?"

"What do you mean? She's not in London. She's in Antibes. She was supposed to get home yesterday, but she was delayed."

Cressida looks confused. "Apparently she's in London now. Or at least she was last night."

A bad feeling settles over me. "What makes you think she's there?"

Cressida wrinkles her brow. She and T exchange a look. "Maybe I read the picture caption wrong. Hold on, let me look."

Cressida sets down T's phone, returning it to its place on the pillow. I watch her look something up on her own cell. In the background, T moves in and out of the frame with stacks of folded clothing. A moment later Cressida holds her own phone up to T's to show me the *Daily Mail Celebrity*'s Twitter page.

"Look at this photo," Cressida says. "That's our Marla having dinner last night with none other than sexy Martin Gaynor."

"No. That's impossible," I say. "Let me pull up the page on my computer. Hold on."

Sure enough, late last night, the tabloid tweeted a photo of Marla sitting at a table with the man I saw pulling out of the driveway that day we went by his house. Martin Gaynor. There was no mistaking that jet-black hair and long, pallid face.

The caption reads, "Spotted! Reclusive punk rocker Martin Gaynor dines with unnamed beauty tonight at a snug table at The Clove Club."

I click on the photo and it takes me to additional pictures of the two leaning in, all cozy-like, at the table. Another shows them looking uncomfortable as they walk away from the restaurant. The final photo shows him holding a door open for her as she climbs into the same car he was driving when I saw him.

I double-check the date. It was last night.

Why would she lie to me? Why not just tell me she was going to London to meet up with Gaynor? That's probably why she insisted on taking the manuscript to Dr. Campbell rather than mailing it, too. She was probably with Martin that night in London before we left for Bristol.

She's free to see who she wants, even relive her groupie days for all I care, but why did she have to lie about it? Why is she so adamant that she's changed her ways?

"Are you okay, love?" Cressida asks.

No, I'm not. I feel like an idiot for trusting her. I should've seen this coming. "I'm fine. I need to go because I need to take care of something before I leave the office."

"Why are you in the office on a Saturday?" Cressida chides. "You're a workaholic."

I shrug. "You know my job has never been the traditional nine to five. It's especially busy in these days before the tour launches."

Tallulah leans in so that her face is in the frame. "No worries, lovie. I'll be there tomorrow to help you."

"I can't wait, T. Text me your arrival info and I'll meet you at the station."

There's a chorus of goodbyes before the call disconnects.

All sorts of thoughts swirl around my brain as I contemplate what to do and how to handle Marla—everything from firing her for lying to me about why she needed the time off to insisting that she buy me out of the Paris apartment, which would amount to selling the place.

Right now I need some breathing room, so I grab my coat and my keys and head out for a long walk to nowhere.

• • •

ON THE MORNING OF the twenty-seventh, Marla texts to tell me her train will arrive at 3:34 p.m.

You little sneak, I think. I wonder if she'll come in with a bogus story about meeting with Étienne Armand.

I contemplate letting her go through the entire spiel before I pull the "gotcha" routine, but the thought of listening to her lie to me twice makes me sick.

Make no mistake—there will be fireworks. I don't know how our fledgling relationship can survive this whopper.

When she gets to the apartment, she's startled to see me sitting there.

"Oh! Hannah. I thought you'd be at the office." She glances at her phone. "It's only four o'clock. Is everything okay?"

"How was your trip?" My voice is flat.

She rolls her bag past me toward the bedroom.

"It was good. I have so much to tell you."

"Do you?"

She gives me a double take. "Yes, I do. Are you okay?"

"How was Antibes?"

"It's gorgeous down there," she says as she toes out of her boots. "I mean, it's the textbook definition of paradise. The weather was beautiful. Sunny with highs in the low sixties. I wish I'd had more time to look around. We'll need to make another trip because Mr. Armand couldn't see me. It was basically a waste of time."

"Really. A no-show, huh? So your lovely holiday and the money you spent going down to Antibes were all for fun? Not a single business-related thing to show for it?"

She frowns as she studies me. "Well, in that regard, yes. I mean, it's my fault. I'll own it, but it was only three days and they stretched over a weekend. So, really it was only one day—Hannah, what's wrong with you?"

"Look, Marla, let's cut to the chase. I know you didn't go to Antibes."

"Yes, I did. I have my train ticket—"

"Stop lying. I know you were in London."

She flinches.

"What do you mean?"

"I saw a picture of you and Martin Gaynor getting cozy at The Clove Club Friday night."

Her cheeks flush and she presses her lips into a thin line. She knows she's busted.

I wait for her to speak first. It takes her a minute to find her voice. She walks around to sit on the sofa across from my chair, and I brace myself for another pile of lies.

"I did go to London, but I went to Antibes first."

She digs in her purse and hands me a piece of paper. "It's my itinerary."

I take it from her and verify that it says Paris to Antibes, Antibes to London, London to Paris. The dates match up.

"Okay, fine. So you thought you'd cloak a little trip to groupie town in family business? You said you'd go down and back in one day or at the most a day and a half, which you knew wasn't going to happen. You even guilted me into the time off by telling me *my* priorities were messed up."

"It's not what you think, Hannah."

"Then you'd better start explaining. What happened with Armand? Did you get your times mixed up?"

"Not exactly. I didn't have an appointment with him."

"Marla! You went all the way down there without an appointment?"

"He wouldn't return my call. I thought I'd drop in and see him in person. But when I got there, he wasn't there."

I throw my hands into the air, and get up and walk into the bedroom to get my purse. I have to meet Tallulah at the train station in an hour. The sooner I can get out of here, the better.

She follows me into the bedroom. "Hannah, don't be mad."

"I'm not mad. I just don't get it. You're a grown woman, and if this is how you want to live your life, that's on you. But you need to take responsibility for the job I hired you to do. In that regard, you did lie to me. You contrived a wild goose chase to hook up with Martin Gaynor."

I grab my handbag and coat and walk to the foyer. Again, she follows me.

"I wasn't hooking up with Martin Gaynor in London. I know that's what you're thinking, but I went because I needed some information."

I shrug into my coat and wait for the rest of her bogus explanation.

"I wanted the circumstances to be different than this when I told you, but . . ."

I wait some more.

"Hannah, I went to London looking for information about your father."

My blood runs cold. I feel like I've been hit in the face with a bucket of ice water.

"I didn't want to tell you until I knew I had something solid. There was no plausible reason for a business trip to London. So I figured if I went to the Armand foundation first, I could justify running by Martin's on the way home."

"London is hardly on the way home from Antibes. It takes a half day to get there."

"Yeah, eleven hours, to be exact." Marla shrugs. "That's why I was gone so much longer than I thought I'd be, but I was out of the apartment and that was half the battle."

My heart is pounding so hard I'm afraid I'll crack a rib.

"Are you saying you have news about my father?"

She chews her bottom lip nervously.

"Not yet."

"Then it's hardly justifiable. I can't believe you'd bait me like that. After all these years? That's a new low, Marla."

I walk to the door.

"Please don't be mad at me. I just— I can't tell you . . . yet."

I turn back to her. "But you do know who my father is?"

She nods. "I can't tell you yet. I need a little more time."

She must think I'm an idiot. As I open the door, I say, "I'm going to ask Levesque to recommend someone to sell the apartment because I can't do this anymore."

June 1930
Paris, France

Dear Diary,

I thought Zelda and Scott Fitzgerald had been traveling. As soon as I finished her wardrobe, she told me they were leaving to get away from the crazy life in Paris. But recently, I learned that she has been in and out of hospitals in Switzerland after suffering a nervous breakdown.

That day at Harry's Bar, she was so obviously distraught; I feel bad that I didn't make more of an effort to help her. However, she seemed in better spirits when we met for her fittings. She was elated with the clothes and even paid me on time.

I had no idea she was teetering so close to the edge until Andres and I bumped into Scott near the Jardin du Luxembourg. When we asked after Zelda, he mumbled something vague. Upon learning he was in Paris alone, Andres insisted we go somewhere for a drink. After a moment's hesitation, he agreed. Once he'd gotten a few down the hatch, he opened up about Zelda's ailments.

Surely having to put one's wife in an asylum takes its toll, but Scott seemed weary and lifeless. It was as if even our company was too much for him to bear. Scott without Zelda is like champagne without bubbles.

Something Scott said in particular haunts me. He said it felt like it was only a few years ago that people were stepping aside to let us, the younger generation, run the world, because our young, fresh minds saw things clearly, with hope and ambition. He hung his head and pronounced that perhaps it was time for us now to pass the mantle to the next generation. If we couldn't live with the intensity of youth anymore, what was the point in even trying?

Twenty-Four

January 29, 2019—10:00 a.m.

Paris, France

Two days after I caught Marla in the Martin Gaynor lie, Dr. Campbell called. Based on the style of the prose, the age of the paper, and typewriter ink, he is as certain as he can be that the manuscript is the work of Andres Armand.

It's fabulous news, but the timing could be better.

The tour kicks off in less than a week. I can't spare the time away, but now, there's new urgency in picking up the manuscript.

Until we figure out our next step, we need to get it into safekeeping.

"Hannah, everything will be fine," says Tallulah. She has settled in well and has been picking up the slack after Marla pulled another disappearing act.

I hadn't wanted to gossip about my mother, the forty-five-year-old groupie, but Tallu needed to know what was what since I hadn't exactly fired Marla. I knew letting her go would open another massive can of worms, so for now I'm letting Marla come and go as she pleases.

When I was at the office, Marla took her suitcase and left. She was gone when I returned. My money is on her being holed up somewhere with Martin, but that's okay. I know I can count on Tallu to hold down the fort while I go to London to pick up the manuscript. I'm telling the truth when I say the trip will take one day.

"Go on," Tallulah says. "If I need anything, you're a phone call away. Everything will be fine."

I check the Eurostar listings. There's a train leaving tomorrow at 5:45 a.m. It will put me in London around 8:30. There's a return passage that leaves shortly after 1:00 p.m., arriving in Paris around 3:30 p.m.

It will be a whirlwind—and an expensive one at that—but I really don't have a choice. Since it is such a quick trip, I justify not texting Marla to say I'm picking up the manuscript without her.

Now that it has been authenticated, the fewer people who know about it, the better. I do, however, let Monsieur Levesque know.

"This is big news," he says on the phone. "When word gets out, it will create a stir. We need to be prepared."

I wonder what he means by *prepared*, but he's already moved on to something else before I can ask.

"This must be the day for good news," he says. "I received an audit of the annuity that has covered the utilities and fees for the apartment all these years. It is the type we now call an inflation-indexed annuity. It was designed to pay out increasingly more over the years to cover the rate of inflation. I don't know if they called it that back when it was originally established, but I do know it was originally purchased in the name of your great-grandmother Ivy. Over the years, it has provided more than was necessary. The excess has gone into an interest-bearing account. It's generous, Hannah. I would say if you combined it with the proceeds of the sale of the house in Florida, it would make quite a large dent in the inheritance taxes you owe on the apartment."

As I hang up, my eyes are dancing and my cheeks are burning. I will tell Marla eventually, but for now, I want to keep it to myself.

The excess from this annuity and the discovery of the manuscript in the apartment have the possibility to change everything, and they've opened a new door: Marla and I now have the ability to liquidate and go our separate ways.

BY THE TIME I get to London and make my way to Dr. Campbell's home, I'm feeling more centered. That is until I enter his living room and see that he has company.

My mother is standing there with a man Dr. Campbell introduces as Étienne Armand. I can hardly focus because I don't understand how she found out about the meeting, but now at least I know where she's been.

I'm not one bit surprised to find her in London.

"Mr. Armand is the president of the Andres Armand Foundation," says Dr. Campbell.

Étienne stands. He's a tall, handsome man with dark hair that's dusted with gray. He has intense hazel eyes that seem laser focused.

He reaches out to shake my hand.

"It is very nice to meet you, Hannah. Your mother and I have been in touch the past few days, and I told her I would be here working with Dr. Campbell to authenticate my great-uncle's manuscript. I thought you'd be arriving together, but that's neither here nor there. Both Campbell and I agree this work seems genuine. We believe you have discovered a missing Andres Armand manuscript."

Marla nods. "I was so happy to hear the news. And I was even happier when Dr. Campbell told me you were on your way to London, Hannah."

She's smiling, but her words are clipped. *How does it feel to be on the other end of deception, Marla?*

"I didn't realize you were in town." Big, toothy smile. "Otherwise I would've let you know, but here we are."

Armand nods. "We must discuss how you came into possession of my great-uncle's manuscript."

Dr. Campbell leaves the room to put on some tea, and we settle into his living room, which is much tidier today than it was when we last visited.

We tell him the story of how we learned of Ivy's apartment and how we found the manuscript under the bed.

"Mr. Armand," I say. "There's more. Further research Marla and I have conducted leads us to believe that we might be relatives."

I tell him the details from Ivy's diary and how they align with Gram's birth date.

Marla asks him, "Would you be willing to take a DNA test to see if we're related?"

AIDEN ARRIVED IN PARIS today, two days before the first tour kicks off.

He shows up at the office with a picnic basket, saying, "I thought we'd better do a test run. Don't you think?"

"Of course. We want to make sure everything is on point."

Standing there, giddy about the two of us sharing a picnic on the grounds of the Eiffel Tower—finally—I have to admit I hadn't let myself believe that he would come through until right now.

I'd been bracing myself for him to back out or for something at the restaurant to take priority. I even had a backup plan. But here he is, two days early with picnic basket in hand.

My doubt has nothing to do with him and everything to do with my trust issues, which I'm beginning not to trust lately. If that makes sense.

Despite Marla's total flake-out, I'm trying not to be such a pessimist. I knew better than to trust her. I'm trying to remove her from the equation and move on. To that end, some things go just as planned, and other things go wrong. That's life, but it's how you spring back that matters. Fall down seven times; get up eight.

So far, knock on wood, Aiden hasn't let me fall, and I refuse to let Marla ruin him for me.

I want to believe in him.

We take a cab from the office to the Champ de Mars. As he spreads a picnic blanket on the grass, the Eiffel Tower looms in the distance like a sentinel standing guard.

"I ordered all the ingredients for the dinner. A friend at Le Cordon Bleu is letting me store it in the refrigerators at the school."

"You're talking about the actual Le Cordon Bleu cooking school? The famous one?"

Aiden laughs. "The one and only. I told you I have connections." He unscrews the lid of a thermos and it makes a slight popping and fizzing sound.

"Is that champagne?" I ask.

He nods and pours it into two paper cups, hands one to me.

"Aiden, they don't allow alcohol on the Champ de Mars," I whisper.

He leans closer and puts a finger to my lips. "If you won't tell, I won't tell."

He raises his cup to mine.

"Santé."

We start with hot onion soup and foie gras on a crispy baguette. Then he unveils the rest of the meal: cassoulet, a mixed-greens salad, and a caramel-and-coffee-infused crème brûlée—the pièce de résistance.

"Aiden, that food deserves Michelin stars."

"From your lips," he says, glancing up at the heavens before his eyes find mine again.

"Where did you learn to cook like that?"

"My mother and grandmother taught me the basics. Then I went to culinary school in London. Plus, I learned that cooking is second only to being a rock star if you want to get the girl."

"Then why aren't you married?" I ask playfully.

For a split second, my mind flashes back to Gabriel and our ill-fated dinner.

Fall down seven times; get up eight.

"I've been waiting for the right woman."

Ohh . . .

I could read so many things into that, but I won't. My mind is scrambling to find small talk to steer us away from that loaded line.

But if it's just a line, I have to wonder, why is he here?

I'm not going to ruin a good night by overthinking it.

"So, your Cordon Bleu friends are storing the food?"

He blinks.

"Yes, and I can also use one of the kitchens to cook. Your timing with this first tour was perfect because Cordon Bleu's new term doesn't start until the end of next week."

"It's really good of you to do this, Aiden."

"I wanted to. For you."

The Eiffel Tower is flashing its bright lasers and lights in the distance, but Aiden and I only have eyes for each other. For a moment, I think he might kiss me. I want to kiss him, but I don't want to make things awkward right before tour time.

So I sit back, breaking the spell. "This seems like the perfect place for a picnic. You're sure it works okay for transporting and serving the food?"

He glances around the park, still looking a little dazed but acting like nothing almost just happened. "Sure, I don't see why not. I'll figure out where to park and use a cart to wheel in the food. If something changes, I'll let you know. But we should be able to find a space in this vicinity."

January is considered the shoulder season for Paris tourists. It gets dark early and the weather is unpredictable. Sunset happens around 5:45, but we've been blessed with relatively mild temperatures in the midforties. Aiden will provide thermoses of hot coffee to keep everyone warm, and the upside to the earlyish sunset is the postdinner light show, compliments of la Tour Eiffel.

"Tallu can meet you here and help you. Emma will probably want to stay with me to see the whole tour. Plus, it will be good for her to get the full effect of walking up to the picnic like a guest."

"Works for me," he says. "We can't reserve a space, but you can look for us around here. Will Marla be helping?"

"That remains to be seen. She might have other things to do."

ON THE MORNING OF the tour launch, Tallulah, Emma, and I arrive at the office at 6:00 a.m., ahead of the 10:00 a.m. departure. Emma came in special for the inaugural run. I'm both giddy and nervous that she will be here watching my performance and helping me shepherd twenty people through Paris's crazy years.

I'm here early to do one last check to make sure everything is in place. I was so grateful when Em and Tallulah volunteered to be here at the crack of dawn to help me. Marla stayed in London a few extra days, which is probably best for both of us because things have been tense since I caught her in the lie.

After I unlock the door and turn on the lights, I pick up messages. The first one is from a reporter.

At first I assume she wants to cover the new tour, and my heart soars. I couldn't buy better advertising. Or, at least, it's not in our budget right now.

However, my elation is short-lived.

"Hello, this is Desirae Montpellier from *The Guardian*. I'm trying to reach Hannah Bond. I'm following up on a tip I received that you might know something about a newly discovered Andres Armand manuscript. Please call me at your earliest convenience."

"What the—?"

"What's wrong?" Tallu asks. She and Emma gather round.

"A reporter has gotten wind of the Armand manuscript. Only a handful of people know about it, but they all know we're not ready for the publicity frenzy it's going to create."

Would Marla do that when she, more than anyone, understands the consequences of announcing it without a plan? Especially on the opening day of the tour. Would she do it out of spite to throw us—me—into chaos?

She has done some pretty bad things in her life, but they've always come from a place of selfishness, not malice or spitefulness. Still, she knew today was the big day and she's not here to help.

"Who would do something like this?" T asks.

I shrug. "I don't know. I'm not sure what to do."

"You shouldn't do anything right now," T says. "Not until you can talk to your attorney."

She's right—I'm not under any obligation to call the reporter back immediately . . . or at all.

"Is there any way you could parlay this into tour coverage?" Emma asks hopefully.

"I don't know." Of course, press like this has the potential to bring a lot of attention to the tour that could translate into bookings. But baiting Desirae Montpellier with the manuscript seems like a cheap publicity stunt. Most important, it feels like Ivy and Andres deserve better.

"Today we need to focus on the tour."

Emma looks a little disappointed, but she nods.

She wouldn't have tipped off Montpellier, would she? We've been friends for so long I can't imagine that she would betray my confidence like that.

Someone did, and sadly, my money is on Marla.

Right now, I can't let speculation distract me. I need to get my head in the game and start channeling Granny Ivy—

No, that doesn't sound right. I need to channel Ivy Braithwaite in her Paris prime.

I bought a blonde bobbed wig with bangs for the occasion. I'm pairing it with Ivy's black-and-gray dress that I found in her closet. Since it's still cold outside, I'll wear her red cloche hat and the long, camel-colored coat trimmed in faux fur.

I'm so busy running through my script and pulling together last-minute odds and ends that the reporter slips my mind. Until Marla waltzes through the door smiling like she's right on time for a girls' day out.

"Good morning, beauties," she sings. "I hope you're hungry. I got us breakfast from Angelina. Café au lait, hot chocolate, *pain au chocolat*, and plain croissants for the boring people. Oh! And I got each of us one of those precious little Mont-Blanc pastries. I couldn't resist. I know it seems like a lot, but when you consider I was tempted to get four of everything on the menu, what I brought you is an exercise in restraint."

She holds up a large handled bag and a beverage tray like she's making an offering. I suppose she is.

"Come, my chickens," she says. "It's a big, big day. We must start with a good breakfast."

As she prances to her desk and clears away the papers and folders littering the top, it takes every ounce of self-control for me not to yell at her to take her sugar-and-carb buffet and get out.

She's an hour and a half late. Oh wait, my bad. She didn't know the call time because she's been pouting since we got back from London. She didn't ask and I sure as hell didn't offer the information.

I won't be able to concentrate until I ask her the burning question. "A reporter from *The Guardian* called asking about a newly discovered Andres Armand manuscript. You wouldn't know anything about that, would you?"

She frowns at me. "Hannah, what are you talking about? Of course I know about the manuscript, but I would be the last person to call the press. You know how I feel about people poking around our home, pilfering through Ivy's and Andres's belongings."

Oh.

I never thought this link to our family would mean so much to my mother, but it does, and she's hell-bent on protecting it. I'm inclined to believe her, but I had also let myself believe she was done with men before Martin Gaynor happened.

October 1939
Paris, France

Dear Diary,

Paris began mobilizing for war when Germany invaded Poland in September. Andres's mood turned dark after he was rejected because of the deafness in his left ear when he tried to sign up to fight.

None of this makes sense to me because the fighting is so far away. It's not even in Paris.

Andres is like an angry bull ready to charge at the slightest provocation. I tried to soothe him by assuring him his condition only made me love him more, but that didn't lighten his mood.

I feel so alone.

Many of our American friends have returned to the States. If you look at the ones who are left in Paris, you'd never know they had a care. They still dance and drink and carry on as if nothing is wrong. Andres thinks such frivolousness is inappropriate. I can't reconcile the urgency that is plaguing him with their untarnished merriment.

I try to assure him that his not being able to fight is a good thing, a blessing that will keep him here with me, but he doesn't see it that way. He gets angry with me, saying that real men live to defend their country from such evil. That's why he has formed a new set of acquaintances. A group of serious men who meet once a week in his apartment and talk of danger.

They don't realize it, but I listen to them from the kitchen and I can hear every word they say.

There is talk of resistance, talk of Andres helping the war effort in unofficial ways, such as delivering packages and conveying messages. Today he asked if I would be willing to open our homes to people of the Jewish faith who might need help. It scares me, but of course I'm willing to help.

I think of Madame Dreyfus, who owns the boulangerie, *and how she gave me a job in my time of need. I hope she's okay. I can't understand how anyone would hurt as gentle and giving a woman as she.*

I ask Andres if he knows when that time might come. He doesn't know. Nobody does. I wish I could calm him. I fear he will pace the floor until he receives word either way.

I will say enough prayers for both of us, that the troops will not move any closer to my beloved Paris. Still, I will visit Madame Dreyfus tomorrow and make sure she and her family are well and safe. I will let her know she can count on us.

All this talk of war reminds me of the international exposition Paris sponsored in 1937 at the Champ de Mars and the esplanade of the Palais de Chaillot.

When we happened upon the pavilions of the Soviet Union, with its hammer and sickle, and of Germany, with its swastika, Andres yelled at the Germans that they were not welcome. For a fraught moment, I feared he and a German soldier would come to blows. It took much cajoling and pleading on my part to get Andres to walk away, but he finally did after I made an appeal for my own safety.

Looking back on that day and knowing what I know now, the cold shadow Germany casts over this city makes me shiver.

God help us all.

Twenty-Five

February 2, 2019—10:00 a.m.

Paris, France

Marla stuck around to help, and she even came in with a last-minute request for a straggler to join the tour. I almost said no because we were at capacity, but she persisted. Apparently, the woman is only in town this week and was so captivated by the sound of the tour that Marla told her she would see what she could do. The softy that I am caved.

I can't wait to find out where she heard about us. Perhaps the seeds Marla claims to have planted with travel writers really are paying off.

"What's her name?" I ask. "I'll add her to the roster."

Marla puts on her readers and holds up the booking slip. "Her first name is Venus. Middle initial D. Last name is Milo."

As Marla spells it, T, Emma, and I break into a chorus of laughter.

"Venus D. Milo?" I say, pen poised. "Are you kidding?"

Marla looks confused.

"Is that her real name, then?" Emma asks.

Marla frowns. "That's what she said. Why should I doubt her?"

"Well, we are very happy to welcome Ms. Milo to the tour," says Emma. "Marla, I'm so proud of you for doing such a bang-up job filling the seats."

Marla beams with pride, and it annoys me because she's been absent more than she's been here recently. At least she showed today when we're desperate for all hands on deck.

The plan is this: Emma will come along with me on the tour, Tallulah will help Aiden set up dinner, and Marla will stay back at the office, answering the phone and fending off any reporters who come sniffing around for the scoop on the manuscript.

"*Bonjour et bienvenu!*" I say to the twenty-one people crowded onto the sidewalk in front of the Heart to Heart Tours office.

"Hello and welcome to the inaugural run of the brand-new Les Années Folles tour. I am so honored that you have decided to join us on this adventure. There is one slight change to the schedule. I have a surprise for you that we didn't advertise. Since you're our very first group, Heart to Heart and the Les Années Folles tour is treating you to dinner tonight on the Champ de Mars, near the Eiffel Tower. We're calling the dinner our moveable feast. You are in for a real treat."

Sounds of delight ripple through the crowd.

After we ask about food allergies, I get into character and reintroduce myself as Ivy. We set out on foot for our first destination: Gertrude Stein's home at 27 rue de Fleurus.

I'm curious to meet Venus D. Milo. As we walk, I have everyone introduce themselves.

Before Ms. Milo takes her turn, I get an urgent text from Marla.

SOS! SOS! I think Venus D. Milo might be the reporter who called this morning. I was processing the credit cards and found out her real name is Desirae Montpellier.

I quickly type a text to Emma, asking her if she can handle Desirae. I can't carry on knowing someone in my group is snooping on me, but I don't want to embarrass Desirae by calling her out, especially if she's a potential press contact.

After Desirae introduces herself as Venus Milo, Emma quietly takes her aside and speaks with her. While they're talking, I'm nervous that Desirae might make a scene or start asking questions about the manuscript in front of the other guests. But when they return, they're both smiling.

A moment later, I get a text from Emma.

No problem. I made a deal with her. If she writes a positive article about the inaugural Les Années Folles tour, you'll give her the exclusive on the Andres Armand manuscript when you're ready. She agreed. I hope that was okay.

Of course!

I know that the story about the apartment and the manuscript will have to come out sometime. Better that we have a chance to develop a relationship with the reporter—and control Ivy and Andres's narrative—before the story goes live.

We head south toward the boulevard Saint-Germain, then walk to 37 rue de la Bûcherie and stop in front of the green-and-gold storefront that is the Shakespeare and Company bookshop.

I explain that this is not the original location of Sylvia Beach's shop and give a brief history of how American George Whitman originally called the shop Le Mistral and renamed it Shakespeare and Company in 1964 after Beach bequeathed the name to him.

"Sylvia Beach opened her celebrated bookstore on the rue de l'Odéon in 1921. It was a gathering place for expat writers. Hemingway and Gertrude Stein first met here. Sylvia Beach was the one who published James Joyce's *Ulysses* in 1922, back when it was considered too scandalous for the mainstream. In 1925, she published Andres Armand's *Un Homme de Parole*, which translates to *A Man of His Word*."

I catch and hold Desirae's gaze. She offers an almost imperceptible nod, but that simple gesture tells me everything I need to know. She is agreeing to play nice.

Later, after we've eaten lunch at the brasserie Les Deux Magots and made our way over to the rue de Rivoli, where the group is busy shopping, Desirae and I have a chance to speak.

"I appreciate your interest," I say. "Would you mind telling me who tipped you off?"

Desirae is a petite woman with curly brown hair and soft amber eyes. She's American. She barely looks old enough to be out of high school, much less working for a paper like *The Guardian*. But more power to her. I never underestimate the capability of a smart woman, no matter her age.

She smiles sweetly. "I wish I could, but a good reporter never reveals her sources."

"I can respect that. This discovery is still new to us, but if you will give us time to get our affairs in order, I will happily give you the exclusive. And I can promise you a bonus story that will make it worth the wait. It shouldn't be much more than a few weeks."

Her eyes are large. "Sounds intriguing. Will you give me a hint?"

"A good source never reveals her story until it's time. I hope you understand."

"Touché," she says. "I look forward to learning more."

"And I look forward to reading your review of the tour."

Later that evening when we arrive at the Champ de Mars, Marla flags us down and leads us to the picnic that she, Aiden, and Tallulah have waiting for us.

The sight takes my breath away: They've set up white blankets decked out with sprigs of lavender and dozens of white candles in short jars. Boards of foie gras, fruit, nuts, and bread are set about for the first course. Aiden stands at the ready in his chef's coat, prepared to ladle out the French onion soup from a large insulated pot.

The group laughs when I explain that alcohol is not allowed in the park and I don't want to lose my license on the first day. Instead, Marla and T distribute mugs of hot cider.

I call the group to attention and raise my glass. "I'd like to quote the great Ernest Hemingway, who said, 'If you are lucky enough to have lived in Paris . . . wherever you go for the rest of your life, it stays with you, for Paris is a moveable feast.' Even if you're visiting, I hope you'll take a piece of Paris home in your heart."

My charges raise their glasses to me amidst a chorus of *cheers*, *santé*, and *hear, hear.* We toast a successful first day for Les Années Folles, new friendships, and the romance of Paris.

April 15, 1940
Paris, France

Dear Diary,

It has been a while since I've written. Forgive me, faithful friend. So much has changed. Our lives have turned upside down. This war that I never believed would amount to much is suddenly of monumental concern. The situation is bad enough for Andres to send me away, home to Bristol to stay with my cousin Abigail. I leave on the ship that sails tomorrow from Calais to Dover.

Andres has given me enough money to stay in a hotel as I make my way to Bristol and to purchase what I might need, as I can only take what I can carry.

I implored him not to send me away. I tried to convey how desperately I do not want to leave him alone in Paris. Alas, he confessed, it is not that he doesn't want me here. He has work to do, and the fewer people coming and going, the better. His apartment has become a workshop for a forger who creates papers that allow Jewish families to assume new identities until they can reach safety. He acts as a courier to transport the papers to the people who need them. He is doing all he can to maintain the appearance of normalcy, so that the neighbors do not become suspicious.

It's not safe for me to be there, but it's just as risky for me to remain alone at my place on the square la Bruyère.

I wish I could do more to help him, but he said knowing I will be safe with my cousin is help enough because our eventual reunion will be his reason to survive. I have resigned myself to believing that my going to Bristol without my beloved is my way of fighting for the resistance. It is my sacrifice until I get settled and find things to do to help combat the Germans—even small things like mending uniforms for the allies and cutting cloth into bandages for the wounded.

This war has changed him in so many ways. Not only has he shown he is willing to put his own life on the line to fight for what is right and good, but he has also promised that once we are reunited, he will make me his wife.

I never thought I would see the day that he would get down on one knee and propose. But he did. He put a gold band with a small ruby on my ring finger. He said it belonged to his grandmother and it was proof of his undying love. I cried—tears of joy mixed with bitter sadness. His promise is the hope to which I am clinging. That, and the belief that Hitler will not prevail.

I set sail tomorrow into what I hope will be a future of prolonged peace. But I shall not rest until Hitler is defeated and Andres and I are together again.

Twenty-Six

February 3, 2019—6:00 p.m.

Paris, France

The final day of the first tour ends at 6:00 after I leave my charges to enjoy dinner at Auberge de Venise Montparnasse. The first run has been a success by all accounts, even if I still have a few things to iron out.

After Emma leaves to catch the train home, I tell Tallu and Marla to take the next two days off. They've worked hard and deserve to relax before the next tour starts, three days from now.

I'm writing up notes in my office when I'm startled by a knock on the door. It's Marla.

"Do you have a minute?" she asks.

"Sure. I thought you'd left with Tallulah." I motion for her to come in, and she sits in the chair across from my desk.

"What's on your mind?"

She starts with awkward small talk—how well the tour went, how pleased Emma seemed to be with our work—and I wonder if she's about to ask me for a raise or something equally absurd.

"So, yeah, I need to talk to you about something."

Here we go.

"I didn't want to say anything to you until I was one hundred percent sure, and I wanted to wait until after the first tour was over."

She licks her lips and then stares at her hands. Even though the silence weighs a million pounds, I give her the time she needs. Maybe it's the opposite of a raise; maybe she's about to quit Heart to Heart.

Strange enough, despite everything, I don't want her to.

After a moment, she takes a deep breath and says, "It's about your father, Hannah. Would you like to know who he is?"

I drop my pen and sit back in my seat.

"Well, yeah. Of course."

She reaches into her pocket and pulls out a folded letter-sized envelope and hands it to me.

I open it and see what looks like a lab report on stationery that says PATERNITY TESTING OF ENGLAND. Subheadings say, "Understanding Your Report" and "Definition of Terms." Following that is a grid of five columns with numbers labeled "DNA Analysis." My eyes skip to the bottom row that's labeled "Paternity Probability: 99.99%."

Marla's name is on the report and so is—

"Who is Darius?"

"He's your father."

"Okay, but this says Darius Gaynor. Like Martin Gaynor? Is that Martin's real name?"

Marla shakes her head. "Darius is Martin's brother."

I can't quite wrap my mind around what she's told me. I guess I'd been expecting her to finally come clean and confess that it was Martin, so the Darius twist throws me. My first impulse is to ask when I can meet him. Then dozens of questions flood my mind and I feel like I'm drowning.

"Darius Gaynor." I test the name. It sounds strange to my ears.

Marla nods like a bobblehead. I hope she will offer more, but she just keeps nodding.

"How did you meet him?" I ask. "I mean, I know you followed Martin Gaynor and the Wellies on the road. But how did you meet Martin's brother?"

"Actually, he was the original drummer for the Wellies, but once they started to catch the eye of A&R types, the producers thought Darius wasn't edgy enough for the image they were trying to cultivate for the band. They basically fired him."

A nervous hiccup of laughter escapes Marla's throat and she clamps her mouth shut.

"Why are you telling me this now? What's changed? And wait—if Darius Gaynor is my father, why were you meeting up with Martin and not him?"

She closes her eyes for a moment, takes a breath in through her nose, and exhales noisily through her mouth. Then looks directly at me.

"I had to make sure. This is still embarrassing to admit, but Darius wasn't the only one that summer. I told you I went a little crazy. First I lost my dad, and then the only other man I ever loved basically ghosted me."

"Are you talking about Darius?"

She nods. "I loved him, Hannah. As trite and starry-eyed as that sounds, I did. He and I connected. He was my first—if you can believe that. He told me he was going to get out of music, get off the road, and quit the drugs. He wanted us to have a life together. I was barely eighteen, but that's what I wanted, too.

"Then they fired him and he left. He left me and all his stuff on the bus and disappeared. He said he hated life on the road, but I guess he'd wanted to leave on his own terms, not get fired from the band that he had founded with his brother.

"I followed the band a little while longer, mainly because I hoped to reconnect with him. I thought he'd come back—that was dumb wishful thinking, I know. When it became clear that wasn't going to happen . . . like I said, I turned to other men. That was my revenge for him dumping me." She huffs humorlessly. "When I found out I was pregnant, I felt in my heart Darius was the father, but I didn't know for sure. I wasn't proud of it, and I didn't want to give you his name since I wasn't sure. Those were the days before the internet, and I didn't know how to find him. He didn't try to find me.

"Because of my situation with Gram, I knew how bad it felt to know a parent didn't want you. I thought you would be better off not knowing than to chance tracking him down and having him reject you.

"I must confess, however, that ten years ago, I googled him on a whim. I saw that he was married with two kids. That sealed the deal for me. Since I wasn't one hundred percent certain he was your father, I didn't want to rock his happy world. But then, on the day we saw Martin pulling out of his driveway, I looked Darius up again and saw he's divorced. I figured I could at least try.

"You know those times recently, when I disappeared and wouldn't tell you where I was? I was figuring out a way to talk to Martin. He seemed like the best place to start. At first he tried to blow me off, but I promised him I wasn't after money, just answers. He said he would help me, but he had stipulations. He would take a DNA test to see if you and he were a match. If so, then he would introduce me to Darius to figure things out. That's why I borrowed your hairbrush, toothbrush, and lipstick. I figured one of those would do it. The lipstick wasn't any help.

"Martin got in touch with me after the DNA results were in. He said he wanted to meet. He only had a short window of time because he was leaving for a Buddhist retreat in Thailand and would be gone several months. He wouldn't tell me the results over the phone—dramatic, I know—and I needed to know one way or the other before he left. That's why I went to London after I went down to Antibes. Now do you understand the reason I couldn't tell you about that leg of the trip? I didn't want to get your hopes up only to dash them. Even after Martin told me his DNA matched yours, I didn't want to tell you until after I had talked to Darius. I needed to make sure he wouldn't reject you.

"But he took the news well and even offered to take a paternity test. Those are the results on that paper, Hannah. You can see it's a near-perfect match."

I nod incredulously.

"So if Darius is my father, that makes Martin Gaynor my uncle."

Tears are streaming down Marla's cheeks. She reaches into her other dress pocket and pulls out a photograph of her looking young, beautiful, and glam-punk. In the photo, her curly hair is dyed bright carrot-red and is slicked back on the sides and molded into a magnificent '90s faux-hawk. She's sitting in the lap of a cute preppy-looking guy who has his arms around her and is gazing at her adoringly.

"That's Darius, Hannah. That's your father."

I see myself in the shape of his face, his nose, his too-full lips. I blink to clear my blurry vision.

Darius Gaynor. My father.

Marla blows out a breath, swipes at the tears. "I haven't even told you the best part. He wants to meet you, if you're interested. He called the night before your tour started. I knew you had a lot on your mind with everything. That's why I waited until now to tell you. Will you please say something so I know what you're thinking?"

"You're sure?" I say. "He really wants to meet me? I don't want to show up and have him be like, 'Who are you? Get out of my life.'"

"I promise you. He wants to meet you."

Okay. Whoa. Slow down. I don't have time to run back to London right now, and we shouldn't rush something like this. I mean, it's been twenty-seven years. What am I supposed to say to him? *Oh, hey, Dad. Nice to meet you. Now what?*

"I don't know, Marla."

She looks crestfallen. "You don't want to meet him? Hannah, how could you not want to meet him?"

"I do, but . . . I . . . I don't know when I can get away. The tour and this—" I make a circular motion with my hands. "It's a lot right now."

"Just leave it to me, okay?" Her blue eyes are shining again. "I'll take care of everything. Don't worry."

I'm worried.

April 16, 1940
Paris, France

Dear Diary,

Andres will arrive any moment to take me to the ship. I am nearly paralyzed by the emotions I'm feeling. I know there are many people who are far worse off than I am, and I keep reminding myself that Andres is doing noble work. I would only be in his way if I stayed. Or worse yet, I might put him and the entire operation in danger.

Early this morning, while Andres worked, I paid a call to Madame Dreyfus's boulangerie *to wish her well and tell her that Andres was still in Paris and would help her should she and her family need anything. I discovered the shop locked up tight during what would have been the busiest hours. No one answered when I knocked. There were no lights on in her small apartment behind the business. I can only hope that she and hers have landed somewhere safe.*

As I stood there, it dawned on me that I should not be so sad about leaving my home. I will return. Madame Dreyfus, however, might not.

I walked back around to the front of the building and glanced up at what was once Helen's and my living room window. My first real home in Paris. The place I tried so hard to get away from when life wasn't going my way.

I closed my eyes and I could almost hear Helen's voice saying, "What if you leave with your tail between your legs and success is right around the corner? You will miss everything."

It's been years since I've seen my dear friend, but she was right.

And yet, there I was once again, standing in Montparnasse and contemplating a return to Bristol.

It will be the first time I've been back to England since arriving in Paris in March 1927.

With a heavy heart, I bid my dear friends a silent farewell and said a prayer that we should meet again in Paris.

Andres has arrived to collect me. The time has come to lock up, but I will leave my heart—and your unfilled pages, dear diary—right here on square la Bruyère until I can return.

Twenty-Seven

February 9, 2019—2:00 p.m.

Paris, France

"The long and short of the story is they sacked me from my own band because I wasn't a squelchy enough punk." Darius Gaynor throws back his head and laughs a loud, deep belly laugh that makes people turn and look. We've been sitting at the table at Les Deux Magots in Saint-Germain-des-Prés for nearly two hours and all I know is I want Marla to marry this guy.

Not my call, I know, but I never dreamed that meeting my father for the first time after all these years would feel like I'd known him forever. No wonder Marla thought he was the love of her life.

When she told him I was tied up with work, he immediately offered to meet me for lunch in Paris.

After he asked me to tell him everything about myself, I learned that just as Marla suspected, Darius had been shaken by being fired from the band he and his brother had founded in their garage.

"What I learned from that, Hannah, was sometimes it takes a swift kick in the arse like that to set us on the path we're supposed to follow. I traded my drum kit for university and studied business accounting. How boring is that? My life hasn't been quite as glamorous as the one your uncle Martin led, but I've been happy."

He pauses and looks at me, searching my face again.

"I wish I could've known you sooner. All these years that we can't get back."

He sighs, and stares into the middle distance before he continues. "It wasn't Marla's fault, ya know. She did the best she could given the circumstances."

"I know that." Or at least now I do.

We settle into companionable silence for a few moments, sipping our coffees as reality sinks in.

"You have a half sister and brother," he said. "Their names are Candace and Johnathan. Candace is a doctor and John is a teacher. Neither is married—too busy working and trying to make their mark on the world. I'd love for you to meet them, but I have to be honest, I haven't had a chance to tell them about you yet. It's all come together so fast."

"It has. We'll take it one step at a time. For now, I'm glad we could do lunch. Thanks for meeting me here, Darius."

"If you're comfortable with it, you can call me Dad."

RATHER THAN JUMPING THROUGH the clinical hoops and expenses that Marla and Martin Gaynor went to when they were trying to figure out on the sly if Darius and I shared DNA, Marla, Étienne Armand, and I agreed to do one of those drugstore DNA tests.

Three weeks later, the results are in. All three of us are enough of a match to suggest that we are cousins. That means Andres

Armand was likely Gram's father, which makes him Marla's grandfather and my great-grandfather.

Just when Marla and I thought we were the only ones we had left, our little family has grown by leaps and bounds.

A COUPLE OF WEEKS later, Étienne asks if he can visit us in Paris. It's a good idea. It's been a month and a half since I promised Desirae Montpellier from *The Guardian* the exclusive on the Andres Armand manuscript story. It's time the family sits down to talk about the strategy.

The family. I love the sound of that.

I told Desirae I've been busy. After the wonderful article she posted about the tour, we're booked solid for the next eight months. The great response has allowed me to train Marla and Tallulah, who has moved to Paris permanently, to handle their own tours and hire a full-time office assistant.

We also hired a literary agent who helped Marla, Étienne, and me sort out what to do with Andres's final manuscript. She sold the rights to the book at auction. That was the easy part. Now I have to wait what feels like years before I can hold my great-grandfather's book in my hands. I'm so impatient, but the agent assured us that these things take time.

The world has been without the manuscript for this long, so I suppose a few more months won't hurt anyone.

Maybe if I keep telling myself that I'll believe it.

We never found out who leaked the news of the manuscript to the press, but I have my suspicions—his name might start with Gabriel and end with Cerny—but it really doesn't matter. Desirae kept her word, so we are eager to reward her with an exclusive. We've decided we will even invite her to the square la Bruyère apartment and share the before photos. She will see the transformation with her own eyes.

But first, Marla and I want to meet with Étienne alone—just family.

The evening he arrives in Paris, Marla and I go to his hotel on rue de la Paix. He invites us up to his suite, saying he has something that is sure to interest us. On the coffee table is a box, not so different from the acid-free number we've used to store the manuscript.

Étienne has ordered wine and a cheese-and-charcuterie board. Once we're all seated, he pours the wine and we toast.

"Thank you for coming," he says. "I want us to enjoy the snacks I have ordered, but before we do, I want you to see what's in the box. For that, we must keep our hands clean."

Marla and I exchange a puzzled glance.

He nods toward the box. "Open it, please. There is something I would like to show you. In fact, I would like to propose a trade. The original hard copy of the manuscript for these letters."

Marla gently lifts the lid off the box. Inside is a stack of letters. I count them. There are ten in all. Marla takes one out.

"It's addressed to Andres." She shows it to me. The address is Antibes, France. It's the same handwriting I've come to know in Ivy's diaries.

"What is this address?" I ask.

"It was our family home and now the location of the Andres Armand Foundation. It is where I work. I think you know part of my mission has been to carry on my great-uncle's legacy. In doing that, I have kept all his documents and papers. That includes drafts of his manuscripts and all of his correspondence. After we met at George Campbell's home in London, I searched through the volumes of correspondence I have in the archives. I found these letters that may provide you with some answers."

I reach into the box and pull out another letter.

Marla lifts the flap of the envelope she's holding and peers in.

"May I read it?" She's nervously fiddling with Granny Ivy's ruby ring, which she's still wearing on a chain around her neck.

"Of course," says Étienne. He looks like a regal gentleman, his dark hair graying at the temples. He is sitting with one leg crossed over the opposite knee in the gilded armchair, wineglass in hand.

Marla and I both remove the letters and begin reading.

"When is yours dated?" she asks.

"April 24, 1940," I say.

"Mine is April 20," she says.

"Read yours first," I say. "Read it out loud."

She begins tentatively.

My Dearest Love,

I am writing to you at your family home as you asked me to do. I made it to England safely. I'm sorry for the delay; it took a while to make passage from Dover to Bristol and get my bearings. I met the nicest man, a US soldier named Thomas Norton. He has been a tremendous help. I showed him my engagement ring. I cannot take my eyes off of it. He knows of you as he has read your books. He says translated versions are quite the rage in the States. He would like to meet you once you arrive in Bristol. Until then, he asked me to convey that he will look out for me and you should not worry.

I will be counting the days until I can be your wife.

With all my deepest love,
Ivy

"Thomas Norton! That's Great-Grandpa Tom," I say. "That's how they met?"

We marvel at discovering the missing puzzle piece.

My letter is short and doesn't offer much information. Just a basic accounting of Ivy's day. The next few are much of the same.

We don't come across anything particularly juicy until the letter dated May 15, 1940.

My Dearest Andres,

I have not heard from you since I set sail for Dover. I must confess I am worried. I have tried to placate myself by believing the mail is delayed because of the German attack on France. There is talk of the French government fleeing Paris. Please tell me that is not so, my love—that it is just hysteria.

What I wouldn't give to know that you are safe and out of harm's way.

Each day I wake with the hope that it will be the day that we are reunited. I have a daydream that I will look up and see you walking toward me, smiling that smile that sets my heart racing. That smile I couldn't resist from the moment I saw you.

I am not the only one depending on you to return to us safely. Darling, soon we will be a family of three. Can you believe it? You will be the best father.

If my condition did not dictate that I stay in Bristol, I would come searching for you myself. Until we can be together again, I will remain true.

Your future wife, the mother of your child,
Ivy

The most heartbreaking letter of them all is dated May 17.

My Dearest,

I have heard the most devastating news, but I refuse to believe it's true. There is talk that you have not survived the war. If, by the grace of God, you are alive, I wanted you to know that I am leaving to go to the States until after our child is born. Please contact Major Tom Norton in Bristol, and he will know how to find me.

Please be safe, my love.

Forever yours,
Ivy

Marla is supposed to read the final letter, but she can't because she's crying. She hands it to me. I'm not much more composed, but I take a deep breath to steady myself before I begin.

June 1, 1940

My Dearest Andres,

I am in Florida now. I need you to know that I will never give up on you. In my heart I will always believe you are alive. I close my eyes and picture you sitting in your chair in the little apartment on square la Bruyère or leaning over your typewriter working. I know how hard it is for you to settle down to write, but once you do, your words are sheer brilliance.

My friend Tom agrees.

My love, I have news that I hope you will understand. You said yourself that times of war call for sacrifices from all, that fighting forces people to make choices they might not necessarily make in times of peace.

I have faced a hard choice.

Since I am pregnant and the situation in Bristol is tenuous, Tom tried to help me arrange passage to the States on a military ship. We soon learned that places aboard the ship were only for Americans or family of American servicemen.

Andres, I know you want what's best for our child. It will be best for the baby to be born in peace and safety. Please find it in your heart to understand that that's why I married Tom Norton.

He is a good soul and he knows I love you. He has agreed to release me from our arrangement once I hear that you are safe and ready to reunite with your family.

In the meantime, our square la Bruyère apartment will be waiting for you. Please go there and contact me when you can.

My love always,
Ivy

Marla and I are both sobbing by the time I reach the end of the letter.

Étienne leaves the room and returns with a box of tissues.

"Andres died on May fourteenth," he says as we do our best to compose ourselves. "From what I can piece together, he was killed before he received Ivy's letters. Our family in the South of France saved the correspondence. Either they didn't try to locate Ivy or they didn't bother because she'd married out of the family."

"I think she was so devastated by Andres's loss that she couldn't bring herself to return to Paris or even sell the apartment because that would mean that she'd given up on him," Marla says. "Her whole life she clung to the idea that he could still be waiting for her in that apartment."

I'm moved by how moved my mother is by today's revelations.

"I think it's also worth mentioning that Tom must've been head over heels in love with Ivy to marry her and raise Gram as his own," I say. "I wonder if Gram knew?"

We will never know, but we do know that Tom did right by her—by both of them.

Ivy and Andres's story is tragic, but somehow, it feels as if our acknowledging their relationship has given them closure. Maybe that's why Ivy left the documents in the trunk in Florida for us to find—so that Marla and I would happen upon them one day and embark on this crazy Parisian adventure of our own. Someday, when I have my own children and grandchildren, I hope I can leave them a key that will unlock half the possibility that Ivy's Paris apartment has unlocked for us.

Epilogue

May 14, 2019—2:00 p.m

Antibes, France

I've always found cemeteries to be uncomfortable places. Not for the obvious reason—that they're full of dead people—but because visiting someone's grave seems morbid.

Doesn't it reinforce the fact that they're gone?

I haven't visited many graves in my life. I haven't had a chance to go back to Florida to visit Gram's grave since the funeral. But on the occasions that Gram and I would go to Granny Ivy's to leave flowers, I never felt close to her there—not nearly as close as I felt to her in the pages of her diaries, or in the Paris apartment.

But a trip to the cemetery is a sign of respect. I get that.

That's why Aiden and I are meeting Marla and Étienne at Andres's grave in Antibes on the anniversary of his death.

Aiden and I stop at a flower shop to buy a bunch of lilies. As we're waiting for our Uber, Aiden says, "I need to talk to you."

He looks so serious it scares me.

There was a time when I would've jumped to conclusions and anticipated the worst.

Not this time.

Instead, I take his hand. "What would you like to talk about, my love?"

"Remember the feast we made for your first Les Années Folles tour?" he asks. "How would you feel about making the dinner a regular feature? It really elevates your tour above the others, you know?"

"It's a great idea in theory. But the logistics might be a little tricky. We both know those Chunnel tickets don't come cheap. And I do two tours a week."

"What if I told you I wouldn't need a Chunnel ticket to make it work?"

I squint at him. "What are you saying?"

"I'm saying that Le Cordon Bleu offered me a job as an instructor. The pay is decent and it will give me a chance to quit Lemon and Lavender, move to Paris, and save for a restaurant of my own."

"You're moving to Paris? Stop it."

He smiles at me and plants a kiss on my lips. "I'm moving the feast to Paris."

AIDEN HOOKS HIS ARM around my waist as we approach my great-grandfather's grave. Earlier, I tied a piece of lace from Ivy's sewing box around the flowers so a small part of her would be here with us. As I lay the lilies at the base of the headstone, I wish that I could sprinkle half of Ivy's ashes here with Andres and leave the other half where she rests now, next to Tom.

I've been thinking about how lucky she was to have the devotion of two men in her lifetime.

Since Andres died so young, their love will live on perfect and true in its incompleteness.

And then there's Tom, the stoic soldier who stood valiantly by her side all those years, loving her in his quiet way and unquestioningly guarding her secret.

Over the past five months, so much has changed. Emma made me a partner in Heart to Heart Tours. I'm in charge of growing the French division of the company. We'll be adding more tours in Paris, such as Haunts of the French Impressionists and the Les Misérables Book Tour. In the meantime, Les Années Folles is quite popular.

Andres's final manuscript, which we named *Pour l'Amour d'Ivy,* will hit the shelves around the holidays. The cover is gorgeous. The publisher commissioned a painting of 1920s Paris with a flapper and a dapper-looking man strolling through Jardin du Luxembourg. It's already garnering rave reviews from the few lucky critics who have gotten their hands on advance copies, and some are even calling it Andres's magnum opus.

A portion of the advance will go to the Armand Foundation, and we're using another portion to pay off the inheritance tax on the apartment. With that, the money we got from the sale of Gram's house, and the excess on the annuity, we're going to be more than okay.

In fact, we were even able to present a sizable check to a watchdog organization for international human rights. We made the donation in Andres's and Ivy's honor. It seemed the best way to pay tribute to him for giving his life to the resistance, and to Ivy for her lifelong dedication to human rights work.

Since Aiden visits often, I've started renting my own little place, freeing up the square la Bruyère apartment for Marla. She remains sober and single, though she and Darius are "talking." She says she's happy with her job at Heart to Heart and wants to devote herself to . . . herself—at least for now. If you ask me, it's only a matter of time until she and Darius finally find their own happy ever after.

In the meantime, Marla and I continue to work on our own

relationship. The fact that we have one is a far cry from where we were when she landed on my doorstep that cold New Year's Eve.

Sure, we still have our ups and downs like most mothers and daughters, but the one thing on which we will always agree is that getting lost in Paris our first day here was the start not only of finding ourselves, but of finding our way to each other.

Acknowledgments

To my fabulous agent, Ann Leslie Tuttle. Thank you for believing in me and knowing "Paris was a good idea" even before the story was fully formed. To my editor, Maggie Loughran. Thank you for getting my sense of humor. Your keen eye and sage advice elevated this story to its full potential. Without you, this book wouldn't be what it is today. To Lauren McKenna, thank you for loving Hannah and Marla's story; I hope I did you proud. Many thanks to the entire team at Simon & Schuster, especially Rachel Brenner, Anne Jaconette, Jennifer Bergstrom, and Aimée Bell.

To Jay, Brendan, Isaiah, Larry, Jim T., Barbara, Wiladean, Juanita, Lynn, Anne, Alex, and Sharon—family is everything.

To Kathy Garbera, Mimi Wells, Lenora Worth, Eve Gaddy, Janet Justiss, Denise Daniels, Cindy Rutledge, Renee Halverson, and Kathleen O'Brien for your unwavering support and everlasting friendship. And to Callie Bowman for the good old days of the on-going story, when we would pass the notebooks back and forth and dream.

Lost in Paris

Elizabeth Thompson

This reading group guide for Lost in Paris *includes an introduction, discussion questions, and ideas for enhancing your book club. The suggested questions are intended to help your reading group find new and interesting angles and topics for your discussion. We hope that these ideas will enrich your conversation and increase your enjoyment of the book.*

Introduction

When a deed to an apartment in Paris turns up in an old attic trunk, an estranged mother and daughter must reunite to uncover the secret life of a family matriarch—perfect for fans of *The Little Paris Bookshop* and *The Beekeeper's Daughter*.

Hannah Bond has always been a bookworm, which is why she fled Florida—and her unstable alcoholic mother—for a quiet life leading Jane Austen–themed tours through the British countryside. But on New Year's Eve, everything comes crashing down when she arrives back at her London flat to find her mother, Marla, waiting for her.

Marla's brought three things with her: the deed to an apartment in Paris, an old key, and newspaper clippings about the death of a famous writer named Andres Armand. Hannah, wary of her mother's motives, reluctantly agrees to accompany her to Paris where, against all odds, they discover Great-Grandma Ivy's apartment frozen in 1940 and covered in dust.

Topics & Questions for Discussion

1. Each chapter consists of Hannah's modern-day point of view and Ivy's diary entries written in the 1920s and '30s, alternating between the present and the past. Why do you think the author chose to structure the novel this way?

2. Early on, Hannah refers to her relationship with Marla as a "dysfunctional mother-daughter reality show." During which points in the novel do we best see examples of their roles being reversed?

3. The story focuses heavily on the relationships between women. Discuss the differences and similarities between Marla and Hannah's relationship and Ivy and Helen's friendship.

4. In the apartment, Hannah and Marla discover mysterious clues about Ivy's life, including a diary detailing evenings of drinking and dancing with Hemingway, the Fitzgeralds, and other iconic expats. Why do you think Ivy hid her life in Paris from her granddaughter and great-granddaughter?

5. Can you pinpoint the moment after arriving in Paris when Marla and Hannah begin to mend their relationship?

6. As Hannah talks through her new Paris tour while walking along the Seine with her mother, Marla stops her and says, "Maybe it's not so much what you say, Hannah, but how you say it." Can you find other instances when Marla feels this way toward Hannah? Why do you think this comment hits Hannah so hard?

7. In her diary, Ivy discusses the volatile relationship between Scott and Zelda Fitzgerald. Discuss Zelda's decision to give up ballet and her belief that Scott stole her work. How do you think the Fitzgeralds' relationship compares to the other relationships in the book?

8. Hannah's potential love interests, Aiden and Gabriel, are secondary to the story's main plot. How do they still drive the plot forward and affect Hannah's character development?

9. On page 122, Marla and Hannah remember Granny Ivy as "stern and matronly." In what ways do you think the war and Andres' death affected and changed her? Do you think she kept the Paris apartment as a way to honor his memory?

10. On pages 128–129, Gabriel says that the Paris apartment is "a city treasure" and that "everyone wants to own a piece of history. Some are willing to pay extra to obtain it." If you were in Marla's and Hannah's shoes, would you keep the apartment or sell it at a high price?

11. Toward the end of the book, Marla unites Hannah and her birth father. Why do you think the author thought this was important to the plot and to Hannah's overall story?

12. Why do you think Hannah agrees to give her mother the Paris apartment? Discuss what you think the apartment and gesture mean to Marla.

13. By the end of the novel, Hannah and Marla have gained an apartment in Paris and newfound family. What else—tangible or intangible—have they gained?

Enhance Your Book Club

1. Plan your own moveable feast! Make a picnic based on the meal that Aiden prepares for Hannah's tour: French onion soup, crispy baguette with foie gras, and crème brûlée. Or improvise, making the menu your own.

2. On page 227, Marla shows Hannah a "French phrase-a-day calendar." Create your own set of French phrases and practice speaking them with your group.

3. While in Paris, Hannah visits the Rodin Museum, the Eiffel Tower, Shakespeare and Company bookstore, and the Seine. Assign each member of your book club one of these famous locations and ask each to research a few facts so your group can create its own "virtual" Paris tour.

4. Ivy was a fashion designer in the 1920s. Research fashion icons of the era, including Zelda Fitzgerald and Coco Chanel, and share some of the key trends of the time.

5. On page 115, Hannah questions, "Why didn't we ask for more details about her life when she was alive?" Reach out to your eldest family matriarch and ask her a set of questions about her past.